Journal of Semitic Studies Supplement 15

HISTORY OF PRINTING AND PUBLISHING IN THE LANGUAGES AND COUNTRIES OF THE MIDDLE EAST

edited by
Philip Sadgrove

Published by Oxford University Press
on behalf of the University of Manchester
2004

OXFORD
UNIVERSITY PRESS

Great Clarendon Street, Oxford OX2 6DP

Oxford University Press is a department of the University of Oxford.
It furthers the University's objective of excellence in research, scholarship,
and education by publishing worldwide in

Oxford New York

Athens Auckland Bangkok Bogotá Buenos Aires Cape Town
Chennai Dar es Salaam Delhi Florence Hong Kong Istanbul Karachi
Kolkata Kuala Lumpur Madrid Melbourne Mexico City Mumbai Nairobi
Paris São Paulo Shanghai Singapore Taipei Tokyo Toronto Warsaw

with associated companies in Berlin Ibadan

Oxford is a registered trade mark of Oxford University Press
in the UK and in certain other countries

Published in the United Kingdom
by Oxford University Press, Oxford

First published 2005

A catalogue for this book is available from the British Library

Library of Congress Cataloguing in Publication Data
(Data available)

ISSN 0022-4480
ISBN 0-19-856875-4

Subscription information for the *Journal of Semitic Studies* is available at the journal website:
jss.oupjournals.org

Printed in Great Britain by Bell & Bain Ltd, Glasgow

Table of Contents

Preface v
Philip C. Sadgrove

Cheng-Hsiang Hsu
A Survey of Arabic-character Publications Printed in Egypt during the Period of 1238–1267 (1822–1851) 1

Olympiada P. Scheglova
The Repertoire of Books in Persian Published Lithographically in Turkestan during 1883–1917 17

Ulrich Marzolph
TULLIP: A Projected Thesaurus Universalis Libri Lithographici Illustrati Persorum 25

Nedret Kuran-Burçoğlu
Osman Zeki Bey and His Printing Office the *Matbaa-i Osmaniye* 35

Christiane Czygan
From London back to Istanbul: The Channel of Communication of the Young Ottoman Journal *Ḥurriyet* (1868–1870) 59

Ami Ayalon
The Beginnings of Publishing in pre-1948 Palestine 69

René Wildangel
The Emergence of the Public: Arab Palestinian Media in British Mandate Palestine 1929–1945 81

Orit Bashkin
Why Did Baghdadi Jews Stop Writing to their Brethren in Mainz? — Some Comments about the Reading Practices of Iraqi Jews in the Nineteenth Century 95

Geoffrey Roper
Arabic Books Printed in Malta 1826–42: Some Physical Characteristics 111

Heather J. Sharkey
Christian Missionaries and Colloquial Arabic Printing 131

Philip C. Sadgrove
The Press, Engine of a Mini-renaissance in Zanzibar (1860–1920) 151

Relli Shechter
From Journalism to Promotion of Goods: Why and How Did Press Publishers Establish Advertising Agencies in Egypt, 1890–1939? 179

Huda Smitshuijzen AbiFarès
Arabic Typography: Call for a Cultural Rebirth 193

Preface

The papers collected in this volume were all presented in some form or other at an international symposium appropriately held in the Gutenberg Museum in Mainz from 8 to 13 September 2002 as a contribution to the activities of the first WOCMES (World Congress for Middle Eastern Studies) held at the Johannes Gutenberg University. To be able to hold such a conference in the Gutenberg Museum in the birthplace of Gutenberg, the father of modern printing, was a particular privilege much appreciated by all those present. There could be no better place than Mainz to document the history of printing in Middle Eastern languages. Alongside the symposium a special exhibition was held in the Museum to illustrate the history of book and newspaper printing in Middle Eastern languages. The exhibition was accompanied by a splendid extensive and beautifully illustrated catalogue, *Sprachen des nahen Ostens und die Druckrevolution: Eine interkulturelle Begegnung / Middle Eastern Languages and the Print Revolution: A Cross-Cultural Encounter,* edited by Eva Hanebutt-Benz, Dagmar Glass and Geoffrey Roper (Wva-Verlag Skulima, Westhofen, 2002) in collaboration with Theo Smets, containing detailed studies by specialists on letterpress printing in the west, oriental scripts from European type foundries, and printing in Hebrew, Arabic, Coptic, Armenian, Syriac, Persian and Turkish. One of the papers published in the catalogue by Hrant Gabeyan, a former employee of Linotype, on his own experiences of modern developments in Arabic typesetting was given at the symposium. Special thanks go the curators and administrative staff of the Gutenberg Museum for their support both to the exhibition and the symposium. The Gutenberg Museum collaborated with specialists from the University of Erlangen-Nürnberg, the Cambridge University Library and other institutions in Germany, Great Britain, France and the USA in arranging the exhibition. The overall project was supported with sponsorship from the Stiftung Rheinland-Pfalz für Kultur, Internationale Gutenberg-Gesellschaft, Agfa-Monotype Corporation, the first World Congress for Middle Eastern Studies (WOCMES 2002) in Mainz, Friedrich-Alexander-Universität, Erlangen-Nürnberg and Schneidersöhne Papier.

At the final session of the symposium I undertook to collect the papers and seek a publisher; my fellow editors on the *Journal of Semitic Studies* agreed to facilitate and support the publication of the proceedings. This volume contains papers on a wide range of subjects reflecting current research on newspaper and book printing in the countries and the languages of the Middle East, covering Egypt, Iran, the Ottoman Empire, Palestine, Iraq, Algeria, Sudan, Zanzibar, Malta, India, Turkistan and England. The languages embraced are Arabic, Persian, Ottoman Turkish, Judeo-Arabic and Hebrew. Many of the articles are accompanied by illustrations of the output of these various presses. Cheng-Hsiang Hsu begins with a survey of Arabic, Turkish and Persian publications printed in Egypt in the period from 1822 to 1851. Olympiada Scheglova gives the general characteristics of the repertoire of books in Persian published lithographically in Turkistan during the period 1883 to 1917. The paper of Ulrich Marzolph gives details of a projected Union Catalogue of Illustrated Persian Lithographed Books. Nedret Kuran-Burçoğlu explores the work of the Ottoman calligrapher, Osman Zeki Bey, and his printing office, the Matbaa-i Osmaniye, active in Istanbul from 1866 to 1927. Christiane Czygan investigates the Young Ottoman newspaper *Ḥurriyet*, that appeared in London from 1868 to 1870. Two papers look at pre-1948 Palestine: Ami Ayalon looks at the modest achievements of the publishing industry amongst the Arab community and René Wildangel at the emergence of a new public through the Arab Palestinian media from 1929 to 1945. Orit Bashkin's paper examines a community in nineteenth century Iraq of Jewish readers, whose literary and cultural artefacts in Hebrew and Judeo-Arabic were produced not only in Baghdad but also in India, Eastern Europe and Palestine. Geoffrey Roper tackles some physical characteristics of the Arabic books printed in Malta by the Church Missionary Society between 1826 and 1842. Heather Sharkey looks at the active role of Christian missionaries in promoting the publication of works in spoken or colloquial Arabic in the 1920s and 1930s. Relli Shechter explains why and how publishers established advertising agencies in Egypt from 1890 to 1939. Finally Huda Smitshuijzen AbiFarès calls for a cultural rebirth of the visual branding of Arab/Islamic culture through new design approaches to Arabic type.

Philip Sadgrove
University of Manchester

A Survey of Arabic-character Publications Printed in Egypt during the Period of 1238–1267 (1822–1851)

Cheng-Hsiang Hsu

National Chengchi University, Taipei

Introduction

It was under the rule of Muḥammad ʿAlī (1805–48) that Egypt entered upon a programme of reforms which affected the military, educational, industrial, and economic life of the country and eventually transformed it from a tributary province of the Ottoman state to a Mediterranean power which was able to challenge the authority of Istanbul. The printing press was one of the key instruments in the implementation of the reform programmes, and was actively fostered and promoted for the publication of many books on military, scientific and technical subjects, as well as many others on subjects, which might be described as useful to the development and modernization of the country. The printing and publishing enterprise promoted by Muḥammad ʿAlī attracted interest among his contemporaries and later scholars, who have produced some works of merit. Amongst these works the most noteworthy are several lists of publications given by some contemporaries, such as J.T. Reinaud (1831), Joseph von Hammer-Purgstall (1832), Count Médem (c. 1837), John Bowring (c. 1837), and T.X. Bianchi (1842), and some studies, which deal with various aspects of the printing/publishing activities of the time.[1]

Despite these useful works and several reference works on Arabic printed books, there has, so far, been no attempt at a complete and systematic review of the publications produced in the reign of Muḥammad ʿAlī, let alone the whole of the nineteenth century. We still have no comprehensive understanding of the range of activities in the field of book-production during this period, and our knowledge of early Egyptian publications still remains very much the same as it was in 1842, when Bianchi made the greatest contribution with his list of 243 publications produced in

1 See Richard N. Verdery, 'The Publications of the Būlāq Press under Muḥammad 'Alī of Egypt', *Journal of American Oriental Society* 91 (1971), 129–32.

Egypt between 1822 and 1842. It is on this list that most later studies and works are based, often with very little addition. What is worse is that many bibliographical inaccuracies seem to have been introduced into not a few of the works and bibliographies written since Bianchi's time.

However, the existence of many contemporary and later bibliographical lists, studies of various kinds in specific fields and published catalogues of printed books have made the possibility of a bibliography of early Egyptian publications more realistic. With the availability of several previously unexploited lists of publications, issued by the Egyptian government between 1260/1844–5 and 1266/1849–50, it has been possible to discover much more detailed information on the activities of book-production as regards prices and in particular the number of copies printed/consumed (i.e. distributed and/or sold) of many works which are given in these officially-issued lists of publications.[2]

This article gives a survey of early Egyptian publications produced from 1822 to the mid-nineteenth century, or more precisely during the period of 1238–67 (1822–51), according to a list of 570 works, or more precisely 472 works in 570 editions, which has been established from a number of the more important and reliable sources.[3] The need for such a bibliography can be particularly perceived from the following comparative table showing the works/editions mentioned in some more important sources and studies.

Surveys of publications

These 570 works, as compared with a maximum 304 works in any previous individual source of importance, will undoubtedly provide us with a better basis for the understanding of various aspects of early printing and publishing activities which took place under Muḥammad ʻAlī. Based on the List, some surveys will be carried out according to the classifications of languages, subjects, and the nature of writing, such as a contemporary writing, a translation or a classical work (i.e. written before 1800 AD), in addition to their chronological output.

Four appendices at the end of this article serve as the basis of surveys. The first (Appendix II) is to show the trend of publications, chronologically, according to the

2 There are three lists, which are known to have been published. However, only two of them were available; they have been abbreviated as 'BūlāqI͟F' and 'BūlāqMK' respectively.

3 This bibliography of 570 works will be hereafter referred to as 'the List' only.

languages of Arabic, Turkish and Persian. The second one (Appendix III) is to survey the publications according to the nature of the publications, which have been classified into contemporary writing, translations, and classical literature. The third one (Appendix IV) is to further classify the publications, within the classifications of the Appendix III, into the categories of general works, philosophy, religion, social science, language, science, technology, arts, literature and history (including geography and travel), along the lines of the Dewey Decimal Classification. The fourth (Appendix V) is a detailed subject output according to decades and languages. The criteria of classification are considered in view of the historical development and social needs of the time.

The Būlāq printing press is generally regarded as the first indigenous Arabic press set up in Egypt by Muslims. It was established by Muḥammad ʿAlī, ruler of Egypt (1805–1849), mainly to facilitate his reform programmes. During the period under study (i.e., 1238–67/1822–51), the vast majority of the 570 works published in Egypt were printed on government presses, and of these the Būlāq press played the most prominent part, with a total of 526 works (or 92.3% of the total) to its credit. Although in the beginning most of works were produced for the government, later some works were printed for private individuals. This indicates that the trend of printing/publishing had developed to meet the need of the general public as well, not wholly to respond to official needs.

The works published under the patronage of the government are termed here as *maṭbū'āt al-ḥukūma* (official publications). They include military manuals, works on administration, medical sciences, mathematics, veterinary science, agriculture, and other sciences (such as chemistry, mineralogy, geodesy, botany, and mechanics, etc.), in addition to that of language, religious writings, literature, and geographical and historical subjects. While those for private individuals are termed as *maṭbū'āt al-multazimīn* (privately-contracted works), and include mainly works of language, religious writings, and literature. The privately contracted works increased significantly from 1251/1835–6.

Among these 570 publications, many deal with military matters (i.e. 86 works or 15.1% of the total), administration (48 works or 8.4%), medical sciences (47 works or 8.2%), mathematics (30 works or 5.3%), veterinary sciences (23 works or 4%), agriculture (10 works or 1.8%), and other sciences (15 works or 2.6%). These 260 works (or 45.6%) and several others are of a utilitarian nature and were intended to facilitate the governmental programmes of reform. Some 40 translations of a literary nature and as many as 264 (or 46.2%) religious, linguistic and literary works of traditional literature (of which at least a third were printed/published at private expense) were also produced with the aim of raising the general level of education and meeting the needs of the reading-public.

The privately contracted publications consist of some 80 Turkish works (including 36 *dīwāns*, 25 religious works, 10 prose-works, 3 works of epistolography, and several linguistic works), 33 Arabic works (including 19 on religion, 8 on literature and 6 on linguistics), and several Persian works of literature. This would indicate that the book-market at the time of Muḥammad ʿAlī was dominated by Turkish works.

However, the needs of the Egyptian government seem to have been met from the early 1830s, by the production of more Arabic works of certain categories, such as scientific and technical works. It is not surprising therefore to note that in the period of this study there were produced, under the auspices of the government, more than a hundred scientific works in Arabic and less than 30 in Turkish, together with more than 40 works of a linguistic nature and less than 10 in Turkish. Official Arabic publications in other fields, such as religion, literature and history (including geography) also generally outnumbered their Turkish counterparts, with the exception of the works dealing with military science and administration, of which 13 Arabic and 70 Turkish were produced in the former category, and 5 Arabic and 15 Turkish were produced in the latter; with a total of 200 Arabic works and some 170 Turkish works being produced by the government.

Chronologically speaking, 26 works were produced in the first period (1238–41/1822–6) of the first decade (1238–47/1822–32), which include 9 military works (8 in Turkish and 1 in Arabic), 9 works of science and technology, 4 on Arabic language, 3 in the field of religion, and 1 on logic. It seems that the primary aim of publications was for their use in the reform programmes. Despite the limitation of the scope and purpose of these early publications, there were certain works, which had a wider benefit for the general public. For instance, we see the publication of some almanacs, which fulfilled general social, economic, and religious needs, while some of the religious and linguistic publications would serve as text-books for traditional education, as many of them (including a work on logic) were texts/works read at al-Azhar.

The importance of the year 1826 lies in that it launched the expansion of reform programmes as well as a systematic educational system in Egypt. Owing to this expansion, not only were printing-presses also installed in many of the administrative, military, educational and industrial establishments, but the Dīwān al-Jihādiyya was also placed in charge of the Būlāq printing-press, which had been under the personal supervision of Muḥammad ʿAlī since its founding in 1822. Thus, in the second period (1242–47/1826–32) of the first decade, the output reached 61, in which there were 18 military works, 5 administrative works, 7 Arabic grammatical works, 5 religious ones, 5 historical, 3 Turkish-Arabic (or Turkish-Persian) vocabularies, 3 on epistolography, 3 poetic works, 2 mathematical works, 2 almanacs/calendars, 2 medical works, 2 Persian prose works and 1 geographical work. Apart from the pedagogical nature of these publications, some of them could also certainly be classed as entertainment for the reading-public (such as those three historical works). It was probably owing to the demand for printed books that all the publications began to be priced for sale from around 1246/1830–1.

In the second decade (1248–57/1832–42), the output was at its height (277 in total, 127 in the first five years and 150 in the second). Works printed by the official presses at private expense began to appear from the eleventh year (1248/1832–3) and increased rapidly during the next ten years. It seems, therefore, that the policy of commercialising the official printing establishments for the benefit of the public had been introduced at this time to meet the demands of the reading-public. In the first five years of this period (1248–52/1832–37), there were 18 privately-contracted works (14 in Turkish and 3 in Arabic), in addition to 3 Arabic works which are regarded in this study as probably privately-printed works. They are mostly in the fields of religion, language and literature. The remaining 106 works include: 23 military, 21 medical, 9 veterinary works, 5 administrative works, 5 mathematical works, 3 almanacs/calendars, 1 on mineralogy, 1 on chemical technology, 13 on Arabic grammar, 1 on ethics, 2 on epistolography, 4 religious, 5 literary works, and 9 historical works.

The strength of the growing book-market for publications can be seen particularly in the next five years (1253–57/1837–42), when some 65 works (or

43.3%) of the total 150 works produced in that period are known to have been published under private patronage. These 65 privately-sponsored works consisted of 49 Turkish works (19 *dīwān*s or poetic collections, 10 religious works, 7 literary works, 3 vocabularies, 1 on epistolography, 1 ethics, and 1 history), 15 Arabic works (7 on religion, 3 grammatical works, 2 literary, 1 on lexicography, and 1 almanac), and 1 Persian poetry. This indicates the predominance of Turkish works in the privately-sponsored publications, and that much of the demand of the reading public was for works of literature, religion, and linguistics, with 62 (out of the total 65) works being produced in these fields.

The remaining 85 works, mostly officially-sponsored, include 52 in Arabic, 24 in Turkish, 4 in Persian, and 4 language unknown. They are 15 in military sciences, 8 Arabic grammar, 7 on religion, 7 on veterinary sciences, 6 in medical sciences, 6 on mathematics, 5 administrative works, 4 historical works, 4 geographical works, 4 Persian literary works, 3 Turkish vocabularies, 3 agricultural works, 2 literary works, 2 on physics, 2 on engineering, and 1 each in the category of almanac, logic, school text-book, geodesy, geology, and botany. This second decade had been marked, in particular, by the large output of Arabic works and translation works.

The expansion in the publication of books seems to have been short-lived, for we see the annual output generally decrease in the third decade (1258–67/1842–51). The decline of publishing may be to a lesser or greater extent a result of Muḥammad ʿAlī's political setback in 1841. In the first five years of this period (1258–62/1842–6), there were 29 privately-sponsored publications (including 20 in Turkish, 7 in Arabic, and 2 in Persian) and 69 officially-published works (24 in Turkish, 43 in Arabic, 1 in Persian, and 1 language unknown). The former includes: 10 Turkish *dīwān*s, 9 religious works, 3 works on epistolography, 2 Turkish vocabularies, 2 Arabic literary works, and 2 Persian literary works. In addition, they published the Arabic regulations for the Jamʿiyyat al-Maʿārif al-Miṣriyya (the Egyptian Society). In the latter category, there were 14 medical works, 9 administrative works, 8 mathematical works, 7 religious works, 6 literary and historical works, 3 works on agriculture, 2 works on geodesy, and 1 each on chemistry and engineering, in addition to 2 lists of publications which were issued by the government around 1260/1844–5 and 1262/1845–6 respectively to be distributed to promote the sale of books.

In the second five years of this period (1263–7/1846–51), the number of privately-sponsored publications has not been ascertained owing to the lack of information. But we can only assume that some of the religious, linguistic and literary works were published under private patronage, as these were the type of works, which had previously been privately-sponsored. The 38 works in these fields include: 16 religious works (9 in Arabic, 6 in Turkish, and 1 in Persian), 14 linguistic works (9 in Arabic and 5 in Turkish), 8 literary works (4 in Arabic, 2 in Turkish, and 2 in Persian). There were 34 works (22 in Arabic, 9 in Turkish, and 3 language unknown), which were published under the auspices of the government and include: 7 administrative works, 5 on medical sciences, 5 historical works, 4 military works, 4 on mathematics, 2 on veterinary sciences, 2 almanacs, 2 travel works, and 1 each on agriculture and physics, in addition to 1 school text-book.

Conclusion

The stagnation in publishing seems to have affected not only official but unofficial publications as well. In particular, we find that there were no Turkish *dīwān*s published in the last five years of the period under discussion. This may indicate the shift in the production of these works from Egypt to other places, especially Istanbul, where we find that Turkish literary works, especially *dīwān*s, were being produced continuously in a steadily increasing stream. Indeed, some Turkish *dīwān*s previously produced in Egypt in an incomplete form were now being published in Istanbul as a complete edition. The halt in the publication of Turkish *dīwān*s in Egypt may also indicate the decline of the Egyptian-Turkish book-trade. More important is that Egyptian printing and publishing activities had developed into Arabic-dominated enterprises in terms of both officially- and unofficially- sponsored publications by the end of Muḥammad ʿAlī's reign.

Many personnel, who had previously worked in Muḥammad ʿAlī's printing/publishing establishments, left their official jobs to act as directors, publishers, and correctors, etc. in new private printing presses. These appeared probably in response to the demand for printed books which was not being met by the government, after it lost its original zeal for promoting the publications of books in the late 1840s, as some works bearing the names of privately-owned printing presses began to appear from this time on. We also find that many published religious, linguistic and literary works of a more traditional nature produced in this period were reprinted in the following decades after 1850. The reprinting of many of these works is proof of the general demand for them; linguistic works seem to have been the most widely read.

Many native Egyptians, who had been trained through Muḥammad ʿAlī's various reform programmes, had contributed a great deal towards the publication of books and periodicals in the second half of the nineteenth century, in which the period of social, political and literary activity is known as the *nahḍa* in the modern history of the Arabs. In this movement, the printing-press has been regarded by many as one of the main factors contributing to its birth. Muḥammad ʿAlī's introduction of Arabic printing actually created a generation of intellectuals, who made significant contributions to cultural life during and after his reign; some even pursued their printing/publishing enterprises outside Egypt.

BIBLIOGRAPHY

AlexMB = Alexandria, al-Maktaba al-Baladiyya, *Fahāris,* 16 Parts (Alexandria, 1343–7/1925–8)

BianchiCG (1842) = T.X. Bianchi, 'Catalogue Général des livres arabes, persans et turcs, imprimés à Boulac en Égypte depuis l'introduction de l'imprimerie dans ce pays', *Journal Asiatique*, Serie 4, 2 (1845), 24–61

BM = British Museum

BowringRE (1837) = John Bowring, Report on Egypt and Canada. Addressed to the Right Hon. Lord Viscount Palmerston, Her Majesty's Principal Secretary of State for Foreign Affairs, &c. &c. &c. (London HMSO, 1840)

BūlāqIF (1845) = Būlāq Printing-press, *Ishbū Fihrist Maḥrūsa-i Miṣrda Maḥkama Jiwārinda Kā'in Kutubkhānada Mawjūd ūlān Kitāblarun 'Adadī Īla Ism wa-Shuhratlarīnī wa-Har Birīnun Fī'ātī Bayān Īdar* (Būlāq 1845?)

BūlāqMK (1846) = Būlāq Printing-press, *Maḥrūsada Kā'in Kitābkhāna-i 'Āmirada Mawjūd ūlān Kitāblarun Miqdār wa-Fī'ātlarī ... etc.* (Būlāq *c.* 1262/1845–6)

CairoDKM = Cairo, Dār al-Kutub al-Miṣriyya, *Fihris al-Kutub al-'Arabiyya al-Mawjūda bi-al-Dār ... etc.*, 1st ed., Vols. II–VI (Cairo 1345–52/1926–33)

DornCO = B. Dorn, 'Catalogue des ouvrages arabes, persans et turcs, publiés à Constantinople, en Égypte et en Perse; qui se trouve au Musée Asiatique de l'Académie', *Bulletin de l'Académie Impériale des Sciences de Saint-Petersbourg*, vol.10 (1866), 182–99

GAL (1949) = Carl Brockelmann, *Geschichte der Arabischen Litteratur,* 5 vols. (Leiden 1937–49)

HammerGOR (1832) = Joseph von Hammer-Purgstall, *Geschichte des Osmanischen Reiches,* 10 vols. (1832; Graz, Akademische Druck- u. Verlagsanstalt, 1963)

IstBK = İstanbul, Belediye Kütüphanesi, *İstanbul Belediye Kütüphanesi Kataloğu,* Osman Ergin Kitaplari, 2 vols. (Istanbul 1953–4)

IstUK = İstanbul, Üniversitesi Kütüphanesi, *Arapça Basmalar Alfabe Kataloğu,* 2 parts, by Fehmī Edhem Karatay (İstanbul Üniversitesi 1951–3)

= -----, *Farsça Basmalar Kataloğu,* by Fehmī Edhem Karatay (İstanbul Üniversitesi 1949)

= -----, *Türkçe Basmalar Alfabe Kataloğu, Memleketimizde ilk Türk matbaasinin Kuruluşundan yeni harflerin Kabulüne Kadar (1729–1928),* Hazirliyan Fehmi Edhem Karatay, 2 parts (İstanbul Üniversitesi 1956)

MedemNI (1837) = Count Médem, 'Notes des livres qui ont été imprimés dans l'imprimerie de Boulaq, dès la commencement jusqu'à l'année courante', in René Cattaui Bey, *Le Règne de Mohamed Aly d'après les archives russes en Égypte,* tome III (Rome 1936), 31–4

ÖzegeTEK (1982) = M. Seyfettin Özege, *Eski Harflerle Basilmiş Türkçe Eserler Kataloğu,* Forma 1–152 (Istanbul 1971–82)

ReinaudNO (1831) = J.T. Reinaud, 'Notice des ouvrages arabes, persans et turcs imprimés en Égypte', *Journal Asiatique,* 8 (1831), 333–43

RiḍwānQMB (1953) = Abū al-Futūḥ Riḍwān, 'Qā'ima bi-Maṭbū'āt Būlāq min Inshā'ihā fī Sanat 1821 ilā Sanat 1842', in the same author's *Tārīkh Maṭba'at Būlāq wa-Lamḥa fī Tārīkh al-Ṭibā'a fī Buldān al-Sharq al-Awsaṭ* (Cairo 1953)

SarkisMMA (1928) = Ilyān Yūsuf Sarkīs, *Mu'jam al-Maṭbū'āt al-'Arabiyya wa-al-Mu'arraba wa-Huwa Shāmil li-Asmā' al-Kutub al-Maṭbū'a fī al-Aqṭār al-Sharqiyya wa-al-Gharbiyya,* 2 vols. (Cairo 1928)

ShayyālQK (1951) = Jamāl al-Dīn al-Shayyāl, 'Qā'ima bi-al-Kutub allatī Turjimat fī 'Aṣr Muḥammad 'Alī fī Jamī' al-Mawādd mā 'Adā al-Funūn al-Ḥarbiyya wa-al-Baḥriyya', in the same author's *Tārīkh al-Tarjama wa-al-Ḥaraka al-Thaqāfiyya fī 'Aṣr Muḥammad 'Alī* (Cairo 1951), 7–27

= -----, 'Qā'ima bi-al-Kutub al-Ḥarbiyya wa-al-Baḥriyya allatī Turjimat fī 'Aṣr Muḥammad 'Alī', in ibid., Appendix 29–36

VanDyckIQ (1895) = Edward Abbot Van Dyck, *Kitāb Iktifā' al-Qunū' bi-mā Huwa Maṭbū' min Ashhar al-Ta'ālīf al-'Arabiyya fī al-Maṭābi' al-Sharqiyya wa-al-Gharbiyya,* compiled by Van Dyck, assisted by al-Sayyid Muḥammad 'Alī al-Biblāwī (Cairo 1313/1895–6)

ZenkerBO (1862) = J.Th. Zenker, *Bibliotheca Orientalis, Manuel de Bibliographie Orientale,* 2 vols. (Leipzig 1846–61)

Appendix I: Egyptian publications mentioned in some important sources

	Language. Sources	Arabic	Turkish	Persian	Unknown	Total
LITERARY	1. ReinaudNO (1831)	19	27	2	-	48 (55)
	2. HammerGOR (1832)	18	33	1	-	54 (56)
	3. MedemNI(1837)	21	38	2	1	62 (76)
	4. BowringRE(1837)	32	50	2	1	85(95)
	5. BianchiCG(1842)	103	124	6	-	233 (243)
	6. BūlāqIF(1845)	73	54	2	2	131 (142)
	7. BūlāqMK (1846)	123	124	4	27	278 (289)
	8. ZenkerBO(1862)	103	125	6	-	234
	9. VanDyckIQ (1895)	85	6	-	-	91
	10. SarkisMMA(1928)	170	6	-	-	176
	11. GAL (1949)	80	13	-	-	93
	12. ShayyālQK (1951)	101	64	-	-	165 (191)
	13. RidwānQMB (1953)	109	130	6	14	259
	14. ÖzegeTEK (1982)	4	122	1	-	127
BIBLIOG	15. AlexMB	64	41	2	-	107
	16. BM	117	54	7	-	178
	17. CairoDKM	134	162	8	-	304
	18. DomCO	66	66	5	1	138 (147)
	19. IstBK	7	19	7	-	33
	20. IstUK	38	16	1	-	55
	Total (in the List)	255	259	14	42	570

- Due to the principles and methods adopted in this study, the number of works listed here may differ from that given in the original source. The figure in each column represents that listed in this study. However, the original number of works mentioned in every source is given, if different, in brackets in the total (i.e. the sixth column). Apart from several catalogues of Dār al-Kutub (mainly CairoFKA, CairoFKT, and CairoDKM), two works were also published on the collection of printed books preserved in that library, i.e. ShurbajīQAM and Cairo, Dār al-Kutub al-Qawmiyya, *Fihris al-Maṭbū'āt al-Turkiyya al-'Uthmāniyya allatī Iqtanathā Dār al-Kutub al-Qawmiyya mundhu Inshā'ihā 'Āmm 1870 hattā Nihāyat 'Āmm 1969*, 1969, 2 vols. (Cairo 1982), of which the latter was not made available until very recently and has not been used in this study. However, in the former 141 Arabic works and 9 Turkish were mentioned with a total of 150 works/editions. Sources have been classified, according to their nature, into either literary or bibliographical (abbreviated as bibliog).

Appendix II: Chronological Survey of Publications According to Language

	Arabic	Turkish	Persian	Unknown	Total
1238 (1822–23)	2	4	-	-	6/6
1239 (1823–24)	2	4	-	-	6/12
1240 (1824–25)	2	4	-	-	6/18
1241 (1825–26)	5	3	-	-	8/26
1242 (1826–27)	7	10	-	1	18/44
1243 (1827–28)	2	5	2	2	11/55
1244 (1828–29)	3	2	-	-	5/60
1245 (1829–30)	1	8	-	-	9/69
1246 (1830–31)	2	7	-	-	9/78
1247 (1831–32)	2	5	-	1	8/86
1248 (1832–33)	4	11	-	2	17/103
1249 (1833–34)	13	7	1	-	21/124
1250 (1834–35)	19	11	-	-	30/154
1251 (1835–36)	14	14	-	1	29/183
1252 (1836–37)	15	15	-	-	30/213
1253 (1837–38)	8	10	1	2	21/234
1254 (1838–39)	12	19	1	-	32/266
1255 (1839–40)	13	15	-	1	29/295
1256 (1840–41)	13	13	1	1	28/323
1257 (1841–42)	20	17	2	1	40/363
1258 (1842–43)	7	11	-	-	18/381
1259 (1843–44)	12	8	1	-	21/402
1260 (1844–45)	14	10	-	1	25/427
1261 (1845)	8	8	2	-	18/445
1262 (1845–46)	10	6	-	-	16/461
1263 (1846–47)	11	-	1	-	12/473
1264 (1847–48)	11	6	-	-	17/490
1265 (1848–49)	5	8	-	2	15/505
1266 (1849–50)	13	5	2	-	20/525
1267 (1850–51)	4	4	-	-	8/533
No Date	1	9	-	27	37/570
Total	255	259	14	42	570/570

Appendix III: Chronological Survey of Publications According to the Nature of the Work

	Contemporary (Arabic/Turkish)	Translation (Arabic/Turkish)	Classical (Arabic/Turkish)	Others	Total
1238 (1822–23)	1/1	1/3	-	-	6/6
1239 (1823–24)	-/2	1/1	1/1	-	6/12
1240 (1824–25)	1/1	-/2	1/1	-	6/18
1241 (1825–26)	1/2	-/1	4/-	-	8/26
1242 (1826–27)	1/5	2/5	4/-	1	18/44
1243 (1827–28)	1/2	-/1	1/2	4	11/55
1244 (1828–29)	2/1	-/1	1/-	-	5/60
1245 (1829–30)	1/4	-/3	-/1	-	9/69
1246 (1830–31)	1/3	-/4	1/-	-	9/78
1247 (1831–32)	-/3	-/2	2/-	1	8/86
1248 (1832–33)	-/3	3/4	1/4	2	17/103
1249 (1833–34)	2/3	7/4	4/-	1	21/124
1250 (1834–35)	6/5	11/5	2/1	-	30/154
1251 (1835–36)	2/-	3/9	9/5	1	29/183
1252 (1836–37)	3/5	8/5	4/5	-	30/213
1253 (1837–38)	1/4	1 /-	6/6	3	21/234
1254 (1838–39)	3/7	9/5	-/7	1	32/266
1255 (1839–40)	3/4	5/4	5/7	1	29/295
1256 (1840–41)	2/2	7/2	4/9	2	28/323
1257 (1841–42)	3/4	12 /-	5/13	3	40/363
1258 (1842–43)	2/6	4/2	1/3	-	18/381
1259 (1843–44)	1/4	8/2		1	21/402
1260 (1844–45)	3/6	9/2		1	25/427
1261 (1845)	1/3	4/1		2	18/445
1262 (1845–46)	2/3	4/-	3/2	-	16/461
1263 (1846–47)	3/-	5/-	2/2	1	12/473
1264 (1847–48)	3/1	4/1	3/4	-	17/490
1265 (1848–49)	2/6	1/-	2/2	2	15/505
1266 (1849–50)	1/5	5/-	5/-	2	20/525
1267 (1850–51)	-/1	1/-	3/3	-	8/533
No Date	-/4	-/4	1/1	27	37/570
Total	54/100	115/73	86/86	56	570/570

Appendix IV: Survey of Publications According to Language, Nature of Work and Subject

		Arabic	Turkish	Persian	Unknown	Total
CONTEMPORARY	General	1	3	-	4	8/8
	Philosophy	-	-	-	-	0/8
	Religion	6	7	-	-	13/21
	Social Sciences	11	30	-	-	41/62
	Language	9	16	-	1	26/88
	Science	9	6	-	3	18/106
	Technology	10	16	-	1	27/133
	Arts	-	-	-	1	1/134
	Literature	5	19	-	-	24!158
	History	3	3	-	1	6/164
TRANSLATIONS	General	-	-	-	-	0/0
	Philosophy	1	-	-	-	1/1
	Religion	-	3	-	-	3/4
	Social Sciences	9	46	-	32	87/91
	Language	-	2	-	-	2/93
	Science	26	6	-	-	32/125
	Technology	61	8	-	-	69/194
	Arts	-	-	-	-	0/194
	Literature	2	-	-	-	2/196
	History	16	8	-	-	24/220
CLASSICAL	General	-	3	-	-	3/3
	Philosophy	1	2	-	-	3/6
	Religion	25	37	1	-	63/69
	Social Sciences	-	-	-	-	0/69
	Language	44	1	-	-	45/114
	Science	2	-	-	-	2/116
	Technology	-	-	-	-	0/116
	Arts	-	-	-	-	0/116
	Literature	13	39	13	-	65/181
	History	1	4	-	-	5/186
	Total	255	259	14	42	570

Appendix Va: Subject Output of General Nature, Philosophy, Religion and Social Sciences

	First Decade 1238-41 (1822-26)				First Decade 1242-47 (1826-32)				Second Decade 1248-52 (1832-37)				Second Decade 1853-57 (1837-42)				Third Decade 1258-62 (1842-46)				Third Decade 1263-67 (1846-51)				Works without Date			Total Language				Total Sub Classes	Total Main Classes
	A.	T.	P.	U.	A.	T.	P.	U.	A.	T.	P.	U.	A.	T.	P.	U.	A.	T.	P.	U.	A.	T.	P.	U.	A.	T.	U.	A.	T.	P.	U.		
General																											4				4	4	11
Bibliography																		2				1							3			J	
Encyclopaedias										1				2															3			5	
Organization																	1											1				I	
Philosophy																																	
Logic	1												1															2				z	4
Ethics										1				1															2			l	
Religion						1												1											2			l	
Tafsīr													1	1				1			2	1						3	3			e	
Ḥadīth																					1							1				i	
Jurisprudence		1			1	1			1	4			2	6			2	2			2	3						8	17			u	
Theology	1	1			1				1	1			3	3			1	4			1	1						8	10			n	
Sects																	1				1							2				^	79
Islamic Ethics																							1							1		j	
Manners/Customs													1								1							2				i	
Mysticism									1	1			1	2				1				1						2	5			?	
History/Biography						1			1	4			2	3			1	2			1							5	10			15	
Social Sciences																											1				1	1	
Administration						2		3	1	2		2		2		4	3	5		1	1	3		3		1	15	5	15		28	48	128
Military	1	8			3	15			2	17			5	9			1	4				5				3	3	12	61		3	76	
Education									1				1								1							3				3	

A. = Arabic Language, T. = Turkish Language, P. = Persian Language, U. = Unknown Language

Appendix Vb: Subject Output in Languages, Pure Sciences and Technology

Years / Subjects	First Decade 1238-41 (1822-26) A.	T.	P.	U.	First Decade 1242-47 (1826-32) A.	T.	P.	U.	Second Decade 1248-52 (1832-37) A.	T.	P.	U.	Second Decade 1253-57 (1837-42) A.	T.	P.	U.	Third Decade 1258-62 (1842-46) A.	T.	P.	U.	Third Decade 1263-67 (1846-51) A.	T.	P.	U.	Works without. Date A.	T.	U.	Total Language A.	T.	P.	U.	Total Sub Classes	Total Main Classes
Language																											1				1	1	
Arabic																					2							2				2	
Arabic Lexicon	1									1			2															3	1			4	
Arabic Morphology	1				4				2				2				2				2							13				13	
Arabic Grammar	2				3				12				9				4				5							35				35	
Turkish Lexicon						3				1				6				2				2							14			14	73
Turkish Prosody																						1							1			1	
Persian																						2							2			2	
Persian Lexicon										1																			1			1	
Pure Sciences																																	
Mathematics	1	2				2			3	2			4				5	3			4				1	1		20	10			30	
Geodesy													1				2											3				3	
Almanac/Calendars	2					1		1	1				1								2					1		7	2		3	12	52
Physics													2								1							3				3	
Chemistry									1								1											2				2	
Geology													1															1				1	
Botany													1															1				1	
Technology																																	
Medical Sciences					1	1			16	5			5	1			11	2			5							38	9			47	
Engineering													2				1											3				3	
Military Engineering		3							1	3				1												2		1	9			10	96
Agriculture					1	1							2	1			1	2			1						1	5	4		1	10	
Veterinary Science									7	2			7				6				2							22	2			24	
Chemical Tech.	1								1																			2				2	

Appendix Vc: Subject Output in Arts, Literature and History

Years / Subjects	First Decade								Second Decade								Third Decade								Works without Date			Total					
	1238-41 (1822-26)				1242-47 (1826-32)				1248-52 (1832-37)				1253 -57 (1837-42)				1258-63 (1842-46)				1263 -67 (1846-51)							Language				Sub- Classes	Main Classes
Subjects	A.	T.	P.	U.	A.	T.	P.	U.	A.	T.	P.	U.	A.	T.	P.	U.	A.	T.	P.	U.	A.	T.	P.	U.	A.	T.	U.	A.	T.	P.	U.		
The Arts																																	1
Music																											1				1	1	
Literature																																	
Arabic (*Inshā'*)					2				1								1				1							5				5	
Arabic Poetry					1				1				2				2											6				6	
Arabic Prose									4				1				2				2							9				9	
Arabic Rhetoric													1								1							2				2	
Turkish (*Inshā'*)						1				1				2				2											6			6	91
Turkish Poetry						2				3				21				10								1			37			37	
Turkish Prose										2				8								1							11			11	
Persian Poetry										2					2				1							1			3	3		6	
Persian Prose							2				1				3				2				2							10		10	
History									1					1			1											2	1			3	
Geography						1			2				3															5	1			6	
Travel									1					1			1				2							4	1			5	
Biography									1																			1				1	35
Ancient History													1	1														1	1			2	
European History						3				2			2					1			4							6	6			12	
Ottoman History						2				2												1							5			5	
Egyptian History									1																			1				1	
Total	11	15			17	37	2	4	65	58	1	3	68	72	5	5	50	44	3	1	45	22	3	2	1	9	27	257	257	14	42	570	
	26				60				127				150				98				72				37								
	86								277								170																

The Repertoire of Books in Persian Published Lithographically in Turkestan during 1883–1917

O.P. Scheglova

Institute of Oriental Studies, St. Petersburg

National book-printing in Turkestan, as well as in India and Iran, gained its foothold in the lithographic form. This was the result of the phenomenon of Islamic culture being closely connected with the many century-old tradition of the art of calligraphy. The first commercial enterprise, which produced books in Oriental languages for sale, was the typo-lithography of S.I. Lakhtin (typography from 1877 and typo-lithography from 1883 to 1893). It was there, where lithographic books were produced for the first time after Khiva in 1874. According to the information of E.K. Betger, the first book published in Tashkent in November 1883 was the *Sabat al-'Ajizin* by Sufi Allayar.[1]

The major part of the oriental books was published in Tashkent and printed by the three largest typo-lithographies, namely those of O.A. Portsev (1887–1917), V.M. Il'yin (founded in 1893, typo-lithography from 1899 to 1912) and G.H. Arifdzhanov (1906–18). Lithographic printing houses also existed in Samarqand, Qokand, Namangan and Marghelan. The largest number of lithographic books, which has survived, is preserved in the Institute of Oriental Studies in Tashkent. Unfortunately, there is no printed catalogue of them. In the year of 1963, the number of the editions in all Oriental languages was equal to 14,620.[2]

The Russian scholar A.A. Semenov, who was the pioneer in studying lithographic book-printing (1912), remarked that the knowledge of the lithographic heritage is equally important for studying the national culture of Central Asia to that of the hand-written legacy. In the Introduction to his unpublished Catalogue of

1 E.K. Betger, 'Iz istorii knizhnogo dela v Uzbekistane (K 70-letiyu poyavleniya pervoy uzbekskoy litografirovannoy knigi)', *Izvestiya AN UzSSR*, 2 (1951), 75–6. About him see M.P. Avsharova and M.S.Viridarskiy, *Evgeniy Karlovich Betger (1887–1956). Ocherk zhiznii deyatel'nosti* (Tashkent 1960).

2 S.A. Azimdzhanova and D.G. Voronovskiy, 'Sobranie vostochnykh rukopisey Akademii Nauk Uzbekistana Uzbekskoy SSR', *Vostokovednye fondy krupneyshikh bibliotek Sovetskogo Soyuza. Stat'i i soobscheniya* (Moscow 1963).

lithographic books (compiled in 1938–40), he outlines three directions of research in this field.[3] In his opinion, the study of the lithographic production can give evidence to: a) 'intellectual requests and enlightenment of the Central Asian population in the pre-revolutionary times', b) 'the development of the lithographic business in the Central Asia' and c) 'the circulation of lithographic books of Indian origin in Central Asia'.

These three aspects have, to a significant extent, been tackled by the scholars, who have worked in Tashkent and Ashgabat during the post-war decades. The study of Almaz Yazberdiyev contains bibliographical evaluation of the material accumulated by 1974 and related to the study of the history of the matter.[4] Series of articles and dissertations are devoted to certain specific aspects of lithographic book printing in Central Asia in the late nineteenth — early twentieth century. However, only the titles of many of these dissertations are available.

The most considerable contribution to the study of the history of the creation of typographic enterprises in Central Asia, the function of certain printing houses and their destiny after the October revolution, as well as the artistic aspects and decoration of the Turkestan editions was made by a scholar from Tashkent Georgy Chabrov (1904–86).[5] He was a historian and an archivist, fond of books and arts and, along with teaching and studying many aspects of Central Asian culture, was constantly interested in lithographic book printing during the whole of his life. One of his last public presentations was his paper entitled the 'Turkestan lithographic book (1874–1917)', which was given in 1983 at the State Public Library in Leningrad (presently the National Library of Russia in St. Petersburg). His last publication was 'Illustration in the Turkestan lithographic book (1908–1916)' in which he deals with illustrations in the works of Persian classical literature also.[6] Unfortunately, his book dedicated to the Central Asian printed and lithographic book was never published.

---

3 G.N. Chabrov, 'Aleksandr Aleksandrovich Semenov kak knigoved', *Kniga. Issledovaniya i materialy*, sb. 3 (Moscow 1960), 408–19.

4 A.Yazberdiyev, *Iz istorii bibliografirovaniya natsional'noy pechati narodov Sredney Azii vtoroy poloviny XIX i pervoy chetverti XX veka* (Ashkhabat 1974).

5 About G.N. Chabrov and the bibliography of his works see B.V. Lunin, *Bibliograficheskie ocherki o deyatelyakh obschestvennykh nauk Uzbekistana*, vol. 2 (Tashkent 1977), 270–3.

6 G.N. Chabrov, 'Illyustratsiya v turkestanskoy litografirovannoy knige (1908–1916 gg.)', *Kniga. Issledovaniya i materialy*, sb. 49 (Moscow 1984), 95–106.

Other authors, such as M.I. Rustamov, R. Mahmudova and the aforementioned A. Yazberdiyev,[7] made additions and a few corrections to the general picture given by G. Chabrov. The dissertations of R. Mahmudova (1971)[8] and R. Holmatov (1989)[9] are devoted to the study of the literature, which was popular in pre-revolutionary Central Asia and the range of people who were involved in book printing. Both of the authors have compiled working catalogues to be able to deal with their subjects with more accuracy, but, unfortunately, these catalogues have not been published either. The history of the circulation and distribution of lithographic editions of Indian origin in Central Asia is reflected in a serious article based on concrete library material by G.L. Dmitriev.[10] In the 70s–90s of the twentieth century the history of book printing was studied by E.A. Akhundzhanov.[11] All the above-mentioned authors and studies deal with either book printing in general, or books in Turkic languages.

This article is dedicated to a narrow question: lithographic book printing in the Persian language in Turkestan. The study is based on the materials preserved in the libraries of St. Petersburg. Catalogues of Persian lithographic books in two collections in this city have been published by me already (those of the Institute of Oriental Studies and the University of St. Petersburg),[12] and the catalogue of the third collection (the National Library of Russia) is expected to come out soon.

The study of academic researches in the field and the available materials allows one to conclude that works in Turkic languages had prevailed in the repertoire of the lithographic publications in the region. Publishing of works in Tajik (the language was usually defined as 'Persian' — *farsi*), especially those which were contemporary

---

7 M.I. Rustamov, *Istoriya knizhnogo dela v Sredney Azii (vtoraya polovina XIX – pervaya chetvert' XX vv.).* Summary of Ph.D. thesis (Tashkent 1968); M.I. Rustamov 'Kniga v Sredney Azii', *Kniga. Issledovaniya i materialy*, sb. 25 (Moscow 1972), 108–26. A bibliography of studies on the subject is given in the aforementioned book by A.Yazberdiyev.

8 R. Mahmudova, *Litografirovannye proizvedeniya i ikh znachenie v istorii uzbekskoy literatury (konets XIX – nachalo XX v.).* Summary of Ph.D. thesis (Tashkent 1971).

9 R.N. Holmatov, *Iz istorii uzbekskoy staropechatnoy arabografichnoy knigi i knizhnoy kul'tury v gorodakh Ferganskoy doliny. 1867–1917 gg.* Summary of Ph.D. thesis (Tashkent 1989).

10 G.L. Dmitriev, 'Rasprostranenie indiyskikh izdaniy v Sredney Azii v kontse XIX – nachale XX vekov', *Kniga. Issledovaniya i materialy*, sb. 6 (Moscow 1962), 239–54.

11 A bibliography of studies by E.A. Akhundzhanov is given in the summary of his Ph.D. thesis 'Istoriko-tipologicheskoe issledovanie istorii knigi i knizhnogo dela v Turkestane. Drevnost'. *Srednie veka*' (Tashkent 1998).

12 O.P. Scheglova, *Katalog litografirovannykh knig na persidskom yazyke v sobranii Leningradskogo otdeleniya Instituta vostokovedeniya AN SSSR*, 2 vols. (Moscow 1975); O.P. Scheglova, *Katalog litografirovannykh knig na persidskom yazyke v sobranii Vostochnogo otdela nauchnoy biblioteki im A.M.Gor'kogo Leningradskogo gosudarstvennogo universiteta* (Moscow 1989).

to the time of their writing, made up just a small percentage of the total flow of book printing. As an example, R. Mahmudova, who studied works of Uzbek literature, gives the number of 700 of such works, which she came across; while in all the catalogues of St. Petersburg collections the similar number is no more than several dozens. Printing of books in Persian was of secondary importance in Turkestan, since the book market was full of cheap Indian lithographic editions in both Persian and Arabic, which were of sufficiently high quality. The books, which had been published in Bombay, Lucknow, Kanpur, Lahore and some other Indian cities and imported to Turkestan, were counted not in numbers but by weight. Turkestan book sellers commissioned popular works to be published in India.

Books dealing with the following subjects were imported to Turkestan: the Qur'ān with its translations and commentaries; authoritative works on Sunni Islam and closely related to it *fiqh* (e.g. the series of works related to *Hidaya-Viqaya*) together with their abridgements, revisions and translations; prayer books; works on Sufism, some encyclopaedias; Arabic-to-Persian and Persian-to-Persian dictionaries; works on grammar and historical compositions. Editions of works of classical Persian literature from the *Shahnameh* of Ferdousi to the poems of the Mughal poets were also mainly represented by the Indian lithographic publications. Things being so, the share of local publishers covered only a small part of the traditional literary repertoire in Persian. The publishers were forced to print only those books, which served practical needs and also were the subject of constant demand.

Collections in St. Petersburg include editions, which were published in the period of active lithographic book printing in Central Asia that is from the beginning of the 1890s up until 1918. It appears that most of the re-editions were made of those books intended for the purpose of teaching at primary schools (*maktab*) and secondary schools (*madrasah*). Books like *Chahaar Kitaab*, poems by Hafiz and Bidil, *Chil Hadith* by Jami and Nava'i were reprinted annually and sometimes even several times a year. Many collections of lithographic books worldwide have abundant copies of such editions. Arabic grammar was studied in *madrasah*s through the *Qafiyeh* of Ibn al-Hajib and other treatises in Arabic and Persian. Arabic works often had marginal abridgements and commentaries in Persian. Such editions were also frequent.

The two first decades of the twentieth century raised the issue of manuals for new-method schools. This was a reflection of social movements in Russia and

Turkestan aimed at organising the education, which would be modern and brought up to the new reality. The activities of the well-known reformer Mahmudhoji Behbudi (1875–1919) in editing school manuals is a good example of this kind. In Samarqand, various printing houses published school-books: *Risala-yi Madkhal-i Jughrafiya-yi 'Umrani* (An introduction to geography, typo-lithography of G.I. Demurov, 1905); 'ABC-book for the Muslim school as per the new method' compiled and published by Hoji Mahmud-khawaja Begbud-khawajaev (typo-lithography of G.I. Demurov, 1906); *Kitabat al-Atfal* (Writing for children, typo-lithography of Ghazarov, 1914).

The Society for the Noble City of Bukhara (*Shirkat-i Bukhara-yi Sharif*) published at Samarqand in 1910 a manual for children in the form of questions and answers (*Tahzib al-Sibyan*) and, in 1913–14, a manual on the elements of Islam and the ritual entitled *Zaruriyat-i Diniyyah* for the first and second year at the *madrasah.*

It is quite obvious that the amount of the published books on theological aspects was considerable. Part of the theological editions, like Islamic catechisms, instructions on ritual and on the reading of the Qur'ān together with certain works on *fiqh* were also published for teaching purposes. A very popular and frequently re-edited book was the work by Sufi Allayar *Maslak al-Muttaqin.* Editions of this work published between 1893 and 1915 are available in St. Petersburg collections.

Such mediaeval works as *Fiqh-i Qaydani,* a fourteenth-century prayer book, and *Dalayil al-Khayrat* by Jazuli (fifteenth century) were repeatedly published beginning from the 1890s. As early as 1893, the lithography of the brothers Kamensky published the manual of ʿAbd al-Haqq Dihlavi (d. 1642) on performing the pilgrimage *Manasik-i Hajj.* Another work by ʿAbd al-Haqq Dihlavi *Takmil al-Iman,* which is a summary of Sunni belief, was later published by the lithography of Arifdzhanov in 1907–8.

In spite of the fact that the book market contained Indian editions of the well-known fourteenth-century authoritative work on the *khanafite fiqh Salat-i Mas'udi* by Sheykh Mas'ud Samarqandi, it was several times reedited in Tashkent in the lithographies of Il'yin in 1904, Portsev in 1910–11 and Arifdzhanov in 1914–15.

The 'table book' of the Muslim jurists, as was remarked by A. Semenov, was the *Hidaya* by Marghinani (twelfth century). Its abridgements, translations, commentaries on it and on its abridgement entitled *Viqaya* were many times published in Central Asia, for example in 1901 in the lithography of Il'yin (*Mukhtasar al-Viqaya* which is actually an abridgement of an abridgement).

It is worth mentioning that the amount of lithographic production increased in the beginning of the twentieth century, and so did the number of books in Persian. Some hagiographic works were published then. In 1908–9 at Samarqand, the lithography of Demurov published the famous twelfth-century opus *Qandiya* by Nasafi and the description of the shrines (*mazar*) of Samarqand. The well-known work *Rashahat* by ʻAli Vaʻiz Kashifi (sixteenth century), the main part of which is dedicated to Khwaja Ahrar, had been many times lithographically printed in India and sold in Central Asia. Nevertheless, in 1911 it was reprinted by the lithography of Arifdzhanov. The lithography of Arifdzhanov, which was the first national lithography in Tashkent, issued a considerable number of works in Persian on various subjects. In particular, the works of Indian theologians and Sufis were published there, and major attention was paid to the Naqshbandi brotherhood.

Such personalities as ʻAbd al-Qadir Jilani (d. in 1166 AD), ʻAbd al-Khaliq Gijduvani (d. in 1179 AD) and Ahmad Sirhindi Mujaddid-i Alf-i Thani (d. in 1624 AD) were the subject of interest, which resulted in publications. Thus, the treatise *Risala-yi Ghausiyah* by ʻAbd al-Qadir Jilani was published in the lithography of Portsev together with its Persian translation and Persian and Uzbek commentaries. Collections of works (*majmu'ah*), which included instructions for the *shaykhs*, were also published. One such book was published in Namangan.

Men of letters of Central Asian origin did not escape the attention of the publishers. Besides the biography of Khwaja Ahrar, certain treatises ascribed to him were published as well, for example in the lithography of Yakovlev in 1910. Among the rare works, which appeared then, E.K. Betger mentions the work *Fasl al-Khitab bi Vasl al-Ahbab* by Muhammad Parsa (fourteenth century) published by the lithography of Arifdzhanov in 1912–13. Another example in this regard is the editions of works by ʻAbd al-Rahman Jami (d. in 1412). His version of the forty *hadith*s was used as a school book, his quatrains (*ruba'i*) were commented upon by the contemporary Samarqand teacher (*mudarris*) Ahmad Vasli and his esoteric treatise was included in the collection of works of the famous Sufis. The hagiographic work *Nafahat al-Uns* by Jami came out in the lithography of Portsev in 1915.

One cannot but acknowledge those rare editions of secular and scientific works drowned in the deep sea of educational and theological publications. Of the few such editions, mention should be made of the encyclopaedia *Jami' al-'Ulum* by Fakhr al-

Din al-Razi (d. in AH 606/1209 AD) and the literary critical work *Shabistan-i Nakat va Gulistan-i Lughat* by Yahya Sibaq Nishapuri (d. in AH 854/1450–1 AD), both of which were published in the lithography of Yakovlev in 1912–13.

As far as the works of belles lettres are concerned, the most significant event was the edition of the *Kulliyat* of Jami at the lithography of Portsev in 1907–8 and the *Haft Aurang* of the same author in the lithography of Yakovlev in 1914. The *Kulliyat* of Jami was reprinted from the Kanpur edition of Nawalkishor, but the publisher put in the margins of the 1914 edition the poem of the Central Asian poet Khaziq.

Among the historical works, the first part of the *Kunuz al-A'zam* by Sirat entitled *Timur-nameh. Kulliyat-i farsi* was published at the lithography of Arifdzhanov in 1913. The publishers often enclosed chronological tables of the Central Asian rulers and chronograms for the famous mediaeval events at the end of large works.

A special place in the repertoire of Turkestan lithographic books is taken by the literary heritage of the authors who lived in the 19th and 20th centuries. This included works on the history of the Central Asia, the history of Islam, impressions of Europe, considerations on ethical and sociological questions by such authors as Mirza Salimi, Ahmad Vasli and ʿAbd al-Ra'uf Fitrat, collections of poems (*divan*) of Hadi, ʿAjizi, Hajji, Fitrat, Ahmad Siddiqi and others. In the total range of publications, the share of these books was small, but yet significant. The language was usually named as Persian (*farsi*), but, in my opinion, these works should be considered as part of Tajik literature.

To conclude, in this brief study the author has tried to give the general characteristics of the repertoire of books in Persian published lithographically in Turkestan.

TULLIP
A Projected Thesaurus Universalis Libri Lithographici Illustrati Persorum

Ulrich Marzolph

Göttingen

Considering the large amount of illustrative data available from the Islamic world, the need for adequate tools for comparative research appears to be compelling. In reality, however, the vast majority of studies in Islamic art deal with specific items or topics, such as particular artists, individual manuscripts, or specific scenes. The lack of a general and comprehensive survey of Islamic iconography[1] is particularly significant for non-specialists dealing with Islamic art, such as historians of literature or folklorists. While these specialists by virtue of their professional interest demonstrate a distinct expertise for the textual backdrop of a given illustration,[2] the illustration's iconographical significance in a wider context would be beyond their apprehension. In consequence, specialists in literature often remain ignorant of significant iconographic aspects, while historians of Islamic art rarely display a profound knowledge of textual aspects relating to the illustrative material they deal with. The projected 'Union Catalogue of Illustrated Persian Lithographed Books,' *Thesaurus Universalis Libri Lithographici Illustrati Persorum* (TULLIP), aims to contribute to closing this gap between the disciplines.

At present, TULLIP is no more than a bulb waiting for adequate conditions to sprout and develop into a full-fledged project. While these conditions are being explored, I would like to profit from the opportunity to present TULLIP's general agenda for further discussion. TULLIP constitutes a follow-up to my earlier study

1 Highly useful surveys of specific topics include M.V. Fontana, *Iconografia dell'Ahl al-Bayt: Immagini di arte persiana dal XII al XX secolo* (Naples 1994); J. Gierlichs, *Mittelalterliche Tierreliefs in Anatolien und Nordmesopotamien: Untersuchungen zur figürlichen Baudekoration der Seldschuken, Artuqiden und ihrer Nachfolger bis ins 15. Jahrhundert* (Tübingen 1996), and, most recently, E. Sims, B.I. Marshak and E.J. Grube, *Peerless Images: Persian Painting and Its Sources* (New Haven, London 2002). The latter work contains a detailed presentation of 'the primary themes of Iranian imagery' (91–330).

2 See, e.g., O. Grabar and C. Robinson (eds), *Islamic Art and Literature* (Princeton 2001).

Narrative Illustration in Persian Lithographed Books.[3] While that study serves as an introduction to a previously unexplored field, it remains my conviction that the genre of illustrated Persian lithographed books is particularly suited for a comprehensive survey of iconographical features: the genre is fairly limited and, hence, surveyable; its imagery is not as complex as that of Persian miniature painting and, hence, more readily available for deciphering and categorizing; large amounts of data are more easily accessible than for any other category of Islamic art; and, finally, the natural way in which text and illustration are combined allows communication between the various disciplines concerned. The present sketch of TULLIP will outline the following points:

The subject: What exactly are illustrated Persian lithographed books?

The scope: Why a *thesaurus universalis*, an international union catalogue of these items?

The bibliographical component: Where and how to acquire the relevant data?

The methodological component: What should TULLIP be expected to document?

The result: How should TULLIP be developed in order to offer optimum conditions for its users?

The Subject

What exactly are illustrated Persian lithographed books?[4] The history of the printed book in Iran is a comparatively recent one.[5] Besides short-lived experiments in the pre-modern era, the art of printing as a continuous practice was introduced to Iran only in the Qajar period.

3 U. Marzolph, *Narrative Illustration in Persian Lithographed Books* (Leiden 2001).

4 For a detailed discussion of the subject see U. Marzolph, 'Zur frühen Druckgeschichte in Iran (1817–*c.*1900). 1: Gedruckte Handschrift/Early Printing History in Iran (1817– *c.* 1900). 1: Printed Manuscript.' in E. Hanebutt-Benz, D. Glass, and G. Roper (eds), *Sprachen des Nahen Ostens und die Druckrevolution: Eine interkulturelle Begegnung/Middle Eastern Languages and the Print Revolution: A Cross-Cultural Encounter* (Westhofen 2002), 249–68 (text), 271–2 (footnotes), 511–17 (description of exhibits), 538–9 (bibliography), and plates 112–21.

5 The most comprehensive survey of this field remains O. P. Scheglova, *Iranskaya litografirovannaya kniga* (Moscow 1979); see also Sh. Bâbâzâde, *Târikh-e châp dar Irân* (Teheran 1378/1999); Marzolph, *Narrative Illustration*, 12–21.

- The first ever book printed in Iran was produced in movable type. It is a collection of *fatwas* relating to the Russian-Persian war, published in 1233/1817.
- The first book printed in Iran by way of the lithographic technique[6] is a copy of the Koran published in Tabriz, dated either 1248/1832, or 1250/1834.
- The first illustrated lithographic book produced in Iran is a copy of Maktabi's *Leili va Majnun* published in 1259/1843. Illustrating lithographic books became a current practice in Iran as of 1263/1847.
- Shortly after the year 1270/1854, printing in movable type ceased altogether. For about two decades, all books published in Iran were produced by way of lithographic printing.
- Even though printing in movable type was taken up again in 1290/1874, lithographed books continued to be produced in large numbers. Gradually, printing in movable type won the upper hand, and lithographic production started to dwindle. The last items of the genre were published around the middle of the twentieth century.

TULLIP is to consider books in the Persian language printed in Iran by way of lithography roughly in the century between 1850 and 1950. One reason for the lasting prevalence of lithography in Iran, besides its aesthetic attraction, was its capacity to combine text and illustration in a comparatively inexpensive way. In consequence, hundreds of illustrated lithographed books were produced in Iran, above all in the areas of classical, religious, and narrative literature. At a later stage, and increasingly towards the latter half of the Qajar period, other genres of lithographed books also contain illustrations, such as travel literature, works of history, medicine, chemistry, astronomy, religious dogmatics or military education, besides translations of European novels and the emerging genre of the Persian schoolbook.[7] Eventually, the illustrations in all of these books will have to be taken into account. As a starting

6 A. Senefelder, *The Invention of Lithography*, translated from the original German by J.W. Muller (Pittsburgh 1998); W. Weber, *A History of Lithography* (New York, Toronto, London 1966); D. Porzio (ed.), *Lithography: 200 Years of Art, History & Technique*, translated from the Italian by G. Culverwell (Secaucus, NJ 1982).

7 For illustrated schoolbooks see particularly M.H. Mohammadi and Z. Qâ'eni, *Târikh-e adabiyât-e kudakân-e Irân*, vols. 1–4 (Teheran1380/2001).

point, research will be restricted to the archive of more than 10,000 individual illustrations that has served as the basis for my monograph study.[8]

The Scope

The most important rationale for proposing a thesaurus universalis, an international union catalogue, derives from the lack of reliable bibliographical documentation.[9] In addition, it relates to the fact that no single library or national conglomerate of libraries holds sufficient quantities of relevant books. Libraries in Iran at first sight would appear to contain promising holdings, yet at second sight prove to be highly problematic. Various reasons account for this evaluation. First, books in Iran were meant to be used. In consequence, many of the books preserved in Iranian libraries are torn and tattered, often missing the first and last pages, and often being in a moderate state of preservation. Second, public libraries are a comparatively recent phenomenon in Iran. Still today, some of the best stocked libraries are held by individuals who eventually might or might not donate their possession (as *vaqf*) to a public or semi-public institution. Hence, neither the Iranian National Library nor any other institution in Iran can be expected to hold but a fragment of the total number of books actually produced. Third, in Iran the awareness of the cultural importance of Qajar book production has only been growing over the past two decades. Up until the restrictions imposed after the revolution of 1978–9, Qajar books were sold and exported in considerable numbers. Meanwhile, most public libraries have stacked their holdings of historical book production in separate sections with limited access. A research trip in the summer of 2002 to important libraries in the five major Iranian cities of Teheran, Shiraz, Esfahan, Mashhad, and Tabriz showed that most libraries pragmatically regard the date 1320, corresponding more or less to 1900, as dividing historical from modern book production. Some of the larger institutions, such as the Teheran National Library and the Library of Congress or the Mashhad Central Library of the Sanctuary have made the bibliographical documentation of their complete holdings, including historical books, accessible by way of online databases in Persian.

---

8 For the archive's scope see Marzolph, *Narrative Illustration*, 230–69.

9 The data on lithographed books in the *Fehrest-e ketâbhâ-ye châpi-ye fârsi az âghâz tâ âkhar-e sâl-e 1345 [1966], bar-asâs-e fehrest-e Khân-Bâbâ Moshâr va fahâres-e Anjoman-e ketâb*, ed. E. Yâr-Shâter, vols 1–3 (Teheran 1352/1973), even though the work remains an admirable and generally useful bibliographical tool, are spurious and unreliable.

In contrast, many of the provincial libraries with limited resources, while shelving their historical books separately, have not even been able to start proper cataloguing.

Outside Iran, a number of major libraries in European and North American cities are known to possess substantial collections of Persian lithographed books rivalling Iranian holdings in respect to both rarity and quality of preservation. No survey of 'the Persian book' can afford to disregard these holdings, above all those in Saint Petersburg,[10] London,[11] Cambridge, Paris, and Berlin. Accordingly, my previous research has taken into consideration the holdings of some 35 libraries in 13 countries, situated above all in Asia and Europe. Future research ought to take into account the holdings of North American libraries (Harvard, Princeton, New York Public Library, University of California at Los Angeles, and others), in addition to those in the Indian subcontinent[12] as well as in the Caucasian and Central Asian republics, such as Azerbaijan, Georgia, and Tajikistan. As a point of specific interest, the available documentation shows that European scholars often regarded Persian historical book production as collectables. Hence, some of the best preserved items are contained in private collections. It might not come as a surprise that several smaller libraries, such as those in the German cities of Frankfurt, Cologne,[13] Halle, or Gotha, whose holdings partly derive from private collections, variously hold extremely rare items that would escape the researcher's attention if those libraries were disregarded. Given this situation, TULLIP will have to rely on a truly international cooperation in order to arrive at a next to complete assessment of Persian lithographic book production.

The Bibliographical Component

In order to acquire the relevant data, the proposed theoretical agenda necessitates human and technical resources in dimensions difficult to realize. Human resources include the preparation of surveys relating to holdings in Iran and its neighbouring Asian countries, Europe, and North America. Particular attention will have to be given

10 O.P. Shcheglova, *Katalog litografirovannykh knig na persidskom yazyke v sobranii Leningradskogo otdeleniya Instituta vostokovedeniya AN SSR*, vols 1–2 (Moscow 1975); ed., *Katalog litografirovannykh knig na persidskom yazyke v sobranii vostochnogo otdela nauchnoi biblioteki im. A. M. Gorkogo Leningradskogo gosudarstvennogo universiteta* (Moscow 1989).

11 E. Edwards, *A Catalogue of the Persian Printed Books in the British Museum* (London 1922).

12 'Â. Noushâhi, *Fehrest-e ketâbhâ-ye fârsi-ye châp-e sangi va kam-yâb-e Ketâbkhâne-ye Ganj-bakhsh* (Islamabad 1350/1971).

13 K. Amir-Arjomand, *Katalog der Bibliothek des schiitischen Schrifttums im Orientalischen Seminar der Universität zu Köln*, ed. A. Falaturi, vols 1–6 (Munich, New York, London, Paris 1996).

to private holdings in Iran, some of which are as rich in terms of holdings as they are difficult to assess. Preparing such a survey will have to rely on a team of researchers from various countries, each contributing with their national expertise. Confining any such survey to the major international libraries containing Persian holdings would be a fatal decision, as any library, and particularly the smaller ones, can reasonably be argued to hold unique items. Technical documentation of the holdings would best be achieved by way of microfilm, as this technique is available in the majority of libraries worldwide. It should be noted, however, that even the Teheran National Library acquired its microfilm equipment as recent as less than ten years ago, and the first items I received from that library in the early 1990s were still prepared as photocopies. Some libraries, particularly the Caucasian and Middle Asian ones, might not command the necessary technical equipment, hence requiring the availability of mobile equipment. Once the relevant items have been documented, they should be made accessible in international data formats, preferably those facilitating their compatibility in various kinds of presentation.

The Methodological Component

In the long run, TULLIP is expected to document a large number of Persian lithographed books containing illustrations of any kind. The data are to be collected in three stages: First, work will be confined to the presently available set of about 10,000 illustrations. Second, new data from Iran should be collected; and third, data from other Asian, European, and North American libraries are to be added. Special care in documentation is to be given to the relation of text and illustration, a relationship that has previously often been neglected. Even though the printed texts of the lithographic period show a lesser degree of variation than manuscript texts, a certain amount of variation cannot be excluded. This evaluation also applies to the position of illustrations within a given text. As illustrations in some of the larger sized books, such as the *Shâhnâme*, fill a whole page from top to bottom, documenting the related text will mean to include at least the preceding and following page or pages. Moreover, the identification of specific scenes will often not be possible without a detailed knowledge of the full text of a given book. As the majority of texts printed in lithographed editions in the Qajar period is not available in modern editions, let alone critical ones, the documentation should not only comprise a given book's illustrations but rather its complete text. In general terms, the systematic documentation and analysis of the illustrations will have to comprise both their iconographical assessment in terms of generic description and detailed catch-word analysis as well as their relation to a specific passage of an individual text.

The Result

In order to offer optimum conditions for its users, it goes without saying that TULLIP is to be developed as a multi-dimensional database, preferably available by way of internet. In addition to basic bibliographical documentation and identification of the illustrations, special care is to be devoted to supplying structured information that in the long run might serve as a basic constituent for a general assessment of Islamic iconography. Various major published systems employed in international iconographical research might serve as a basis for the development of an individual structure of iconographical description, while taking into account the particular requirements of the Islamic data.

A major source of inspiration for the creation of the required database will be the ICONCLASS system as developed by Dutch art historian Henri van de Waal.[14] ICONCLASS is an iconographic classification system, essentially devised to supply ready-made descriptions for works of art, whether two-dimensional illustrations or emblematic imagery or three-dimensional sculptures. ICONCLASS works with a strict hierarchical order, starting with ten major categories labelled with the numbers 0 thru 9: (0) Abstract, Non-representational Art; (1) Religion and Magic; (2) Nature; (3) Human Being, Man in General; (4) Society, Civilization, Culture; (5) Abstract Ideas and Concepts; (6) History; (7) Bible; (8) Literature; (9) Classical Mythology and Ancient History. Already this outline shows the system's obvious rootedness in Western culture. Data from the Persian and Islamic context will rarely fit into categories (0) thru (6), virtually none into category (7), and the overwhelming majority into categories (8) and (9). This situation suggests that in order to use ICONCLASS for the classification of illustrations in Persian lithographed books one would have to expand the main categories of literature and mythology whilst

14 Besides the information available by way of internet (http://iconclass.let.ruu.nl) see, e.g., R. van Straten, *Iconography, Indexing, Iconclass: A Handbook* (Leiden 1994).

diminishing the less important ones. In the context of Qajar lithographed books, literature implies the three categories of classical literature, particularly mystical, religious, pedagogical or otherwise instructive literature; religious literature, above all the works relating to the genre of *maqâtil* or *rouze-khvâni*, i.e. works treating the martyrdom of Hosein b. 'Ali at Karbala that is of pivotal importance for the definition of the Shiite creed; and works of a narrative, fictional, or otherwise primarily entertaining character.

The second published system of iconographical identification to serve as a source of inspiration for TULLIP is François Garnier's *Thesaurus iconographique*.[15] This system has originally been developed with the practical purpose of cataloguing works of art in French museums, and has since been applied to tens of thousands of items. Garnier's system is much more detailed and, apparently, less predisposed than ICONCLASS. Moreover, it allows classification on various levels that are classed in the two large groups of *thèmes* ('general subjects') and *sujets* ('specific subjects'). Levels range from (1) general specifics of representation, (2) nature, (3) the human body and natural environment to (16) geographical (17) biblical, (18) mythological, (19) historical subjects. As a particularly interesting point, Garnier's system also takes into account implicit aspects of representation, such as (21) *courant de pensée* ('intellectual background') and (22) *périodisation* ('imagery depicting certain periods').

Other systems whose experience might prove useful for developing TULLIP's system of iconographical classification include the Princeton *Index of Christian Art* or the *Marburger Inventarisations-, Dokumentations- und Administrations-System (MIDAS)*.[16] At any rate, whatever the source of inspiration, TULLIP will have to develop its own system specifically adjusted to its purpose. Beyond the factual description of a given illustration, additional data will have to position the illustrations both diachronically and synchronically, the latter category supplying links to identical illustrations both in editions of the same work of literature as well as in other works. In addition, a detailed analysis of components such as background, gestures, and

15 F. Garnier, *Thesaurus iconographique: système descriptif de représentations* (Paris 1984).

16 L. Heusinger, *Marburger Informations-, Dokumentations- und Administrations-System (MIDAS)*, 4th edn (Marburg 2000).

material culture will enable a multi-dimensional comparison of these aspects across different works as well as editions of the same work.

The only internet presentation at least partly aiming at a similar goal known to me to date is the *Shahnama Project*, parts of which are available on an internet site published by Princeton University,[17] while a major project funded by the Arts and Humanities Research Board of the British Academy under the supervision of Charles Melville (Cambridge) and Robert Hillenbrand (Edinburgh) is ongoing.[18] The Princeton website contains the documentation of all illustrations in five *Shâhnâme* manuscripts located in Princeton libraries, plus a survey of the dispersed leaves of the so-called Great Mongol (formerly 'Demotte') *Shâhnâme*.[19] Viewing includes thumbnail surveys, identification of scenes, and related text passages from the English translation (Warner). The complete list of illustrated episodes in the various *Shâhnâmes* worldwide, an amended version of the list originally compiled by Edward Davis and Jill Norgren,[20] provides an extremely useful starting point for the general iconographical identification of *Shâhnâme* episodes in lithographed editions.[21] Similar listings have been published for two other major works of Persian literature, the poet Nezâmi's *Khamse*[22] and the corpus of fables commonly known as *Kalila va Dimna*.[23] Similar comparative corpora have already been prepared by the present author for other works frequently published in lithographed editions, such as the Persian translation of the *Arabian Nights* (*Hezâr va yek shab*), the seventeenth century collection of proverbs, Mohammad-'Ali Hablerudi's *Jâme' al-tamsil*, or the most popular work of *rouze-khvâni*-literature, Jouhari's *Tufân al-bokâ'*.

By surveying a limited range of illustrated books, TULLIP will succeed in supplying basic data for a general survey of Islamic iconography. As the analyzed genre is both highly specific and chronologically late, these data will have to be

17 http://humanitas.princeton.edu/shahnama/
18 http://www.oriental.cam.ac.uk/shah
19 O. Grabar and Sh. Blair, *Epic Images and Contemporary History: The Illustrations of the Great Mongol Shahnama* (Chicago, London 1980).
20 E. Davis and J. Norgren, *A Preliminary Index of Shahnameh Illustrations* (Ann Arbor 1969).
21 See U. Marzolph, 'Illustrated Persian Lithographed Editions of the Shâhnâme,' in *Edebiyât* (in print); id., *Images of Power: Illustrated Persian Lithographed Editions of the Shâhnâme* (Teheran in print).
22 L.N. Dodkhudoeva, *Poemy Nezami v srednevekovoi minyaturnoi zhivopisi* (Moscow 1985).
23 E.J. Grube, 'Prolegomena for a corpus publication of illustrated Kalīlah wa Dimna Manuscripts', *Islamic Art* 4 (1990/91), 301–481; see also U. Marzolph, 'The Lithographed Kalīlah. Illustrations to Tales from the Anvār-i Suhaylī and Kalīla va Dimnah Tradition in Lithographed Editions of the Qājār Period', *Islamic Art* (in print).

developed and adjusted in order to fit the broader context. One of the numerous questions that TULLIP might help to answer is concerned with the relationship between lithographic illustration and popular iconography. When considering book production in the Near and Middle East, one has to keep in mind that books do not only contain printed words. In largely illiterate societies such as nineteenth century Iran, the illustrations included in lithographed books might even have conveyed stronger and more lasting impressions than the printed word, similar to the impact exercised by illustrations in other popular media, such as tile-work, stucco-work, glass painting or picture carpets.

Osman Zeki Bey
and
His Printing Office the *Matbaa-i Osmaniye*

Nedret Kuran-Burçoğlu

Yeditepe University, Istanbul

Introduction

Osman Zeki Bey was an Ottoman calligrapher who lived in the second half of the nineteenth century in Istanbul. He was the printer who was given the first legal permission to print the Qur'ān, by the Palace. This paper which is based on family documents and research done by the great granddaughter of the printer aims to present Osman Zeki Bey's life story within the socio-cultural context of his time,[1] as well as giving information about his printing office the *Matbaa-i Osmaniye* and its publications. By doing this it also aims to highlight a particular phase of the Ottoman history of printing.

Osman Bey, the Printer

The calligrapher Osman Zeki Bey who got the first legal permission from the Ottoman Palace to print the Qur'ān, the holy book of Islam, was the first Chamberlain (*Başmabeynci)* at the Palace during the reign of Abdülhamid II. His birth date is unknown. His burial date is given on his tombstone as 1888 (1301).

His father, Hakkakzâde Mustafa Hilmi Efendi was a well-known calligrapher and his name 'Hakkakzâde' indicates that Osman Zeki Bey's grandfather had been a

1 The author of this paper started her research on Osman Bey's Printing Office and its publications in January 2000. The initial research that had been mainly based on the author's family documents, focused on Osman Bey's life and general information about his Printing Office. That part was completed the same year and the following two articles were published: Nedret Kuran-Burçoğlu,.'Saray'dan İlk Defa Kur'an-ı Kerim Basma İznini Alan Hattat: Matbaacı Osman Bey', *Tarih ve Toplum Dergisi.* 35, issue 209 (2001) 312–20, Istanbul: İletişim Yayınları; Nedret Kuran-Burçoğlu, 'Matbaacı Osman Bey', *Journal of Turkish Studies: Essays in Honour of Barbara Flemming* Edit. by Şinasi and Gönül Tekin; guest editor: Jan Schmidt, 26/II (2002), 97–112, Harvard University: NELC. The second article covers some additional information about family members that is reflected in the family tree.

well-known engraver. Mustafa Hilmi Efendi had received calligraphy lessons from Hattat Ömer Vasfi Efendi, great master of *nasih* and *sülüs* who was known as 'Lâz Ömer', and had married the daughter of Ibrahim Sükûti Efendi, who had also been a famous calligrapher and at the same time the guard of the Palace of Esma Sultan.[2] Starting from 1819 on, Mustafa Hilmi had taught calligraphy in the schools that had been founded by Nakşıdil Valide Sultan, the mother of Sultan Mahmud II, and by Bezmiâlem Valide Sultan, the mother of Abdülmecid, in Fatih and Çemberlitaş, respectively.[3] His son Osman Zeki was among the pupils whom he had trained as calligraphers. Mustafa Hilmi Efendi must have been a prolific person who had written three copies of *Mushaf-ı Şerif* (*glorious Qur'ān*) upon the order of Sultan Mahmud II, and received his compliments for the excellent job he had done. His famous work is called *Mizânü'l hatt alâ vaz'il-üstâd-i's selef* (*Measurement of Calligraphy and Styles of Preceding Masters*),[4] which was written in the first half of the nineteenth century (see Figures 2 to 6). Furthermore, Mustafa Hilmi Efendi produced innumerable calligraphies for mosques, inns, soup-kitchens and schools, as well as wrote the inscription on the tombstone of his father in law Ibrahim Sükûti Efendi, who had died in 1834 (1250 H), and was buried in Edirnekapı.[5] Mustafa Hilmi Efendi himself died in 1852, and was buried in Ayaspaşa Cemetery near Taksim.

Not much is known about the life story of Mustafa Hilmi Efendi's son Osman Zeki Bey. However, the cited information above indicates that he was born into a family of calligraphers and engravers. Elder family members claim that he originated from Safranbolu, an old Ottoman settlement near Zonguldak. He died in Istanbul in 1888 (1301) and was buried in the Sultan Mahmud II Cemetery, in Çemberlitaş (Figure 7).

Historian Johann Strauss indicates in his article, 'Le livre français d'Istanbul (1730–1908)' that Osman Zeki had grown up in the vicinity of the Palace during the rule of Abdülmecid (1839–61), and that he had been the closest friend of the Sultan.[6]

---

2 İbnülemin Mahmud Kemal İnal, *Son Hattatlar* (İstanbul 1955), 213.
3 Ibid., 213; also in Şevket Rado, *Türk Hattatlar*, (İstanbul), 208; and in Abdülkadir Dedeoğlu (ed.), 'Introduction', *Mizânü'l-hatt* (İstanbul 1986).
4 The first part of this book was reprinted by Abdülkadir Dedeoğlu with the following title: *Mizânü'l hatt*, in 1986, in Istanbul.
5 İnal, Op.cit., 213.
6 Johann Strauss, 'Le livre français d'Istanbul, 1730–1908', *Revue des mondes musulmans et de la Méditerranée* 87–8 (1999), 277–301

This could explain his important position as the first Chamberlain at the Palace, during Abdülhamid II's rule (1876–1909), as well as his authorization by the Sultan to set up the *Matbaa-i Osmaniye* (*Typographie et lithographie Osmanié*) and print the Qur'ān, the holy book of Islam. To receive this permission from a Sultan like Abdülhamid II, who was known to be a person who did not trust his men, must have been quite an honourable privilege for Osman Zeki. Having been his old friend he must have gained the Sultan's confidence and was given this important mission. Another explanation for Abdülhamid's patronage could have been to keep the whole activity of the press under the control of the Palace. The categories of the books that had been chosen for publication in the *Matbaa-i Osmaniye* seem to justify this hypothesis.[7] Osman Zeki Bey's respectful position within the Palace team was also reflected in his title. He was designated as 'Serkurenâ-i Hazret-i Şehriyâri Osman Zeki Bey', meaning, 'Chief Chamberlain Osman Zeki Bey, affiliated to the Sultan.'

With the legal permission to print the holy book of Islam, that had been denied to others before him since the foundation of the printing office in the Ottoman Empire by İbrahim Müteferrika and Said Bey, in 1727,[8] Osman Zeki Bey must have evoked anger and hatred amongst the scribes and calligraphers of his time, as a great number of them would lose their jobs. The printed Qur'āns were cheap and easier to obtain than the handwritten ones. In a short time it was printed in large numbers and sold not only in the Ottoman Empire, but also in neighbouring Muslim countries. Thus the *Matbaa-i Osmaniye* fulfilled an important mission, it contributed to the spread of Islam, the third monotheistic religion after Judaism and Christianity, among a large number of people, and it also brought a large revenue to its owner. As he was a well trained calligrapher himself, Osman Zeki Bey showed great care in keeping to the

7 See part 2, paragraph 1.

8 Johann Gutenberg's discovery, the printing press had been brought to Istanbul in 1492 by the Jews who had escaped from Spain and found refuge in the Ottoman Empire. In 1567, seventy-five years later the Armenians founded a printing office in Istanbul, which was followed by the press set up by the Greek Orthodox Patriarchate in Fanarion, in 1627. The first Ottoman printing office was founded by İbrahim Müteferrika, a Hungarian convert, and Said Efendi, in Müteferrika's house in Yavuzselim, in 1727. (Kut 1994: 308, in Kuran-Burçoğlu, 'Matbaacı Osman Bey', 99). As the opposition of the calligraphers and scribes was quite powerful, these two initiators had to use a clever strategy, in order to overcome this obstacle. Thus they first got the *firman* (decree) of the Sultan Ahmed III, the *fatva* (formal declaration) of the Sheikh-ul-Islam Yenişehirli Abdullah Efendi, and the consent of the Grand Vizier Damat İbrahim Pasha, and through these they could secure the success of their initiative (Franz Babinger, *Stambuler Buchwesen im 18. Jahrhundert* (Leipzig 1919) However their permission was limited to secular books, the permission to print the Qur'ān, the Hadith, and other sacred texts was denied to them.

aesthetic values of the holy book. Hence after a meticulous analysis, Hâfız Osman's handwritten version of the Qur'ān was selected as the best model to be printed, and lithography was found the most appropriate technique to be used in printing it (Figure 8).[9]

Osman Zeki Bey had a large family. His wife Fatma Zehra Hanım bore him three sons and three daughters. His daughters Sabiha, Nudiye and Fıtriye got married to well-known Generals of the Empire. One of his sons, Ömer Vasfi[10] became the Director of the Foreign Correspondence at the Palace, and his oldest and youngest sons Cevat and Saim worked in the *Matbaa-i Osmaniye.* As a man of vision Osman Bey had bought a large site in Istanbul in 1870s, in a newly developing area of the city, which still bears his name. This area is nowadays at the crossroads of Halâskârgazi and Rumeli Streets between Şişli and Harbiye. The whole family of Osman Bey lived in that area in the mansions he had built for himself and for his children until this place was transformed from a residential to a commercial area. Some buildings there still belong to his family members.

Matbaa-i Osmaniye

There are different opinions about the foundation date of the *Matbaa-i Osmaniye.* As it will appear below, a Greek journalist who visited it in 1888, gives this date as 1878. Johann Strauss gives it as 1868 (1285).[11] However in the list of the printed books of the *Matbaa-i Osmaniye* in the National Library in Ankara there are three books listed that had been printed prior to this date. According to this list, the earliest publications of this office was Yirmisekiz Mehmet Çelebi's *Sefaretnâme-i Mehmet Efendi,* which was printed in 1866 (1283), and the two others that followed were Seyyid Vahid Paşa's *Sefaretnâme-i Fransa,* and Yirmisekiz Çelebi Mehmet Efendi's *Şerefnâme-i Fransa,* both printed in 1867 (1283).[12] This indicates that the *Matbaa-i Osmaniye* was already active in 1866.

9 This miniature Qur'ān is an item in Kuran-Burçoğlu's family collection.

10 Ömer Vasfi, who had been the great grandfather of the author of this paper, died at an early age, in 1895. He is buried with his two brothers, Cevat and Saim, one sister, Nudiye and his parents, Osman Zeki Bey and Fatma Zehra Hanım in the cemetery of Sultan Mahmud II, in Çemberlitaş.

11 Johann Strauss, 'Alexandre Pacha Carathéodory (tr.): *Traité du quadrilatère attribute Nassiruddin-el Toussy (Kitab shakl al-qatta')',* in *The Beginnings of Printing in the Near and Middle East: Jews Christians and Muslims.* edt. by Lehrstuhl für Türkische Sprache, Geschichte und Kultur. Universität Bamberg/Staatsbibliothek (Wiesbaden 2001), 78.

12 They are ordered under the following numbers: 723, 722, 768.

For this printing press in Çemberlitaş Osman Bey had procured equipment, and even foremen and typographers from Germany. According to a contemporary observer it was 'sans contredit, la plus belle et la mieux outillé de tout la ville.'[13] In his above mentioned article Strauss states that most of the printing offices — Imprimeries & lithographies — that had been printing semi-official books during the reign of Abdülaziz (1861–76), had closed down towards the end of the nineteenth century. The *Matbaa-i Âmire*, the imperial printing office, which had also been going to shut down in 1902, had not printed books in western languages.[14] These facts had obviously motivated the newly founded the *Matbaa-i Osmaniye* to fill this gap, and print along with the holy book Qur'ān also official publications, as well as books in eastern and western languages. Thus in a short time it became an unrivalled press that printed public documents, border protocols, international agreements, directories, educational books, dictionaries, as well as great literary works, such as the works of well-known Islamic and Ottoman personalities as Gazâli, Namık Kemal, Halid Ziya Uşaklıgil and Cevdet Paşa.

A detailed description of the *Matbaa-i Osmaniye* was given by a Greek journalist, who visited it in 1888. In his essay that he published under his column, in the daily newspaper *Epistevrisiyi,* on April 8, 1888 in Athens, the journalist compares it with the printing offices in Athens that he had thought were the best printing offices of their time before he visited Osman Bey's press. In this essay in which the columnist designates the *Matbaa-i Osmaniye* as 'the best printing office in the Orient', he describes the space of the office as well as the equipment of the press.[15]

The site plan of the press justifies the Greek journalist's description. (See Figure 9).[16] The journalist states that the printing office had been founded in 1878, and moved to that two-storied rectangular building in Çemberlitaş in 1884. The name of the press that hung on the building was written in three languages, in French, German and Turkish. In the building there were halls and rooms in different sizes. The large hall in the middle contained 18 presses that were run by steam engines. Nine of these were used for lithographies, and the rest for typographies. Next to these 18 presses,

13 *Le Temps*, 9 Septembre 1890 in Strauss, 'Alexandre Pacha'.

14 Strauss, 'Le livre français'.

15 The translation of this essay into Turkish done by the translator Malyakas Efendi is in Kuran-Burçoğlu's family archive.

16 Family archive.

there was a manually operated press and five paper-cutters. In the opposite room there were cameras and equipment for film-development. The next room was used for letter casting. In the third room books were bound.

The columnist furthermore claims in his essay that the *Matbaa-i Osmaniye* had along with the equipment that was necessary for lithography, typography, all the necessary equipment for stereotypography, photography, hallography, xylography and galvanoplasty. However, the main function of the press was to print the huge number of Ottoman books.

Apart from the technical information the Greek columnist also gives in-house details of the life in the press. The workers in the press earned 6 to 30 piasters a day according to their qualification and performance. Another interesting detail is about the lunch that was served in the dining hall of the press for the personnel. The menu, which was prepared by the owner of the press himself, was typed in gold letters in two languages, in French and Turkish, on a cardboard and hung at the door of the hall. This is an indication that the staff of the press was taken good care of by their boss, Osman Bey, and later by his two sons, Cevat Bey and Saim Bey who took over the press.

In his visit to the press, the Greek journalist found the opportunity to watch the printing of the Qur'ān in 6,000 issues and was impressed by the efficiency and precision the Ottomans had gained in this printing business. For him this should also be seen as a sign of the importance given to furthering science and education, and efforts to propagate them in the Empire, as well as a sincere effort to develop and improve the state. Abdülhamid II must have played a significant role in this endeavour. Johann Strauss, in his article entitled, 'Zum Istanbuler Buchwesen in der zweiten Hälfte des 19. Jahrhunderts'[17] confirms this and states that the activity of the printing presses, that had started to increase during the reign of Abdülaziz (1861–76) continued to increase during Abdülhamid II's reign (1876–1909), and that this Sultan had collected books for the library of his Palace, and that he had books translated from European languages which he had found interesting.

A final point the Greek journalist makes in his essay is about how he was impressed by the modesty of the people he had observed in this press.

17 Johann Strauss, 'Zum Istanbuler Buchwesen in der zweiten Hälfte des 19. Jahrhunderts', *Osmanlı Araştırmaları* 12 (1992a).

According to the documentation of the Turkish National Library the *Matbaa-i Osmaniye* seems to have flourished after 1881 and was very active until 1927. Osman Bey's oldest son Cevat Bey seems to have run it quite successfully and had made this unique printing office of the holy book an unrivalled institution for official publications. After Cevat Bey's death in 1911 his younger brother Saim Bey took over the press. In 1920s it was sold to Darüşşafaka, a well-known Turkish charity organization. In 1928 it was closed down and its building demolished.

Publications of the Matbaa-i Osmaniye

It is interesting to note that the first secular publication of the *Matbaa-i Osmaniye* that appeared in 1866 was Yirmisekiz Mehmet Çelebi's book *Sefâretname-i Mehmet Efendi.* Yirmisekiz Mehmet Çelebi was namely the father of Said Efendi, who was one of the two founders of the first Ottoman Printing Office in 1727. Said Efendi got this inspiration in his stay in Paris with his father Yirmisekiz Mehmet Çelebi, who was an important Ambassador of the Ottoman Empire. His famous book had been translated into French, under the name *Relation de l'Ambassade de Mehémet Effendi à la cour de France en 1721,* and was published in Paris in 1757. This first publication in Turkish was realized by the *Matbaa-i Osmaniye.* This choice should be taken as an indication of Osman Zeki Bey's commitment to printing.

As was mentioned above, the *Matbaa-i Osmaniye* became known at first for its Qur'ān publications. However, soon it started to publish secular books and with the growing demand official documents and educational books. It also printed books in eastern and western languages. The list of its publications, prepared by the Turkish National Library details 996 items within a time span of 62 years, that is from 1866 to 1928 (page 52).[18] This distribution shows that the printing office was very active between the years 1881 and 1906, after that there was a stagnation in 1907, a year before the Second Constitution, and then again it became very busy until 1927, a year before it closed down (Figure 10). This also shows that the printing office continued its mission not only during the last 57 years of the Ottoman Empire but also during the first 5 years of the Turkish Republic.

18 Qur'ān publications are not included in this list.

A rough categorisation of the printed books and documents in the *Matbaa-i Osmaniye*[19] shows that almost half of them (420 items) were official publications related to state affairs (pages 53–4), then come scientific and technical texts (115), followed by educational publications (100), texts related to rhetoric, language and literature (90), religious texts (85), histories (55), military publications (25), medical publications (20), dictionaries (10), calligraphy (5).[20] That the majority of the books that were printed by the *Matbaa-i Osmaniye* were state documents indicates how close this printing office had been to the Palace. The large number of technical and educational books indicates how much importance was given to education in those years that mark a change in the Ottoman culture towards western norms.

The quality of the printed books of the *Matbaa-i Osmaniye* was quite high, as the cover page of *Musavver Tarif-i Hayvanat* exemplifies (Figure 11).[21] The title page of this book (Figure 12) which was written by Mehmed Emin and published in the *Matbaa-i Osmaniye* by Serkurenâ-i Hazret-i Şehriyâri Osman Zeki Bey, in 1310 (1893) gives an important note about the copyright of the printing office which shows that it was a thoroughly professional institution (of the nineteenth century!) and was protecting its rights.

19 It is important to note here, that research concerning this last part of the paper is still in progress, and the works have not been examined properly by the author yet.

20 The titles of 40 items in the list are ambiguous and therefore could not be classified. Further research will reveal their proper place within this categorization.

21 *Musavver Tarif-i Hayvanat* is in Kuran-Burçoğlu's family collection.

Figure 1. Osman Zeki Bey's Portrait.

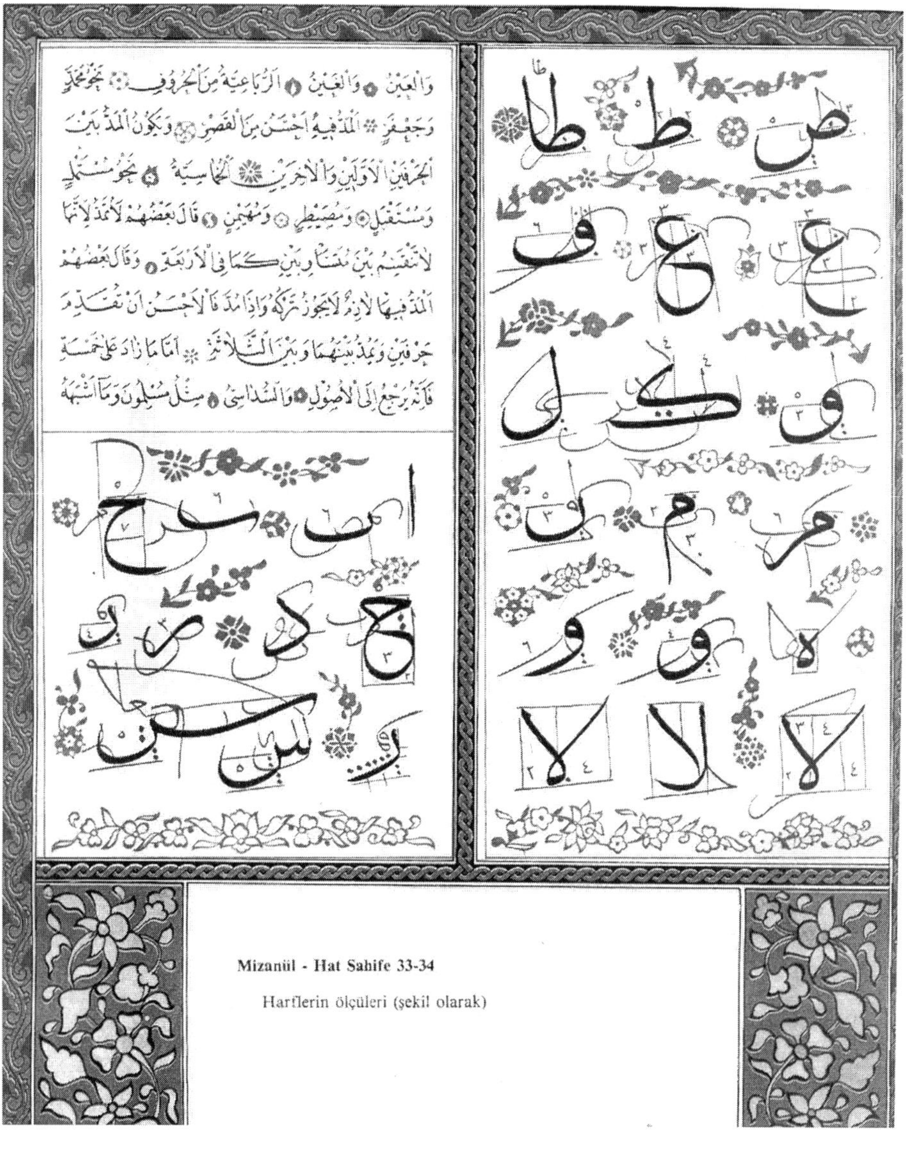

Figure 2. The ideal proportions of Arabic letters drawn by the calligrapher Mustafa Hilmi.

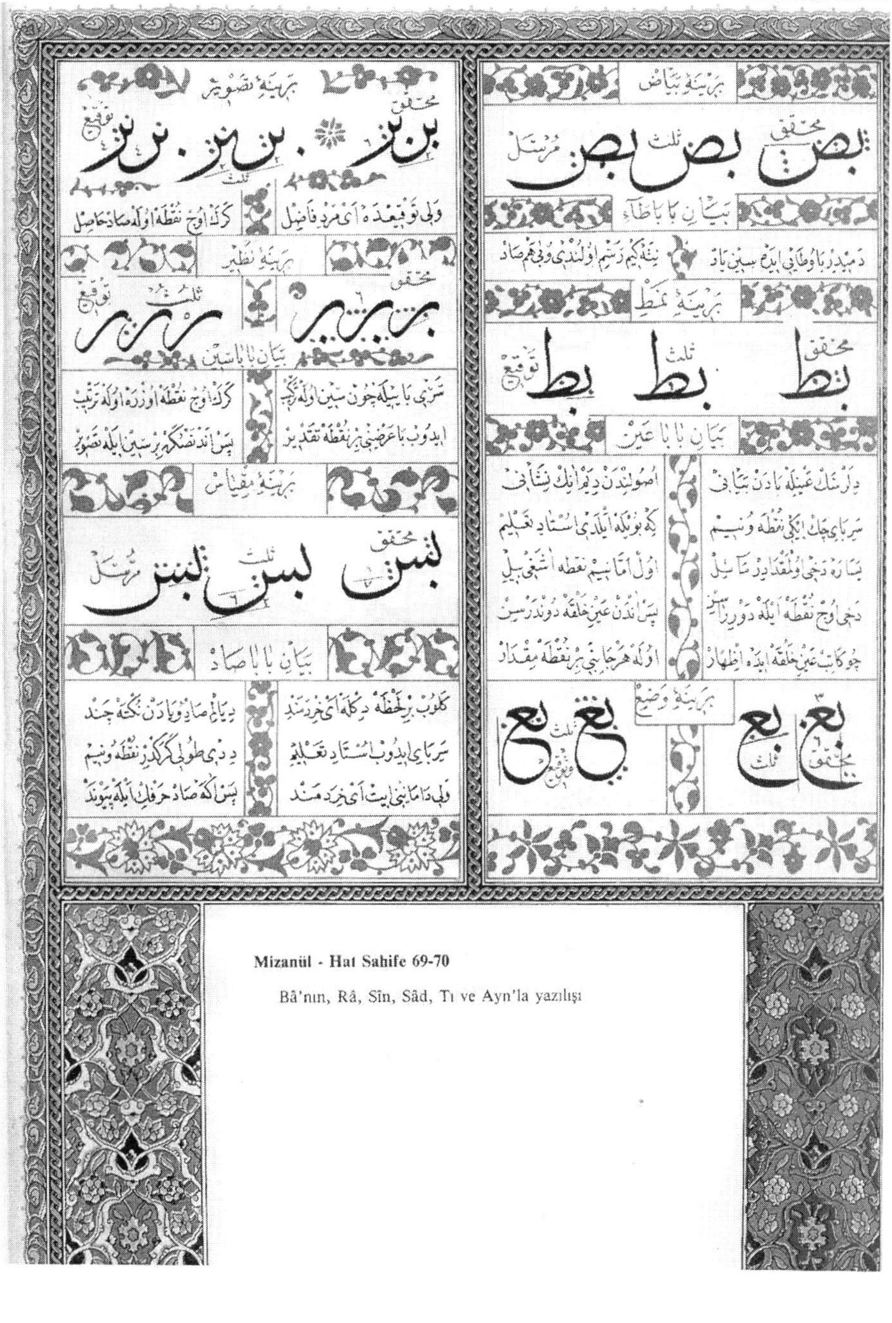
Mizanül - Hat Sahife 69-70
Bâ'nın, Râ, Sîn, Sâd, Tı ve Ayn'la yazılışı

Figure 3.

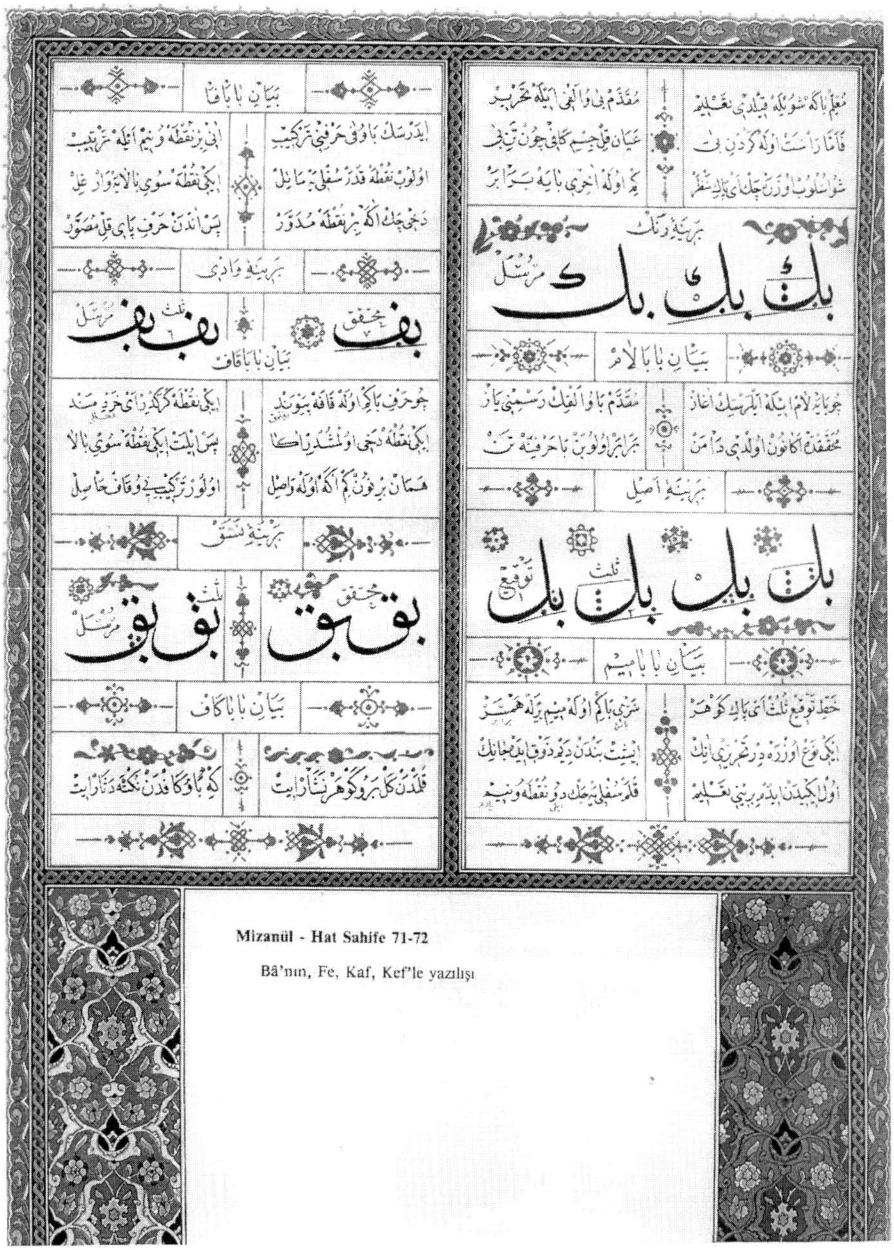
Mizanül - Hat Sahife 71-72
Bâ'nın, Fe, Kaf, Kef'le yazılışı

Figure 4.

Mizanül - Hat Sahife 229-230

Hattatlar Silsilesi (Devamı)
Şah-ı Cihan Ruh-u Alem Abdül-Mecid Han, Ademzâde Emin Efendi, Muhammed Zihni Efendi, Seyyid Muhammed Zihni Efendi, Eyüplü Seyyid Muhammed Raşid Efendi, Sükûtî İbrahim Efendi, Damadı Mustafa Efendi.

Figure 5.

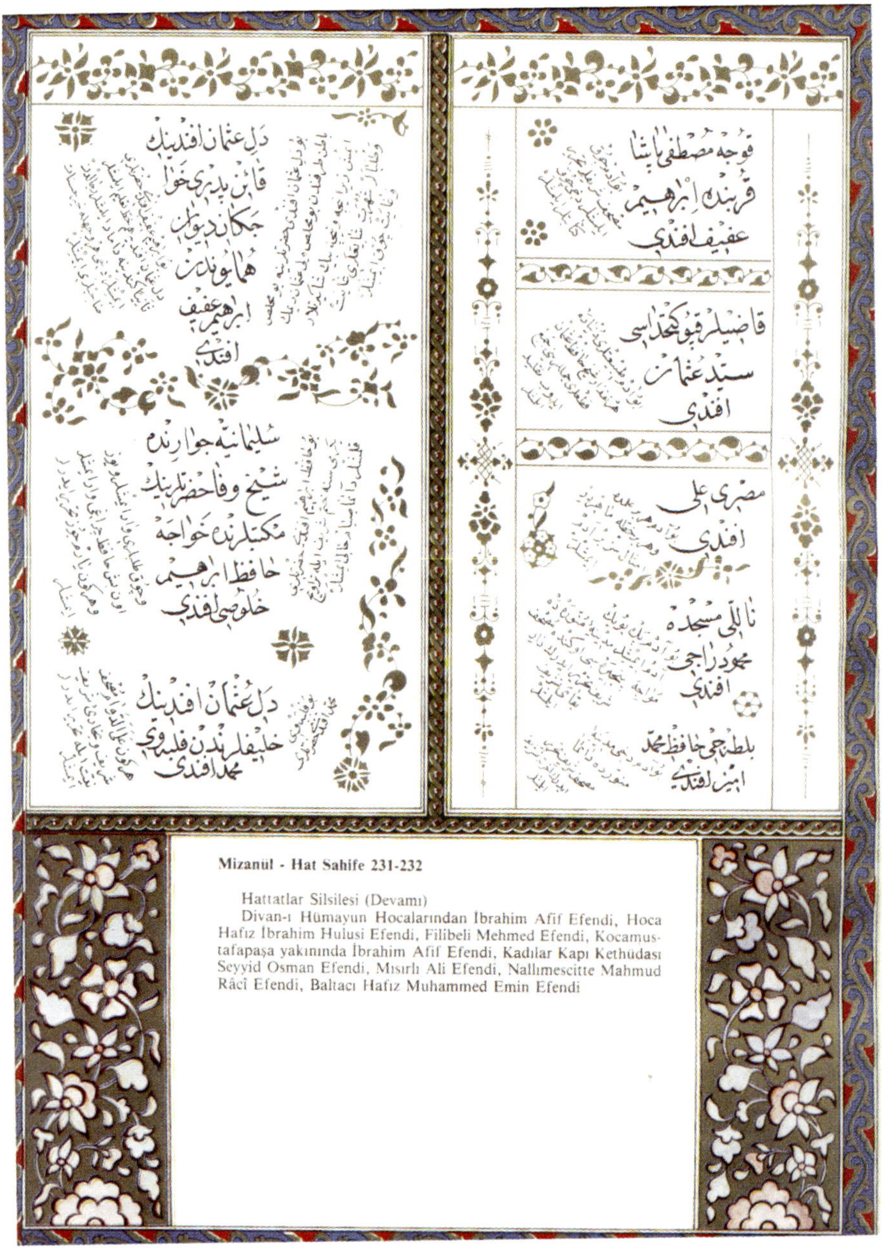
Mizanül - Hat Sahife 231-232
Hattatlar Silsilesi (Devamı)
Divan-ı Hümayun Hocalarından İbrahim Afif Efendi, Hoca Hafız İbrahim Hulusi Efendi, Filibeli Mehmed Efendi, Kocamustafapaşa yakınında İbrahim Afif Efendi, Kadılar Kapı Kethüdası Seyyid Osman Efendi, Mısırlı Ali Efendi, Nallımescitte Mahmud Râcî Efendi, Baltacı Hafız Muhammed Emin Efendi

Figure 6.

Matbaaci Osman Bey Sulalesi'nin Kabirleri ile ilgili bazi Bilgiler:

1.6. Ada, 133. Kabir: Hattat Hafiz Osman Zeki Bey, vefati: 1301 (Hicri 1301=1884; Rumi 1301=1888) (A.I.A.: 1306 = 1890)[22]

Matbaaci Osman Bey'in Kitabesi:

Huve'l-Hallaku'l-baki	هو الحلاق البقي
Ser kurena-yi hazret-i sehriyari	سر قرناي حضرت شهرياري
Iken irtihal-i dar-i beka iden	ايكن ارتحال دار بقا ايدن
merhum ve magfuru'l-muhtac	مرحوم مغفور المحتاج
ila rahmet-i Rabbuhu'l-gafur	الى رحمة ربه الغفور
Ulum-i aliyeden me'zun	علوم عاليه دن مأزون
ve mesahir-i hattatin el-Hac	ومشاهير خطاطين الحاج
Hafiz Osman Zeki Beg'in	حافظ عثمان ذكي بكيك
Kabirlerider ruh-i serifine Fatiha	قبرلريدر روح شريفيه فاتحة
1301	١٣٠١

Figure 7. Osman Zeki Bey's tomb stone and the inscription on it.

22 *Asirlar Boyunca Istanbul* Ansiklopedisi'nde yayimlanan 'Sultan Mahmud Turbesi Bahcesindeki Kabirlerin Listesi ndekiler (s. 223) (bkz. belge 3) ile mezar taslari uzerindeki tarihler birbirini tutmadigi icin, yazinin ekler kisminda her iki kaynaktaki tarihler birlikte verilmis, adi gegen ansiklopedideki tarihleri ayirmak icin bunlarin yanina (A.L.A.) harfleri eklenmistir.

Figure 8. The signature page of one of these Qur'ān issues printed in *Matbaa-i Osmaniye*, in 1301 (1888) which is a miniature. It measures 2.5 cm in width, 3.5 cm in length and 1.5 cm in thickness. It is bound and has a tortoise shell cover. A small magnifying glass is attached to it with an ivory chain.

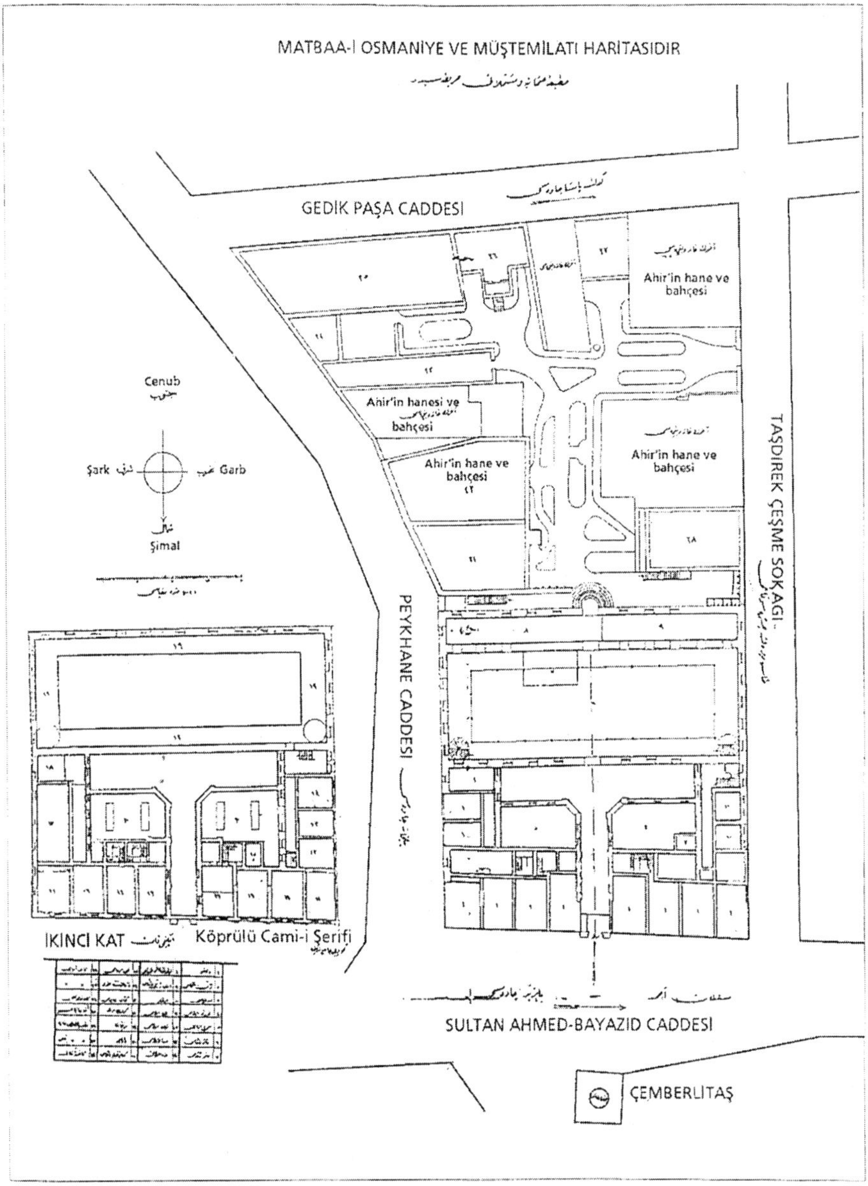

Belge 1: Matbaanın planı.

Figure 9. The site-plan of *Matbaa-i Osmaniye.*

MATBAACI OSMAN BEY

TABLE 1

Distribution of Printed Books According to Years

1859	1	1869	-	1879	-	1889	21	1899	15	1909	23	1919	14
1860	-	1870	-	1880	1	1890	21	1900	8	1910	53	1920	8
1861	-	1871	-	1881	5	1891	21	1901	12	1911	23	1921	10
1862	-	1872	2	1882	22	1892	73	1902	14	1912	32	1922	8
1863	-	1873	1	1883	26	1893	10	1903	12	1913	40	1923	9
1864	-	1874	-	1884	27	1894	26	1904	10	1914	43	1924	15
1865	-	1875	-	1885	46	1895	21	1905	15	1915	15	1925	31
1866	1	1876	-	1886	31	1896	14	1906	4	1916	24	1926	20
1867	2	1877	-	1887	23	1897	3	1907	1	1917	14	1927	11
1868	-	1878	-	1888	31	1898	15	1908	5	1918	14	1928	1

As the dates of publication of 51 works are not listed in the National Library's list, this table covers 945 items.

MATBAACI OSMAN BEY TABLE II

I Official Prints / State Publications (approx. 420)

1. Normative and Prescriptive Texts
    - i. Directions and Explanatory Texts (*Tarifnameler*)
    - ii. Regulations, Codes and Statutes (*Nizamname ve Düzenlemeler*)
    - iii. State Orders and Instructions (*Talimatnameler*)
    - iv. Decrees (*Kararanameler*)
    - v. Laws and Annotations (*Kanunlar ve Kanun Şerhleri*)
    - vi. Contracts (*Mukavelenameler*)
    - vii. Declarations (*Beyannameler*)
    - viii. Stipulations (*Şartnameler*)
    - ix. Laws and Decrees of Foreign Countries
2. Treaties and Agreements
    - i. Treaties with Foreign Countries
    - ii. Border Protocols with Neighbouring Countries
3. Evaluation of Current Political and Economic Issues
4. Commentaries and Reports
5. Statistics, State Records, Budgets of State Institutions
6. Official Correspondence
7. Public Reviews and Periodicals.
8. Yearbooks and Almanacs
9. Directories, Lists and Tables
10. Conversion of Measurements
11. Calendars

II Scientific and Technical Publications (approx. 115)

III Educational Publications (approx. 100)

1. School Textbooks
2. Practical Education

IV Rhetoric, Language and Literature (approx. 90)

1. Essays
2. Narratives i. Literary ii. Social
3. Novels
4. Drama
5. Poetry
6. Travel accounts
7. Translated Literature

V Religion, Ethics, Morality, Conduct, Sufism (approx. 85)

VI History (approx. 55)

VII Law (approx. 30)

VIII Military Publications (approx. 25)

IX Medicine (approx. 20)

X Dictionaries (approx. 10)

XI Calligraphy (approx. 5)

Unclassified (approx. 40)

<u>II Educational Publications</u>

1. School Textbooks

    i. Language and Literature (see paragraph III below)
    ii. Geography
    iii. History
    iv. Mathematics (Geometry, Algebra)
    v. Biology

2. Practical Education
    i. Agriculture
    ii. Zoology
    iii. Housekeeping
    iv. Leisure
    v. Industry
    vi. Calligraphy

<u>III Language and Literature</u>

1. Literature
    i. Rhetoric and Style
    ii. Poetry
    iii. Drama
    iv. Novel
    v. Narratives, Essays
    vi. Travel Accounts
    vii. Biography
        i. Historical Personalities
        ii. Lives of Saints (*Menakıpnameler*)
    viii. Translations

2. Language
    i. ABC's
        i. Turkish
        ii. Foreign
    ii. Grammar
        i. Turkish
        ii. Ottoman
        iii. Persian
        iv. French
        v. German
    iii. Reading Skills
    iv. Foreign Language Ed.

<u>IV Dictionaries</u>

<u>V Scientific and Technical Publications</u>

i. History
ii. Geography
iii. Topography
iv. Meteorology
v. Cosmography
vi. Chemistry
vii. Engineering
viii. Accounting
ix. Law
x. Medicine
xi. Veterinary

<u>VI Religion, Ethics and Sufism</u>

<u>VII Military Publications</u>

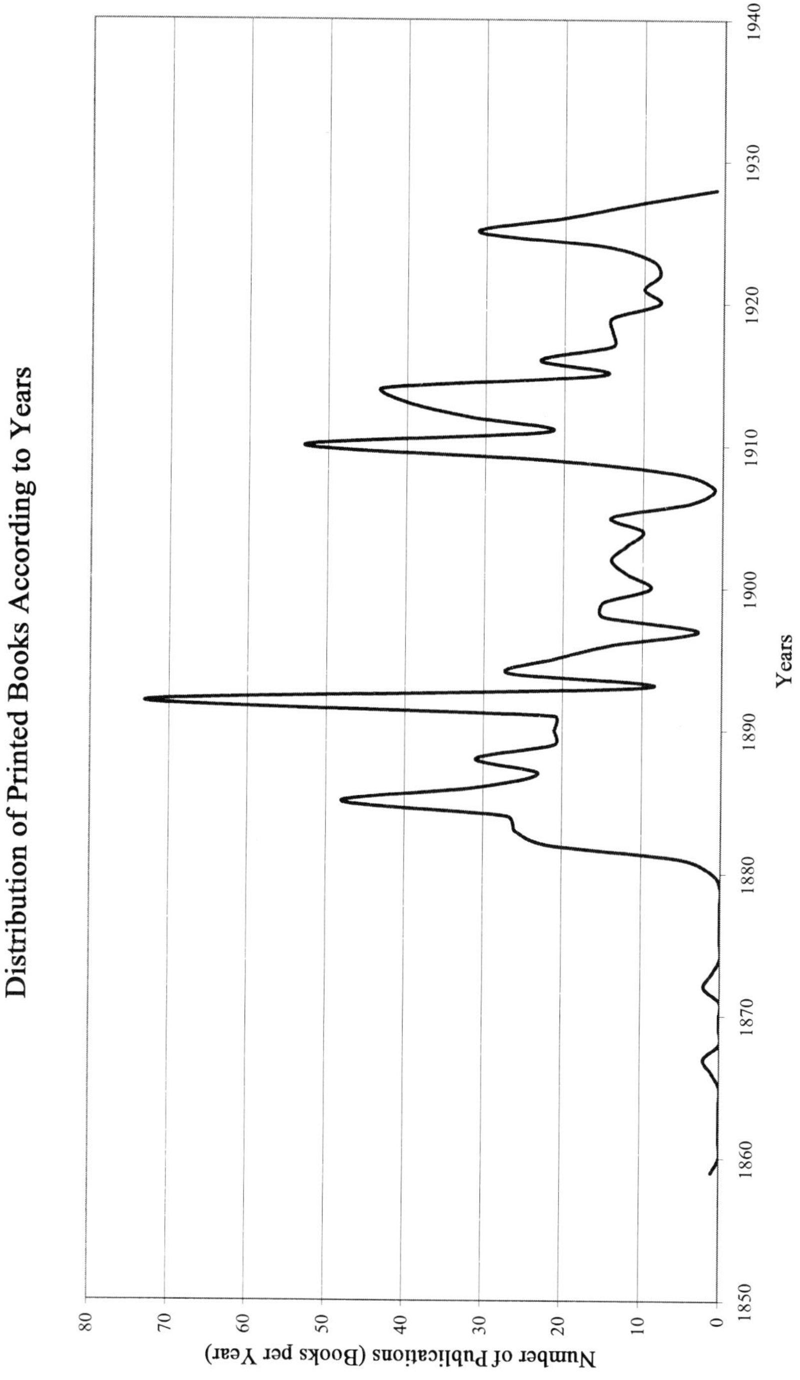

Figure 10. Chart of Table 1.

Figure 11. Cover page of *Musavver Tarif-i Hayvanat.*

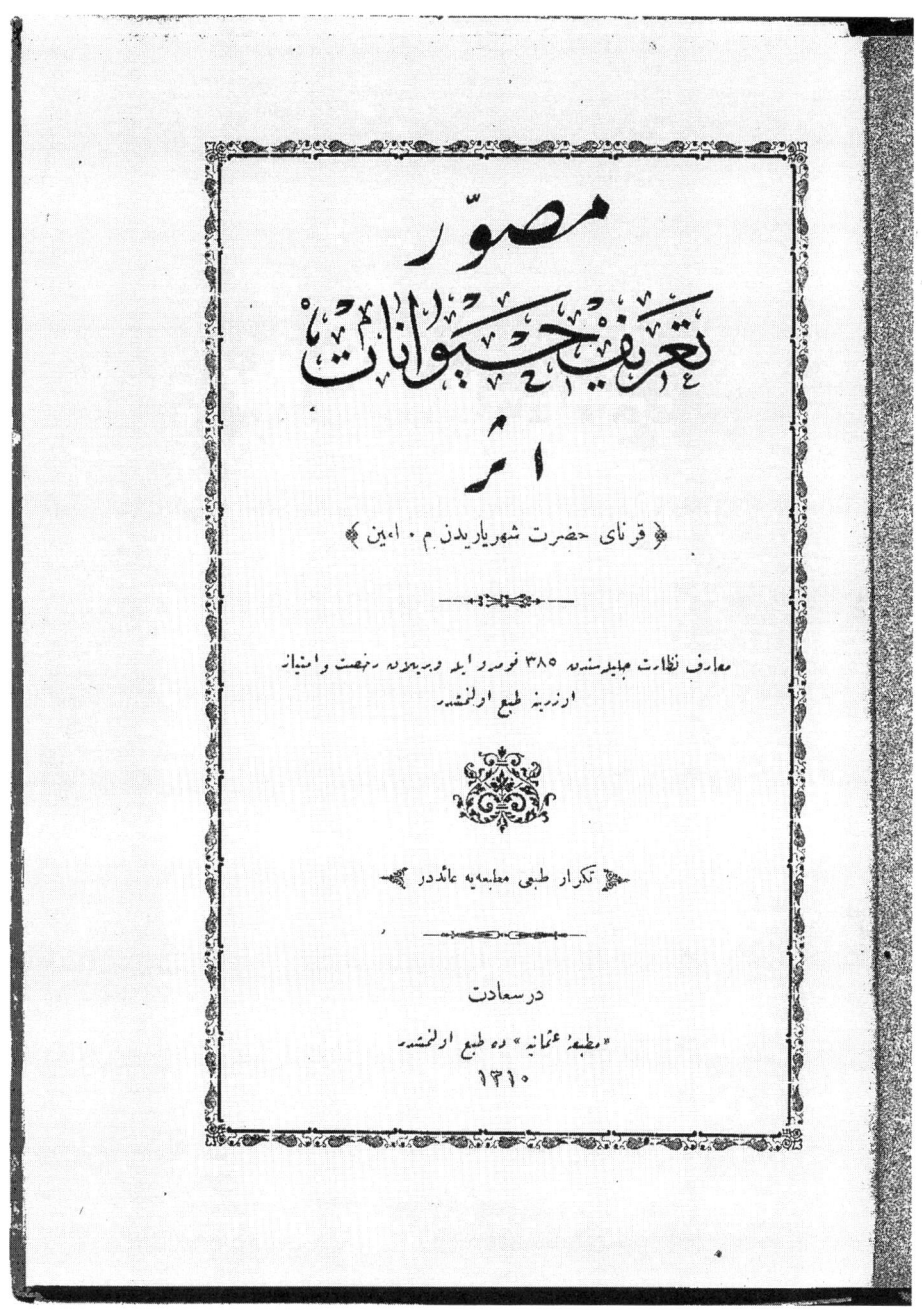

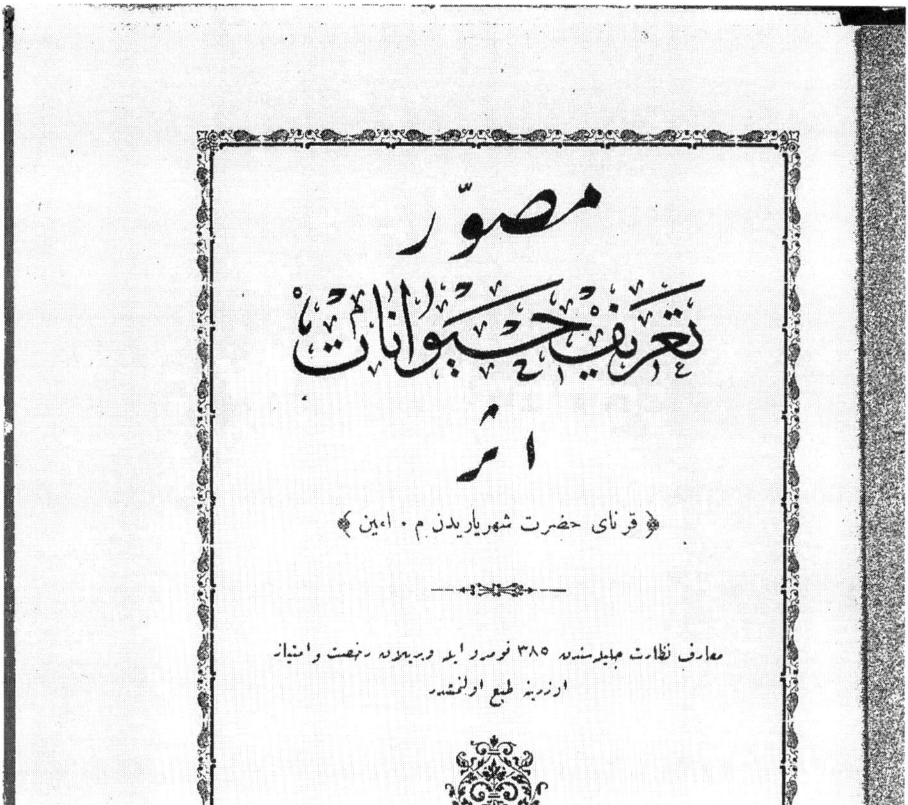

مصوّر

تعریف حیوانات

اثر

قرنای حضرت شهریاریدن م ۰ امین

معارف نظارت جلیله سنده ۳۸۵ نومرو ایله و یریلان رخصت و امتیاز

اوزرینه طبع اولنمشدر

تکرار طبعی مطبعه یه عائددر

درسعادت

«مطبعهٔ عثمانیه» ده طبع اولنمشدر

۱۳۱۰

Figure 12. Title page of *Musavver Tarif-i Hayvanat.*

From London back to Istanbul: The Channel of Communication of the Young Ottoman Journal *Ḥurriyet* (1868-1870)

Christiane Czygan

University of Hamburg

Almost 300 years after Johannes Gutenberg's *Wiegendrucke*, the first Turkish printed works by Ibrahim Müteferrika appeared in 1719/1720. The emergence of a Turkish press was thus postponed. While the first European newspapers had appeared at the beginning of the seventeenth century, products of the Turkish press were not launched before the nineteenth century. The first Turkish newspaper, titled *Taqvim-i Veqa'ı'* (Calendar of Events) was established by Sultan Maḥmud II (1808–39) in 1831. Several decades passed until in 1860, *Tercüman-ı Aḥval* (Interpreter of Conditions) the first newspaper financially independent of the government, appeared. Numerous further publications followed in the sixties, among them *Taṣvir-i Efkar* (Tablet of Opinion), which at its peak, is said to have reached a circulation of 24,000 copies. Although this number quoted by Roderic Davison is possibly too high, it illustrates its significance.[1]

The flowering of the Turkish press was aided both by a scarcely developed system of government sanctions and little government interference. Judicial involvement first took shape with the demand for official permission for every kind of publication in 1842. Although some further steps towards official control were undertaken, such as the demand to submit all publications to the *Meclis-i Ma'arif* (Council of Education) before publishing, the absence of an official manual for sanctions meant, that the constraints on publishers remained few. It was not until 1864 that the first Publication Act *Maṭbu'at Niẓamnamesi*, appeared.[2]

This new press medium offered a new dimension for political participation. It is striking that as the free press was growing, numerous political activities, some in the

1 R.H. Davison, *Reform in the Ottoman Empire 1856–1876* (Princeton 1963), 185.
2 Server İskit, *Türkiyede Matbuat Rejimleri, II: Tahlil ve Tarihçe* (Istanbul 1939), 8–12; Server İskit, *Türkiyede Matbuat İdareleri ve Politikaları* (Istanbul 1943), 15–22.

shape of secret societies, sprouted up. It is an interesting question, to what extent this new press provoked heated political discussion in Istanbul.

Among the Turkish publicists were young, well-educated bureaucrats, who had begun to use the press as a medium to search for new political structures. They were dissatisfied with the results of the *Tanẓimat*, which designates the reform period between 1839 and 1878 in the Ottoman Empire. The *Tanẓimat* were considered to be an insufficient method to stabilize the empire. From their perspective the growing number of revolts in the European border regions of the Ottoman Empire as well as European interference were related to misgovernment by the political elite.[3] Their criticism was specifically focused on the Grand Vezir ʿĀli Pasha. One of its most sophisticated expressions was Dhiya Bey's satirical poem *Ẓafername* (Letter of Victory).[4]

Greater restrictions on the press occurred in spring 1867 with the enactment of the *Qararname-i 'Ali (Sublime Decree)*, which repealed the former *Maṭbu'at Niẓamnamesi* temporarily and contained an institutional shift from the *Meclis-i Ma'arif* towards direct governmental control.[5] At the same time numerous bans on publications were imposed. In addition to these limitations on the press, critical publicists, such as ʿAli Su'avi, Namıq Kemal and Dhiya Bey, were either imprisoned or pressured to leave Istanbul. The Egyptian Prince, Muṣṭafa Fadhıl Pasha, residing in Paris after his expulsion from the Ottoman Empire in 1866, invited the aforementioned through a mediator, to flee to Paris.[6] They accepted and left Istanbul in spring 1867, shortly followed by Nuri, Reshad, Meḥmed Bey and Āğah Efendi, who were wanted because of their relationship to conspiratorial groups.[7]

Although some questions still remain open concerning their political involvement before their flight, it seems to be clear that it was first in Europe, that they came together and formed a common cause.

---

3 Malcolm Yapp, *The Making of the Modern East 1792–1923* (London 1987), 115–16; Enver Koray, 'Yeni Osmanlılar', in Hakkı Dursun Yıldız (ed.), *Yüzellinci Yılında Tanzimat* (Türk Tarih Kurumu Yayınları VII: 142, Ankara 1992), 550–5.

4 Dhiya Bey, *Ẓafername-i sherḥi* (Istanbul n.d.), 3–23.

5 İskit, *Türkiyede Matbuat İdareleri*, 24–6.

6 Ebu'dh-dhiya Tevfiq, 'Yeŋi 'Othmanlılar ta'rikhi: 12', in *Yeŋi Taṣvir-i Efkar* n.s. 14 (1327/1909), 2–3.

7 Ebu'dh-dhiya Tevfiq, 'Yeŋi 'Othmanlılar ta'rikhi: 21', *Yeŋi Taṣvir-i Efkar* n. 88, 4; 'Yeŋi 'Othmanlılar ta'rikhi: 22', in *Yeŋi Taṣvir-i Efkar* n. 89, 4.

While they first called themselves in the French press, under Muṣṭafa Fadhıl Pasha's leadership, *Jeune Turquie*,[8] they later used, after Muṣṭafa Fadhıl Pasha's return to Istanbul, the name *Yeŋi 'Othmanlılar Cem'iyeti*, generally translated as *Young Ottomans* or *Young Ottoman Society*.[9] Although their political positions were quite different, these seven men fostered through their different perspectives the spirit of the Young Ottomans, giving the 'movement' its specific heterogeneous shape.

In Paris the Young Ottomans had already aroused public interest through their publications in the French press. Dhiya Bey's dispute with the journal *Le Mémorial Diplomatique*, published in *La Liberté* and settled before the court indicates its extent.[10] However, with these publications they were unable to reach an Istanbul readership. Which prior considerations led to the decision to produce a Turkish language newspaper destined for the domestic Ottoman public remain speculative. At first glance, London as the place of choice for publication seems somewhat strange as the Young Ottomans lacked a command of English and were leaving an extensive network of personal contacts behind in Paris.

So, why was London chosen? Two important premises might have influenced their decision:

1. The British repeal of the Newspaper Stamp Bill in March 1855;
2. The liberal press laws towards a non-English press.

The repeal of the Newspaper Stamp Bill reflected the major parliamentary approach that the free market displaced governmental control by self-regulation.

In India Sir Charles Metcalfe had already supported vernacular newspapers in 1835 with the repeal of a rigid licensing system. A free press was perceived as a relatively safe forum for dissent. Instead of undermining British rule it was seen as a means of increasing the stability of the British empire.

However, in the 1870s this attitude became less liberal and the latitude given towards Oriental languages was strongly challenged. It culminated in the Oriental

8 Dhiya Bey, 'A Monsieur le Directeur du Journal la Liberté', *La Liberté* (18.06.1867), 2.

9 Sherif Mardin, *The Genesis of the Young Ottoman Thought* (Princeton Oriental Studies 21, Princeton 1962), 396–408.

10 Dhiya Bey, 'La Jeune Turquie', *La Liberté* (26.06.1867), 1; Le Mémorial Diplomatique, *Imputations Diffamatoires contre Ziya Bey* (n. 43, Paris 29.06.1867), 2.

Languages Act in 1878, which resulted in severe restrictions on non-English language journalism.[11]

While in Great Britain restrictions on the press were repealed in the period between 1855 and 1880, in France control remained relatively severe and the abolition of stamp duty did not happen until 1881.

In 1847 one journalist of the magazine *Punch* formulated the difference between French and British journalism:

> A French journalist has two great chances. He may either become Prime Minister or an inmate of a Government prison ... An English journalist ... has one great chance ... if he has extraordinary talent, perseverance, and industry - to remain unknown.[12]

Geneva and Brussels were considered as alternatives to London. According to Namıq Kemal's somewhat egocentric version of events, the decision for London was mainly made on the basis of his demands.[13]

To realize the publication of the newspaper *Ḥurriyet* (Freedom) at a distance from the centre of the Ottoman Empire, but aimed at the Istanbul public, a variety of obstacles had to be overcome. Hardly any information was left by the Young Ottomans themselves concerning the technical procurement, necessary for the publication of the newspaper. There seems to have been very little common interest in this subject, which explains why there is no mention of it in *Ḥurriyet* and very little in the private correspondence of Namıq Kemal.[14]

Although the newspaper *Mukhbir* (Correspondent) was a short-lived common project, the practical experiences gained therefrom, were of use in the subsequent publication of *Ḥurriyet.* In August 1867 they began to publish *Mukhbir*, which was identically titled to the forbidden newspaper in Istanbul. Differences of a rather more personal than political nature split ʿAli Su'avi from the rest of the group. The Young Ottomans harshly criticized his dominant position in *Mukhbir* and reproached him for having plotted against some of them.[15] In May 1868 Dhiya Bey and Namıq Kemal

11 Aled Jones, *Powers of the Press: Newspapers, Power and Public in the Nineteenth-Century England* (Cambridge 1996), 10–26.

12 *Punch* 13 (1847), 123; cited in Jones, *Powers of the Press*, 119.

13 Fevziye Abdullah Tansel (ed.), *Namık Kemal'in Husūsī Mektupları I: İstanbul, Avrupa ve Magosa Mektupları* (Türk Tarih Krumu Yayınlarından n.s. 22, Ankara 1967), 145–7.

14 Ibid., 146–7.

15 Ebu'dh-dhiya Tevfiq, 'Yeŋi 'Othmanlılar ta'rikhi: 105', *Yeŋi Taṣvir-i Efkar* n. 172 , 4; 'Yeŋi 'Othmanlılar ta'rikhi: 55', *Yeŋi Taṣvir-i Efkar* n. 122, 4.

explicitly declared *Mukhbir* as a common project to be finished and decided to produce a new publication.[16]

Āğah Efendi was charged with installing the printing office. For *Mukhbir* he had already overcome the typological obstacles related to the language. The Arabic character printing blocks had already been brought to London from Āğah Efendi's own print shop in Istanbul.[17] They were than transferred from the office of *Mukhbir* to new premises at no. 4 Rupert Street, where *Ḥurriyet* was subsequently published. From Istanbul, Melik Efendi, a printer was then engaged. Further typographical details came to light, thanks to Ebu'dh-dhiya Tevfiq's chronicle of the Young Ottomans, which appeared some forty years later in the newspaper *Yeŋi Taṣvir-i efkar* (New Tablet of Opinion).

> Su'avi, Mukhbir'i (Hammersmith) de George Bertrand'ıŋ maṭba'asında tertib ettiriyor idi. Çünke Āğah Efendiniŋ ḥurufı o maṭba'ada bir da'ire-i makhṣuṣaya vadh' edilmish idi. Ḥurriyet ise, Mukhbir'iŋ bulındıghı maṭba'ada çıqarılmaq istenilmediğinden, kharflarıŋ oradan qaldırılmasına lüzum khaṣıl oldı. O cihhetle Londra'da Saint James maḥallesinde (Rupert) soqaghında ṣuret-i makhṣuṣada bir khane kiralanaraq "Jön Türkleriŋ maṭba'a-ı merkeziyesi" nam ile bir maṭba'a açıldı ki, o tarikhde eŋ ziyade shöhreti olan "Walter sistemi" bir de ṭab' makinesi alındıghından, maṭba'a ufaq olmaqla beraber, Londra'da açıldıghı cihhetle Yeŋi 'Othmanlıların shan ve ḥaythiyetlerile mütenasib idi.[18]

> Su'avi had arranged the types for printing *Mukhbir* in George Bertrand's printing office, located in Hammersmith, as Āğah Efendi's Arabic character printing blocks were deposited there in a separate office. As they desired to publish *Ḥurriyet* at a different printing office to *Mukhbir*, this necessitated moving the type blocks to another location. A house was then rented in Rupert Street (in St. James') for this purpose and given the name central printing office of the Young Turks. A printing machine with the Walter system, amongst the most famous of that period, was purchased. Their new venture in London, complete with their own small printing office, befitted the repute and standing of the Young Ottomans.[19]

The above-mentioned Walter printing machine was first used by the publishers of *The Times*. John Walter II had in 1814 first installed, a new kind of cylindrical printing machine, which was able to supersede manpower by the power, inherent in the cylinders. T. Walter, who continued the work of his father, gave the order to

16 Tansel (ed.), *Namık Kemal'in Husūsī Mektupları I*, 137.
17 M.K. Bilgegil, *Ziyā Paşa Üzerinde bir Araştırma* (Atatürk Üniversitesi Yayınları n.s. 100, Erzurum 1970), 117–21.
18 Ebu'dh-dhiya Tevfiq, 'Yeŋi 'Othmanlılar ta'rikhi: 68', *Yeŋi Taşvir-i Efkar* n. 135, 4.
19 Ibid., trans. by the author.

construct a new printing machine, which was intended as an improvement on the new type of rotation machine, developed by the American William Bullock in 1860. J. Calverley was the constructor, given this task. The modified rotation press was first installed for *The Times* in 1866, with four cylinders being arranged in a vertical manner one above the other. This facilitated the printing of both sides of the same sheet of paper. This printing machine was thus named after its sponsor, T. Walter.[20]

It remains rather doubtful, whether the Walter press was really purchased by the Young Ottomans. The Walter press seems to have been the most innovative of that period, realized for a huge daily readership and not for some thousand copies, to be sent far away, which meant that the speed of printing could not have been such an important premise.

Ḥurriyet, which first appeared on the 29th of June 1868 was explicitly cited as an organ of the *Yeŋi 'Othmanlılar Cem'iyeti*, although it was mostly written by Dhiya Bey and Namıq Kemal. Namıq Kemal ended his collaboration with the 63rd edition, due to the desperate financial situation and dissension about sponsoring. Nevertheless Dhiya Bey continued to publish *Ḥurriyet* until its cessation with the 100th edition in Geneva in July 1870. Due to the intervention of the Ottoman ambassador in London, Dhiya Bey had been called to court, as a result of one article published in *Ḥurriyet* against ʿĀli Pasha. He ignored this call and escaped to Geneva,[21] where he published the last 11 editions of *Ḥurriyet*. With only a few exceptions *Ḥurriyet* appeared weekly.

The financial backing of Muṣṭafa Fadhıl Pasha, which had at first offered them a bohemian lifestyle in Europe, gradually dried up after his reconciliation with the Sultan and subsequent return to Istanbul. Although, according to Ebu'dh-dhiya Tevfiq, Muṣṭafa Fadhıl Paşa still provided the financial backing for the setting up of a print shop for *Ḥurriyet*,[22] with increasing official disapproval of the newspaper, his remittance became more and more irregular until it finally ceased completely in Spring 1869.[23] This put the Young Ottomans in an extremely difficult financial situation. One facet of this dilemma is reflected in one of Namıq Kemal's letters to his father in September 1868:

---

20 Hans-Jürgen Wolf, *Schwarze Kunst: Eine illustrierte Geschichte der Druckverfahren* (Mainz 1981), 251–5.
21 Ebu'dh-dhiya Tevfiq, 'Yeŋi 'Othmanlılar ta'rikhi: 68', *Yeŋi Taṣvir-i Efkar* n. 135, 4.
22 Ibid., 4.
23 Bilgegil, *Ziyā Paşa*, 123.

> … daha mebālig teshrif etmedi. Yarın-obir gün gelir sanırım. Geldiği zeman, nihāyet dereceye kalma bir ihtiyat olarak saklanılacaktır. İnsha'llāh maslahat, ekmek yediğimiz yere fenālık derecesine gelmez. Eğer o pereseye gelirse, nefsimce mümkün değil, ac kalsam kabûl etmem; … Bilmem öteki budalanın ne vakit aklı bashına gelecek. He r türlüsünü ihtār ettik; bundan bashka elimizden ne gelir?[24]

> The sum of money has not arrived yet. I suppose that it will arrive very soon. When it comes, we will at last, have an amount to set aside for cases of necessity. I hope that the affair here will not cumulate into a harmful one. If it comes to such a point, for myself personally it is out of the question that I will accept a situation in which I will submit to hunger. … I don't know when the other fool will come to his senses. We have done every kind of reminding, what else can we do?[25]

How was *Ḥurriyet* channelled back to Istanbul?

The delivery of *Ḥurriyet* must have been a risky and uncertain undertaking. To date little information on this subject has come to light. However, we can assume that they probably made use of some of the contacts, which they had already used to channel *Mukhbir*. For example Namıq Kemal had addressed his desire for support to a customs official, named Rif'at Aḥmed Efendi, who was asked to facilitate the import of *Mukhbir* over the borders of the Ottoman Empire.[26]

The distribution of *Ḥurriyet* and *Mukhbir* in Istanbul seems to have been organised differently. While *Mukhbir* appears to have been distributed only by one person, called Yorgi Istenfalis, who was engaged for this purpose by Muṣṭafa Fadhıl Pasha, *Ḥurriyet* probably reached its readership via more than one channel. This strategic shift might have been provoked by stronger governmental controls, the lack of Muṣṭafa Fadhıl Pasha's financial support as well as rumours about the former distributor, who was accused by ʿAli Su'avi of having used deceitful methods for his personal financial gain.[27]

For *Ḥurriyet* Ebu'dh-dhiya Tevfiq quotes a French bookseller in Beyoghlu, called Coq, who used his own spectacular method of distribution.

> Üçüncü numerası geldiği günlerde, Beyoghlında shimdiki gözlükçi (Verdou)'nıŋ bulındıghı dükkan, ki (Qoq) isminde bir Fransız kitabcısı idi; *Ḥurriyet*i iki nüskha olaraq

24 Tansel (ed.), *Namık Kemal'in Husūsī Mektupları I*, 156.
25 Ibid., trans. by the author.
26 Ibid., 131.
27 'Ali Su'avi, 'Yeŋi ʿOthmanlılar ta'rikhi', *ʿUlum* n.3, vol 2 (1286/1869), 781; cited in Tansel (ed.), *Namık Kemal'in Husūsī Mektupları I*, 130.

> içli ṭıshlı camekanına yapıshdırmısh ve bu ṣuretle gelüb geçenler bi-perva camekanıŋ öŋünde tevaqqufla oqumushlardır.[28]

> At the time, when the third number arrived, in Beyoghlu there had been in the actual shop of the optician Verdoux a French bookseller, named Coq. He displayed two editions of *Ḥurriyet* quite openly in his shop window. Passers by stopped in front of the window and read it free from concern.[29]

According to this related story, the police of Beyoghlu were then sent to remove the newspapers from the window. Although Monsieur Coq was already in his sixties, he did not hesitate to use physical force to prevent the police entering his bookshop.[30]

We have no information relating to the number of copies per edition. But even if we assumed figures deductively, these would tell us very little about the real size of readership among the Istanbul public, as newspapers were read aloud before an audience in the coffee-houses and other public places. Although we have to consider the ban on *Ḥurriyet*, which might have limited the feasibility of this tradition in the public, it probably caused only a shift from public towards more private places, without dampening its attraction. The importance of *Ḥurriyet* might also be evaluated by the Grand Vizir's involvement. ʿĀli Pasha tried to intervene in a reconciliatory way offering to buy 2,000 copies of *Ḥurriyet*, if the Young Ottomans were willing to change its content.[31] Although it is not possible to provide any exact information concerning the resonance of *Ḥurriyet*, one can assume that it helped pave the way for the realization of the first constitution in 1876.

Far from the official grasp, the Young Ottomans were able to develop political concepts of state, propagating different positions referring to aspects of the Enlightenment and also those involving ideas of nationalism together with ideas of Ottoman Islamic tradition. Their freedom from official political restraints made *Ḥurriyet* a medium, which today offers us a unique opportunity to gain access to their world of thinking.

---

28 Ebu'dh-dhiya Tevfiq, 'Yeŋi ʿOthmanlılar ta'rikhi: 86' *Yeŋi Taṣvir-i Efkar* n. 153, 4.
29 Ibid., 4, trans. by the author.
30 Ibid., 4.
31 Tansel (ed.), *Namık Kemal'in Husūsī Mektupları I*, 154; Mardin, *The Genesis*, 51.

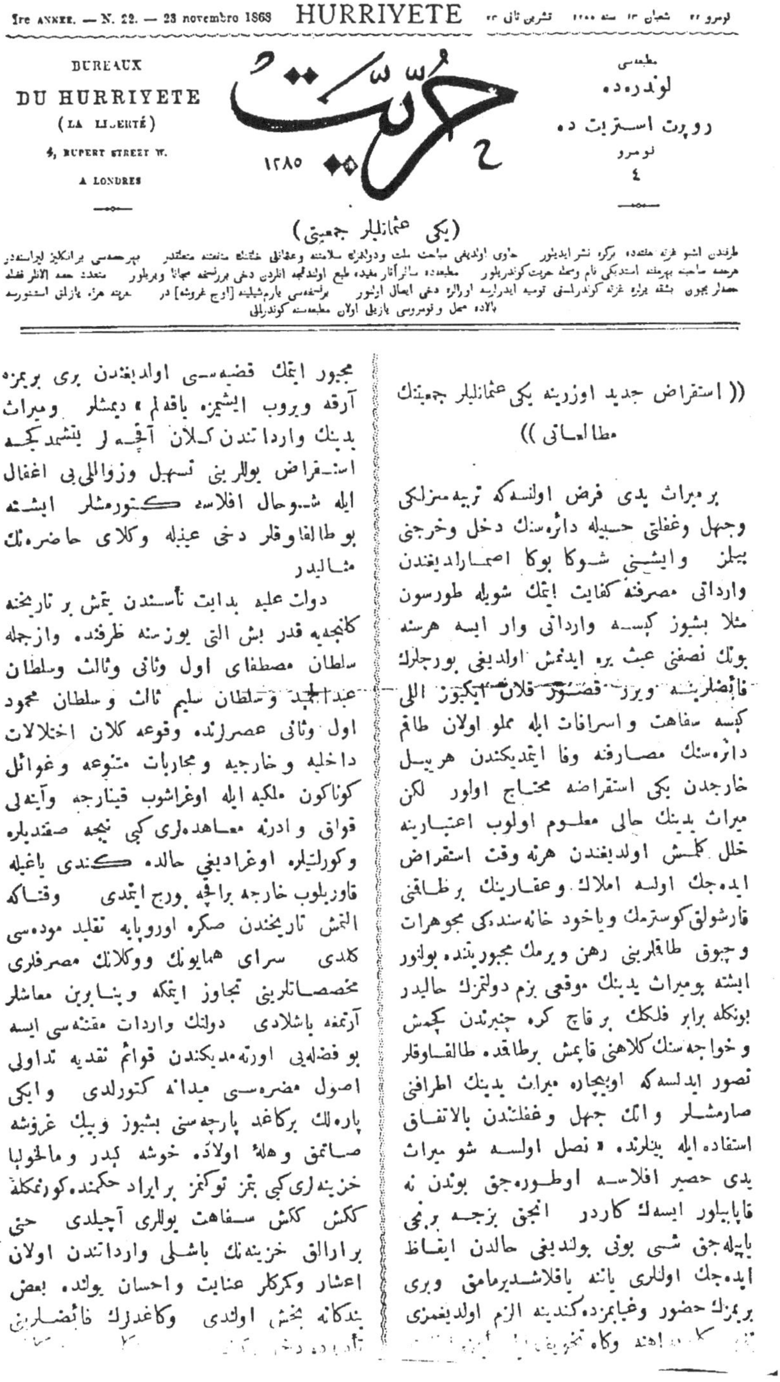

1re ANNÉE. — N. 22. — 23 novembre 1868 HURRIYETE

BUREAUX
DU HURRIYETE
(LA LIBERTÉ)
4, RUPERT STREET W.
A LONDRES

حريت

۱۲۸۵

لوندره‌ده
روپرت استریت‌ده

(یکی عثمانلیلر جمعیتی)

((استقراض جدید اوزرینه یکی عثمانلیلر جمعیتنك مطالعاتی))

Figure 1. Hurriyet

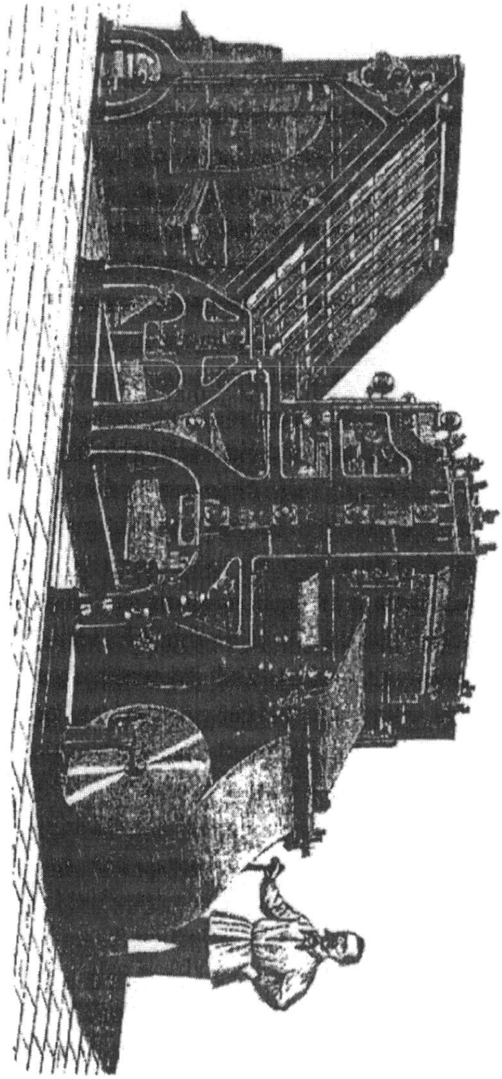

Figure 2. Press

The Beginnings of Publishing in pre-1948 Palestine

Ami Ayalon

Tel Aviv University

What happens to a printed text once it is out of the printer's shop?[1] How does it become public property and how is it consumed? After all, printing, an amazing device no doubt, is no more than a production implement and further processes are involved in turning written texts into consumer goods. Indeed, printing is a link in the chain of mechanisms by which ideas are transmitted from author to audience. Earlier links include the formulation of ideas as intelligible statements and rendering them as presentable manuscripts, and printing, in turn, is followed by publishing — advertising, distributing, and selling — which make the product accessible to the public. Where this last process ends another, equally complex process begins: consumption. Aside of reading in different modes, solitarily or collectively, quietly or vocally, the consumption of printed texts also entails their mental assimilation, sometimes debating their contents with others, and always a dialogue with the author, explicit or implied. The fate of a text once it is born thus forms a multi-phased and multicoloured tale.

Historians, sociologists, anthropologists and ethnographers have explored aspects of the production and consumption of written texts, mainly in Western societies. We already have a considerable corpus of scholarship on the history of printing and publishing in Europe and its cultural offshoots, on the evolution of libraries, bookstores, private book collecting and literary societies, as well as on who read what and how, the intercourse between writer and audience, and the formation of public opinion. In the Middle East, by contrast, work on such matters has barely begun. In cultural history, as in most other fields, the study of Arab societies still lags way behind that of Europe, not least when modern times are concerned, for reasons that are too well known to detain us here. In the pages below I propose to make a very

1 The author acknowledges the support of the Israeli Science Foundation in the preparation of this article.

modest contribution to the study of Arab publishing, focusing on one individual case, that of the Arab community in pre-1948 Palestine. The confines set for this article allow no more than a quick glimpse at two limited sections of the scene: the advent of printing and the emergence of bookshops, two central links in the chain of the publishing trade at its inception. It may be noted in passing that this is a particularly difficult terrain to plough in the Middle East, since evidence is ever wanting; and that in Palestine the problem is all the more intricate, due to the devastating impact of the 1948 *nakba* on historical evidence. Still, testimonies do exist and, when creatively exploited, they permit us to tell a meaningful story.

The development of publishing in pre-1948 Palestine had two prominent features. First, the process was short and markedly intensive. While elsewhere in the region — primarily in Egypt and the Lebanon — a vivid cultural-literary blossoming had taken place from the mid-nineteenth century onward, Palestine had remained on the sidelines of this activity until much later. A handful of precursors aside, its cultural awakening and the concomitant emergence of publishing activity were telescoped into the half-century after 1900, especially the post-World War I decades, and then cut short rather abruptly by the mid-century crisis. Second, even when such an industry began to evolve in Palestine, it was overshadowed — and actually checked — by the dynamic ventures in its neighbourhood. By the time Palestine took its first step in this arena, Egypt and, to a lesser extent, Lebanon had already become lively regional foci of creativity, potent enough to constrict the growth of local publishing industries around them. Palestine, like most of the region's other countries, thus remained a satellite of the Egyptian and Lebanese literary endeavours, whose written products were regularly consumed by the Palestinian educated class. We have few data on this influx of imported texts, but there is ample evidence to show that it was substantial, perhaps to the extent of dominating the market in Palestine, at least with regards to books.[2]

Under the circumstances, pre-1948 Arab Palestine made up a rather modest publishing arena. Of the humble yield of its products, the bulk was newspapers, a

2 For a discussion of imported texts from Palestine's neighbourhood, see Ami Ayalon, 'Modern Texts and their Readers in Late Ottoman Palestine,' *Middle Eastern Studies* 38:4 (2002), 17–40, and idem, *Reading Palestine: Texts and Audience, 1900–1948* (Austin forthcoming), Ch. 2.

novel commodity whose history in the country began only after 1900.[3] By the mid-1940s the Palestinian periodical press had reached a total circulation of perhaps 20,000, an impressive progress explainable by the growing public thirst for information, which, in turn, was generated by the rapid shifts in the country's political landscape. Books, by contrast, addressed different (and less urgent) needs and there was a small demand for them that was met, in part, by imports. Local book making was therefore very limited. A full record of it is yet to be assembled, but available data seem to suggest that it did not exceed an annual output of 20 titles on average from 1900–48 (being more energetic at the end than at the outset).[4] Notably, in some significant way book printing was a by-product of the journalistic enterprise, especially so in its early years, as we shall see.

In the discussion below we will be concerned mainly with non-periodical publishing, leaving aside the exciting story of Palestinian journalism, except when it affected the advent of the book industry. Basically, book production in Palestine represented collaborative efforts of two kinds: author-printer and author-bookseller. The former, born shortly after the introduction of printing into the country, was by far the most common type of operation until the end of the period. The latter, indeed a variation of the former, developed only in the wake of World War II.

Printing

A Jewish press had operated in Safad, northern Palestine, already in the late sixteenth century, turning out books in Hebrew for about a decade before it closed down. The country's next press was another Jewish venture, set up in 1832 in the same town by Yisrael Bak and his son Nissan, who in 1841 moved their shop to Jerusalem. It was followed by several initiatives launched by Christian evangelical societies in Jerusalem. The earliest of these, and by far the busiest depot until the end of the century, was the one founded by the Franciscans in 1846 near the Old City's New Gate. It printed scores of books and pamphlets in several languages, including Arabic,

3 That is, if we disregard a reported feeble attempt to publish an official state bulletin back in 1876, of which we know nothing other than its name. See Yusuf Khuri, *Al-Sihafa al-'Arabiyya fi Filastin 1876–1948* (Beirut 1976), 3. Another official Ottoman organ appeared briefly in 1903 (see below), but the real beginning of the Palestinian Arab press was only in 1908, following the Young Turk Revolution.

4 For a detailed discussion of this issue, see *Reading Palestine*, ibid.

dealing with a variety of subjects, from theology to geography.[5] Anglican and Protestant societies and the local Greek-Orthodox and Armenian communities in the city subsequently founded presses that printed in Arabic, all in the nineteenth century, which put out books and leaflets dealing mostly with religious-educational matters.[6] Some reports also point to the existence, alongside the missionary and communal enterprises, of several private presses in pre-1900 Jerusalem: *al-Matba'a al-Ma'muniyya* (1876), the Dumyan brothers press (1892), a printing shop owned by Martin Lasfu (1892) and *al-Matba'a al-Wataniyya*, which Alfonse Antun Alonzo ran from 1892–4. We know little about them beyond their names. Nor is there evidence to support an obscure reference in an 1898 official Ottoman publication, to similar activities taking place outside of Jerusalem.[7] Further exploration is obviously needed before this scene is clear.[8]

Yet another private printing shop that started operating around the same time was that of Jurji Habib Hananya, about which we know slightly more. Apparently a typical instance of the country's nascent publishing projects, it would be worth our while to look at it more closely. Hananya (1857–1920), a Greek-Orthodox Jerusalemite, seems to have been employed for some time in one of the presses in that

---

5 M.T. Petrozzi, 'The Franciscan printing press,' *Christian News from Israel*, 20:26 (1971), 64–9. A bibliography of Arabic works printed in Palestine from 1847 onward lists 65 items produced by the Franciscan press during the nineteenth century and another 51 during the first half of the twentieth; see Rasim Jabbara, *Al-Bibliyughrafiyya al-'Arabiyya fi Filastin 1847–1947* (al-Tayyiba, Israel 1996), passim. Jabara's list exists only in draft form, and I am grateful to the author for allowing me to consult it. Undoubtedly less than complete, it is nonetheless the most comprehensive record of this kind so far.

6 Details in Ya'acov Yehoshua, *Ta'rikh al-Sihafa al-'Arabiyya fi Filastin fi'l-'Ahd al-'Uthmani, 1908–1918* (Jerusalem 1974), 7–13; Muhammad Sulayman, 'al-Matabi' al-Filastiniyya wa-Atharuha al-Thaqafi fi'l-'Ahd al-Turki,' *Ru'ya* (Gaza), 13 (October 2001), 78–82; 'Abd al-Rahman Yaghi, *Hayat al-Adab al-Filastini al-Hadith, min Awwal al-Nahda hatta al-Nakba* (Beirut 1968), 77–80.

7 Sulayman, 77, quoting an Ottoman *Salnameh* from 1316/1898, which refers to private Arabic printing activity 'in the narrow alleys of old Jerusalem, Haifa and Jaffa.' This reference was first quoted by Sulayman in a study he had published in 1987 (probably adopted from Yehoshua, 7). In his 2001 article cited here, he notes that 'since the publication of that book in 1987 until today, my extensive toiling and all forms of exploring and inquiring [into the matter] have led to no [new information] worth mentioning in this regard.'

8 Yehoshua, *Ta'rikh*, ibid; Sulayman, ibid. Yehoshua also mentions two Jewish presses, that of Yitzhaq Hirschenson (1876) and that of Yitzhaq Levi (1896), both of which were equipped with Arabic characters as well as Hebrew ones. Frequent discrepancies between the secondary sources regarding dates of foundation and other details suggest that the early development of printing in Palestine is still awaiting a more systematic study. For example, Yaghi, relying on various sources, quotes impressive but somewhat dubious figures relating to the output of some pre-1900 presses in Jerusalem, for which no evidence is known to be extant. Jabbara's *Bibliyughrafiyya* mentions a modest total of 14 items printed before 1900 by Jerusalem presses other than the Franciscan (and a few others without a date of publication printed between 1847 and 1948).

city before launching his own business. In 1894 he applied for a printing license. Such a request normally entailed protracted waiting in Hamidian times, and Hananya moved ahead to begin his activities anyway, acquiring Latin characters and buying printing time from presses in the city to perform freelance jobs during the tourist season. Resourceful and ambitious, he then imported Arabic letters and a simple leg-operated machine and put them to use secretly in his home, taking private assignments from Ottoman officials and others and handling them at night while carrying on with his other commitments during the day. Repeatedly quarrelling with the authorities, Hananya persisted in this difficult routine until February 1898, when he eventually obtained the desired printing license. The following year he applied for permission to publish a newspaper, an application he would subsequently repeat numerous times and back it with sizeable bribes but to no avail. Meanwhile, he made a living from printing 'the circulars (*dafatir*) of all government departments' as well as the local Ottoman official organ, *Quds-i Sharif/al-Quds al-Sharif*, launched in 1903 and lasting for five years. More impressive, by the time the Hamidian censorship dam collapsed in summer 1908, Hananya's business had to its credit — by his own account — a total of '281 books (*kitab*^{an}), among them 83 in Arabic.'[9] Aside of Hananya's own testimony, however, no evidence has yet come to light that would confirm these remarkable but somewhat questionable figures. Most likely, a yield of this scale, if true, comprised mainly small-size pamphlets, leaflets and perhaps single-sheet products rather than real 'books'.[10]

Having gone through trial and error in rough times, Hananya was ready for the new opportunities offered under 'the rising sun of freedom.' Within six weeks of the changeover in the Ottoman capital, his semi-weekly newspaper *al-Quds* was out in the market — one of the country's very earliest periodicals. It was among 15 Arabic newspapers and journals that appeared in a frantic outburst before the end of 1908, reflecting the new liberal spirit in the empire.[11] The license to print prompted the

---

9 Opening article of *al-Quds* (Hananya's paper), 5–18 September 1908, quoted in Yehoshua, *Ta'rikh,* 41–4, and see also 10–11. On p. 10 Yehoshua erroneously indicates the date of the license as 1906, an error also adopted by Sulayman, 82.

10 Jabbara's bibliography lists only 5 works printed in Hananya's press (also called Matbaʿat *Jaridat al-Quds*), only one of them before 1908 — see below. In addition, *c.* 20 other titles are mentioned as having been printed in Jerusalem until 1908, for which no printer's name is given.

11 Details in Khuri, *al-Sihafa,* 7–15. Another 19 papers appeared in Palestine between 1909 and 1914; ibid, 16–26.

emergence of presses, set up specifically for the purpose of publishing newspaper and voicing opinion. Such were the printing shops producing *al-Insaf*, *al-Najah* and *al-Nafir* in Jerusalem, *al-Akhbar*, *Sawt al-'Uthmaniyya* and *Filastin* in Jaffa and *al-Karmil* in Haifa before 1914, all modest enterprises that used imported machinery, often second-hand, to manufacture the rudimentary organs authored by their owners. Others, eager to pronounce views but unable to buy the needed equipment, hired the services of existing presses (Hananya's own shop printed one other journal, or more, alongside his own *al-Quds*).[12] But putting out newspapers was a small operation even for these humble businesses, and they looked for additional jobs, advertising such innovative products as commercial letterheads and envelopes, personal cards, wedding invitations and the like. They would gladly print books, if and when they were available for publication.

But books were slow to appear. Pre-World War I Palestine was overwhelmingly illiterate and the size of its book-consuming audience was Lilliputian. The number of authors was still tinier. Prior to the introduction of printing into the country, members of the small educated elite had subscribed to foreign journals and bought books from neighbouring provinces and Europe; while the handful of local writers went abroad to print their composed or translated works.[13] Writing in Palestine was far too limited in scope to keep the machines of the newly launched presses rolling. Preceding the country's literary awakening, the development of printing thus had to rely mainly on publishing newspapers, a novel brand of commodity whose consumer market was yet to be formed. Hananya's business was illustrative of this activity. With a twice-weekly paper as its mainstay, the press constantly looked for more jobs but found little. 'Few as [presses in Jerusalem] are, there is no adequate work for them,' he complained.[14] In 1900 he was hired to print the catalogue of the new Khalidiyya library, an 87-page, Spartan-looking booklet.[15] Other Hananya-produced works that came down to us include a 28-page tourist guide in 1908 and three tracts on language

12 Ibid, 7; Yehoshua, *Ta'rikh,* 78, 86.

13 Husam al-Khatib, *Harakat al-Tarjamah al-Filastiniyya: min al-Nahda hatta Awakhir al-Qarn al-'Ishrin* (Beirut 1995), appendix; Nasir al-Din al-Asad, *al-Ittijahat al-Adabiyya al-Haditha fi Filastin wa'l-Urdun* (Cairo 1957), 42.

14 Quoted in Yehoshua, *Ta'rikh,* 12.

15 Al-Maktaba al-Khalidiyya, *Barnamaj al-Maktaba al-Khalidiyya al-'Umumiyya* (Jerusalem: Matbaʿat Jurji Habib Hananya, 1900).

from 1912, likewise skinny opuses of 60–70 pages each.[16] There might have been a few more, of which we have no trace. This was probably characteristic of the scale of private printing efforts in pre-World War I Palestine. We know little on the manner in which such works were circulated; with few bookstores around before the War (see below), the dissemination of printed items must have been slow and cumbersome, and on the whole limited in scope. Hananya himself ran into financial difficulties, typically resulting from the unfriendly market conditions, and was forced to close his business, leaving the country for Alexandria in 1913 or 1914.[17]

So much for the printer's share. To view Palestine's early publishing from the author's angle, we may look at Khalil Baydas (1875–1949), owner of the literary weekly/monthly *al-Nafa'is al-'Asriyya.*[18] A Greek-Orthodox like Hananya and a graduate of Russian missionary schools in Palestine and Syria, Baydas had translated Tolstoy and Pushkin novels and published them in Beirut and Cairo for several years prior to 1908.[19] In November of that year, three months after the Revolution, he launched his journal in Haifa, teaming up with a new local press called *al-Matba'a al-Wataniyya.* The following year he published a novel he had adapted from the Russian, hiring the same printer to bring it out.[20] In 1910 Baydas moved with his journal to Jerusalem, where he continued to publish it regularly until the War, scoring remarkable success.[21] Seeking to acquaint his readers with the treasures of Russian literature, he devoted a large portion of the journal to translations from that language, usually his own. But he also issued separate works, rendered from Russian and other tongues and often presented as *riwayat,* or short stories — apparently small-size chapbooks (as their modest price would suggest) — but also more massive works.[22] Both *al-Nafa'is al-'Asriyya* and some of these separate literary items were produced

16 Jabbara, *al-Bibliyughrafiyya,* see entries under Salim Ilyas al-Qari (1908) and Muhammad Salim Ibn Qutayna (1912).

17 Yehoshua, *Ta'rikh,* 48–50.

18 Jan Daya, 'Al-Nafa'is al-'Asriyya,' *Shu'un Filastiniyya,* 87–88 (February–March 1979), 168–80.

19 Details in al-Khatib, first page of the appendix; *al-Kitab al-'Arabi al-Filastini: Ma'rad al-Kitab al-'Arabi al-Filastini al-Awwal fi Nadi al-Ittihad al-Urthuduksi fi'l-Quds, min 11–20 Tishrin al-Awwal 1946* (Jerusalem 1946), passim.

20 *Ahwal al-Istibdad,* a translation of a book by Tolstoy (Haifa: al-Matba'a al-Wataniyya, 1909); Khatib, *al-Kitab,* ibid.

21 Daya, 'Al-Nafa'is al-'Asriyya,' 170; Yehoshua, *Ta'rikh,* 94. While in Haifa the paper was entitled *al-Nafa'is.* The name was expanded to *al-Nafa'is al-'Asriyya* once it was restarted in Jerusalem.

22 Baydas's journal used to advertise such books and booklets. See e.g. Vol. 5, issues 1 (January 1913) and 4 (April 1913), back covers, featuring 19 and 20 items respectively. Most items sold for 1.50–2.50 Franks each (equivalent to 6–10 Ottoman qurush), a rather modest price.

in Jerusalem by *Matba'at Dar al-Aytam*, the Syrian orphanage press, an ambitious endeavour which by then had acquired a reputation as the country's best.[23] The initiative in this publishing operation was most likely the author's, who selected the texts, prepared the manuscripts and then promoted the final products in his journal. Once again, with bookstores still in the future, the printed items were distributed directly by the author and potential customers were urged to order them 'from the management of *al-Nafa'is al-'Asriyya* in Jerusalem.'[24]

Palestine's political, economic and educational wheels shifted to a higher gear after World War I and private printing shops proliferated quickly. A bibliography of Arabic works published in Palestine until 1947 mentions no less than 115 presses that were involved in their production in the post-War years, including 40 in Jerusalem, 35 in Jaffa, 22 in Haifa and the rest in Acre, Nazareth, Nablus, Bethlehem, Gaza, Ramallah, Lydda, Safad and Hebron.[25] The majority of books and leaflets were produced through simple collaboration with the authors, usually initiated by the latter. Serving as his own editor and copyreader, the writer would hire the services of a press, which would also advertise the work in its own-printed or other newspaper. As for distribution, bookshops that emerged in Palestine after the War gradually became popular conduits for the purpose. Some of them also got involved in publishing, as we shall now see.

Bookstores as Publishers

Data on the front cover of *Ta'rikh Filastin,* a volume published in Palestine in 1923, reveal the story of its production. 'Its publication,' it reads, 'was handled (*'ana bi-nashrihi*) by Bulus and Wadi' Sa'id, owners of *Maktabat Filastin al-'Ilmiyya*, and it was 'printed in *Bayt al-Maqdis* press in Jerusalem.'[26] Production was thus a dual process, representing a joint author-bookshop-printer venture. This was a rather rare kind of undertaking at the time, but it would become quite common in the 1940s.

---

23 Yaghi, *Hayat,* 79; W.D. McCracken, *The New Palestine* (London 1922), 262. The Syrian orphanage was founded in 1860 as a German Protestant project. Among the different vocations in which the children were trained was printing, an endeavour apparently begun around the turn of the century.

24 E.g., *al-Nafa'is al-'Asriyya,* Vol. 5, issues 1 (January 1913) and 4 (April 1913), back covers.

25 Jabbara, *al-Bibliyughrafiyya,* passim.

26 'Umar Salih al-Barghuthi and Khalil Tawtah, *Ta'rikh Filastin* (Jerusalem: Matba'at Bayt al-Maqdis, 1923).

Until close to World War I, the notion of a bookstore was barely known in Palestine. A survey of Jerusalem shops in the late 1860s, conducted by a contemporary observer, found only two booksellers among the 1,932 businesses he recorded, an Armenian and a Jew.[27] Old-style individual book dealers may have operated in some places there already in the nineteenth century, circulating mainly traditional manuscripts; but given the limited demand, this could hardly have been a thriving trade. During the last third of that century, the number of visitors to the holy city was on the ascent and local traders began to cater to their needs, among others in tourist guides (primarily, of course, in foreign languages). Thus, Boulus (Bulus) Meo's famous souvenir shop near the Jaffa Gate carried, along with 'olive, wood and pearl' items, also 'tourist guidebooks,' as its front door sign indicated.[28] More such dealerships opened elsewhere in the city and possibly in the town of Jaffa, the country's main port of entry. Sometime before World War I, the brothers Bulus and Wadi' Sa'id — who would later publish *Ta'rikh Filastin* — opened their *Maktabat Filastin al-'Ilmiyya* or 'Palestine Educational Company' in Jerusalem, a firm that would become one of the country's biggest after the War.[29] A bookshop is also reported to have opened in Haifa in mid-1914, only to close down within several months due to the War.[30] Commensurate with the scanty demand, the scope of these initiatives must have been, on the whole, very small at that stage.

The number of bookshops in Palestine grew markedly after the War. But if books made in the country were few, what did they sell? Ads in the post-War press tell us that the merchandize carried by these businesses was highly variegated. In mandatory Palestine, a bookshop, or *maktaba,* represented a colourful institution. Beyond trading in local and imported books, such places often sold newspapers, school and office supplies, Christmas cards and gifts, toys, household aids, and more. Some of them offered bookbinding services. Others lent books for a periodic fee.

---

27 Charles Warren, *Underground Jerusalem* (London 1876), 491–2. There were also seven bookbinders, six Jews and a Muslim.

28 See Ruth Victor Hummel, 'Reality, imagination and belief: Jerusalem in 19th- and early 20th-century photographs (1839–1917),' in Sylvia Auld and Robert Hillenbrand (eds), *Ottoman Palestine* (London 2000), Vol. 1:261 (presenting a photograph from *c.* 1881 that shows the shop and its sign); Walid Khalidi, *Before Their Diaspora* (Washington DC: Institute for Palestine Studies, 1984), 62, picture no. 40 (where it appears in a section covering the period prior to 1918).

29 Their post-war ads indicated that the shop had been in operation since 1910; e.g., *Filastin,* 9 September 1921, 3; *al-Nafa'is al-'Asriyya,* 9:4 (August 1922), 111.

30 *Al-Zahra,* 2:7/8 (1922–3), 185–6.

Thus, the Sa'id brothers' company, expanding its trade to Jaffa (as well as to Cairo and Alexandria), carried 'all scholarly and cultural books in Arabic and foreign languages, writing materials, school and business supplies,' current periodicals, Arabic, English and Hebrew 'Royal' typewriters and even 'Columbia' gramophones.[31] Such businesses became quite numerous during the mandate; by 1945, when a 'union of Arab bookstore owners in Palestine' was founded, no less than 51 of them had joined in — from Acre to Jerusalem, from Tiberias to Gaza.[32] More to the point, toward the end of the period some of the more enterprising businesses began to enter into publishing, cooperating with existing presses or buying their own printing equipment.

A closer look at one such venture would illustrate this development.[33] Fawzi Yusuf, a young man from Jerusalem, moved to 'fulfil an old dream' in 1935 by opening a bookstore in the Old City, which he named *Maktabat al-Andalus*. He rented a small place, previously a shoe store, refurbished it and commenced his trade. The shop at first sold mostly writing materials, but Yusuf aspired for more. Identifying a rising demand for printed texts, he began to import Egyptian schoolbooks, literary works and journals. Within three years he already had his own bureau in Cairo, upgrading his services and acting as an agent of leading Egyptian periodicals, which he distributed through contracting shops in Jaffa, Haifa, Lydda and other towns. On the eve of World War II he introduced yet another innovative service, allowing his customers to borrow books for a monthly sum. The War cut the supplies from Egypt and forced Yusuf to close down his Cairo office. Resourceful and resilient, he moved to devise new projects that would keep him afloat on the rough waters. 'We did not remain idle with our arms crossed,' Yusuf recalled (speaking of himself in the first-person plural):

> Rather, we sought new directions for our initiative and began thinking of printing schoolbooks locally … The idea was crowned with success. A group of teachers prepared the texts needed for our schools, each in his field of specialization, and we had the books

---

31 Ads in *al-Nafa'is al-'Asriyya*, ibid; *Filastin*, 9 November 1921, 4, and 30 April 1929, 7.

32 Israel State Archive, P326/630 — letter by the union's secretary to Khalil al-Sakakini dated 11 March 1945. The letter also refers to several additional bookstores that had declined to join the union.

33 This description is based on Fawzi Yusuf, *Khamsun 'Aman fi Khidam al-Haraka al-Thaqafiyya: Maktabat al-Andalus 1935–1985* (Jerusalem 1985), 16–22, 27, 30; idem, *Shay' min Hayati* (Jerusalem 1980), 47–9.

> printed locally. We thereby fulfilled a precious desire: the writing and printing of books at home became a reality ... To guarantee continued production, we began importing the required [quantities of] paper directly from the mills.
>
> Our store came to supply schools with the necessary texts ... The Department of Education encouraged this scheme, and sometimes bought quantities of them for its depositories. We also paid visits to schools and bookstores, offering them the books we printed.[34]

This was an exemplary case of a project born out of necessity. Yusuf combined forces with a well-known press, Bandali Mushahwar's *Matba'at Bayt al-Maqdis* near the Old City's Jaffa Gate (which, we shall recall, was the printer of *Ta'rikh Filastin*, mentioned above).[35] He also came up with an assortment of original paper products carrying his shop's logo, outwitting his competitors and helping his business to survive the dire circumstances. Once the war was over, *Maktabat al-Andalus* could resume its book dealings in full swing. By now it was experienced in production and in a position to become a small-size publisher, issuing school texts and children's books.

Fawzi Yusuf's story was replicated by other businesses of a similar kind that sprang up in mandatory Palestine. The bookstore-cum-stationery formula, the centrality of selling imported products, the marketing of school texts along with other works, were all features of the post-Ottoman era, which *Maktabat al-Andalus* shared with several other traders. The market of consumers developed tardily, and booksellers had to engage in diverse tactics to survive. The more creative among them became embryonic publishers, entering into book production toward the end of the period. Most active, aside of Yusuf's shop, were *al-Maktaba al-'Asriyya* and *Maktabat al-Tahir Ikhwan* in Jaffa, both founded in the 1930s, and the Jerusalem *Maktabat Filastin al-'Ilmiyya* of the veteran Sa'id brothers.[36] A growing share of the books appearing in the country during the later years of the mandate were, thus, not only distributed but also printed by these shops.

34 Yusuf, *Shay'*, 48; idem, *Khamsun 'Aman*, 30.

35 Jabbara's bibliography mentions 122 items published by this press between 1920 and 1948. Jabbara, *al-Bibliyughrafiyya*, passim.

36 Of the two Jaffa shops, the former produced 20 books or more during the 1940s, the latter at least 16; the Sa'ids issued at least 7 recorded titles. Figures gathered from Jabbara's bibliography, passim. See also Yaacov Shim'oni, *Aravey Eretz Yisrael* (Tel Aviv 1947), 397–8.

By 1948, Palestine had made important strides toward developing its own publishing industry. Where a mere handful of presses had existed in 1900, dozens of them were now running. Where bookstores had been rare, scores of them were now engaged in lively trade countrywide. Other changes, not discussed in this paper, were equally vital in this development: the expansion of the periodical press, a promoter of books and a public trainer in reading; the emergence of social-cultural clubs, loci of literary activities; and, perhaps most important, the dynamic spread of education. These changes provided indispensable underpinnings for the publishing edifice. On the whole, however, the achievements were modest at that early stage, as reflected in the meagre local printed harvest (this was especially conspicuous when juxtaposed with the immeasurably richer output of the country's smaller but better educated Jewish community at the time).[37] Such limited accomplishments should be hardly surprising, given the very low point of departure and the mighty impact of literary activity in neighbouring countries. The fateful events of 1948 befell Palestine while still laying the foundations for its own publishing trade, cutting short what seemed to be a promising beginning.

37 Cf. the somewhat hasty but still telling comparison by Ishaq Musa al-Husayni between Arab and Jewish publishing in mandatory Palestine. Husayni contrasted the 209 Arabic books published between 1919 and 1946, which he had managed to trace, with 349 Hebrew books published in the country in one year, 1933–4. Ishaq Musa al-Husayni, *'Awdat al-Safina* (Jerusalem 1945), 37–40. In the same vein, see E. Mills, *Census of Palestine 1931* (Alexandria, Printed for the Government of Palestine by Whitehead Morris, 1933), I:214, 219.

The Emergence of the Public: Arab Palestinian Media in British Mandate Palestine 1929–1945: Arab Palestinian History and the Arab Press as a Neglected Subject

René Wildangel

Zentrum Moderner Orient, Berlin

Compared to the nearly endless literature on Mandate Palestine, studies dealing primarily with the political, economical, social and cultural history of the Arab community, and such studies making wide use of Arab primary sources in particular, are — with some remarkable exceptions — under-represented. This is not a new phenomenon and has arguably, apart from obvious practical explanations as the language barrier facing western scholars, a lot to do with political realities. In his famous book *The Arab Awakening* that was published in 1938, George Antonius complained that Arab sources were frequently disregarded in contemporary accounts of the Mandate Period. While writing about the Permanent Mandate Commission in Palestine he refers to the Arab newspapers in Palestine:

> Even such sources as the Arabic Press of Palestine, which provide a valuable body of comment on the operation of the mandate as it effects the Arab population, are not used. Petitions and memoranda drawn up in Arabic have to be submitted at Geneva in translation. It requires more than mere transposition to turn good Arabic into readable English or French, and the Arabs of Palestine are so notoriously unskilled in the art of presenting their case in a foreign language that the rendering is usually a travesty.[1]

The under-representation of Arab sources in different accounts of the period also concerns the later years of the Mandate and the period of the Second World War in Palestine; there is something like a tradition of excluding Arab experiences during the Mandate from historical accounts. While often obviously disregarded for political reasons, many sources were lost in the turmoil Palestinian Arabs were forced to live in after 1948. Years of occupation and displacement did not only handicap the

1 George Antonius, *The Arab Awakening: The Story of the Arab National Movement* (London 1938), 338.

development of an Arab Palestinian historiography, but also brought with them the loss and expropriation of primary source material.

The history of the Palestinian Arab community in the later Mandate years, when several members of the traditional elite, especially the circle of the Palestine Arab Party (PAP) around Mufti Hajj Amīn al-Ḥusaynī, had left the country or had been forced out by the British administration after the violent escalation of Arab protests during the years 1936–9, has often been characterized as a chapter of a society left leaderless, inactive and disoriented. On the other hand quite an effort was made to analyse Arab Palestinian activities in exile, foremost concerning Hajj Amīn and his collaboration with the Axis Powers. However, Arab Palestinians obviously did not — literally and symbolically speaking — disappear from Palestine during the War years. Even with prominent leaders being out of the country and much of their own public life being tightly controlled by the British Authorities — without any doubt an 'Arab Public Sphere' and an 'Arab Public Opinion' continued to exist and even further developed, with the Arab Press being a central factor during these years. Only recently a literature on Arab Palestinian cultural and social history 'from below' - reaching beyond the common political narratives has started to develop. Most of the older studies dealing with Mandate history focussed on British and Zionist policies as the progressive and decisive forces 'making' history in Palestine.

The history of the Arab community in Palestine has in this regard mostly been referred to as a history of failure: the failure of a passive player to formulate and execute its own policies to counter-balance the Zionist state project and the failure of an 'old-fashioned' and 'back-ward' society to keep up with the immense speed of modernization and change in Palestine. Additionally, as the most common narrative goes, the two large communities, Arabs and Jews, are presented as two isolated entities without contact and exchange. Only in recent years has this picture been changed by new studies in the field of Mandate history, with a trend to 'write Arab experiences into history.'[2] Such new impulses came for example with the studies of

2 Beshara Doumani, 'Rediscovering Ottoman Palestine', in Ilan Pappé (ed.), *The Israel/Palestine Question: Rewriting Histories* (London, 1999), 11–40; *Rediscovering Palestine: Merchants and Peasants in Jabal Nablus, 1700–1900* (Berkeley 1995); 'Rediscovering Ottoman Palestine: Writing Palestinians into History', *Journal of Palestine Studies* 21:2 (Winter, 1992), 5–28.

Zachary Lockman and Deborah Bernstein on Jewish-Arab workers' relations,[3] that open the view to a more complex discourse in the field, or with Ted Swedenburg's 'Memories of the revolt',[4] that tries to recapture Arab experiences and perceptions of the 1936–9 revolt.

However, the Arab media in Palestine itself has not been extensively addressed from a cultural-historical or sociological perspective. The coming study by Ami Ayalon on 'reading in pre-1948 Palestine'[5] will in this regard close a gap in the history of Mandate Palestine, concerning an interface between the social, intellectual and political history of Arab Society.

Only a few works have been written on the general subject of the Arab press in Palestine. Most of them collect the historical information available without far reaching reflection, as do Muḥammad Sulaymān, who gives a general overview on Palestinian newspapers and its legal boundaries during the Mandate days,[6] Yūsuf Khūrī, who prepared a helpful list of all Arab Palestinian newspapers and journals edited between 1876 and 1945 in Palestine[7] and Qustandī Shawmalī who published books and articles on major Palestinian newspapers, including indices and source material.[8] However these studies barely constitute a fact-presenting perspective. With his influential work on the emergence of Palestinian Identity Rashid Khalidi has shown how fruitful an analysis of Arab newspaper material can be: he analysed papers between 1908 and 1914 and demonstrates in which way the press in these years shaped a 'perfect example of the kind of 'imagined community' (...) which Benedict Anderson has written about', with the newspapers being the main distributor of the

3 Zachary Lockman, *Comrades and Enemies: Arab and Jewish Workers in Palestine 1906–1948* (Berkeley 1996); Deborah Bernstein: *Constructing Boundaries: Jewish and Arab Workers in Mandatory Palestine* (Albany 2000)

4 Ted Swedenburg, *Memories of Revolt: The 1936–1939 Rebellion and the Palestinian National Past* (Minneapolis 1995).

5 Also compare the article by Ami Ayalon in this volume.

6 Muḥammad Sulaymān, *Al-Ṣiḥāfa al-Filasṭīniyya wa-Qawānīn al-Intidāb al-Barīṭānī* (Nicosia 1988).

7 Yūsuf K. Khūrī, *Al-Ṣiḥāfa al-'Arabiyya fī Filasṭīn 1876–1945* [The Arab press in Palestine] (Beirut 1976).

8 Qustandī Shawmalī, *Al-Ṣiḥāfa al-'Arabiyya fī Filasṭīn: Fihris al-Nuṣūṣ al-Adabiyya fī Jarīdat Filasṭīn* [Bibliography of Literary Texts Published in the Newspaper 'Palestine'] (Jerusalem 1990); *Jarīdāt Filasṭīn 1911–1967* [Newspapers in Palestine 1911–1967] (Jerusalem 1992); *Al-Ṣiḥāfa al-'Arabiyya fī Filasṭīn: Jarīdāt 'Mir'at al-Sharq' 1919–1939* [The Arab Press in Palestine: The Newspaper 'Mirror of the East'] (Jerusalem 1992).

common ideas, symbols and vocabulary that hold together this constructed community.[9]

Following up on this thought, I will try to outline the cultural and social context of the Arab Media in the later years of the Mandate and analyse its role regarding the emerging concept of the 'Public' in Palestine between 1929 and 1945.

Some remarks on the concepts of the 'Public' and their relation to the Arab Palestinian case

In a recent book on public opinion Slavko Splichal commented that

> it has been symptomatic since the beginning of the second half of the twentieth century that all dissertations on public opinion begin with a note that there is an extensive literature on the public and on public opinion, but clear and unequivocal definition of the concepts are not to be found.[10]

If we keep the state of the academic literature on Mandate Palestine in mind and ask for concepts of 'public' in Mandate Palestine, it becomes clear that we bring together two fields with an extraordinary amount of literature, that has however little to say about the question of public opinion and the public sphere in Palestine.

Classical theories on the concept of the 'public' usually reviewed emerging concepts of the public in Western European society. While Hannah Arendt defined the public in her political philosophy in a very general way as 'everything that appears in public can be seen and heard by everybody and has the widest possible publicity'[11] Habermas' groundbreaking study on the 'Structural Transformation of the Public Sphere' examines the western-liberal societies from a historical perspective; however he does not present a universal concept. The 'public sphere' in his understanding is linked to the democratic age and the western enlightenment project. In this context Habermas gives the following, well known definition:

> The bourgeois public sphere may be conceived above all as the sphere of private people come together as a public; they soon claimed the public sphere regulated from above against the public authorities themselves, to engage them in a debate over the

9 Rashid Khalidi, *Palestinian Identity: The Construction of Modern National Consciousness*, (New York 1997), 143.

10 Slavko Splichal, *Public Opinion: Developments and Controversies in the Twentieth Century* (Lanham 1999), 3.

11 Hannah Arendt, *The Human Condition* (Chicago 1998), 50.

> general rules governing relations in the basically privatised but publicly relevant sphere of commodity exchange and social labour. The medium of this political confrontation was peculiar and without historical precedents: people's public use of their reason.[12]

This is a description of the beginning of civil society in Europe during the 18th century; it includes several of the main attributes and ambiguities of the terms 'public' and 'publicness': The private-public dichotomy, the original feudal character of the public as 'representative publicness' and the opposite implication of publicness as a democratic or civil power if used 'from below'. Generally, the concept of the 'public' has different connotations and changed its meaning in different historical contexts and their specific economical, social and cultural conditions. However, the emergence of the public in a modernist sense is clearly linked to the development of the press and the media sector as an independent factor. Many of the changes, that took place in Europe between the sixteenth and nineteenth century, were experienced in Palestine in a very condensed form during Mandate times. While it would be ignorant to deny the origins of public life and the press during Ottoman times, the Mandate and its specific quasi-colonial situation created an environment of external modernization that ultimately led to an unprecedented social transformation of Arab society. 'Traditional' and 'modern' concepts of the public continued to coexist during the Mandate: if one uses the concepts derived from Habermas, this includes the existence of a representative publicness, the creation of a bourgeois sphere and elements of a liberal economy and the emergence of a critical public:

- The 'authoritarian' publicness or representative publicness that is generated by the British Mandate Administration (jurisdiction, public administration, representative character of the Mandate Commissioner and his government) and corresponds with Habermas' concept of Representative Publicity.

- The publicness of the traditional old Arab Society that has a partly private character (the family, the private household, coffee houses, the Hammam, the religious institutions) - Habermas: Private Autonomy.

- Finally a publicness generated by a politically alert and economically more independent social group of Arab writers, journalists, intellectuals, businessmen and other professionals mainly in the urban centres that includes members of the traditional elite and of a new middle class — Habermas: Bourgeois/ Civil Society.

12 Jürgen Habermas, *The Structural Transformation of the Public Sphere: An Inquiry into a Category of Bourgeois Society* (Cambridge, Mass. 1991), 27.

The press is the most important agent of this third type of a newly emerged independent public sphere. Especially in the latter part of the Mandate after 1929 this new Arab public sphere was created due to internal and external developments influencing Arab society.

Similar to other historical cases (e.g. colonial India) this public sphere was built up under the ambiguities of the colonial situation, and the ambiguities of the colonizer's policies, that ultimately oscillated between restricting and encouraging public activity among the colonized.

Modernization, Social Change and the Rise of the Media

In addition to the British institutionalised public sector, such as the educational or health care sector, and the traditional loci of Arab society there was a new public sphere created from within Arab society and shaped by the Arab media. This sphere was dominated by certain circles of the Arab elite and professionals in Palestine and constantly expanded in the period of the Mandate. Social developments in the Arab community, such as growing literacy and the desire to read contributed to this trend. One of its main expressions was the founding of political clubs, that finally lead the way to the newly founded Arab parties of the 1930s: even if these organizations partly represented traditional social (i.e. clan or family) divisions they were an expression of this new public sphere and of 'private people coming together as a public' (Habermas). The more or less openly party affiliated newspapers also were an important step towards a more differentiated and structured discourse.

While in the first period long before 1929 Palestinian consciousness and identity had been constructed, as Khalidi has shown, the late Mandate years brought its consolidation and heterogeneity at the same time. The press in Palestine played an important part in both processes. Anderson's idea of the imaginative construction of the nation also brings in the role of the press as a decisive factor: a constructed community depends on the constant reassurance and equal distribution of its common imagination and ideas, and in the 'age of technical reproduction' (Walter Benjamin) it is the media that executes this function. At the beginning of the century there was no publishing industry in Palestine. By 1929 this situation had significantly changed: not only had a wide range of Arab press items been established, also a readership, a recipient and consuming public had been created in a few years, a process that elsewhere took centuries. Palestine finally had entered an era that is usually referred to as the 'age of mass communication' which was further comforted by modern technical standards of communication, such as the telephone, telegraphy, and the broadcasting system. Additionally, distribution and transportation facilities were improved and contributed to rising circulations. The degree to which the media was influential on society thus significantly rose after 1929.

The years after 1929 also were a time of rising unrest and conflict in Palestine and especially a time of unprecedented change within Arab society in Palestine. The external modernization process influenced by the British administration and the Jewish organizations had, as already mentioned, ambiguous effects on the Arab Palestinian community.

This process comprised a quickly growing population with a marked trend to urbanisation and industrialisation, the latter especially during the war years, when around 100,000 Arab wageworkers were employed. The population rose from 800,000 in 1929 to 1.2 million Arabs in 1945 (Jews 160,000 to 570,000). In spite of this rapid growth some 'progress' was made in the field of education, although British educational policies far from satisfied the growing Arab demand for education. However, secondary education was increased and the number of boys' schools raised from 283 to 398 and girls' schools from 31 to 80, still leaving female education far behind.[13]

In the first 15 years of the Mandate, Government schools only included a two-year secondary education period, while from 1935 on this education was extended to a four-year period. Apart from the Governmental schools and colleges the importance of private schools was constantly increasing too, as for instance such foreign teaching institutes as the British run St. George College or the American University in Beirut. The expanded literate public was now no longer a specialized and purely intellectual elite — from the 1920s on, an increasing number of Arab Palestinian citizens was making use of the information spread by the media.

The technical modernisation process in the country had changed the communication landscape and also transformed the role of the recipients as readers,

13 A.L. Tibawi, *Arab Education in Mandatory Palestine* (London 1956), 48.

listeners or consumers of this new kind of information. Finally the emergence of a younger generation forming a group of professionals, such as lawyers, administration officials and businessmen, that were partly educated in the West or in Western style institutions, plays an important role. This new social group — whether it is called a 'New Middle Class' or not — also started to erode the vertical political cleavages of the elite and the old concepts of legitimacy derived from family or clan origin (that nonetheless remained an influential factor).

The development of the media and its growing influence on society was closely connected to this changing social environment. The rising level of education and literacy contributed to a rising demand for newspapers and information in general, while on the other hand obviously the increased circulation of papers contributed to a stronger demand for study and education.

1929–1939: Newspaper Expansion

In the 1920s some 20 newspapers existed in Jerusalem, with a small circulation and their impact on the public being relatively limited. Although British authorities — until 1921 through military rule, then with the help of the newly established Mandate government — controlled the Palestinian press, censorship did not play such an important role as in later years: as long as the political situation was quiet, the British administration took little interest in Arab journalistic activities, even if new Press laws were issued by the Mandate Authorities in 1923 to replace the old Ottoman regulations. Thus there was relatively free room for the development of the Arab press until 1929, when it entered a new stage: Rising tension between Arabs and both Jews and the Mandate power increasingly turned the press into a motor for mobilising public opinion and into a political factor that was now more closely and suspiciously watched by the British government.

Traditionally, Zionist policies and Jewish immigration had formed a central subject for all Arab newspapers in Palestine. But with rising polarisation within the Palestinian political landscape newspapers also became the mouthpieces of the various political groups, increasing tendencies of social, religious and political factionalism.

The Mufti and his followers, at the beginning of the 30s still powerful, but harshly criticized by a growing opposition were supported by *al-Jāmi'a al-'arabiyya* and the nationalistic and Islamic *al-Jāmi'a al-islāmiyya* (circulation approximately 2,000) and produced their own newspaper, *al-Liwā'*, which was edited by Jamāl al-Ḥusaynī, a cousin of Hajj Amīn. The opposition, usually referred to with the Arab term *mu'āraḍa*, consisting of other families struggling for power and influence with the Mufti, was largely represented by the 1921 founded *Filasṭīn*, which had a circulation of 4,000–6,000 and was edited by ʿĪsā al-ʿĪsā and his brother. A new party, the younger generation's *Istiqlāl* was supported by *al-Difā'* with a circulation of approximately 4,000–6,000. [14] However the number of effective readers was significantly higher, because newspapers were shared and sometimes read out publicly to the illiterate, i.e. in rural areas.

In these years modern technology, like the quickly expanding telephone system (after 1920), with higher mobility, optimised ways of distribution and improved communication channels, whilst raising the effectiveness of the Palestinian media. The constantly improving form and content of the newspapers also contributed to its importance in public discourse. It is in these years, one could argue, that finally an attentive 'Palestinian public' was created through these developments: the politically active and educated 'reader', who was not only a consumer of feature pages on Arab poetry and arts or a distant follower of political events, but was himself an active part of a new kind of political discourse within Arab society. By 1935 the newspapers had become an irreversible factor for producing opinion and political attitudes in the Arab community. British and Jewish observers also acknowledged that. *Filasṭīn* quoted an article on the Arab press from the Jewish newspaper *ha-Davar* that had commented on its progress:

> Since 1929 till now the Arab newspapers in Palestine have made huge steps towards internal and external progress and improvement and concerning their circulation as well. It is not long since there was no daily Arab newspaper in Palestine and now there are in Jaffa alone three large daily newspapers.[15]

Filasṭīn is perceived as an important, while independent and sometimes oppositional voice in the national struggle, whose high quality and accuracy in

14 Circulation of Arab Palestinian newspapers: PRO CO - 323 346/10.
15 *Filasṭīn,* June 7th, 1935.

reporting are acknowledged in the article. The British administration was also fully aware of the power of the media and its role in the growing tension of the 1930s. The Central Investigation Department (C.I.D.) emphasized the importance of the Palestinian papers:

> In this connection it must be stated that in shaping public opinion the press is becoming increasingly an important factor. The Arab reading public is on the increase and some peasants in their villages read newspapers. That this is so is perhaps obvious from the fact that the public now supports three daily papers.[16]

Especially during the Arab general strike and the violent protests between 1936 and 1939 the newspapers voiced the concerns of most Arabs in Palestine: the growing Jewish immigration, the Arab land sales, the economic decline and the opposition to the policies of the Mandate power were the subjects that unified the different Arab factions and dominated public opinion. The press in this regard realised a function attributed to the media in the classical modernist enlightenment sense: the public sphere and public opinion that the Mandate power tried to generate and control, was actively recreated and partly claimed by the Arab media and the Arab community itself. This clearly posed a threat to British rule in the country, so that strict censorship and control was introduced: During the violent period of 1936–9 some Palestinian newspapers were closed down or temporarily suspended. This especially concerned the Muslim owned organs of the Mufti-faction and the Islamic authorities, while more moderate newspapers like *al-Difā'* and *Filasṭīn* had a slightly easier time. The distribution of Egyptian, Syrian and Iraqi newspapers, which were imported by air and widely read in Palestine, was also controlled.[17] In 1938 eleven newspapers were suspended for periods between one week and six months, among them the moderate *Filasṭīn* (one week) and the Christian *al-Karmil al-Jadīd* (the former *Karmil*) for six months.[18]

The Propaganda Battle, Broadcasting in Palestine and the War 1939–1945

At the same time efforts were made to prevent an imminent foreign infiltration of Palestinian media, especially from Italy and Germany. While Italy openly tried to

16 PRO CO 733 – 257/11 8.9.1933, report by H.P. Rice.
17 PRO CO 733 – 346/10.
18 PRO CO 733 – 375/16.

promote its propaganda goals in the country, increased German activities started in 1938, when the newspaper *al-Jāmi'a al-islāmiyya* was supported by the German News Agency *Deutsches Nachrichtenbüro* (DNB) and its representative in Palestine, Dr. Franz Reichart.[19]

Printing techniques and new means of communications were not only used by the newspapers and the official media in Palestine, other groups understood and used the modernised channels of mass communication: thus the printing of propaganda leaflets — outside of the institutionalised press — became an important means during the rebellion of 1936, making propaganda an important element in the inner-Arab struggles as well as in the conflict with the Mandate authorities and the Zionist institutions. A famous propaganda campaign was directed against the old traditional Ottoman *Tarboosh* headgear in favour of the national *Kafiyah*, which also voiced threats against anyone ignoring the appeal.

Even records were produced in this propaganda battle for public opinion under the most adventurous circumstances: organized by Arab Palestinian leaders, recordings were made in Aleppo, Syria, with nationalistic songs written by Arab Palestinian songwriters. These nationalistic songs were pressed on wax discs, and then sent to London for professional editing in 1939, where they were produced by Columbia Records and then distributed throughout the Near East to strengthen the nationalistic struggle against the British authorities.[20]

With the propaganda war between the Axis and the Mandate Power, the importance of broadcasting in Palestine also rose. The Italian Service from Bari and later the German service put pressure on the Palestine Government to improve their own programme.

According to a memorandum by the Colonial Office from autumn 1933 approximately 1,000 Palestinians were listening to overseas broadcasting, most of them to the Bucharest station, which was easy to receive with an ordinary wireless set. This memorandum also emphasized the need for a British station in Palestine as 'one of the few colonies under civilized administration which possesses no system of wireless broadcasting'. Moreover it would have a special significance due to the high

---

19 See Ralf Balke, *Hakenkreuz im Heiligen Land: Die NSDAP-Landesgruppe in Palästina* (Erfurt 2001), 118 f.

20 PRO FO 684 – 12.

illiteracy among the Arab population, especially in the rural areas, where only 200 schools, mainly boys' schools, existed for more than 800 villages, with girls receiving less or no school education at all. The memorandum mentions the Soviet Union as an example, where 'every village, school or factory possesses a radio set'.[21] In December 1933 a Broadcasting Committee was formed by the HC and only a year later a transmitter station was erected near Ramallah, while programmes were produced in studios in Jerusalem. The programme consisted of English, Hebrew and Arabic programmes and was directed by a British director with two additional sub-directors. The Arab Palestinian poet Ibrāhīm Tuqān was the first Arabic Sub-Director. Apparently the reception of the program among the Arab population was remarkable: the station received letters from listeners as far away as Istanbul and Aden; in Palestine itself there were around 8,000 Arab license holders, suggesting that the number of listeners was remarkably higher than that. Some coffee shops had receivers to serve their customers. According to Foreign Office Reports, Arabs in Palestine generally welcomed the British Service in Palestine and kept sending 'encouraging reports, comments and suggestions.'[22] A majority of the Arab community in Palestine preferred the British produced news to foreign transmission, i.e. the German broadcasts from Athens and Berlin and the Italian station, that were largely taken for what they were — Axis propaganda programmes.

There was a remarkable number of Arabs committing themselves in support of the British War effort by working for the broadcasting service. One of these journalists was ʿAjāj Nuwayhiḍ, who wrote about his experiences in his memories.[23] When he was approached by the British broadcasting director and asked to lead the Arabic department, he presented a number of conditions to the director: he was only willing to lead an independent Arabic department, with a free choose of employees and a secure budget, and without any British control over the broadcasting. While this proposal was rejected by the British side, Nūwayhiḍ was approached again after the beginning of the war with his conditions accepted: the news should only have to be checked by an administration official, who was moreover an old associate of the Istiqlāl Party. Moreover the history of the broadcasting service, similar to the press

21 PRO CO 733 – 246/10.
22 PRO FO 371 – 23251.
23 ʿAjāj Nuwayhiḍ: *Sittūn ʾĀman maʿa al-Qāfila al-ʿArabiyya* [Sixty Years with the Arab Caravan] (Beirut 1993).

and other printed publications of the time shows, that Arab Palestinians had created an independent public opinion within the public sphere of the Mandate administration, that could even be maintained during the World War.

With the beginning of the War, Britain introduced a most restrictive policy in Palestine that also affected the press. Only three of the traditional daily newspapers were kept open by the British authorities during the Second World War:

Filasṭīn, edited since 1911 by ʿĪsā al-ʿĪsā and his brother Yūsuf, *al-Ṣirāṭ al-Mustaqīm* with its editor ʿAbd Allāh al-Qalqīlī, and *al-Difāʿ* whose proprietor was Ibrāhīm al-Shanṭī; some other publications appeared during the war, such as the newspaper of the communist party (*al-Ittiḥād*) and others. But the atmosphere in Palestine had lost its violent anti-British tone not only due to British military and administrative pressure and the expulsion of nationalist leaders, but also due to the firm conviction among opposition circles, that co-operation with the British side for the duration of the War would serve Arab Palestinian interests best. The moderate daily press supported this view during the war, and public opinion in Palestine was now clearly influenced by that — even if anti-British sentiments still existed.

There was a clear consciousness among Arab Palestinians, that the developments in Europe and in the war also had a strong relevance for the future of their own country. The existing newspapers, especially *Filasṭīn* and *al-Difāʿ* took a moderate view in these times, including a resolute stance against the Axis powers and Nazism. Another paper in Jaffa, *al-Akhbār*, that approached Nazi-Germany with numerous very critical reports throughout 1937 and 1942, was later closed down. In February 1942 the newspaper under its editor Bandalī Ḥanā al-Gharābī and its editor-in-chief Doctor Muḥammad Najīb characterized Hitler as 'the greatest enemy of humanity.' [24] The most traditional Palestinian Arab newspaper *Filasṭīn* had also published critical articles since 1933 and provided its readers with accurate and very detailed information about the course of the war, partly through news agency notices and also reports by several of its own correspondents.

However, the readership during the war still comprised only a limited part of the Arab Palestinian public. In the rural milieu — at this time with approximately 55 to 65 percent still a majority[25] — these dailies were scarcely read, although news used to

24 *Al-Akhbār*, 18.2.1942, 1.
25 Bernstein, 'Constructing Boundaries', 25.

spread fast through oral communication channels and the public announcement of news and information.

Arab Media and the Emergence of the Public Sphere

It is obvious, that the press played a central role in the consolidation of Arab Palestinian identity as an imagined community as described by Rashid Khalidi. But in the 1930s and 1940s, in interdependence with the immense external and internal changes to this community, the media had another importance more than merely distributing national symbols; it gave a main impulse for the creation of a genuinely new Arab public sphere and the platform for a rational discourse. This becomes clear through the discussion on the war events and the cooperation with the Mandate power in the war against the Axis. Moderate Arab circles in Palestine actively supported the British war effort, although opposition against Jewish immigration and the respective British policy was at the same time widespread.

The leading newspapers, the participation in the broadcasting service or the foundation of new organisations and unions during the last phase of the war show this rising degree of Arab political participation; this process, that might have been the key for the formulation of an effective Arab Palestinian policy after 1945, was however halted by the turbulences of the post-war development. While in the 1930s and 1940s a new form of Arab Palestinian public had been established, these structures were largely destroyed with the events of the year 1948, i.e. the expulsions and the difficult conditions for Arab Palestinians in their new host countries, where it was impossible to rebuild their own public sphere and difficult to take part in the public life.

Why Did Baghdadi Jews Stop Writing to their Brethren in Mainz? – Some Comments about the Reading Practices of Iraqi Jews in the Nineteenth Century

Orit Bashkin*

Introduction

This paper examines a community of Jewish readers in nineteenth century Iraq, whose literary and cultural artefacts were produced not only in Baghdad but also in India, Eastern Europe and Palestine. Such an inquiry requires us to deconstruct an Arab and an Iraqi national discourse, which depicts the Ottoman past as an era of bleakness and decline. This national discourse correspondingly ignores the linguistic and cultural realities of the late Ottoman era during which Iraqi intellectuals were immersed in Ottoman, Central Asian, Arabian and Indian intellectual traditions and 'privy to the debates on reform current amongst scholars of these areas'.[1] The Zionist narrative imagined the Oriental backwardness of Iraqi Jews, thus perceiving their immigration to Israel as a liberating exodus. Finally, the categories of 'East' and 'West' limited previous historical studies on the nature of readership in Iraq as scholars found it difficult to envisage a reading community whose literary products circulated between Baghdad, Berlin, Bombay and Odessa.

The Jewish-Iraqi community in the nineteenth century was relatively affluent because Iraqi Jewish merchants were engaged in global trade, particularly in the trade with India.[2] Since the beginning of the nineteenth century, Iraq served as a centre to Persian, Indian and Yemenite Jewry as Iraqi rabbis like ʿAbd Allah Sômekh (died 1899) published important religious and liturgical works. During the nineteenth century, Jews opened charity clubs and societies. Following the initiative of the

* I thank Amy Motlagh.

1 Dina Rizk Khoury, *State and Provincial Society in the Ottoman Empire: Mosul, 1540–1834* (Cambridge and New York 1999), 17

2 On the Indian-Iraqi relationship, see Thabit A.J. Abdullah, *Merchants, Mamluks, and Murder: the Political Economy of Trade in Eighteenth Century Basra* (Albany 2001); Hala Fattah, *The Politics of Regional Trade in Iraq, Arabia, and the Gulf, 1745–1900* (Albany 1997); Meir Litvak, 'Money, Religion and Politics: The Oudh Bequest in Najaf and Karbala', 1850–1903', *International Journal of Middle East Studies* 33 (Feb. 2000), 1–21.

Russian Isaac Luria and the Austrian Herman Rozenfeld, the Jewish French society, *Alliance israelite universelle* established in 1869 the *Alliance* school in Baghdad.[3]

Iraq's print culture during the nineteenth century was comparatively fledgling.[4] Nonetheless, Jews tried to emulate the journalistic activity of their Muslim neighbours; Rabbi Barûkh Mošeh Mizraḥî published a paper called *Ha-Dôver* ('The Orator') in Judaeo-Arabic between 1863 and 1871. Rabbi Šelomoh Bekhôr Ḥoṣîn strove to obtain a license from the Ottoman authorities to print his own newspaper but was refused.[5] Consequently, the Jewish community sought to read papers published outside of Iraq. Jews read journals published in Lebanon and Syria such as *al-Muqtaṭaf*, whose editors mentioned Baghdadi Jews as one of their first groups of subscribers in Iraq.[6] Likewise, their command of Hebrew enabled them to read the Hebrew press published in Europe and Palestine. Meanwhile, Iraqi Jewish immigrants who settled in India distributed local publications in Judaeo-Arabic that were purchased by Baghdadi readers.

In what follows, I explore the participation of Iraqi Jews in the European and Indian journalistic enterprises in order to examine the role the foreign press played in the Jewish Iraqi community, to consider the various images of enlightenment presented in these papers and to scrutinize the ways in which Iraqi Jews defined their

---

3 On Iraqi Jewry, see Nissim Rejwan, *The Jews of Iraq: 3000 Years of History and Culture* (London 1985); Nissim Kazzaz, *The Jews of Iraq in the Twentieth Century* (Jerusalem 1991) (Hebrew); Avraham Twinah, *Exiles and Saved – Jewish Education in Baghdad, 1832–1951* (Ramla 1975) (Hebrew); Avraham Ben Yaacob, *The Jews of Babylon – From the End of the Ge'onim Period to the Present* (Jerusalem 1960) (Hebrew); Yizhaq Avishur, 'Reconstructing Literary Systems and Linguistic Change Amongst Iraqi Jews in the Modern Age (1759–1950)', in Joseph Shitrit (ed.) *Mi-Kedem u-Mi-Yam* (no. 6, Haifa, 1991), 236–54 (Hebrew); R. Senir, 'The Arabic Literature of Iraqi Jews – Internal Dynamics of Cultural Systems and Mutual Relations with the Arabic Cultural System', ibid, 254–80 (Hebrew); Sasson Somekh, 'introduction', *Dīwān Murād Mikhā'īl – al-A'māl al-Shi'riyya al-Kāmila* (Shifa' 'Amr 1988), 7–18 (Arabic); Sasson Somekh, 'Lost Voices, Jewish Authors in Modern Arabic Literature', in Mark Cohen and Abraham L. Udovitch (eds), *Jews and Arabs: Contacts and Boundaries* (Princeton 1989), 9–21.

4 The Ottoman governor Midḥat Pasha initiated the establishment of the government bulletin *al-Zawrā'* (1869), although some claim that Da'ūd Pasha instigated the government press with a journal allegedly titled *jurnāl al-'Irāq*. Foreign newspapers like Maḥmūd II's official *Takvîm-i vekâyi* or the Arabic *al-Jawā'ib* found their way to Baghdad. Mosul hosted a Dominican publishing house that printed the journal *al-Mawṣil* (1889). On the press, see Ami Ayalon, *The Press in the Arab Middle East* (New York and Oxford 1995), 91–5, 118–19, 188–9; Rafā'īl Buttī, *Al-Ṣiḥāfa fī al-'Irāq*, (Cairo 1955)

5 Nissim Kazzaz, 'Jewish Journalists in Iraq', *Kesher* 7 (1990), 36–40 (Hebrew).

6 L.M. Kenny, 'East versus West in al-Muqtaṭaf, 1875–1900: Image and Self-Image', in D.P. Little (ed.), *Essays on Islamic Civilization – Presented to Niyazi Berkes* (Leiden 1976), 143.

identity vis-à-vis their Muslim neighbours on the one hand, and European Jews on the other.

The European Journals

Jacob Obermeir, who was the local agent of the journal *Ha-Maggîd* ('The Speaker'), reported that *Ha-Maggîd, Ha-Ṣefirah* ('The Awakening'), *Ha-Melîṣ* ('The Intercessor') and *Ha-Ḥavaṣelet* ('The Lily')[7] were commonly read by Jews in Baghdad.[8] These journals are usually categorized as part of the *haskalah* movement, an assortment of literary, philosophical and cultural currents, which began in late eighteenth century Germany. The intellectuals of *haskalah* called for a rational understanding of Judaism, for assimilation into the European communities, and advised Jews to familiarize themselves with scientific and global innovations.[9]

Iraqi writers and readers of the haskalah journals can be divided into two groups. The first group was comprised of European merchants and teachers who settled in Baghdad whereas the second group was of Baghdadi Arab Jews. The accounts of the first group closely follow the orientalist 'imaginative geography' utilized by European travellers.[10] The interest in Iraq was common in orientalist literature because of its

7 *Ha-Maggîd* (1856–1903) was published in Lyck (Eastern Prussia) and in Berlin and edited by the Russian Eliezer Liphman Zilberman, and later by David Gordon and Jacob Samuel Fox. *Ha-'Ôlam* (1907–50) was published in Eastern Europe (Köln, Vilna, Odessa, London and Berlin) and was an official organ of the Zionist movement. *Ha-Melîṣ* (1860–1904) was published in Odessa and Saint Petersburg and edited by Alexander Zederbaum and later by Aaron Isaac Goldblum and Judah Leib Gordon. *Ha-Ṣefirah* (1862–1934) was edited by the mathematician Haim Zelig Slonimski and later by Nahum Sokolow and was published in Warsaw. *Ha-Ḥavaṣelet* (1863–4; 1870–1911) was published in Palestine and edited by Israel Beck, Michal ha-Kohen and Dov Frumkin. *Ha-Ḥavaṣelet* was probably the newspaper with which Iraqi Jews most identified, because it was produced in the Ottoman Province, Palestine and related to familiar themes — problems Jews had with local *wālīs* and their relationship with their Muslim neighbours. I chose to include it because it enjoyed both European and Iraqi readership, contained stories by Iraqi Jews and accounts by Jewish European travellers.

8 Kazzaz, *Jews*, 146.

9 I use in this paper the definition of *haskalah* as employed by Uzi Shavit. As Shavit notes, the term gradually evolved from Moses Mendelson's initial conceptualization to encompass such terms as *Bildung, Aufklärung*, culture and enlightenment, but I prefer to apply the term *haskalah* for the purpose of this paper. See Uzi Shavit, *Ba'alôt ha-Šaḥar, Haskalah, Poetry and Modernity* (Tel Aviv 1996), 7–37 (Hebrew). See also: Ismar Schorsch, *From Text to Context: the Turn to History in Modern Judaism* (Hanover 1994); Michael A. Meyer, *The Origins of the Modern Jew; Jewish Identity and European Culture in Germany, 1749–1824* (Detroit 1967); David Sorkin, *The Transformation of German Jewry, 1780–1840* (New York 1987).

10 As suggested by Edward Said, 'imagined geography' is the universal practice of 'designating, *in one's mind*, a familiar space which is "ours", as opposed to an unfamiliar space, which is "theirs"'. Moreover, imagined geography inscribed not only the characteristics of an unspecified space, but also the features of the traveller's essence, for the process of constructing recognizable and

significance to both Biblical and Islamic history and its prominence in famed texts like the Arabian Nights. Iraq had momentous impact on Jewish culture for its place in the Biblical tradition as the homeland of Abraham and the place of the first Jewish exile. Subsequently, Jews travelled to Iraq during the nineteenth century and composed their own travel literature.[11]

The first orientalist theme recurrent in the Hebrew journals was a growing interest in archaeological excavations in Iraq and in its depiction as a land standing in perpetual ruin. Jacob Obermeir provided general historical information about Baghdad's Sassanid and Abbasid histories and frequently described his visits to Babylonian and Assyrian sites. In his portrayal of such sites, he was aided by the works of travellers like the Jewish Benjamin of Tudela and the Muslim Ibn Batuta. He often referred to Biblical heroes that lived in 'Babylon': Jonah, Nimrod, and Ezekiel, whose famous tomb is found in Iraq.[12] The accentuation of the ancient was part of the *haskalah*'s desire to produce a scientific study of the Bible based on archaeology. Nonetheless, Jacob Obermeir believed that the ruins of Baghdad, once the centre of empires, were part of a divine plan to punish the descendants of the Babylonians: 'The Almighty has paid the daughter of Babylon for what she has done to the sons of Jacob. Blessed be He, who destroyed the evil Babylon'.[13] This narration colours the orientalist motives with specific Biblical and Jewish overtones.

The second characteristic in the writings of the Jewish-European group was the depiction of Baghdad as the antithesis to an enlightened community. *Ha-Ḥavaṣelet* reported that 'most Babylonian Jews are mindless and ignorant'. The Jews of Kurdistan were regarded as the worst of these savages:

---

unrecognizable spaces compelled the traveller to 'find himself at the Orient'. See Edward Said, *Orientalism* (New York 1979), 168, 171–2, 216.

11 The Lithuanian rabbi Davîd de Beyt Hillel, who hoped to find the lost Jewish tribes, travelled to India and Baghdad in 1827. In 1848, Israel Benjamin, also known as the second Benjamin, originally from Moldova, visited Baghdad and published his travel accounts in 1856 in French. The book was translated into German (1858) and into Hebrew (1859). Wolf Schor (born in 1850, Poland) visited Baghdad in 1881, as part of a tour to India, Syria and Kurdistan, and published his narratives in Peretz Somlenskin's journal *Ha-Šaḥar* ('the Dawn') and in journals in Baltimore and Chicago. Yôm Tôv ben Davîd Ṣemaḥ, a Bulgarian Jew came to Iraq in 1869 and published his impressions in French. See Me'ir Benayahu, 'Introduction – Voyages of Jews to Babylon', in Meir Benayahu (ed.), *Masa' Bavel by Rabbi Davîd Sulayman Sasūn* (Jerusalem 1955), 13–59.

12 Jacob Obermeir, 'A Travel to the Ruins of Babylon', *Ha-Maggîd* 20:33 (16/8/1876), 287; Jacob Obermeir, 'A Travel to the Ruins of Babylon', *Ha-Maggîd* 20:36 (13/9/1876), 314; Jacob Obermeir, 'These are My Travels', *Ha-Maggîd* 24:7 (11/2/1880), 57.

13 Jacob Obermier, 'A Travel to the Ruins of Babylon', '*Ha-Maggîd* 20:33 (23/8/1876), 287.

> They are stubborn and impatient and strike each other senselessly and violently for the pettiest of causes. Murder and robbery are to them the mildest of offences. Nevertheless, they are all kind-hearted, and act benevolently towards their brothers. However, they are ill-bred and boorish *as the rest of the people who dwell in such places*, and believe in witchcraft, spirits, devils, charms, talismans and similar nonsense ... the boys are raised as wild animals. Torah and education are virtually unknown ... They have no knowledge of fine manners or morals. The state of women there is very peculiar. Apart from the regular house-chores, they guard the houses, the donkeys and the sheep ... but the men perform tasks in powers unfamiliar to human strength [emphasis mine][14]

Iraqi Jews, then, have neither interest in nor knowledge of *haskalah*. The image of the women as traditional and religious is utilized to characterize the backwardness of Iraqi space. The explanation offered for this horrific state is the resemblance between Middle Eastern Jews and the rest of the Turkish and Arab subjects of the Ottoman Empire.

The Iraqi Jews, however, because of their resemblance to the Arabs, preserve some sort of authentic Judaism, which is not to be found in Europe. The cantors in Baghdad, for example, chant better than any other community and have kept the purest dialect of Arabic, because of their dwelling close to the deserts and because of their commercial relations with 'the nomad Ishmaelites'. The similarity to the Arabs, in this case, allows Jews to captivate the ancient nature of Hebrew, lost by modern Jews.[15]

This European literature often exhibited feeling of closeness and sympathy with Iraqi Jews since readers assumed that all Jews were brethren. In consequence, even if the East was essentially different from the West, Jews were somewhat distinct from the rest of their society and thus had a potential to progress. Furthermore, as these writers were denizens of Baghdad and knew their Jewish-Arab neighbours were aware of their publications, they took care to notice the similarities between various Jewish communities. Baghdad was therefore depicted as a model of successful integration of Jews in a non-Jewish society. Seen from this vantage point, the tolerant atmosphere in Baghdad was the antithesis of European anti-Semitic approaches. When the Ottoman governor helped a Baghdadi Jew, accused of blasphemy, *Ha-Ḥavaṣelet* noted that the Jews were fortunate that this incident occurred in the lands of Edom (Arabia) for had

14 Moses Weinberg, 'Asia: Babylon, Kurdistan, Yemen and India', *Ha-Ḥavaṣelet* 21:45 (28/8/1891), 557–8.

15 'Asia-Baghdad', *Ha-Maggîd* 20:20 (22/3/1876), 103.

it occurred in Europe, it 'would have excited the hearts of the foes of Israel and would have given them an opportunity to spread false rumours about us'.[16]

Even when European writers depicted Iraq as an uncultured society, they still perceived the potential for change. The first possibility of change lay in Baghdad's glorious history. Iraq was previously a centre of reason and science, and caliphs like the Abbasid al-Ma'mūn esteemed knowledge and learning.[17] Other venues of change appeared to be the reforms taking place in the Ottoman Empire, particularly the equality between believers of various faiths. The 'enlightened Ishmaelites' and the Turkish government 'had abandoned the thoughts of the past', endeavoured to follow 'the principles of tolerance and humanity' and consequently Baghdadi Jews adopted 'the spirit of the time' and 'resembled the West'.[18] Isaac Luria wrote that public safety prevailed in a Baghdad once known to be 'the city of thieves and muggers'.[19] The city's hospital accepts people from *all religions* and the newly established telegraph lines and train services should make Baghdadi Jews 'closer to the enlightened people of Europe'. 'Light would come even to our dark dwellings, because, God willing, *all follow the light*, and telegraph and trains are the messengers of reason and science' [emphasis mine].[20] Reform and science are therefore global and inevitable processes that should and would occur in Iraq.

The most important agency of change, assumed writers, was Jewish-European instruction. Isaac Luria testified that he took it upon himself to school Iraqi Jews 'in the ways of modern civilization'. As a founder of a new school, he had managed to establish firm grounds for the pursuit of science and education. This newly awakened spirit would enable Baghdad to recapture its past glory. God, argued Luria, had sent him to Baghdad to distribute the seeds of knowledge amongst Iraqi Jews.[21]

This inner Jewish orientalist discourse reflects textual tensions between different sets of expectations. It continuously shifts between the category of East/West and subsequently the racial dichotomy Arab/European, which differentiated between European and Arab Jews on the one hand, and the category of religion, which

---

16 'Babylon', *Ha-Ḥavaṣelet*, 27:3 (9/10/1897), 17.
17 Jacob Obermeir, 'Baghdad', *Ha-Maggîd* 19:45 (24/11/1875), 397.
18 Isaac Luria, 'Asia-Baghdad', *Ha-Maggîd* 14:37 (21/9/1870), 291.
19 Isaac Luria, 'Asia-Baghdad', *Ha-Maggîd* 14:38 (28/9/1870), 300.
20 Isaac Luria, 'Baghdad', *Ha-Maggîd* 8:5 (3/2/1864), 28.
21 Isaac Luria, 'Baghdad', *Ha-Levanon* 7:32 (2/9/1870), 266. On the school, see also Luria, 'Baghdad', *Ha-Maggîd* 9:14 (5/4/1865), 108.

highlights Jewish uniformity and negates the differences between groups of Jews, on the other. Although the Hebrew newspapers embraced the ideas of Enlightenment, European Jews positioned themselves as guides and supervisors and hence did not permit the Iraqi Jews to independently manage their affairs, a feature very relevant to Kant's definition of enlightenment.[22]

The second group of readers and writers were the Baghdadi Jewish elite. These Arab Jews utilized the press as a global billboard and some, like Rabbi Šelomoh Bekhôr Ḥoṣîn, regularly published letters and news-items. Rabbi Ḥoṣîn reported about plagues in Basra and Baghdad, the sufferings of the Jews in Persia, complained about floods in Baghdad and asked for financial assistance in order to pay to Muslims upon visiting the grave of Ezekiel. Iraqi Jews also used the press to assist their European brethren. Rabbi Ḥoṣîn, for example, followed closely the lot of Mina Hirsch, whose husband left her in Europe and travelled to North Africa. He read about the case, and when the treacherous man reached Baghdad, Ḥoṣîn wrote to *Ha-Maggîd* about his whereabouts and that 'he had promised Isaac Luria to return safely to his wife'. Regrettably, Mr. Hirsch did not keep his promise and hence the Baghdadi Jews tried to pressure him to divorce his wife. Ḥoṣîn informed Mina over the pages of *Ha-Maggîd* that if she wished to obtain any further information about her husband or the divorce, she should contact him via the press or a private letter.[23]

Baghdadi Jewish readers underlined the fact that enlightenment had indeed reached Baghdad. They announced their commitment to better the ways of those who do not observe the light of science and are bound by the shackles of stupidity and ignorance.[24] *Ha-Maggîd* published on its front page a letter by Ḥoṣîn informing readers about the commitment of Baghdadi Jews to promoting innovation in the study of the Torah based on manuscripts never published before.[25]

22 According to Kant, enlightenment indicates a type of maturity, a stage in which a man is able to use his own intellect and reason without being guided by others. See Immanuel Kant, 'Beantwortung der Frage: Was ist Aufklärung?' (1784) in E. Bahr (ed.), *Was ist Aufklärung?: Thesen und Definitionen* (Stuttgart 1974), 7–19.

23 Šelomoh Bekhôr Ḥoṣîn, 'Good News', *Ha-Maggîd* 13:2 (13/1/1869), 16; on Mina, see also Šelomoh Bekhôr Ḥoṣîn, 'A Terrific Plea', *Ha-Maggîd* 13: 40 (20/10/1869), 320.

24 Šelomoh Bekhôr Ḥoṣîn, 'Asia-Baghdad', *Ha-Maggîd* 12:49 (16/12/1868), 387. See also Efrayim Levinhausen, 'Baghdad', ibid.

25 Yehôšua' Davîd and Šelomoh Bekhôr Ḥoṣîn, 'The Awakening Society', *Ha-Maggîd* 6:48 (11/12/1862), 1.

However, Iraqi Jews occasionally accepted the orientalist narrative, especially when asking for financial help. ‘Unlike our European brethren, who reside in perfect peace for freedom has already been established in their lands, we the people of Babylon, reside in the bitter Babylonian exile, tortured and tormented’.[26] Furthermore, when Iraqi Jews sent letters that seemed contradictory to the *haskalah*’s ideas, editors used them as evidence to the backwardness of Iraqi Jews. For example, Baghdadi rabbis published a petition against the opening of a school for girls, labelling it as ‘objectionable to laws of decency’ and threatened to reprimand girls who attended the school by not writing their marriage contracts. The editors added to this item that: ‘this is the preaching of intolerance’ that ‘reached the Gates of Babylon’.[27]

Nonetheless, since European Jews also published stories about struggles within the European world, between the old and superstitious rabbinical and Hassidic leaders and the enlightened modern Jews, Baghdadi Jews accentuated that the Jewish world was divided not between Eastern and Western Jewry but rather between enlightened and ignorant Jews. Mo reover, the majority of Iraqi readers responded rapidly to stories they felt portrayed their community as primitive or traditional, and supplied evidence to reaffirm their claims.

An item that aggravated Iraqis was letters to *Ha-Maggîd* send by Jacob Obermeir critiquing Rabbi Yôsef Ḥayîm (born 1835) for standing in the way of reforming the Jewish educational system. The rabbis ex-communicated Obermeir, read the ex-communication document in the synagogues and wrote letters and petitions to *Ha-Maggîd* and *Ha-Levanôn* on the matter. Subsequently, Obermeir sent letters of apology to these newspapers. Coincidentally, he concurrently received news about his mother’s death, which were seen by the community as divine punishment. No Jew agreed to pray with him during the seven days of morning and finally, he publicly requested the community’s forgiveness.[28]

The reluctance of Iraqi Jews to be placed within orientalist rubric is fully articulated in *Ha-'Ôlam*’s interview with Yeḥzq’el Sasūn (Sasôn) (born 1860), who served as an Iraqi representative in the Ottoman Parliament. The reporter was impressed by Sasūn’s physical features:

---

26 Yehôšua‘ Davîd and Šelomoh Bekhôr Ḥoṣîn, ‘Asia-Baghdad’, *Ha-Maggîd* 7:11 (12/3/1863), 84.
27 ‘Baghdad’, *Ha-Ḥavaṣelet* 16:31 (7/5/1881), 248.
28 Ben Yaacob, 190–6.

> Sasūn Effendi is tall (he is the tallest of the Turkish Parliament member). His face attests to his enormous spiritual endeavours and when he converses, his eyes penetrate the soul of his companion and an unexplained smile, combining contempt and self-satisfaction appears. His dark skin certainly exemplifies his Baghdadi origins, especially seen against his short white beard. Despite his European manners, Arab influence is obvious in the way he talks and moves.

It seems, at first, that Sasūn accept an orientalist European discourse as he bemoans the state of 'Mohammedan fanaticism' in Baghdad and the 'half-savage' features of Muslim culture. Yet, he differentiates between Islam and Arab culture, which he cherishes and in which he desires to integrate. Sasūn Effendi accepts the reporter's assumption regarding the profound influence of Arab culture in Iraq and argues that Jews emulate every aspect of Arab life. The 'Muslim fanaticism' consequently is recognized as an obstacle in the way of complete integration in Arab society. The reporter accordingly laments that Mr. Sasūn 'sees no purpose in studying Hebrew, for he considers it a liturgical language. ... Zionism is utterly strange to him ... He wished to demonstrate to me that there is nothing that ties together Jews of different nations'.[29] The text echoes tensions between Sasūn's desire to adopt a European orientalist discourse regarding the nature of Islam and his pride in Arab culture, and between the reporter's admiration of Sasūn, who achieved a position coveted by many European Jews and his puzzlement at an Arab Jew entirely contemptuous of the Zionist project.

At that time when the terms 'Jew', 'citizen' and 'Oriental' were negotiated both in European imperialist, nationalist and racial theories, and in the Ottoman Empire following the *tanẓīmāt,* Iraqi and European Jews had likewise defined their identity vis-à-vis an assortment of others (Christian/Jewish, Muslim/Jewish, European/Arab) in the pages of the Hebrew journals. These publications generated a continuous dialogue between producers of orientalist literature and the objects and subjects of these descriptions for nearly fifty years. The orientalist nature of these journals, however, had encouraged Iraqi Jews to publish elsewhere, in their own language, in India.

29 'A Conversation with Sasūn Effendi – The Jewish Delegate from Baghdad', *Ha-'Ôlam,* 3:8 (10.3.1909), 11–12.

The Indian Journals

Jews from Baghdad and Basra immigrated to India when Iraqi trade integrated into the world system and settled in Bombay, Surat and later in Calcutta.[30] The Iraqi Jews in India continued speaking and publishing in Judaeo-Arabic and maintained strong religious and cultural links with the Baghdadi community to whom they turned for advice. The Sasūn family of Bombay, for example, brought tutors from Baghdad to David Solomon Sasūn (1880–1941) that provided instruction in the Bible, Hebrew and Arabic. When one teacher travelled to Baghdad, other Baghdadi teachers would replace him. This cultural exchange initiated the movement of texts from Iraq to India. Synagogues in Bombay contained religious scripts produced in Baghdad. As the Indian-Iraqi community became wealthier, Jews published texts in Judaeo-Arabic in India and owned printing houses. The texts published in these printing houses included liturgical literature, such as stories mimicking the Muslim genres of *Qiṣaṣ al-anbiyā'* (tales of the prophets) about Jewish prophets, rabbis and martyrs and popular literature like the anthology *Qiṣṣat al-Mathal*, a collection of 500 popular proverbs. Gradually, texts were produced first for the Indian market and then sent to Baghdad.[31]

Jewish journals in India included the following publications: *Ṭālib al-Khayr li-Qawmihi – Dôreš Tôv le-'Amô* ('Seeker of Good for its People')[32], *Peraḥ* ('Flower')[33], *Maggîd Meyšarim* ('Speaker of Truth'),[34] *Šôšanah* ('Rose')[35] and *Ha-Mevaser* ('The Announcer').[36] The papers considered themselves Jewish publications. *Ṭālib al-Khayr* added the title *The Hebrew Gazette* to its front page and *Peraḥ* and *Ha-Mevaser* added

30 Jews arrived in Bombay and Surat in the mid eighteenth century. The community in Bombay in 1889 was of 9,023 Jews and in 1901 13,919 Jews. The term 'Baghdadi' later included all Arabic speaking Jews in India. On Jewish life in India, see Joan G. Roland, *Jews in British India* (Hanover and London 1989); Thomas A. Timberg, 'Indigenous and Non Indigenous Jews', in Nathan Katz (ed.), *Studies of Indian Jewish Identity* (New Delhi 1995), 135–52.

31 On cultural and religious contacts between Jews in Baghdad and Bombay, see Avraham ben Yaacob, *The Immigration of Babylonian Jews to India and Integration there, Seen through the Medium of the Local Judeo-Arabic Press* (unpublished Ph.D. dissertation, Jerusalem 1986) (Hebrew); Yitzhak Avishur, 'Literature and Journalism in Judeo-Arabic by Iraqi Jews in Indian Print', *Pe'amim* 52 (1992), 101–15; Yitzhak Avishur, *The Babylonian Hakham from Calcutta: Rabbi Shelomo Twena and his work in Hebrew and Judeo-Arabic* (Tel-Aviv 2002); Benayahu, 'Introduction', 9–59.

32 *Dôreš Tôv* (1855–66), Biweekly, Bombay, edited by a club associated with the Sasūn family. It was later converted into a weekly.

33 *Peraḥ* (1878–89), Weekly, Calcutta, edited first by Rabbi Mošeh Meyuḥas and in its third year by Mošeh Shim'ôn Kohen of Syria.

34 *Maggîd Meyšahrin* (1889–1901), Weekly, Calcutta, edited by Rabbi Šelomoh Twinah.

35 *Šôšana* (1901–2), Weekly, Calcutta, edited by Sulayman ben Yehôšua' 'Ezra'.

36 *Ha-Mevaser* (1873–9) Calcutta, Weekly, edited by Yeḥezq'el b. Sulayman b. 'Abd Allah Ḥanîn

the subtitle *The Jewish Gazette*. *Ṭālib al-Khayr* likewise published details about weekly prayers. As Ben Yaacov notes despite differences in length, quality of paper and level of Arabic[37] all journals shared common features.[38]

The first and most obvious feature of these papers is the linkage between the emergence of the press and the colonial trade system as indicated in many items about rates, merchandise, prices, shares and the British commercial interests in India. *Peraḥ*, *Ṭālib al-Khayr* and *Ha-Mevaser* included in their opening pages details about the movements of ships to and from Basra, Bombay, Liverpool, London, Rangoon, Shanghai and Singapore. The following advertisement was placed by Mošeh de Yaʿqob Abū ʿAzīz in *Peraḥ*:

> Trade had extended as a result of the linking of peoples to each other, by money or by reason or by knowledge. People come from land and sea, selling their goods, as the sea of trade widens immensely. Since the city Calcutta, which I have chosen as a home to my family, is an important point of the trade coming from all the Indian states, I hereby take the honour of informing the readers of this new journal, and particularly my friends and relatives in the cities of Europe and Syria, that I am ready to serve them in all my capacities. I am well known amongst the small and large merchants[39]

The importance of local trade was attested by the fact that Ashkenazi Jews bought ads in *Peraḥ*, presumably because they believed middle class Jewish readers would be interested in their merchandise. Herr Bernard Schnich, for instance, who identified himself as an Ashkenazi Jew, asked his brethren to come and assist him by shopping at his clothing shop.[40] Another example is Herr Moses Williams who offered his services for merchants as a 'commercial informant' knowledgeable in European languages.[41] Jews, then, were aware of the fact that they were living in 'the age of empires'. This term, adopted from Eric Hobsbawm's work, specifies that in the years 1875–1914 distant parts of the world were interwoven into an economic mechanism

37 The Arabic of *Ṭālib* was quite horrifying at times, and jumbled *fuṣḥā* and *'āmmiyya*. The first page of the first issue suggests that people wrote in the same way they spoke. Thus, we find the title the *Tālib al-Khayr li-Qawmoho* (instead of *li-qawmihi*) and the misuse of *alladhī*. The Arabic of *Peraḥ* resembled the normative classical Arabic, although colloquialism often surfaced in commercials and advertisements.

38 Ben Yaacov, ibid.

39 *Peraḥ* 1:3 (6/7/1878), 4.

40 *Peraḥ* 1:2 (28/6/1878), 4.

41 The add reads: 'The undersigned offers himself as commercial informant for Austro-Hungary, Germany and Switzerland. Writers in English, French or Hebrew. Moses Williams, University of Vienna, Austria'. See *Peraḥ*, 11:32 (18/1/1889), 1.

of trade and communications.[42] Readers thus saw the journals as commodities travelling in this world, which helped them to locate themselves in the imperial system and to gather information about its various components.

Secondly, these journals aspired to emulate in their structure the Hebrew journals. The inclusion of columns like 'Jewish News' and 'World News' was probably inspired by the structure of the Hebrew press. Indian editors translated stories and news from *Ha-Melîṣ, Ha-Maggîd, Ha-Ḥavaṣelet, The Jewish Chronicle* and *Der Israelite* (Mainz). They were possibly inspired by the Hebrew *Ha-Mevaser* and *Ha-Maggîd* when choosing titles for their own publications. The journals' self-perception as products of science and education also resemble the European products. One of the aims of *Ṭālib al-Khayr* was to propagate Jewish education. *Peraḥ* had sections dedicated to global news (*akhbār al-buldān*) and to 'the news of the Jewish community' (*akhbār khāṣṣat al-yahūd*) reporting about Jews residing in England, Italy, Spain, Eastern and central Europe. Like the *haskalah* journals, the papers offered Biblical studies, but, unlike the Hebrew journals, also older methodologies of explicating the sacred texts, namely the *sharḥ*[43] and translations of liturgical works into Judaeo-Arabic. The importance of the *sharḥ* literature is attested in a letter published in *Ha-Mevaser*:

> To the man of high wisdom and astuteness, our beloved brother and friend, the publisher of *Ha-Mevaser*! ... We know that your intelligence, knowledge and reason have given you the reputation of an important man, and we wish your journal to prosper for the benefit of the Israelite nation, for your mission is that of the Heavens — to increase wisdom, science and reason ... Many desire to read and to see the shining light of biblical interpretation in the language of Arabia known to the people of Babylon, and their branches in Eastern India. I was therefore awakened and published in Livorno a Bible with commentary.[44]

Hillel Yôsef, who wrote this ad, explains that his translation is vital for people who have not mastered classical Arabic, since the translation will also elucidate the meaning of incomprehensible Arabic words. Making the holy scripts accessible to the reading public was significant to writers. Interest in translation was not reserved to sacred texts. *Peraḥ*'s literary section incorporated translated stories from Hebrew,

---

42 Eric Hobsbawm, *The Age of Empire, 1875–1914* (London 1987).
43 *Sharḥ* – the translation and clarification of biblical texts into Judaeo-Arabic.
44 Hillel Yôsef, *Ha-Mevaser* 2:33 (24/4/1874), 1.

French, German and classical Arabic. Some translations from German and French were adaptations from Hebrew translations originally published in the Hebrew journals. *Peraḥ* printed the story *Ibn al-ḥarāmī* (the thief's son), from the *Arabian Nights.*[45] Often times, Jews who contributed to these publications were rabbis, although they considered themselves part of a scientific and enlightened movement. They saw no contradiction between science and religion and identified themselves as an elite, eager to make use of textual and economic innovations offered by Ottoman, British and European elites, while preserving their Iraqi, Arab and Jewish characteristics.

Thirdly, the Iraqi-Jewish journals produced in India were seemingly Iraqi publications since their language and themes mirrored the life of the Baghdadi community. Baghdadi and Indian Jews also used this press as a billboard to announce the deaths, births and weddings of members of the community, both in India and in Iraq. Baghdadis addressed their brethren for help in the struggle against floods and diseases. *Peraḥ* had a section devoted to the news of Baghdad (*akhbār baghdād*). As Abraham Ben Yaaqob notes the paper devoted considerable space to discussing Ottoman Baghdadi politics and stories of crime in Baghdad. The journals praised wālīs like Midhat Pasha (1869–72), known as the 'father of peace' (*avî ha-šalôm*), for his reforms and Ḥajjī Ḥasan Rafīq Pasha for threatening to banish any Muslim who falsely accused a Jew of blasphemy.[46]

Maggid Meyšarīm published three letters from Sydney, Australia written by Iraqi Jews that appeared in issues 46 (26/8/1897), 47 (2/9/1897), 48 (9/9/1897). The letters narrated the history of the Sasūn family in Baghdad and its escape to Persia and then to India. The accounts include information about the tyranny of the last Mamluk governor of Iraq, Da'ūd Pasha (1816–31), as well as about the leaders of the Jewish community and their relationship with the Jewish leadership in Istanbul. Such publications could not have been published in Arabic. For example, they tell the story of Abraham Šalôm, who converted to Islam and changed his name to Ibn Yayy. He informed Da'ūd Pasha about the fortunes of affluent Jews, thus making them a target for Da'ūd's confiscation policy. The reason for his conversion, we are told, was his

45 The *Arabian Nights* was printed in Bombay in Judaeo-Arabic in 1886 in order to teach the reading audiences useful and practical lessons. See Avishur, 'Literature', 108–9.

46 Ben Yaacob, *Jews,* 151–6.

infatuation with a Muslim woman, whom he obsessively visited, carried publicly and shamelessly on his shoulders and bought her everything, 'even vegetables'. The writers were sure that Ibn Yayy was struck by the evil eye and wished he would be burned in hell.[47] Such a negative portrayal of a converted Jew would have been extremely problematic if published in the Ottoman province, but the location of the press outside of Iraq and in Hebrew characters allowed writers to freely voice their criticisms.

These news items were read differently by various audiences. The reports on crime in Baghdad indicated to Baghdadi readers that the Jews in India were interested in their misery and simultaneously assured the Indian Jewish community that their decision to immigrate to India was correct. The English press read by Jews, which had its own stereotypes regarding the negative nature of Muslim governments might have inspired the accentuation of the hardships of Jews under the Ottoman-Muslim government in Iraq. Religious ties to Baghdad were vital to the Baghdadi immigrants predominantly because in the linguistic, religious and ethnic Indian milieu, such ties provided a sense of identity that distinguished the community from both the Indian Jews and from their Muslim and Hindu neighbours.[48]

Fourthly, as the community established itself in the Indian locale, the press became less and less relevant for Iraqi Jews. Commercials for the local opera house or for athletic shoes bought only in Calcutta[49] reflect a middle-class community looking towards assimilation with Britain, rather than with Baghdad. Indian, colonial and international affairs were important to readers. For example, the war in Kabul and its aftermath occupied the front pages of *Peraḥ*.[50] In 1887 *Peraḥ* produced a letter by D. Sasūn to the Chief Clerk of the High Court of Justice on behalf of Jews who refused to serve on jury duty on Saturdays. 'Jews are by their religion precluded from attending to any description of work or business on that holy day … when compelled

47 A translation and commentary of the texts appeared in Ben Yaacob, *Immigration,* 127–35.

48 The Arab Jews in India were reluctant to integrate into the older existing Indian Jewish communities, i.e. the Bene Israel and the Jews of Cochin, and often refer to them as 'black Jews'. There were hardly any marriages between the two communities because Baghdadi Jews questioned the religiosity of their Indian brethren.

49 *Peraḥ* 3:46 (13/5/1881), 1; see also *Peraḥ* 20:25 (10/12/1880), 1, a commercial for Victoria's Theatrical Company.

50 'News of the War from Kabul', *Peraḥ* 1:32 (31/1/1878), 1; 'News of the War from Kabul', *Peraḥ* 1:31 (24/1/1879), 1; 'News of the War from Kabul' *Peraḥ* 1:27 (3/1/1879), 1; 'News of the War from Kabul', *Peraḥ* 1:29 (10/1/1879), 1.

to serve on a Jury on Saturday they are forced to break one of the most solemn ordinances of their creed'. Therefore, the British defy their own enlightened principles that allow perfect freedom to subjects in matters of religion.[51] In response, the clerk of the court allowed the Jews not to attend the court meetings on Saturdays. This story was important for Baghdadi Jews for it indicated that enlightened governments permit freedom of faith, a very topical issue in the Ottoman Empire at the time. For Indian readers it demonstrated the degree of their successful integration, epitomized also in the power of the Sasūn family.

The Indian press in Judaeo-Arabic corresponds to Benedict Anderson's conceptualization of print capitalism, as it is closely linked to markets and involves shipping news.[52] Yet, Judaeo-Arabic did not characterize either the language of the colony (India), or that of the metropolis, but was rather a language uniting Baghdadi Jews in India and Iraq. What determined the relationship between the Judaeo-Arabic reading communities in India and in Iraq was their position in the imperial system. The middle-class Indian Jewish elite shared both its language and its religion with the Jews of Iraq, and this brought about the vision of Iraq as a cultural centre. Nevertheless, as the Baghdadi community was established in India and became pro-British, the Arab nature of the Iraqi press was negatively perceived. By the 1920s the Jewish Indian press continued to exist, but mostly in English.

Conclusions

Following the Young Turks Revolution (1908), Jews began to publish Ottoman Arabic journals in Baghdad. After the establishment of the Iraqi State, Iraqi Jews became avid readers and contributors to the Arabic press.[53] With the rise of the Iraqi nation state, and the gradual Zionization of the Hebrew journals, the Judaeo-Arabic press virtually disappeared. The nineteenth century Jewish Iraqi community of readers was multilingual. In the Ottoman Empire, Arabic script (used for Arabic, Ottoman and Persian) was a sacred form of writing, linked to sacred dynasties and holy practices

51 S.D.Sasūn, 'A Letter by S.D. Sasūn', *Peraḥ* 1:41 (18/7/1878), 8. A copy of the original letter is attached to *Peraḥ*'s microfilm in the National Library, Jerusalem.

52 Benedict R. Anderson, *Imagined Communities: Reflections on the Origin and Spread of Nationalism* (London and New York 1991).

53 Editor Anuwār Sha'ūl and publisher Salman Shina printed the journal *al-Miṣbāḥ* in Arabic (1924–8). In 1929, Sha'ūl edited the Arab journal *al-Ḥāṣid,* which lasted for almost a decade and was an Arab rather than a Jewish publication.

such as pilgrimage. For the Jewish Iraqi community, Arabic was an ingredient amongst other imperial languages, the other being Ottoman Turkish and English (administrative and imperial languages in Iraq and in India) and French (the language taught in the *Alliance* schools). Hebrew was not only a liturgical language, but also an imperial language because it functioned as a means to converse with and respond to the writings of European Jews.

It seems to me that all writers, both in the European-Hebrew journals and in the Judaeo-Arabic publications attempt to answer the question 'What is Enlightenment?' They all relate to the complex historical processes, which shaped their daily lives, and to 'types of political institutions, forms of knowledge, projects of rationalization of knowledge and practices'.[54] Surely, they did not provide such sophisticated answers as Kant's, but they do expose and critique such processes as colonial trade, education systems and print capitalism. Given their Iraqi, Ottoman and Arabic nature, these publications can be seen as part of the cultural revival of the Middle East in the nineteenth century, specifically the Arabic *nahḍa.* Rather than searching for the specific moment when the *nahḍa* began or constructing a particular order for its spread (first in Egypt and Lebanon, later in Palestine and Iraq), it is preferable to explore the *nahḍa* as an ethos, as movements of ideas concurrently coming from diverse centres. Different people, at different places in the nineteenth century, spoke of science and progress, although they had very different conceptions of who was enjoying the rays of light, and who was to remain in darkness.

---

54 Michel Foucault, 'What Is Enlightenment?' in Paul Rabinow (ed.), *The Foucault Reader* (London 1984), 32–51.

Arabic Books Printed In Malta 1826–42: Some Physical Characteristics

Geoffrey Roper

The Arabic press run by the English Church Missionary Society in Malta between 1825 and 1842 produced over a hundred editions of Arabic and Turkish books, tracts and newspapers for readers in the Middle East at a time when indigenous printing was still in its infancy. These included not only Christian texts and tracts, but also secular educational texts intended for Muslim, Christian and Jewish pupils in the new schools and colleges of the Middle East, as well as a newly literate adult population. These text-books dealt with the Arabic and English languages, mathematics, geography, astronomy, zoology, history and art; also translations of English literature, and a periodical in the style of a newspaper.[1]

They were distributed in quite large numbers: figures from the missionary archives and records indicate that a total of over 150,000 Arabic and Turkish books and 8,600 'newspapers' from Malta arrived in the Middle East and North Africa between 1825 and the mid-1840s.[2] At the time, this represented a drastic increase in the availability of reading material: neither traditional manuscript production, nor the earlier imports of European printed books, nor the output of books from most of the local presses can have approached these levels in a comparable period of time. Only the Būlāq Press in Egypt exceeded the Malta production figures:[3] but their output was aimed at a quite different readership, the already educated adult elite.

The main destinations of the Malta books were Egypt and Lebanon, where missionary educational establishments were in operation, and which, in the Muḥammad ʿAlī period, were relatively open to foreign influences. But significant quantities were also distributed in the Maghrib, Palestine, Syria, Iraq and Turkey, with some copies also finding their way to the Hejaz, Yemen and Eritrea.[4]

---

1 For a history of the press, and a full bibliography of its Arabic and Turkish publications, see Geoffrey Roper, *Arabic Printing in Malta 1825–1845: Its History and its Place in the Development of Print Culture in the Arab Middle East,* Ph.D.Thesis, (University of Durham 1988).

2 Ibid., 270–2.

3 Abū 'l-Futūḥ Riḍwān, *Tārīkh Matba'at Būlāq wa-Lamḥa fī Tārīkh al-Ṭibā'a fī Buldān al-Sharq al-Awsaṭ* (Cairo 1953), 138–9 and 259–60.

4 Roper, *Arabic Printing,* 272–302.

What impact did all these books make on their Arab readers? Obviously this relates partly to the texts, which they contained; but the intention here is to examine a different aspect of the question. The effects which books have on their readers' thought processes depend also on their physical characteristics, on the way in which the texts are packaged and presented. So what did the Malta books look like, and how did they differ from what Arab readers of the time might have found in other reading matter? Of necessity this can be only a brief survey of some of the relevant characteristics.

Perhaps the most important feature of a printed book is its type-face. The first Arabic types used in Malta were supplied by the London printer and type-founder Richard Watts. These were almost identical to, and most probably from the punches and/or matrices of, the founts prepared by the English typographer William Martin, who was a pupil of the famous Baskerville. He cut them from models provided by the orientalist Charles Wilkins at the beginning of the nineteenth century.[5] Two type-faces were supplied to Malta — English and Great Primer sizes — and they were exclusively used until the late 1830s. Any larger size of lettering, as required sometimes for headings and titles, had to be specially engraved or lithographed.

These Martin/Watts type-faces were a considerable improvement on many earlier ones used in England and northern Europe generally. But although they are quite elegant in appearance, they do not really correspond to any authentic Arabic *ductus*, or style of writing, and certain features, such as the opaque 'eyes' in letters such as *fā*, *qāf* and *wāw*, must have seemed somewhat alien to Arab readers. The use of the Persian form of the numeral 4 (which probably came from Wilkins's Indian models), and Western numerals and letters for sheet signatures, would also have contributed to the 'foreign' look. It seems that, in consequence, the early Malta books did encounter some criticism from their Arab recipients on account of their type-style and appearance. An internal memorandum in the missionary archives, dated December 1831, notes that 'The Arabs generally dislike the characters of the books issued from our Press.'[6]

---

5 CMS Archives: CM/O39/31a, Jowett to the Secretaries, 29.5.1824; CM/O39/44, Jowett to Secs., 7.3.1825; CM/L1/69, Bickersteth to Jowett, 8.4.1825; CM/L1/295 and CM/L2/3, Coates to Jowett, 7.7.1830 and 15.9.1830; Geoffrey Roper, 'Arabic Printing and Publishing in England before 1820', *British Society for Middle Eastern Studies Bulletin* 12 (1985), 22–4.

6 CMS Archives: CM/O18/11, Brenner to Coates, 3.12.1831.

Because of this, and also because the Watts types were wearing out, completely new Arabic founts were brought into use in 1838. These were prepared and cast entirely in Malta,[7] under the supervision of George Badger and the famous Lebanese writer Fāris al-Shidyāq.[8] The latter had been a copyist in his youth in Lebanon, and this undoubtedly contributed greatly to the preparation of good calligraphic models.[9] George Badger — later a noted orientalist — had considerable mechanical skill and typographical experience — he had previously worked as a typographer at the American Press in Beirut.[10] This, combined with his feeling for Arabic, ensured that Shidyāq's models were reproduced as faithfully and elegantly as possible on the punches that were cut.

Three sizes of alphabet were created, of which the largest, Double Pica, was quite calligraphic: as well as being used for headings and titles, some entire texts were set in it, such as Shidyāq's own reading-book, *Al-Laṭīf fī Kull Ma'nā Ṭarīf* (1839) and the Biblical *Kitāb al-Zāri'* of 1840, which one Arab typographical historian has described as being 'of extreme beauty of script and excellence of typography.'[11] The two smaller ones — Great Primer and English — were designed to replace the Watts types, and were also considerably more authentic than their predecessors, being fair reproductions of good *naskhī* styles. All three type-faces reflect some of the characteristics of Shidyāq's handwriting, particularly the strong bold horizontals, which can be seen in his extant autograph manuscripts.[12]

The impression made by lines of type is affected not only by the type-face, but also by the type-setting: this is especially true of Arabic typography, which must imitate cursive script. Careless or disjointed type-casting or composition can greatly mar the appearance of the text and alienate the reader. A few of the early Malta publications do suffer from this; but most of them are carefully set, with the cursiveness well maintained. Typographical spelling errors, however, are not

7 CMS Archives: CM/O18/14, Brenner to Coates, 11.9.1832; CM/L2/406–407, Coates to Schlienz, 30.3.1836; CM/O18/33 and 44, Brenner to Secs., 14.1.1837 and 6.9.1838; CM/O65/47, Schlienz to Secs., 10.3.1837.

8 CMS Archives: CM/O18/33, Brenner to Secs., 14.1.1837.

9 Geoffrey Roper, 'Fāris al-Shidyāq and the Transition from Scribal to Print Culture in the Middle East', in George N. Atiyeh (ed.), *The Book in the Islamic World: The Written Word and Communication in the Middle East* (Albany 1995), 209–31, 211 and 213.

10 Geoffrey Roper, 'The Beginnings of Arabic Printing by the ABCFM, 1822–1841', *Harvard Library Bulletin* N.S.9 / 1998 (1999), 59–60.

11 'Huwa ghāya fī jamāl al-khaṭṭ wa-jūdat al-ṭab'', Riḍwān, *Tārīkh*, 25.

12 E.g. Leeds Arabic MS.128, Cambridge UL Or.1446.

infrequent, despite the proof-reading efforts of the missionary printers and their assistants. Among other things, the compositors seem to have had continual difficulty with Eastern Arabic numerals, frequently muddling 2 and 6, or 7 and 8, or reversing the order of digits. Most of these errors occur in the earlier books: by the late 1830s the vigilance of Shidyāq and Badger was brought to bear, and eliminated most such misprints. Printed errata lists are appended to some volumes, a new feature of Arabic books at the time.

The arrangement of the text on the page, and the accompanying typographical features which serve to present it and package it as a book, are also of crucial importance in determining its impact on readers. The books produced at the early Turkish and Egyptian presses were usually modelled quite closely on traditional manuscript layouts and styles of presentation. The Arabic and Turkish books from Malta, on the other hand, introduced a number of new features derived from the European printed book, while at the same time retaining a sensitivity to Middle Eastern norms which was often lacking in Arabic books printed in Europe. Some traditional features are sometimes found, such as, in a few cases, decorative headings, corresponding to manuscript *'unwāns* (although these are generally much less elaborate than their counterparts in Istanbul or Būlāq books); also, occasionally, the use of ruled borders around the text, red ink for headings or rubricated key words, and sometimes tapered colophons.

On the other hand, unlike manuscripts, and contrary to the practice in most Egyptian and Ottoman printed books of the period, the Malta books contain no printed marginal glosses or commentaries, and there are no catchwords to link one page of text to the next. Instead, several of them introduce footnotes, a novel way of presenting ancillary information in Arabic books. At the top of the page, another novel feature is sometimes found: running heads, repeating the title of the chapter or section as an aid to those referring to the book.

Most ordinary manuscripts, and many printed books from the Middle East until the late nineteenth century, lack title-pages. The Malta books, however, with only a few exceptions, do provide them. Usually (but not always) they set out the place and date of publication as well as the title. The author's name, however, is only seldom given: in most cases the omission is understandable, as many of the books have no identifiable authors, being biblical anthologies, reading books, prayers or such like, or are translated from English authors, with names like Bickersteth, Pinnock, etc., which, if transliterated into Arabic, would appear as nothing but gobbledegook to Arab readers; but it is perhaps surprising that Shidyāq's name is missing from the title-pages of the books of which he was the author;[13] and that the names of the Arab authors ʿAbd Allāh Zākhir and Jibrīl Farḥāt do not appear on the title-pages of the Malta editions of their works.[14]

Many of the title-pages are adorned with quotations from biblical or other sources, and some have wood-engraved vignettes, mostly taken or copied from contemporary English editions. Some have decorative engraved panels or borders, sometimes incorporating patterns produced by the repetition of ornamental types known as fleurons, or small foliate, floral or crystal devices. These reintroduced to the Arab world elements of the arabesque, originally taken by Europeans from Islamic models, and now re-cast (literally) in a new form. Such compositions were subsequently used quite frequently on Middle Eastern printed books, until the end of the nineteenth century and beyond. Some books have large or elaborate engraved lettering for the title or part of it: in particular, the word *Kitāb*, in large letters with the *bā'* placed over the *kāf*, appears in identical form on several title-pages, and must have been engraved on a block which was reused. A few title-pages were produced entirely by lithography, with attempts at calligraphy for the titles and sometimes elaborate decorative ensembles: one notable example is the first edition of Farḥāt's *Baḥth al-Maṭālib* of 1836, with a very elaborate design incorporating rather incongruous ancient Egyptian motifs.

Tables of contents, with page numbers, are also to be found in a number of the Malta publications. While this was not entirely unknown in Arabic books, it was still uncommon in that period. Other tables and charts also appear within the texts of certain books.

The page layouts likewise set new standards, being considerably more spacious and easier on the eye than most ordinary Arabic manuscripts or contemporary printed books from the Middle East. Margins are reasonably wide, and are unencumbered by glosses or commentaries. The spacing between lines and between words is also quite

---

13 *Al-Bākūra al-Shahīya*, 1836; *Al-Lafīf fī Kull Ma'nā Ṭarīf*, 1839; (with George Percy Badger) *Al-Muḥāwara al-Unsīya*, 1840.

14 Zākhir,ʿAbd Allāh, *Kitāb al-Burhān al-Ṣarīḥ*, 1834; Jibrīl Farḥāt, *Kitāb Baḥth al-Maṭālib*, 1836.

generous, leaving a reasonable overall ratio between black and white, which contrasts markedly with the normal appearance of a page of a Būlāq or Istanbul book of the same period. Many of the Malta texts are also divided into paragraphs (albeit often rather long ones), which is not true of most of their local counterparts.

Punctuation, in the modern sense, was not used in Arabic in the manuscript era, although sometimes circles, rosettes or groups of dots were used to indicate the ends of passages, such as verses in the Qur'ān.[15] Early printed books in the Middle East did not depart from scribal tradition in this respect. The Malta press for the most part did likewise, and the only marks in most of their books are asterisks or dots enclosed in inverted heart-shaped devices, conforming in their use with the traditional Arabic system. There was, however, one serious attempt to introduce modern punctuation, and it came not from the Europeans at the press, but from the Arab scholar Fāris al-Shidyāq. His approach to the Arabic language was a combination of conservatism in his determination to maintain classical norms of grammar and style, and radicalism in seeking ways to revitalise it for use in the modern world. By the late 1830s he had become familiar with European books and literature, and had observed the usefulness of punctuation marks in clarifying the structure and meaning of passages of prose. In 1836 he published at the Malta press his English grammar in Arabic, *Al-Bākūra al-Shahīya*, and was careful to set out in detail the punctuation signs, their names and uses. Then, three years later, in 1839, when he came to publish his primer and reading book of literary Arabic, *Al-Lafīf fī Kull Ma'nā Ṭarīf*, he boldly decided to introduce these Western punctuation marks into it. He announced his decision in the preface to the book, setting out the signs and their uses, and calling for their general adoption.

This remarkable proposal for a significant change in Arabic orthography was, however, far ahead of its time. Although all these punctuation marks appear throughout *Al-Lafīf*, they were, apart from the full-stop, very seldom used in other Malta books, and are even missing from some for which Shidyāq himself was entirely responsible. A few commas, dashes, colons and quotation marks appeared in books published in 1839 and 1840. Exclamation and question marks are not found anywhere outside *Al-Lafīf*. In the Middle East, Shidyāq's appeal fell on deaf ears, and he himself soon gave up the idea. In the second edition of *Al-Lafīf*, published in Istanbul in 1881 at Al-Jawā'ib Press, of which he was the director, all the punctuation marks

15 Johannes Pedersen, *The Arabic Book*, G.French (trans.), R. Hillenbrand (ed.) (Princeton 1984), 79.

were omitted, as well as the relevant section of the introduction. It was not until the twentieth century that full punctuation became widely adopted in Arabic.

Another new feature of printed books for Arab readers was the use of pictorial illustrations. From 1832 the German artist Carl-Friedrich Brocktorff (resident in Malta) and his son Ludwig (or Luigi) were employed to prepare both wood-engravings and lithographed drawings and maps.[16] These were mostly copied from the illustrations in the English originals from which Arabic books were translated, such as *Robinson Crusoe*. Some fine lithographed maps were also published in the form of an Arabic atlas (1835).[17]

The formats and sizes of the Malta Arabic books vary considerably. Apart from the oblong folio atlas and a calligraphic copying book,[18] and quarto drawing lessons,[19] none of them exceeded the standard octavo size of the 1840 dialogues (*Al-Muḥāwara al-Unsīya*). Many, however, especially the early tracts and primers, were much smaller — mostly 16mo, little more than pocket size. This was presumably both for reasons of cost, and to facilitate their transport and distribution by travelling missionaries.

It remains to mention the Arabic publications in newspaper format printed in Malta in 1833 and 1834. They seem usually to have contained six pages, consisting of one sheet folded, with a half-sheet tipped in. They measured, when folded, 25 x 21 cm. The upper 11 cm. of the first page contains the title, *Akhbār al-Qāṣid*, in large engraved calligraphic lettering, surmounted by a wood-engraved vignette, on either side of which are printed the year, the issue number and the names of the month in the Eastern Christian and Coptic calendars, in small type. The main text, in two columns divided by a rule, is set in Great Primer Arabic from the old Martin & Watts fount. The imprint appears in small type at the foot of the back page. The 'news' is simply

16 On the Brocktorff family and their artistic output in Malta, see Nicholas de Piro, *The International Dictionary of Artists Who Painted Malta* (Valletta 1988), 33–7; their employment by the CMS is recorded in the CMS Archives: CM/O65/21, Schlienz to Secs., 30.6.1832; CM/O67/6, Weiss to Jowett, 28.8.1833; their names also appear on several of the engravings and lithographs.

17 Carmel G. Bonavia, *Bibliography of Maltese Textbooks 1651–1979* (Msida 1979), n. 35, 29; Eva Hanebutt-Benz, Dagmar Glass, and Geoffrey Roper (eds), in collaboration with Theo Smets, *Middle Eastern Languages and the Print Revolution: A Cross-cultural Encounter* (Westhofen 2002), n. 86, 495.

18 No title or imprint [1835]. British Library obl.fol.14546.f.1.

19 *Ba'ḍ Qawā'id fī Uṣūl al-Rasm* [1835].

the 'good news' of the Christian gospel. But for most, if not all, of its readers, it will have been the first publication in newspaper format which they had ever seen.[20]

The role of the Malta press in standardising layouts and methods of presentation of printed Arabic texts had a significant impact. Some of the new features which it introduced correspond with several which Elizabeth Eisenstein mentioned, in her seminal work on the printing press as an agent of change, as significant in the systematisation of thought-processes in the formative era of European print culture. The use of title-pages engendered 'new habits of placing and dating' as well as helping the later development of new standards of cataloguing and enumerative bibliography. The use of footnotes, running heads and abbreviations, as well as Shidyāq's experiments with punctuation, all served to 'reorder the thought of readers' and to create a new 'esprit de système.'[21]

The plates and engravings in some of the Malta books also broke new ground. The views and story illustrations incorporated perspective, which was still a very new convention in Arab pictorial representation, and one which, as McLuhan and others have pointed out, implied a new reordering of consciousness by the adoption of a fixed point of view.[22] The lithographed diagrams, which accompanied an astronomical work published in Malta in 1833,[23] were another important new feature of the Arabic book. Technical illustrations were sometimes found in Arabic manuscripts; but, as David James has aptly observed, 'in the absence of the printing press, transmission of technical data depends upon the accuracy of the scribe. The problem becomes doubly difficult when information has also to be communicated in the form of diagrams ... [which] were regarded by the copyists as little more than an exotic appendage, frequently misplaced and sometimes omitted.'[24] With the introduction of standard, repeatable, engraved diagrams incorporated into printed books, the presentation of such information became transformed.

---

20 The only previous Arabic publication in newspaper format was the Egyptian official gazette *Al-Waqā'i' al-Miṣrīya*, which had started publication five years earlier, in 1828.

21 Elizabeth L. Eisenstein, *The Printing Press as an Agent of Change* (Cambridge 1979), 105–6.

22 Marshall McLuhan, *The Gutenberg Galaxy: The Making of Typographic Man* (Toronto and London 1962), 111–14.

23 [James Mitchell] *Kitāb al-Durr al-Malḍūm*, 1833.

24 David James, 'The *Manual de artillería* of al-Ra'īs Ibrāhīm b. Aḥmad al-Andalusī with Particular Reference to its Illustrations and their Sources', *Bulletin of the School of Oriental and African Studies* 41 (1978), 257.

In this the Malta press shared with the Būlāq press a pioneering role in the Arab world; and what was true of diagrams was equally true of printed maps, in which field the Malta atlas of 1835 also broke new ground. In Tunisia the first atlas was printed in 1860[25]; in Egypt regular Arabic map printing did not begin until 1870,[26] although copies of the Malta atlas itself were made there at an earlier date.[27] As Eisenstein has pointed out, 'heightened awareness of distant regional boundaries is encouraged by the printed output of more uniform maps containing more uniform boundaries and place names.'[28] This in turn may have played some part in developing national and political self-awareness among Arabs.

Let us conclude by pointing to an even more fundamental epistemological development. Many of these Arabic primers from Malta, and others, which later followed their example, were arranged on the principle of gradation. They started with the simplest basics, and then gradually introduced increasingly challenging and complex matter, a pattern, which was reflected in the typographical layout as well as the textual content. This now seems an obvious way to design teaching materials. But this was not generally characteristic of earlier texts used in Arab elementary schools. This new feature perhaps almost subliminally may have promoted the idea of progress — of gradually increasing knowledge, and moving forward intellectually, technologically and culturally.

This is characteristic also, as Eisenstein has pointed out, of the world of printed books in general, where past knowledge and intellectual achievements can be taken for granted and built upon, instead of continually having to be retrieved through the hand copying of texts and commentaries.[29] Perhaps this re-orientation, introduced in the second quarter of the nineteenth century from Malta and elsewhere, may have influenced at least part of a generation of children and students who later became the

25 Muḥammad al-Ṣāliḥ Al-Muhaydī, *Tārīkh al-Ṭibā'a wa-'l-Nashr bi-Tūnis* (Tunis 1965), 11. Turkish maps had been printed at Istanbul in the eighteenth century and atlases in the early years of the nineteenth. Cf. [J.T.] Reinaud, *Notice des ouvrages arabes, persans, turcs et français, imprimés à Constantinople* (Paris 1831). Also in *Bulletin Universel des Sciences* (Nov. 1831), 6.

26 Muḥammad Maḥmūd Ṣayyād, 'Fann al-Kharā'iṭ wa-'l-Maṭba'a al-'Arabīya', *Majallat al-Kitāb al-'Arabī*, 41 (1967), 13.

27 Lord A.W. Lindsay [25th Earl of Crawford], *Letters on Egypt, Edom, and the Holy Land*, 5th edn (London 1858), I, 33; Dār al-Kutub [al-Miṣrīya], *Fihrist al-Kutub al-'Arabīya al-Mawjūda bi-'l-Dār.* Al-juz' al-sādis. (Cairo 1933), 70; A. Demeerseman, *L'imprimerie en Orient et au Maghreb: une étape décisive de la culture et de la psychologie sociale islamiques* (Tunis, 1954), 2–3 n.10. Also in *IBLA*, 17 (1954), 2–3 n.10

28 Eisenstein, *The Printing Press*, 83.

29 Eisenstein, *The Printing Press*, 113–24

modernizers and progressives of the late-nineteenth-century *nahḍa*, or Arab renaissance.

SOURCES

The most important sources are the Malta books themselves. The best single collection of them is in the British Library in London. Other significant holdings are to be found at the Bodleian Library in Oxford (including especially the Malan collection in the Indian Institute Library housed there), Cambridge University Library, New College Library in Edinburgh, Dār al-Kutub in Cairo, Universitätsbibliothek Tübingen, Österreichische Nationalbibliothek in Vienna, Deutsche Morgenländische Gesellschaft in Halle and the Harvard Divinity School in Cambridge, USA.

Archives

Church Missionary Society, kept in Birmingham University Library

Letter-books (outgoing): CM/L …

Original papers: CM/O …

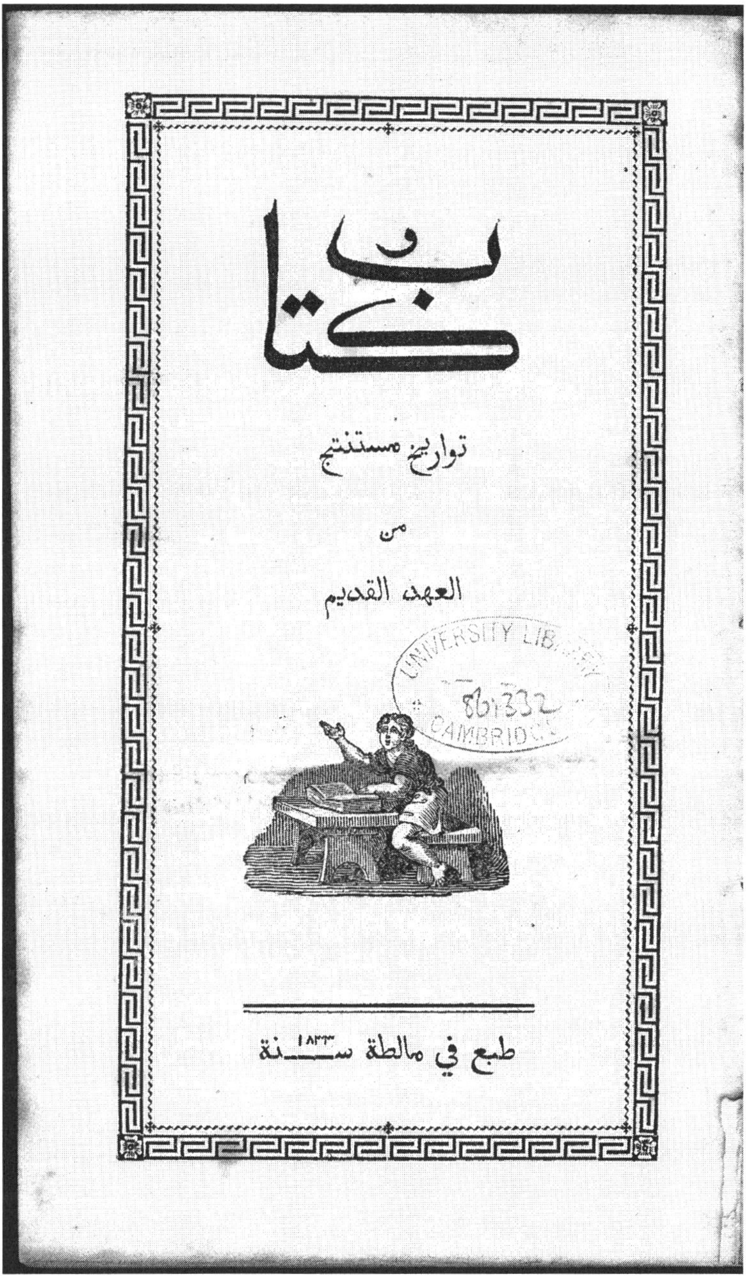

كتاب

تواريخ مستنتج

من

العهد القديم

طبع في مالطة سنة ١٨٣٣

Figure 1. [Bible: O.T.] *Kitāb Tawārīkh mustantaj min al-'Ahd al-Qadīm* [Book of histories extracted from the Old Testament (Rome 1671 version)]. Malta 1833. Cambridge University Library, 8828.d.28. Title within Greek-style border; word *Kitāb* calligraphically engraved; woodcut vignette of European origin

Figure 2. (FARḤĀT, Jibrīl.) *Fī 'l-wa'ẓ* [On preaching]. No imprint [Malta 1841.] Cambridge University Library, 8828.d.29. Title set in the large 1838 type, within an elaborate engraved European Gothic architectural panel.

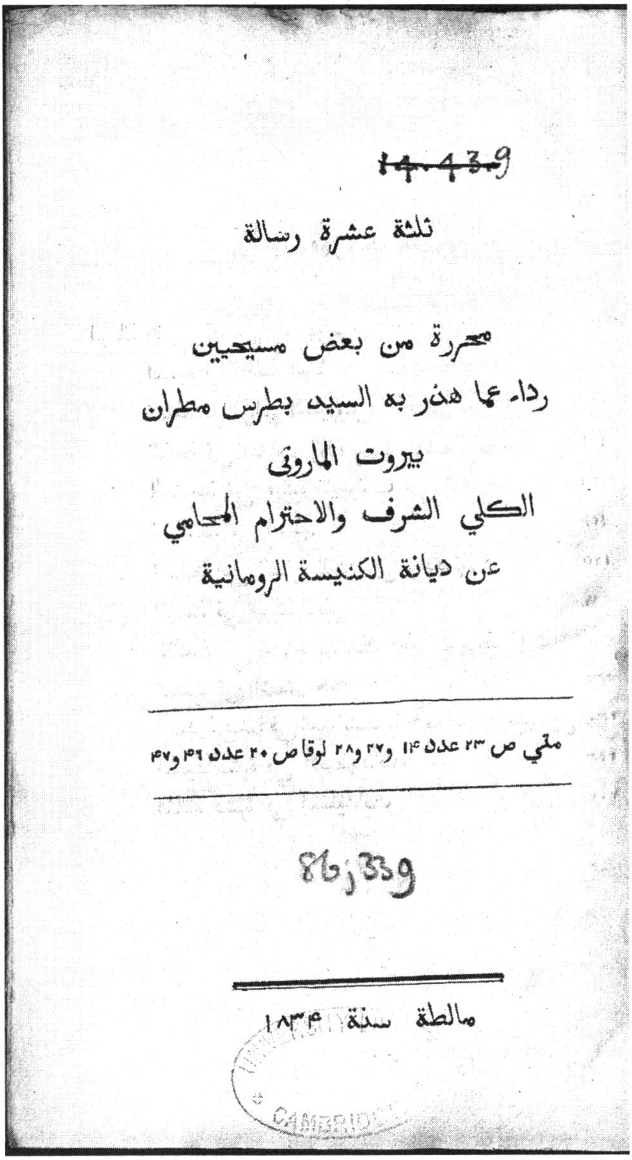

ثلثة عشرة رسالة

محررة من بعض مسيحيين

رداء عما هذر به السيد بطرس مطران

بيروت المارونى

الكلي الشرف والاحترام المحامي

عن ديانة الكنيسة الرومانية

متي ص ٢٣ عدد ١٤ و٢٧ و٢٨ لوقا ص ٢٠ عدد ٤٦ و٤٧

مالطة سنة ١٨٣٤

Figure 3. [BIRD, Isaac.] *Thalatha 'ashara risāla* [13 letters]. Malta 1834. Cambridge University Library, 8828.d.33. Title-page, set in the original types of Richard Watts, from the Wilkins/Martin design. First word of title misspelt (*alif* omitted). Printed by the CMS on behalf of the American missionaries in Beirut.

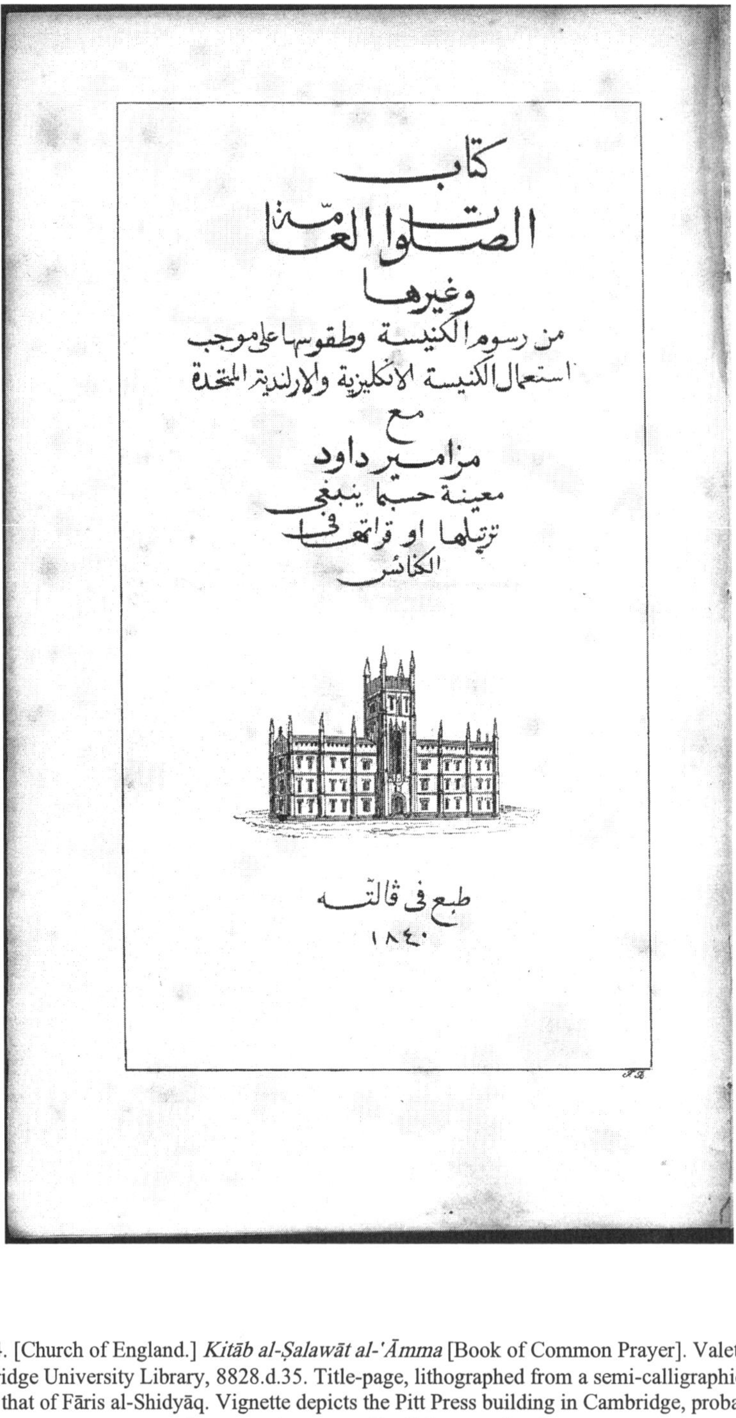

كتاب
الصلوات العامّة
وغيرها
من رسوم الكنيسة وطقوسها على موجب
استعمال الكنيسة الانكليزية والارلندية المتحدة
مع
مزامير داود
معينة حسبما ينبغي
ترتيلها او قراءتها في
الكنائس

طبع في ڤالتّه
١٨٤٠

Figure 4. [Church of England.] *Kitāb al-Ṣalawāt al-'Āmma* [Book of Common Prayer]. Valetta 1840. Cambridge University Library, 8828.d.35. Title-page, lithographed from a semi-calligraphic hand, probably that of Fāris al-Shidyāq. Vignette depicts the Pitt Press building in Cambridge, probably taken from a contemporary English prayer-book.

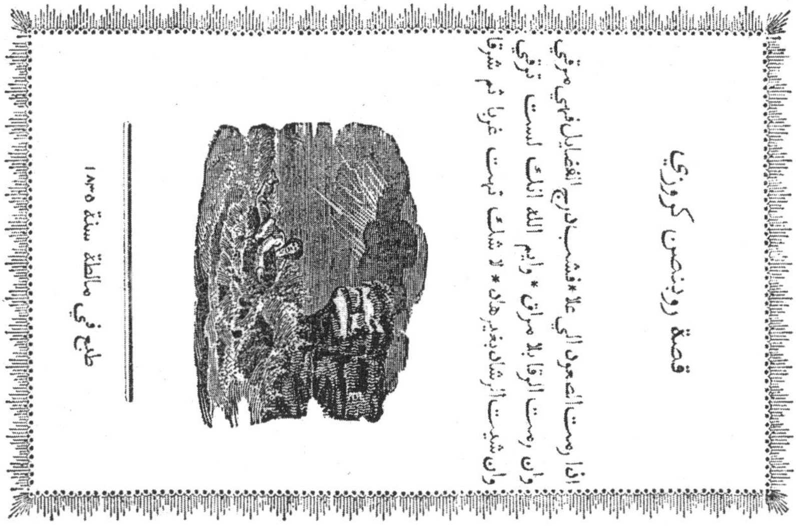

Figure 5. [DEFOE, Daniel.] *Qiṣṣat Rawbinṣun Kurūzī* [The story of Robinson Crusoe.] Malta 1835. Cambridge University Library, 8828.d.37. Title-page set in Watts types, within border constructed from ornamental typographic sorts. Wood-cut vignette. Frontispiece apparently lithographed from a wood-cut original.

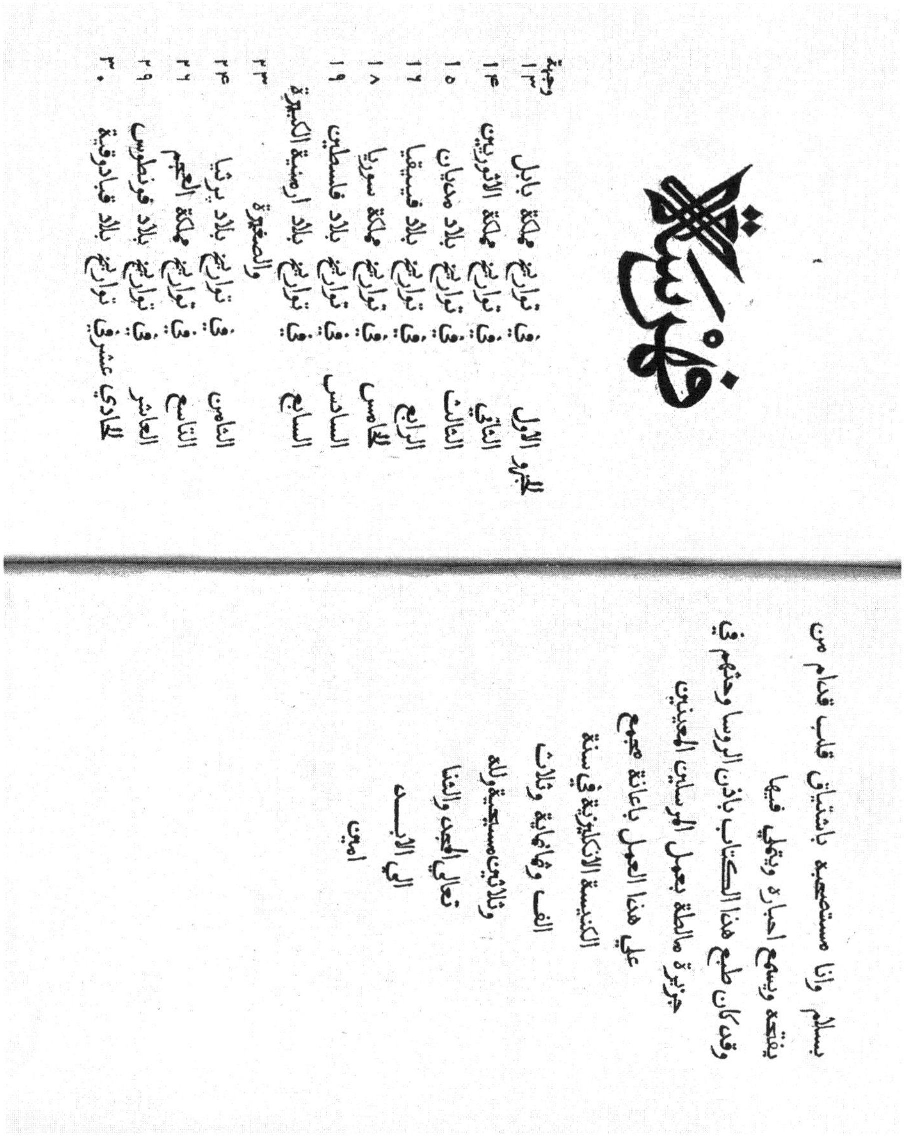

Figure 6. [PINNOCK, William.] *Kitāb Tawārīkh mukhtaṣar* [Concise book of histories (from *A catechism of universal history*)]. [Malta] 1833. Cambridge University Library, 8828.d.46. Set in Watts types. A traditional MS-style tapered colophon is followed by a more modern table of contents, with the engraved heading *Fihrist* containing a rather fanciful rendering of the final *tā'*

كتاب

تواريخ مختصر ينبي عن ممالك وبلاد عديدة

وما حدث فيها

من قديم الزمان الي عصرنا هذا

١٨٣٣

Figure 7. [PINNOCK, William.] *Kitāb Tawārīkh mukhtaṣar* [Concise book of histories (from *A catechism of universal history*)]. [Malta] 1833. Cambridge University Library, 8828.d.46. Title-page set in Watts types, with word *Kitāb* calligraphically engraved; woodcut vignette of European origin, depicting a missionary engaged in a literary discussion with a 'native'.

سـنة ١٨٣٣ — نمره ١

بشهر كانون الثاني — شهر طوبه

اخبار القاصد

تشتمل علي سته قضايا

القضيه الاولي تعلن حياة الناس المسيحيين الفاضلين الذين كانوا ساكنين في بر مصر وسوريا وفلسطين من ابتدا انتشار الديانه المسيحيه حتي الان

القضيه الثانيه تخبر عن انتشار الانجيل الالهي في اربع اقطار المسكونه

القضيه الثالثه تتضمن اخبار الكتب المقدسه

القضيه الرابعه تخبر عن حسن التربيه

القضيه الخامسه تتضمن بعض ايات ثمينه مفيده ماخوذة من الكتب المقدسه

القضيه السادسه تحوي بعض نموذجات مقتبسه من كتب مفيدة

خبر وجيز عن حياة السيد المسيح له المجد

السيد المسيح له المجد ولد من عذرة طاهرة قديسة تدعي مريم في بيت لحم قرية صغيرة في ارض يهوذا مشهورة كون داود النبي ولد فيها * وميلاده حدث وقتما فسد الزمان وجنس البشري احتاج الي معونة قوته * فاتيانه كان موعودا من زمان مديد * فاوليك الذين كانوا قاطنين بين شعوبه شعروا فى احتياج المخلص وانتظروه مع الحمية الحقيقية ثم بعد ذلك ولد ميلادا عجيبا مشهورا * وتبجل من الملايكة العلويين واستقام في صبوته تحت الطاعة العظيمة وتربى تربية حسنة مقدسة * وبعد ذلك شب فى القامه والمجد

وصار فتي وفرح كافة الناس وعاش متخفيا حتي صار عمره ثلاثين سنة ثم ان يوحنا صابغه ظهر في نهر الاردن مملوا من الروح الطاهر والغيرة الحارة ومن الاتضاع القلبي ثم انه بشر الشعوب قايلا ان المخلص قد ظهر وتهددهم بان يسهلوا طريق السيد المسيح له المجد * فخدمة يوحنا كانت انه يعد طريق المخلص فقط ولاجل ذلك وبخ الخطاة وامرهم بان يتوبوا ويمهدوا الطريق * وايضا دعاهم لاجل التطهير (فاما يوحنا المعمدان فانتهت حياته في السجن وهناك قطع راسه ومات) ثم ان السيد له المجد اتي وتعمد من يوحنا في نهر الاردن اجتهارا قدام ساير الناس * ثم كشف ذاته لهم من بعد

Figure 8. *Akhbār al-Qāṣid* [News of the straight path], no.1. Malta 1833. Bulletin in newspaper format, 25x21 cm., set in two sizes of the Watts types, with engraved calligraphic title surmounted by a woodcut vignette.

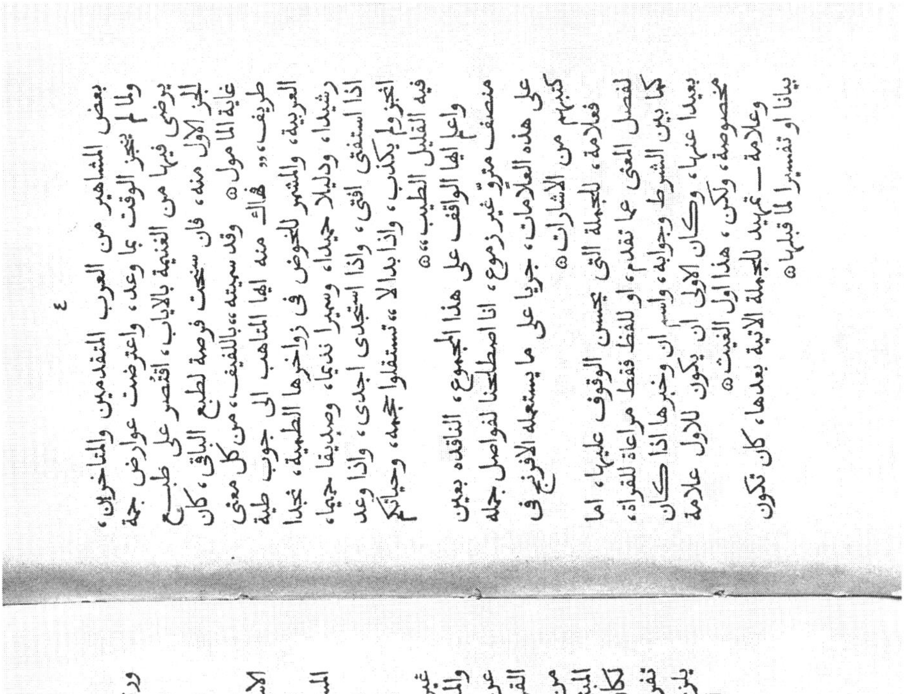

Figure 9.[FĀRIS al-SHIDYĀQ.] *Al-Lafīf fī kull ma'nā ṭarīf* [The throng, on every exquisite meaning.] Malta 1839. Cambridge University Library, Moh.315.d.18. Set in the smaller size of 1838 types. Two pages from the introduction, setting out the punctuation marks (*'alāmāt*) and explaining their use.

Christian Missionaries and Colloquial Arabic Printing

Heather J. Sharkey

University of Pennsylvania

Introduction

In the nineteenth and early twentieth centuries, Christian missionaries played active roles in the development of modern Arabic publishing. First in Malta, and later in Beirut and Cairo, they printed works that ranged from the Bible to classroom textbooks and thereby influenced the content, style, and even typographic formatting of modern Arabic literature.[1] Yet while the great majority of missionary publications were produced in literary Arabic (*al-fuṣḥā*), the formal language which has historically been the accepted medium for written discourse, missionaries in the 1920s and '30s also published some works in the regionally and socially variable spoken or colloquial Arabic (*al-'āmmiyya*) of the non-elite, ordinary people.

The missionaries who published works in the Arabic colloquial hoped that it would take off as a print language and in the process extend literacy rates among peoples they wished to evangelise. But ultimately it failed to do so, while efforts to promote the *'āmmiyya* provoked opposition among educated Arabic-speakers who insisted on the cultural primacy of the *fuṣḥā* as the expressive literary vehicle for all Arabs. The resentments that missionaries stoked — through their language policies and, much more broadly, through their evangelical work — still smoulder today.

This article considers missionary objectives in promoting colloquial Arabic as a print language, the controversies that ensued from their efforts, and the long-term consequences of their *'āmmiyya* experiments. The main focus is on Egypt during the interwar period of the twentieth century, years when the missionary enterprise was at

The author would like to thank Knut Vikør, for delivering the author's conference paper at the Mainz symposium on printing, and Peter Gran, for offering a valuable suggestion on sources.

1 Geoffrey Roper, *Arabic Printing in Malta, 1825–1845: Its History and Its Place in the Development of Print Culture in the Arab Middle East*, unpublished Ph.D. thesis (University of Durham 1988); Dagmar Glass, *Malta, Beirut, Leipzig and Beirut Again: Eli Smith, the American Syria Mission and the Spread of Arabic Typography in Nineteenth-Century Lebanon* (Beirut 1998).

its peak and when mission-supported colloquial publishing was enjoying its short-lived heyday.

The Missionaries and Their Movement

The missionaries who promoted colloquial Arabic were British and American Protestants, men and women, who in the 1880s began to express a growing commitment to work in Muslim societies. In discussing their goal of converting Muslims to Christianity, they arguably absorbed and adapted the aggressive expansionist rhetoric of the British Empire in the late Victorian and Edwardian periods.[2] Certainly they took a combative line toward Islam itself. In 1906, for example, an American missionary in Punjab declared that Islam was Christianity's 'only rival for the conquest of the world' and urged his fellow missionaries to scramble for souls in Africa, India, and China.[3] Along a similar vein, in 1910, a British missionary in Iran praised his colleagues in the Islamic world as 'Crusaders of the twentieth century' who were conducting 'spiritual warfare' in order to 'bring Christianity back to the East ....'[4]

These missionaries to Muslims were not operating in mutual isolation. On the contrary, they belonged to a global Anglo-American enterprise whose leaders boldly called for 'the evangelisation of the world in this generation'.[5] Drawn together through a growing ecumenical 'inter-mission' movement that bridged denominational differences,[6] Christian missionaries gathered in regular conferences to discuss techniques for evangelising among Muslims and published several conference-paper volumes (many for internal, private circulation only) that set out their common plans and objectives.

---

2 See Clifton J. Phillips, 'Changing Attitudes in the Student Volunteer Movement of Great Britain and North America, 1886–1928', in Torben Christensen and William R. Hutchison (eds), *Missionary Ideologies in the Imperialist Era: 1880–1920* (Århus 1982), 131–45 and esp. 131, 136.

3 Rev. E.M. Wherry, 'Introduction', in E.M. Wherry (ed.), *Methods of Mission Work among Moslems* (New York 1906), 10–11.

4 Rev. W.A. Rice, *Crusaders of the Twentieth Century, or the Christian Missionary and the Muslim: An Introduction to Work among Muhammadans* (London 1910), xlv–xlvi.

5 John R. Mott, *The Evangelization of the World in This Generation* (New York 1905); William R. Hutchison, *Errand to the World: American Protestant Thought and Foreign Missions* (Chicago 1987), 90–124; William R. Hutchison, 'A Moral Equivalent for Imperialism: Americans and the Promotion of 'Christian Civilization, 1880–1910', in Christensen and Hutchison (eds), *Missionary Ideologies*, 167–78.

6 Consider, for example, *Minutes of the Egypt Inter-Mission Council* (Cairo 1922), a copy of which is preserved in the Presbyterian Historical Society archives in Philadelphia.

Meanwhile, working on the ground in their respective mission fields, missionaries attempted to reach out to Muslims of all ages and social classes by establishing rural and urban schools, orphanages, clinics, and hospitals. In these various institutions, they tried to spread their Christian message by distributing Bibles and religious pamphlets but encountered a basic obstacle: few people could read their books and brochures because of low literacy rates widely prevailing. Before World War I, in the Middle East as in India and Southeast Asia, literacy remained a relative rarity and was still a monopoly of male elites. To communicate broadly, therefore, missionaries decided that they would have to speak and perhaps also write in the language of the masses. For missionaries in Arabophone lands, whose bases of operation ranged from the Maghreb east to Bahrain, writing in the language of the masses meant writing in the *'āmmiyya*, that is, in one of Arabic's widely variable colloquial forms.

Writing the Spoken: Efforts to Systematize Colloquial Arabic

In the late nineteenth and early twentieth centuries, the era of high European imperialism, missionaries in Africa and Asia participated in a wide range of 'colonial linguistic projects' — codifying alien languages and pursuing philological study in order to map the ethnic terrain.[7] Among peoples who had historically been non-literate, this work of linguistic systemization formalized and reified particular dialects as regional languages, thereby catapulting them to the top of emergent language hierarchies. For example, in southern Rhodesia (later Zimbabwe), where there had been 'a graded continuum of Shona dialects' before the twentieth century, competing Protestant and Catholic missionaries had by 1930 'produced three mutually distinct [Shona] languages within their territorially delimited spheres of influence'.[8] Through comparable processes, from Indonesia to Madagascar, new 'missionary lingua francas' came into being within imperial domains[9] and gained some currency as print languages — if only via Bible translations. Meanwhile, in regions that already had literacy traditions, missionaries engaged in advanced philological and grammatical

7 Joseph Errington, 'Colonial Linguistics', *Annual Review of Anthropology* 30 (2001), 19–20.
8 Ibid., 24, drawing upon Terence Ranger, 'Missionaries, Migrants and the Manyika: The Invention of Ethnicity in Zimbabwe', in Leroy Vail (ed.), *The Creation of Tribalism in Southern Africa* (Berkeley 1989), 127.
9 Errington, 'Colonial Linguistics', 25.

study and worked to produce Christian literatures capable of reaching out to local audiences, often directing their persuasive efforts toward local literate elites.

Missionaries tended to take the latter approach toward the Arab peoples, who had a long and strong tradition of literacy and enjoyed a lingua franca in the Arabic *fuṣḥā,* the vehicle for learned (and usually written) discourse that educated Arabs could understand regardless of marked variations in their informal speech (i.e. their *'āmmiyya*s). Arabic also had a deep tradition of linguistic scholarship, which had roots in studies of the Qur'ān, a text regarded not only as the sacred Islamic scripture but also as the ultimate model of beautiful Arabic. Over many centuries, Islamic philologists and grammarians had analysed the Qur'ān's language and articulated standards for Arabic expression that writers were encouraged to follow. In other words, they had endeavoured to maintain a normative literary language in spite of the divergences in Arabic dialects, which grew more pronounced as Arabic-Islamic culture expanded territorially and assimilated or incorporated non-Arab peoples. Written Arabic thus achieved a high degree of fixity, though it never became static. On the contrary, changes in the language subtly and constantly occurred over the centuries — for example, as Arabic literati borrowed or coined new words in response to shifting social milieus.[10]

By the late nineteenth century, when British and American missionaries began to pursue their work among Muslims, Arabic could boast a firmly established written tradition with an illustrious literary past. Nevertheless, the pace of linguistic change had already begun to accelerate as the rapid growth of print culture and rising literacy rates encouraged new modes of literary experimentation among an expanding pool of readers and writers. Far from existing as a timeless or classical language, therefore, the *fuṣḥā* was on its way to becoming a 'Modern Standard Arabic' (to use the late twentieth-century English parlance) with a wealth of new vocabulary words and stylistic conventions.[11] The bulk of missionary production in Arabic appeared in this literary language and targeted educated male elites.

10 Roger Allen, *The Arabic Literary Heritage: The Development of Its Genres and Criticism* (Cambridge 1998), 17–24; B. Weiss, 'Arabic Language', in Julie Scott Meisami and Paul Starkey (eds), *Encyclopedia of Arabic Literature*, vol. 1(London 1998), 101–2.

11 M.M. Badawi, *A Short History of Modern Arabic Literature* (Oxford 1993), 1–18; see also Ami Ayalon, *The Press in the Arab Middle East: A History* (New York 1995).

Nevertheless, from the early twentieth century some missionaries began to express an interest in extending their program to larger audiences of the barely literate, those who knew how to read little more than the Arabic alphabet. Their thinking was that if they could produce works in the language that the barely literate actually spoke (as opposed to the formal *fuṣḥā* language that people could only learn through years of focussed study), then they would stand a chance of overcoming the high educational barrier that Arabic literacy had historically posed.

Missionaries were not the first to seize on this idea of writing and printing the plebeian vernacular. In the early 1880s, just before and after Britain's colonial Occupation of Egypt in 1882, a small group of Europeans and Americans in Cairo had already voiced doubts about the capacity of the Arabic *fuṣḥā* to function as a mass medium. These foreigners had suggested that literary Arabic's sharp divergence from colloquial Arabic, in vocabulary, pronunciation, and syntax, made it inaccessible to all but the highly educated minority and that it therefore posed an obstacle to modern social progress.

The first to stake these claims had been a German named Wilhelm Spitta (1853–83), who arrived in Egypt in 1870 to direct Khedive Isma'il's Vice-regal Library. Spitta became an enthusiastic student of the spoken, everyday language and published a grammatical study of the Egyptian *'āmmiyya* as well as a collection of colloquial tales.[12] Anticipating the missionaries by more than twenty years, Spitta advocated the adoption of colloquial Arabic as a written language in lieu of the *fuṣḥā*. Convinced that the Arabic script was a factor contributing to Egypt's low literacy rates, in part because of its non-representation of short vowels, he devised a new 'Egyptian alphabet', based on Roman letters (i.e. a modified Latin print orthography), for rendering colloquial phonetics. Spitta was thus the first to call for the elevation of colloquial Arabic — specifically in a Romanised Cairene form — as a language of print culture.[13]

As the nineteenth century ended other Westerners took up and expanded on Spitta's Arabic agenda, while expressing keen admiration for what they regarded as

12 Wilhelm Spitta, *Grammatik des arabischen Vulgärdialectes von Aegypten* (Leipzig 1880); Wilhelm Spitta, *Contes arabes modernes* (Leiden 1883).

13 [Daniel] Willard Fiske, *An Egyptian Alphabet for the Egyptian People*, 2nd edn (Florence 1904), 1–34. Spitta's system entailed exclusive use of lower-case letters and dispensing with conventions of capitalization — a reform that, in Fiske's view, marked an advance over the spelling conventions of European languages. Fiske, *An Egyptian Alphabet*, 23–4.

the structural logic and dynamism of the colloquial language. The German Karl Vollers, for example, who worked as a director at Cairo's Dar al-Kutub, asserted that modern Arabic dialects were 'not mere degenerate forms of the classical idiom', as Arabic scholars had often suggested, but rather languages with histories and lives of their own.[14]

Further emphasizing the colloquial's independence, J. Selden Willmore, a British judge in the Cairo Native Court of Appeal, boldly if dubiously asserted that Cairene colloquial Arabic had closer affinities to Hebrew and Aramaic than to the Arabic of the Qur'ān. (Willmore was perhaps evincing the kind of 'fantasmic representation of authoritative certainty in the face of spectacular ignorance', which was a hallmark of colonial linguistics).[15] Willmore further averred that Cairene Arabic deserved to be a language of literature and warned that unless Arabs adopted a simpler written language (closer to the vernacular), Arabic as a whole 'would be gradually ousted, as the intercourse with European nations increases, by a foreign tongue'.[16] Meanwhile, Daniel Willard Fiske, an American literary scholar (and expert on the Icelandic sagas and Dante) championed Arabic typographical reform and the widespread application of Spitta's Romanised alphabet, calling the Arabic script itself a kind of educational and visual 'torture'.[17] By the time missionaries began to promote colloquial Arabic printing in the first years of the twentieth century, they were able to join this small but vocal chorus.

Missionaries and the Barely Literate: Colloquial Arabic's Appeal

Upon arriving in Egypt, British and American missionaries devoted years to Arabic study, even as they pursued their routine of evangelistic, educational, medical or administrative work. For many, learning Arabic was an ongoing struggle. One missionary, for example, described it as a looming mountain to be crossed, and remarked that the humbling and discouraging experience of five years of 'plodding' in

---

14 K. Vollers, *The Modern Egyptian Dialect of Arabic: A Grammar*, trans. F.C. Burkitt (Cambridge 1895), 2.

15 S. Greenblatt, 'Kidnapping Language', in *Marvellous Possessions: The Wonder of the New World* (Chicago 1991), 89 cited in Errington, 'Colonial Linguistics', 20.

16 J. Selden Willmore, *The Spoken Arabic of Egypt* (London 1901), viii, xii.

17 Fiske, *An Egyptian Alphabet*, 25.

Arabic study had forced him into 'a deeper devotional life in order to keep up good-cheer'.[18]

Originally, missionaries had formally studied only Classical Arabic (here implying a focus on early and medieval Islamic texts) and were expected to pick up the colloquial in the course of daily work. That approach began to change in 1912, when W.H.T. Gairdner, a prominent member of the British Church Missionary Society (more commonly known as the CMS), decided that he should teach new missionaries not the literary Arabic of the Qur'ān, but rather the spoken language of ordinary Cairenes: this, he felt, would be more practical and immediately useful. Gairdner's efforts to analyse and teach this language culminated in a textbook that he published in 1917, simply titled *Egyptian Colloquial Arabic.* Emphasizing the development of daily conversational skills, his book appeared in later editions and also provided the model for other colloquial Arabic textbooks, such as one devised by missionaries for use in the northern Sudan.[19] In the words of his biographer, Gairdner had 'discovered that, far from being only a rather slovenly and degraded form of the written tongue, [colloquial Cairene Arabic] was a living language following very exact grammatical and phonetical rules of its own'.[20] In other words, Gairdner's research into Arabic dialectology led him to feel the same kind of admiration for the colloquial that Spitta, Vollers, Willmore and others had earlier expressed.

In 1922, five years after Gairdner's book appeared, an interdenominational group of American missionaries convened in Cairo to survey the Christian literature available for Muslim audiences and to suggest plans for future development. 'One common fact at once emerges', they wrote in their report, 'The Moslem World is learning to read.' They noted that more Muslims were attending schools, that literacy rates were rising, and that demand was growing among educated males for technical books, encyclopaedias, and even cheap detective stories.[21]

---

18 Presbyterian Historical Society, Philadelphia (henceforth abbreviated PHS), UPCNA RG 209-1-02: J.W. Acheson Papers, Acheson to Anderson, Cairo, 18 March 1918.

19 W.H.T. Gairdner, *Egyptian Colloquial Arabic: A Conversation Grammar and Reader* (Cambridge 1917); other revised editions were published in 1926 and posthumously in 1944 and 1953. This book was the model for R.S. Macdonald and Mary Wright (comps) '*Da Kitab*' *A Sudanese Colloquial Grammar*, ed. J. Spencer Trimingham (Cairo 1939).

20 Constance E. Padwick, *Temple Gairdner of Cairo* (London 1929), 222–5.

21 American Committee on Survey [sic] of Christian Literature for Moslems, *The Power of the Printed Page in the World of Islam* (Cairo 1922), 4, 10.

But they also sounded a cautionary note, observing that many Muslims were learning how to read little more than the Arabic alphabet. They identified a growing class of people 'who, through the spread of education, have had enough schooling to teach them the phonetic values of the Arabic alphabet, but who, as they mouth out their syllables, fail to get the sense of what they read in classical Arabic, because they have not gone far enough to learn the literary vocabulary'. To cater to this 'great and populous borderland between literacy and illiteracy', the American missionaries advocated printing simple illustrated texts that would use the colloquial language.[22] In 1925, a British woman missionary supported a similar venture. 'Moslem lands today', she wrote, 'with the modern increase of primary education, have a new population of half-readers or stuttering readers who cannot attain to the glories of high literature, but who are, like all normal human beings, hungry for stories'.[23]

The Goals and Achievements of the Missionaries' Colloquial Printing

In the early 1920s, therefore, British and American missionaries began to promote the development of printed colloquial Arabic materials, sometimes pooling their efforts to do so. Five points can summarize their aims and motives in these endeavours.

The first and most basic point is that missionaries wanted to evangelize among Muslims, and believed that they could reach out to the illiterate and barely literate masses by printing texts in the language spoken by humble people. Female missionaries were especially eager to reach out to women, including those who lived in relative seclusion, but female literacy rates were minute in the early twentieth-century Arab world — thus making colloquial materials seem especially useful for women's evangelical work.[24]

Second, Protestants believed that men and women should be able to read, understand, and personally interpret the Bible in the vernacular — that is, in the

22 Ibid., 21.

23 Constance E. Padwick, 'Some Types of Literature in the World of Islam', in John R. Mott (ed.), *The Moslem World of Today* (London 1925), 155–65, see esp. 162–3.

24 On missions and women in the Islamic world, see, for example, Annie von Summer and Samuel M. Zwemer, *Daylight in the Harem* (Edinburgh 1911); Caroline M. Buchanan, 'Movements in the Life of Women in the Islamic World: The Near and Middle East', in Mott (ed.) *The Moslem World of Today*, 209–27; Guli Francis-Dehqani, 'CMS Women Missionaries in Persia: Perceptions of Muslim Women and Islam, 1884–1934', in Kevin Ward and Brian Stanley (eds), *The Church Mission Society and World Christianity, 1799–1999* (Richmond 2000), 91–119.

common language or dialect spoken by ordinary people.[25] In other words, they believed that the Bible should not be the exclusive and esoteric preserve of a clergy or educated elite. In the Middle East, missionary efforts to translate portions of the Bible into colloquial Arabic were part of a worldwide translation project through which missionaries translated scriptures into such diverse languages as Ibo, Tamil, and Malay — in many cases helping to codify or revive languages in the context of modern print culture.[26]

Third, missionaries found colloquial Arabic appealing because it did not seem bound to the Islamic literary tradition centred on the Qur'ān. Along these lines, some missionaries hinted in the 1920s and early '30s that their promotion of colloquial Arabic as a print language might enable Christianity to grow within Muslim societies at a time when the collapse of the Ottoman Empire and its caliphate had led to political and ideological fragmentation.[27] In non-Muslim regions (notably, for example, in the Nuba Mountains of Sudan), some believed that colloquial Arabic — particularly when rendered in Roman or Latin print — could act as a communications barrier to Islamisation.[28]

Fourth, missionaries seemed to believe that colloquial Arabic had a genuinely promising future as a print language, and that local variants would flourish in tandem with the rise of country-specific nationalisms. One commentator thought that colloquial Arabic's prospects were especially bright in Algeria, where colonial

25 The Wycliffe Organization of Bible translators and its affiliate, SIL International (formerly known as the Summer Institute of Linguistics) continue to promote Bible translations on the grounds that all languages are gifts of God and '[e]very language deserves to see its language in print and to have some literature written in it'. Linguistic Creed of SIL International at http://www.sil.org/sil/linguistic_creed.htm (Accessed December 31, 2002).

26 Errington, 'Colonial Linguistics'. Consider, for example, the role of nineteenth-century Christian missionaries in producing Tamil language translations, grammars, and lexicons which contributed to the assertion of Dravidian sub-nationalism and Tamil print culture in southern India. Sumathi Ramaswamy, *Passions of the Tongue: Language Devotion in Tamil India, 1891–1970* (Berkeley 1997); V. Ravindiran, 'Discourses of Empowerment: Missionary Orientalism in the Development of Dravidian Nationalism', in Timothy Brook and André Schmid (eds), *Nation Work: Asian Elites and National Identities* (Ann Arbor 2000), 51–82. For a brief but thought-provoking commentary on the impact of missionary Bible translation, see Lamin Sanneh, *Encountering the West: Christianity and the Global Cultural Process: The African Dimension* (Maryknoll, NY 1993), 18.

27 See the following essays in Mott (ed.), *The Moslem World of Today*: John R. Mott, Foreword, vii–xii; D.S. Margoliouth, 'The Caliphate Yesterday, To-Day, and To-Morrow', 31–44; and Anonymous, 'The Institution of the Caliphate and the Spirit of the Age', 45–58.

28 This view is implicitly expressed in W. Wilson Cash, *The Nubas Calling: A Challenge to Pioneer Missionary Adventure among Sudan Hill Tribes* (London 1933), 11, 24–5. See also Heather J. Sharkey, 'Christians among Muslims: the Church Missionary Society in the Northern Sudan', *Journal of African History* 43 (2002), 51–75.

education was creating an educated class that was highly proficient in French but weak in classical Arabic.[29] Moreover, colloquial Arabic supporters frequently compared the Arabic *fuṣḥā* to Latin and the *'āmmiyya* to Italian, suggesting that the former was stilted, moribund, and on its way to extinction and that the latter was vibrant and modern.[30]

A fifth and final motive is that few Christian missionaries knew literary Arabic well or felt confident with the Classical texts they had studied, but on the contrary learned colloquial Arabic while interacting with patients in clinics, children in schools, and so on. Conversant in and comfortable with everyday Arabic speech, missionaries welcomed the idea of printing materials in a simple conversational medium that they themselves could understand. The lack of literary Arabic language skills may have been especially pronounced among women, many of whom served on short-term missionary contracts or came in their capacity as wives (in the latter case often doing mission work along with their husbands but without being treated, or paid, as official missionaries).[31] Indeed, although women were increasingly important to the missionary enterprise of the period, they seldom pursued work of Islamic or Arabic scholarship.[32]

These were the motives that prompted missionaries to call for the printing of colloquial Arabic materials. However, assessing their colloquial output is difficult because their printed materials, intended for the semi-literate and therefore the non-powerful, appear to have been ephemeral and rarely if ever made their way into the libraries and other scholarly institutions that preserve the high culture of intellectuals.

---

29 American Committee on ... Christian Literature for Moslems, *The Power of the Printed Page*, 51.

30 For example, Spitta cited in Fiskę, *An Egyptian Alphabet*, 6–7; Vollers, *The Modern Egyptian Dialect*, 3–4.

31 I was particularly struck by the pattern of short-term female missionary work in the Nile Valley when consulting certain documents (notably the 'Original Papers, Northern Sudan mission, 1931–34') preserved in CMS archives at Birmingham University. Regarding women and missions in this period more generally, see Fiona Bowie, 'Introduction: reclaiming women's presence', in Fiona Bowie, Deborah Kirkwood, and Shirley Ardener (eds), *Women and Missions: Past and Present, Anthropological and Historical Perceptions* (Providence, R.I. 1993), 1–19; Mary Taylor Huber and Nancy C. Lutkehaus, 'Introduction: gendered missions at home and abroad', in Mary Taylor Huber and Nancy C. Lutkehaus (eds), *Gendered Missions: Women and Men in Missionary Discourse and Practice* (Ann Arbor 1999), 1–38. On the status of missionary wives, see Francis-Dehqani, 'CMS Women Missionaries in Persia', 100–3.

32 An exception was the British missionary-scholar Constance E. Padwick, who was affiliated to the Nile Mission Press in Cairo. Padwick produced two biographical works on British missionaries to Muslims as well as a study of Muslim prayer-manuals, which remains in print today. Constance E. Padwick, *Temple Gairdner of Cairo* (1929); *Henry Martyn: Confessor of the Faith* (London 1922), and *Muslim Devotions: A Study of Prayer-Manuals in Common Use* (London 1961; Oxford 1996).

In other words, mission records make it much easier to gauge missionary intentions than actual accomplishments insofar as colloquial printing is concerned.

Judging from reports, however, this much is clear: By the 1920s, British and American missionaries were printing colloquial Arabic texts on cheap paper, in single sheets or in thin booklets; they were also tailoring these materials to regional audiences, for example, in Algiers, where American missionaries printed local folk tales. They were using their colloquial publications in schools and clinics, and during home visits when female missionaries visited women. At conferences and in reports, missionaries stressed the need for a wider range of colloquial literature, calling for more Christian stories, more materials catering for women, and more texts discussing hygiene, social responsibility, and aspects of daily life.[33] They appear to have used these instructional texts in tandem with pictorial materials, such as large coloured pictures of Jesus, Moses, and other Biblical figures, or glass-plate lantern-slide images projected onto screens.[34]

One of the largest publishers of colloquial texts was the Nile Mission Press in Cairo, which by 1922 had produced Bible passages and commentaries, two hymn books, and stories about the life of Jesus and the Creation and Fall of mankind. The Nile Mission Press used these materials in Egypt and also exported them abroad, for example, to American missionaries in the Maghreb and Bahrain.[35] The Nile Mission Press had a global reach: in 1925, it shipped special consignments intended 'for [missionary] work among Arab sailors in a port of British Columbia' as well as to Ecuador, South Africa, and China.[36]

Most of these printed materials presumably reproduced colloquial Arabic using the Arabic script, for indeed mission reports seldom engage in discussions about

33 American Committee on ... Christian Literature for Moslems, *The Power of the Printed Page,* 21–3, 50–1. In 1931 a British missionary in the Northern Sudan issued a plea for more colloquial materials in a document now preserved in the CMS archive at the University of Birmingham: CMS G3/SN/O/1931/3: Notes on CMS Work in the Northern Sudan, by Mr. S.A. Morrison.

34 Regarding coloured pictures, see PHS, UPCNA RG 209-1-01: Papers of J.W. Acheson, 'Inspiring News from the Southern Sudan', attached to a letter dated March 16, 1925; regarding lantern slides, see Rev. W. Goldsack, 'How to Reach and Teach Illiterate Moslems', in Wherry (ed.), *Methods,* 31. Lantern-slide shows were used widely among separate male and female audiences, for example, in northern Sudan. Church Missionary Society archives, University of Birmingham, CMS G3 E O 1925: Lilian V. Jackson to Mr. Manley, dated CMS Girls' School, Omdurman, March 17th 1925.

35 American Committee on ... Christian Literature for Moslems, *The Power of the Printed Page,* 31–3, 44–8, 53.

36 PHS, UPCNA RG 209-1-04: J.W. Acheson Papers, 'A Summary of N.M.P. Annual Report for 1925' (Nile Mission Press), attached to a letter from Acheson to Edie dated March 16, 1925.

orthography and typography. However, in at least one case — in the Nuba Mountains of Sudan — British missionaries in the early 1930s consciously chose to render the Arabic colloquial in the Latin alphabet and in this manner published a textbook for teaching Nuba children how to read. In this Nuba Mountains case, missionaries believed or hoped that 'Romanised Arabic' would thwart the spread of Islam among people who were still practicing traditional religions by propagating a form of literacy that would nevertheless cut its users off from mainstream Arabic texts.[37] Their behaviour was characteristic of a period when Christian missionaries regarded Islam as an arch-enemy battling for African souls.

Finally, there was another important genre of colloquial Arabic book that missionaries actively published: namely, textbooks targeting English-speaking audiences of missionaries, colonial officials, and assorted other expatriates who needed or wanted to learn the everyday language. Most of these textbooks used a combination of Arabic and Latin typeface for rendering the colloquial. Gairdner's 1912 volume was the pacesetter but others followed, such as the *Egyptian Colloquial Arabic Reader* (1927), by the American Presbyterian missionary Earl Edgar Elder.[38]

The Demise of Colloquial Printing

The heyday of colloquial Arabic printing was brief, occurring in the interwar period of the 1920s and '30s. Missionaries' enthusiasm for developing a colloquial Arabic literature diminished as they gradually downgraded or abandoned their plans for evangelising among Muslim peoples. Various shifts were occurring in mission thought, Arab societies, and global politics to bring about this change in priorities. Three relevant trends stand out here.

First, by the 1930s, mainline American and British Protestant organizations were beginning to lose some of the optimism, militancy, and cultural arrogance which had convinced church leaders of an earlier generation that rapid, worldwide, mass evangelisation was both possible and desirable.[39] Perhaps the book which best

37 Sharkey, 'Christians among Muslims', 68–71.

38 Gairdner, *Egyptian Colloquial Arabic*; Earl Edgar Elder, *Egyptian Colloquial Arabic Reader* (London 1927).

39 Hutchison, *Errand to the World*, 146–75. The term 'mainline' here refers to Protestant organizations such as the Presbyterians, Anglicans, Congregationalists and Methodists; it does not refer to pentecostal organizations which pushed a new wave of missions to Muslims in the late twentieth century.

exemplified this new soul-searching was *Re-thinking Missions after One Hundred Years*, published in the United States and undertaken by a 'Laymen's Foreign Missions Inquiry' in 1932.[40]

Second, Christian missionaries throughout the Islamic world were beginning to reckon with the fact that relatively few Muslims had converted despite their years of vigorous efforts. Pressure was mounting within missions to redirect limited resources and energies into areas where Christianity was expanding dramatically, notably, in sub-Saharan Africa.[41] Financial pressure became especially acute in the 1930s as the Depression eroded foreign mission budgets.

Third, with the collapse of the British and French empires in the Middle East after World War II, Christian missionaries lost the protection of the foreign powers which had allowed them to pursue their aims on the ground without much regard for Muslim sentiment. After decolonisation, Christian missionaries knew that they would be remaining in the Middle East only at the sufferance of Muslim governments and that to evangelise among Muslims would be to risk wholesale expulsion.[42] In the years ahead foreign Christian organizations in the Arab world abandoned or de-emphasized their religious mission while continuing to provide social services, or refocused their attention onto local Christian minorities and expatriates.[43] At the same time, the actions that some postcolonial governments took to nationalize missionary schools — for example, in Egypt and Sudan in the late 1950s — sharply curtailed missionary options.[44] In this context some Christian thinkers began to emphasize the idea of cultural encounter and exchange in their relations with Muslims, thereby participating

40 Laymen's Foreign Missions Inquiry: Commission of Appraisal, *Re-thinking Missions: A Laymens' Inquiry after One Hundred Years*, ed. William Ernest Hocking (New York 1932).

41 Consider the case of northern Sudan during the Anglo-Egyptian period (1898–1956) where CMS missionaries gained only one Muslim convert during fifty years of work. Their colleagues in southern Sudan, by contrast, sponsored conversions by the score. Sharkey, 'Christians among Muslims'.

42 Jacques Waardenburg, 'The Contemporary Period, 1950–1995', in Jacques Waardenburg (ed.), *Muslim Perceptions of Other Religions: A Historical Survey* (New York 1999), 85–101.

43 For example, regarding the balancing act performed by the American University in Cairo vis-à-vis the Egyptian government after the establishment of Israel in 1948 and the Free Officers coup of 1952, see Lawrence R. Murphy, *The American University in Cairo: 1919–1987* (Cairo 1987).

44 Regarding Egypt, see, for example, Sohirin Mohammad Solihin, *Copts and Muslims: A Study on Harmony and Hostility* (Leicester 1991), 44–5. Regarding Sudan, where the nationalization of missionary schools had a major impact on the southern region, see, for example, John O. Voll, 'Imperialism, Nationalism, and Missionaries: Lessons from Sudan for the Twenty-First Century', *Islam and Christian-Muslim Relations* 8:1 (1997), 39–52.

in what the next generation of theologians began to describe as the interfaith dialogue movement.[45]

In any case, by the 1950s, colloquial Arabic appeared doomed as a print language. Pan-Arab ideals were flourishing, and standard literary Arabic was providing critical cultural ground for transcending national boundaries. Standard literary Arabic arguably became the most important platform of Arab identity as formalized by membership in the Arab League, which grew after 1945 to embrace not only the countries of the Arabian Peninsula and the Fertile Crescent but also the whole of northern Africa.

In the late twentieth century, the dramatic expansion of state-sponsored education made the Arabic *fuṣḥā* more widely accessible still, even as substantial segments within Arab countries — for example, more than half the female populations of Egypt and Morocco — remained unable to read and write.[46] Against this context, the colloquial enjoyed only limited applications in print. Some novelists, for example, rendered the *'āmmiyya* in dialogue to convey a setting or to suggest a character's class or ethnic background,[47] while some poets (building upon centuries-old local traditions of Arabic oral poetry) composed verse in dialect in an attempt to reach out to audiences beyond the elites while signalling their social commitment. However, this *'āmmiyya* poetry tended to gain more recognition as folk art than as work of high cultural merit, reflecting the *fuṣḥā*'s continued paramountcy as the expected language of literary expression.[48]

---

45 Hugh Goddard, *A History of Christian-Muslim Relations* (Chicago 2000); Timothy Yates, *Christian Mission in the Twentieth Century* (Cambridge 1994), especially 133–92.

46 According to UNESCO, 56.1 per cent of Egyptian women and 63.9 per cent of Moroccan women were illiterate according to 1986 and 1994 figures respectively. United Nations Statistics Division, 'Indicators on Literacy', http://www.un.org/Depts/unsd/social/literacy.htm (Accessed August 18, 2002).

47 Marilyn Booth, 'Colloquial Arabic Poetry, Politics, and the Press in Modern Egypt', *IJMES* 24 (1992), 419–40. There were late nineteenth- and early twentieth-century precedents for using the colloquial to render dialogue — for example, in Muḥammad Ḥusayn Haykal's 1913 novel, *Zaynab*. Roger Allen, *The Arabic Novel: A Historical and Critical Introduction*, 2nd ed. (Syracuse 1995), 34.

48 Marilyn Booth, 'Poetry in the Vernacular', in M.M. Badawi (ed.), *Modern Arabic Literature*, The Cambridge History of Arabic Literature (Cambridge 1992), 463–4. Regarding the (limited) uses of the colloquial in Arabic literary works of the early and middle Islamic eras, see, for example, Madiha Doss, 'Réflexions sur les débuts de l'écriture dialectale en Égypte', *Égypte/Monde Arabe* 27–8: 3–4 (1996), 119–45.

The Arab Rejection of the *'Āmmiyya*

Ultimately, colloquial printing failed to catch on, less because of the collapse of missionary willpower and financing, and much more because native Arabic-speakers mounted sustained opposition to the idea of elevating the colloquial as a literary language. Strikingly, the colloquial faced resistance from both the Arabic literati and the moderately educated, and among both Muslims and local Christians.

In a 1964 study, the Egyptian historian Naffūsa Zakariyya Sa'īd traced the history of the European and American bid (*da'wa*) to promote the colloquial Arabic language in Egypt after 1880 and adamantly rejected it. 'The call to take the colloquial as a tool for literary expression', she wrote, 'and its displacement (*iḥlāl*) of the Arabic *fuṣḥā* ... exposed Arabic expression to the most violent crisis that it has known during its long history' ... and formed part of a 'biased imperialist call' aiming toward the elimination or extermination (*qaḍā 'alā*) of the literary Arabic.[49] She asserted that men like the British judge J. Selden Willmore, who supported the literary adoption of the colloquial rendered in Latin print, had an inner desire 'to realize one of the goals of British Imperialism, namely the separation of Muslims and Arabs from their past and the destruction (*taftīt*) of their linguistic unity ....' Such Westerners were aiming for the cultural dispossession (*ḥirmān*) of the Arabs, 'but the Egyptians caught on' to their scheme.[50]

Some of Egypt's most distinguished literati shared this vehement opposition to the colloquial agenda. Taha Husayn averred that 'the colloquial lacks the qualities to make it worthy of the name of a language', and expressed hope that with the cultural elevation of the masses, its corrupt forms would disappear. The Nobel laureate Najib Mahfuz was bolder still; describing colloquial Arabic as a sickness, he declared, 'I consider the colloquial one of the failings of our society, exactly like ignorance, poverty and disease'.[51]

Reflecting on Egyptian attitudes toward the Arabic language at the end of the twentieth century, the socio-linguist Niloofar Haeri noted that Egyptians from across the educational spectrum assigned tremendous cultural value to the Arabic *fuṣḥā,* often regardless of their level of mastery in this medium or even of their likelihood to

49 Naffūsa Zakariyya Sa'īd, *Tārīkh al-Da'wa ilā al-'Āmmiyya wa-Atharuhā fī Miṣr* (Alexandria 1964), i, xiii.
50 Ibid., 25–6, 37.
51 Allen, *The Arabic Novel,* 35–6.

use it in writing or formal speech. Egyptians variously described the *fuṣḥā* as an emblem of Arab or Islamic cultural authenticity, as an expressive vehicle for building Arab unity, and as a tool for counteracting foreign domination or the legacies of colonialism and the Christian missionaries. With regard to language policies in particular, some Egyptian intellectuals (along with other Arab scholars) expressed their mistrust of European and American attempts to promote colloquial Arabic and pointed to possible ulterior motives, above all secularisation, Westernisation, and fragmentation — the last an inevitable consequence of any system that would promote local *'āmmiyya* dialects over the trans-regional *fuṣḥā*.[52]

These concerns and suspicions have had an impact on scholarship insofar as they have tended to leave the scholarly field of dialectology — the linguistic study of local Arabic dialects — to foreign (i.e. non-Arab) linguists.[53] A recent Arabic study on the historical emergence and development of the Arabic dialects, written by Abd al-Ghaffar Hilal, a dean at Cairo's al-Azhar University, is no exception to this pattern. Hilal praises God for revealing the Qur'ān in Arabic and emphasizes the role of the Qur'ān — and of the scholars who studied it — in setting a linguistic standard for unifying the otherwise fragmented and dispersed Arab peoples during the Islamic era. He describes the Islamic grammarians and philologists of past centuries as language guardians who tried to guide the masses toward 'exemplary Arabic' (*al-'arabiyya al-namūdhajiyya*) and to purge the language of colloquial influences that would have otherwise weakened its unifying force.[54]

While many Muslims cherish the *fuṣḥā* because of its connections to the language of the Qur'ān, Christian Arabs have favoured the *fuṣḥā* for literary and religious expression as well, regarding it as an elegant and prestigious language and as a dignifying medium. Of course, many missionaries also appreciated its power in rendering Bible translations. This was the case with the American missionary to Syria, C.V.A. Van Dyck, who strove in the late nineteenth century to produce a fresh Arabic *fuṣḥā* translation of the New Testament, which would be sufficiently graceful in its language to appeal to both Muslims and Christians, from Casablanca to Baghdad, while being suitable for evangelistic and educational work as well as for regular

52 Niloofar Haeri, 'Form and Ideology: Arabic Sociolinguistics and Beyond', *Annual Review of Anthropology* 29 (2000), 63, 68–9, 71.
53 Ibid., 64.
54 'Abd al-Ghaffār Hilāl, *al-Lahajāt al-'Arabiyya: Nash'atan wa-Taṭawwuran* (Cairo 1998), 5–6.

worship. Van Dyck's final product was deemed so successful that the American Bible Society and British & Foreign Bible Society agreed to circulate his text jointly in what one church historian describes as a 'landmark' of co-operation between Christian Bible societies.[55]

In the early twentieth century Christian missionaries did attempt to translate portions of the Bible into Arabic dialects, but did not produce full versions in the colloquial, perhaps because audiences were not receptive. Consider the Sudan, where Egyptian Christians helped missionaries to translate portions of the Bible into Sudanese Arabic: these efforts resulted in 1927 in the publication of a Latin-print colloquial Arabic version of the Book of Mark, and in 1955 in an Arabic-script colloquial version of the Book of Luke. Attempting to explain why these colloquial versions never caught on among Sudanese Christian converts, a Bible historian wrote in 1998: 'On the whole Arabic speakers still have a resistance to writing the colloquial language or to using the colloquial language for literature held in any sort of esteem. Folk tales, yes; dialect poetry, yes; but a book of sacred import such as the Bible should be dignified in its language and therefore only the Classical or Literary Arabic is worthy'. Clearly unaware of the early twentieth-century history of Romanised Arabic among missionaries who hoped it would thwart the spread of Islam, this writer speculated that the colloquial translation of Mark may have been rendered in Latin print 'because it was felt by Sudanese [Christians] that the colloquial language was not worthy of the [Arabic] script ....'[56] Instead, Arabic-speaking Protestants in the Sudan used Van Dyck's Arabic *fuṣḥā* translation of the Bible, notwithstanding some of its archaic-sounding vocabulary.[57]

The Sudanese experience suggests that colloquial Arabic may have been a stepping stone for the barely literate, but that learners aspired to more. Proper literacy remained standard Arabic literacy — *fuṣḥā* in Arabic script.

55 E.F.F. Bishop, 'The Arabic Bible after a Century', *The Bible Translator* 15 (1964), 167–72.
56 Janet Persson, *In Our Own Languages: The Story of Bible Translation in Sudan* (Nairobi 1998), 17–18.
57 Ibid., 17.

Conclusion: Missionary Legacies and the Impact of Colloquial Printing

The missionary experiment in developing colloquial Arabic literature was short in duration and limited in scope and yet it nevertheless had a social impact. Above all, it fuelled continuing debates and controversies about Arabic educational policies, the role of the Arabic language in maintaining an Arab-Islamic heritage and identity, and the historical legacies of Christian missionary work among the Arab peoples.

To emphasize the positive while assessing the educational import of the missionary experiment, one could argue the following: In devising a colloquial Arabic literature for the barely literate, missionaries prioritised the educational needs of marginalized groups, including women and the poor, at a time when only privileged social groups had access to rigorous education in standard literary Arabic. In do doing, missionaries were pioneers in two fields: first, in the development of children's literature, that is, of printed materials catering especially to the needs and interests of the young; and second, in the pedagogy of literacy for adults. That is, missionaries recognized that there is a spectrum of literacies and developed materials to help minimally literate adults maintain and perhaps extend their skills.

Yet missionary efforts in colloquial Arabic printing were undeniably part of a larger evangelical project that occurred under the aegis of Western imperialism. Understood thus, Christian missionaries had a very negative long-term impact insofar as they seeded an enduring legacy of ill will among many Arab Muslims and arguably prompted them to adopt their own version of the Christian-Muslim 'clash of civilizations' worldview. Evidence of lingering resentment surfaces in a late twentieth-century Arabic genre of anti-missionary treatises. Written by a multinational assortment of Muslim Arab thinkers (including Lebanese, Egyptians, Saudis and others) these works stress the cultural threat that Christian evangelism and Western culture has posed to Islamic societies in an era of European and later American imperialism.[58]

Several accusations recur in these Arabic writings. Their authors argue, for example, that Christian missionaries demeaned and demoralized Muslims by

58 See, for example, Muṣṭafā Khālidī and ʿUmar Farrūkh, *al-Tabshīr wa-al-Istiʿmār fī al-Bilād al-ʿArabiyya: Ard li-Juhūd al-Mubashshirīn Allati Tarmī ilā Ikhdāʿ al-Sharq lil-Istiʿmār al-Gharbī*, 2nd edn (Beirut 1957); ʿAbd al-ʿAzīz ibn Ibrāhīm al-ʿAskar, *al-Tanṣīr wa-Muḥāwalatuhu fī Bilād al-Khalīj al-ʿArabī* (Riyadh 1993); Malik Manṣūr, *Wasāʾil Imbiryāliyya fī al-Takhrīb al-Thaqāfī* (Baghdad 1977).

denigrating their heritage; that they fomented sectarian conflicts, notably in Lebanon; that they contributed to the political mood among British colonizers that facilitated the Zionist appropriation of Palestine; and significantly for the history of Arabic printing and language study, that they undermined pan-Arab unity by promoting the codification of variant colloquial Arabic writing systems. According to many of these authors, missionary schools and hospitals masqueraded as charity but in fact carried out cultural assaults, by secularising and westernising those they claimed to serve. Despite their efforts and ruses, one of these writers asserted in the 1990s, the missionaries 'made a mistake, because Islam is a tall building which no one can destroy'.[59] These last words, apparently an allusion to the 1993 bombing attack on the World Trade Center in New York City, serve as a reminder that the history of Christian missionaries in the Middle East remains politically charged, and that the history of their efforts in printing and language reform is inextricably bound to larger controversies involving cultural interaction and conflict.

59 Muṣṭafā Fawzī 'Abd al-Laṭīf Ghazal, *al-Ḥiyal wa-al-Asālib al-Munḥarafa fī al-Da'wa ilā al-Tabshīr* (n.p, n.d.), 6. I read this book in the library of the American University in Cairo in July, 2001 — less than two months before the September 11th attacks in the United States. Its rhetoric against 'Jewish Crusading' institutions (p. 69) — a category into which it places the United Nations — is evocative of the discourse of the so-called Qā'ida network. The book also targets the American University in Cairo itself. Referring to the university's early twentieth-century missionary roots, it declares, 'There is no argument about it, the American University in Cairo was and still is a center for Christianisation to a dangerous extent' (p. 29).

The Press: Engine of a Mini-renaissance in Zanzibar (1860–1920)

Philip C. Sadgrove

University of Manchester

The islands of Zanzibar, to which the Omani ruler Seyyid Saʿīd moved his court in 1840, changed in a few decades from a quiet backwater to an important trading centre, creating a small Arab-ruled East African state. The island's Arab and Swahili population as well as conducting trade with the African hinterland and the Arabian Peninsula increased their commercial links with American, British and French merchants. As a consequence of these activities British Indians in increasing numbers settled and traded there. Zanzibar was largely a country of immigrants, of Omani, Hadhrami and Shihiri Arabs, Indians or Banianis, Comorians, Swahilis and African slaves; in 1895 the British First Minister Sir Lloyd Mathews estimated the population as being composed of 140,000 slaves, 27,000 freed slaves, and 30,000 freeborn Swahili, including the indigenous Hadimu. In 1905 there were reckoned to be 15,000 Arabs, and 10–12,000 British Indian inhabitants; in 1911 Europeans numbered 234, Indians and Cingalese 8,305, and Portuguese Indians 440. In 1910 the total population of the island of Zanzibar was 114,069 and the sister island of Pemba 83,130; the capital Zanzibar Town had 35,262 inhabitants. Added to these figures there was always a large floating population, a constant stream to and fro with the monsoon winds of passengers of dhows of Somalis, Shihiri and Baluchi Arabs, and natives of the Kutch.[1]

The British Anglican missionaries of the Universities' Mission to Central Africa soon after their arrival on the island from about 1865 in the reign of Saʿīd's son, Sultan Mājid (1856–70), introduced on the island of Zanzibar the first press in East Africa, the Universities' Mission Press; on August 31 1864 the Right Reverend Bishop Tozer and Reverend Dr. Steere had arrived in Zanzibar. The press mainly

1 Public Record Office, FO 4716, 1909–10, 13 and FO 5176, 1911–2, 7. My thanks go to the staff of the Zanzibar Archives for their generous help to me in carrying out this research. This research has been funded by a British Academy small research grant, a Leverhulme Research Fellowship, and a Hayter Parry award at the University of Manchester.

printed religious texts in English and the Southern Swahili dialect, Swahili translations of the Gospels and the Old Testament, Swahili language books, handbooks for other African languages, Swahili short stories, etc., to service the missionary activities on the African mainland and for the small African Christian community in Zanzibar. Under a great obligation to the French Roman Catholic Mission Steere printed their *Catechism* in French and Swahili at the UMCA press. The missionaries were helped by local scholars in the preparation of the translations: Sheikh Abd al-Aziz bin Abd al-Ghani al-Amawī (1832–96), one of the leading ulema of the coast and a *qāḍī* in Zanzibar, was co-translator with Richard Lewin Pennel of the Gospel of St Luke into the Kiunguja (Zanzibari) dialect of Swahili, *Anjili ya Luka ilivyofasirika kwa maneno ya Kiunguja* (1872) and helped Bishop Steere with his translation of the Bible into Swahili and an Arabic Psalter.[2]

Swahili was the language of the indigenous population of the coast. Though the islands had an Arab-ruling political class, who were the wealthiest merchants, the owners of the largest clove plantations, and the employers of the largest numbers of slaves, Swahili remained the lingua franca. Though thousands of Zanzibar natives claimed to be 'Arabs', what they really meant was that they at least possessed a modicum of Arab blood in their veins. As early as the 1860s the British Consul C.P. Rigby noted that the majority of the island's landed families no longer used Arabic in conversation or daily life; even the Sultan Barghash spoke 'very softly and smoothly in splendid Swahili.' By the 1910s very few people in Zanzibar continued to use Arabic; the Sultan himself used Kiswahili within his home, but knowledge of Arabic remained an important marker of social status, education and religious training.[3] By 1932 the medium of instruction throughout the schools was Swahili.

Sultan Sayyid Barghash b. Saʿīd (1870–88), before coming to power, had spent time in exile in Bombay, so was familiar with all the trappings of the modern world. His reign was a period of reform and modernisation in Zanzibar. Like his contemporary Khedive Ismāʿīl of Egypt, Barghash was a lavish spender of money and a great builder of palaces. He took a more active interest than his predecessors in

2 Edward Steere, *A Handbook of the Swahili Language: As Spoken at Zanzibar* (London 1924), vii–viii.

3 Norman R. Bennett (ed.), *The Zanzibar Letters of Edward D. Ropes, Jr., 1882–1892* (Boston 1973), 13 and Laura Fair, *Pastimes and Politics. Culture, Community, and Identity in Post-abolition Urban Zanzibar, 1890–1945* (Athens, Ohio 2001), 167, n. 76, 200 from C.P. Rigby, *Report on the Zanzibar Dominions* (Bombay 1861), 5.

Zanzibar town itself and initiated a number of public improvements, building roads, an aqueduct giving the town a much-needed supply of fresh water and several important new buildings. He signed an agreement in 1873 to end the trade in slaves in Zanzibar, and subsequently closed down all public slave markets.

In 1875 he had travelled to Europe on a state visit to England, stopping in Egypt en route. It may be during this trip that he decided his country needed an Arabic printing press, Egypt perhaps being the inspiration for his decision. Under Khedive Ismāʿīl the Egyptian Arabic press had come into its own; as well as publishing a number of Arabic newspapers, public and private presses in Egypt were multiplying, printing new and classical Arabic texts and responding to an expanding public thirst for new genres of Arabic writing and access to the vast treasury of Arab intellectual history. Barghash may well have been encouraged by his links with a number of Arab intellectuals and other foreign friends to acquire his own printing press. Barghash brought back printing machines using Arabic and Roman scripts, and recruited printers from abroad to run them. The presses were used to print books and other publications, most of which were Ibāḍī religious texts.[4] The publishing of Ibāḍī texts began for the first time in the 1880s at presses thousands of miles apart in Algiers, Tunis, Cairo and Zanzibar.

Al-Maṭbaʿa al-Sulṭāniyya (the Sultanate Press) in Zanzibar, the first Arabic press in East Africa, began its book-publishing activities in 1879–80. Though the number of Ibadi texts published over the next forty years by the press was not large, the works chosen for publication were significant for the Ibadi community at large, which up to then had had no access in printed form to the religious literature of the sect. Details are not available, but it seems probable that the largest number of copies of the print runs of the Ibadi texts, though not large, were exported to Ibadi communities in Oman and beyond. Though Oman had the largest Ibadi community, there were no printing presses there in this period and Omani writers had to arrange publication of their works further afield. In the spirit of this period of the Arab renaissance, in which many young Arab intellectuals, particularly in Syria (*bilād al-Shām*) and Egypt, were challenging accepted values, promoting new political and social concepts and experimenting with new literary genres, such as the theatre, the novel and short

4 Mariam Mohamed Abdulrahman Hamdani, *Zanzibar Newspapers 1902 to 1974* (Dar es Salaam: Tanzania School of Journalism, 1981), 1.

stories, the Sultan's press seems to have considered one of its principal tasks to stimulate contemporary Ibadi scholarship by authors thousands of miles away in Oman and Algeria. The very first publication of the press, appearing over the years 1879/80–1886/87, was a complete system of Islamic theology and law according to the Ibadi school, by a contemporary Omani *'ālim,* Jumayyil b. Khamīs al-Saʿdī (1791/2–?), the *Qāmūs al-Sharīʿa,* written between 1844–63.[5] In 1884 Barghash bought another Arabic press from the famous Jesuit Fathers' Press (Maṭbaʿat al-Abā' al-Yasūʿīyyīn) in Beirut and recruited Lebanese workers to run it.

Few works were published perhaps because of the costs and labour involved. The Sultanate Press typeset its Arabic works; with a small staff and the challenge of multi-volume works it would have been a mammoth task to have attempted to produce more. As well as contemporary works of scholarship, the press printed a number of canonical works, considered as primary texts on the Ibadi religious sciences. In 1886 it published a classical compendium of Ibadi law, *al-Mukhtaṣar,* by the Omani *faqīh,* Shaykh Abū'l-Ḥasan, ʿAlī b. Muḥammad al-Bīsyāwī (fl. 11th cent.), selected from his *al-Jāmiʿ*. Between 1886/87 and 1890/91 the press published a gloss in three volumes, called *Kitāb Ḥāshiyat al-Tartīb,* by a Jerban, Muḥammad b. ʿUmar, Abū Sitta al-Jarbī al-Sadwīkashī (d. 1677), based on *al-Jāmiʿ al-Ṣaḥīḥ,* an arrangement by Yūsuf b. Ibrāhīm al-Warjalānī (d. 1175), of an authoritative Ibadi collection of *ḥadīth, al-Musnad,* by the Azdī al-Imām al-Rabīʿ b. Ḥabīb al-Farāhīdī (d. 786). The first work of the great Algerian scholar and *mujtahid,* Shaykh Muḥammad b. Yūsuf Aṭṭafayyish (1820–1914), published at al-Maṭbaʿa al-Sulṭānīya, was his lengthy commentary on the Qur'ān, *Tafsīr al-Qur'an al-Musammā Ḥimyān al-Zād ilā Dār al-Ma'ād;* this incomplete work was published in thirteen parts between 1887 and 1897.

Under Barghash's successors, Khalīfa b. Saʿīd (1888–90), ʿAlī b. Saʿīd (1890–3), Sayyid Ḥamad b. Thuwaynī (1893–6) and al-Sayyid Ḥamūd b. Muḥammad (1896–1902), the press continued its limited new publication projects and completed the volumes of works started in his reign. In 1898 it published another basic text at Maṭbaʿat Jāzīt *al-Shānba, Madārij al-Kamāl fī Naẓm Mukhtaṣar al-Khiṣāl,* by a leading contemporary Omani scholar and historian, ʿAbd Allāh b. Ḥumayd al-Sālimī

5 Though in its entirety it consists of 90 volumes, only seventeen volumes were printed. The first ten volumes were edited by a Zanzibari, Yaḥyā b. Khalfān b. Abī Nabhān al-Kharūṣī.

(1869/70–1914), a rhymed summary of the basic text, *Mukhtaṣar al-Khiṣāl*, by Abū Isḥāq, Ibrāhīm b. Qays b. Sulaymān al-Hamadhānī al-Ḥaḍramī (fl. 1126–27).[6] Another book published by the press was Abū'l-ʿAbbās, Aḥmad b. Muḥammad b. Bakr's *Hādhā'l-Kitāb al-Musammā bi-Abī Mas'ala* in 1900–1.

Barghash had close ties with a Syrian publisher and journalist, Luwīs Ṣābūnjī (1838–1931), who gave publicity to Zanzibar in his Arabic journal, *The Bee/al-Naḥla,* published in London, in which religious reform was preached to Muslims. The Sultan may have met Ṣābūnjī during his visit to London; Ṣābūnjī wrote an Arabic account of Barghash's visit to England, depending on notes (*ruqaʿ*) taken from the English newspapers and French publications, written by Zāhir b. Saʿīd, secretary to the Sultan. This work, *Tanzīh al-Abṣār wa'l-Afkār, fī Riḥlat Sultān Zanjībār,* was published in London in 1879.[7] It contains a most amusing illustration of Barghash's attendance at Ascot and Doncaster races, culled from some illustrated paper of the period; the drawing depicts Barghash with another Arab standing in an open carriage with conventional race-glasses in his hand, watching the finish of the race. Around the carriage cluster the cream of London society, including apparently royalty. The men wear high top-hats and long whiskers, and the ladies the strange fashions of the period.[8]

Ṣābūnjī, an Arabic teacher, had taken priest's orders and served the Congregation of the Propaganda at Rome. He had later thrown off the cassock and became much more in sympathy with Islam than with his own faith. He had a wide acquaintance with questions, half political, half religious, which were being discussed among Muslims. He had done the main work for Dr George Percy Badger in compiling the *Arabic-English Lexicon* (1881) under his name. Ṣābūnjī published Arabic newspapers in Beirut, Egypt, London and Istanbul from the 1870s to the 1890s. In the late 1870s and 1880s he was based in England. He is said to have spent eight years in the service of Barghash as his special agent, until the sultan's death; the sultan wrote to him every month, insisting that he be kept informed of events by every post. According to Wilfred Scawen Blunt, traveller and espouser of nationalist causes,

6 A great Ibāḍī Imam and poet from the Hadramawt, who led raids on India and made himself master of the Hadramawt.

7 Republished Oman: Wizārat al-turāth al-qawmī wa'l-thaqāfa, 1981; 2nd pr. Oman: Wizārat al-turāth al-qawmī wa'l-thaqāfa, 1988.

8 Major Francis Barrow Pearce, CMG, *Zanzibar: the Island Metropolis of Eastern Africa* (London 1920), 265–6.

who later employed Ṣābūnjī as his secretary, 'there was a mystery about the financing of this little journal, and the motives prompting its issue, which I never quite fathomed. His [Ṣābūnjī's] own account of it was that his chief patron was the Sultan of Zanzibar, a very enlightened and liberal-minded ruler. But I was never quite satisfied with this explanation, and I have since had reason to believe that the funds to support it, and the suggestion of its politics came, in part at least, from the ex-khedive Ismaïl.' The *Bee* was violent against the Ottoman Sultan Abd al-Hamid and denounced him as the usurper of the title of Emir al-Mumenin and Caliph; Ismāʿīl was very angry with the Ottoman sultan for his betrayal of him to Europe by agreeing to issue a decree deposing him as ruler of Egypt in favour of his son.[9]

Another of Barghash's contacts, the British Arabist, the Rev. Badger, member of the Muscat-Zanzibar Commission of 1860, encouraged him to exploit the Arabic press in Istanbul, through *al-Jawā'ib,* the newspaper of the Lebanese intellectual, Aḥmad Fāris al-Shidyāq, to argue Zanzibar's case in the international arena. Other Arab papers reached Zanzibar; on its foundation in 1876 the Egyptian *al-Ahrām* newspaper hoped to sell copies in Syria, Iraq, Turkey, Europe, Algeria, Tunisia, and Zanzibar and as far afield as Bombay and Calcutta. Van den Berg mentions that by the 1880s reformist Arabic papers like the pan-Islamic *al-Jawā'ib, al-Waṭan* from Cairo, *al-Ahrām* from Alexandria, and Muḥammad 'Abduh's *al-Urwa al-Wuthqā* from Paris were reaching Shafii readership as far away as Indonesia; from this it can be implied that East African Shafiis as well, because of their close ties, may have been reading the same journals and newspapers.[10]

The Zanzibar and Omani sultans funded the publication of a number of books in Cairo, not all by Ibadi writers. Copies of books printed at their expense and with dedications to the sultans on specially printed pages, often in expensive bound versions, were sent to the palace in Zanzibar. The Zanzibar sultans also later subsidized a number of Arabic newspapers by taking out regular subscriptions and making other donations: *Jarīdat al-Iqbāl* and *Thamarāt al-Funūn*, Beirut; *Jarīdat al-Mirsād,* Marseilles; *al-Ta'rīkh al-Yawmī, al-Baṣīr* and *al-Faḍīla,* Alexandria; *al-Ma'lūmāt,* Istanbul; *Ṭarāblus al-Shām,* Tripoli; *al-Maḥrūsa, al-Hilāl, al-Mu'ayyad, al-*

9 Wilfred Scawen Blunt, *Secret History of the English Occupation of Egypt* (New York 1969), 66. None of Ṣābūnjī's correspondence survives in the Zanzibar archives.
10 Randall L. Pouwels, *Horn and Crescent. Cultural Change and Traditional Islam on the East African Coast, 800–1900* (Cambridge 1987), 206 and 206, n. 83.

Manār, al-Ḍiyā', Jarīdat al-'Umrān, Jarīdat al-Būsta, Jarīdat al-Ikhlāṣ, Jarīdat al-Rāwī, al-Rā'id al-Miṣrī, and *al-Ṣabāḥ* in Cairo, *al-Khilāfa* in London, and *Abū Nazzāra* in Paris.[11]

The first paper in East Africa, a small Swahili quarterly booklet, *Msimulizi (The Reporter),* was the magazine of Kiungani College in Zanzibar, edited and printed in October 1888 by 'the boys themselves', African theological students of the Universities' Mission to Central Africa. More of a literary and religious magazine than a newspaper with a limited audience and a narrow range of interests it carried local news on the mission's activities at its houses at Mkunazini and Mbweni near Zanzibar Town. An article by a teacher at Mbweni, Mildred Maua, was the first contribution by a local person. From 1895 it was not printed for nearly a decade, reappearing in March 1904 and lasting to the First World War.[12]

The first issue of the weekly *The Gazette for Zanzibar and East Africa,* appeared on 1 February 1892 published by a British trading company in Zanzibar, Forward Brothers and Co. The Universities' Mission press in Kiungani printed the first issue. In a letter introducing the paper the editors said:

> We have today the honour of publishing the first newspaper ever issued in East Africa and in doing so we venture to assert that we are taking a most important step in the mercantile progress of Zanzibar and one which claims the support of all who are interested in the prosperity of the place.

The first public notice by the British Diplomatic Agent and Consul General, G.H. Portal, CB., informed British protected persons that *The Gazette* 'will henceforth be regarded as the official channel of communication to the public;' Zanzibar had become a British protectorate in 1890. Before an assembly of 4,000 merchants in 'the large new shed' at the Customs House on the day of the paper's publication Portal had declared Zanzibar a free port. Immense enthusiasm prevailed of Zanzibar taking her place 'amongst other leading ports of the world which have recognised the fact that a duty on imports is a serious obstacle in the way of a large extension of trade.' Copies

11 Thomas Philipp, *Ǧurǧī Zaidān: His Life and Thought* (Beirut 1979), 40.

12 The first issue had twelve sides. See A.E.M. Anderson-Morshead, *The History of the Universities' Mission to Central Africa, vol. 1, 1859–1909* (London 1955), 1, 185 and Martin Sturmer, *Sprachspolitik und Pressegeschichte in Tanzania* (Vienna 1995), 181–3. Copies of *Msimuliza* can be found in the library of the United Society for the Propagation of the Gospel in London, in SOAS library (i, 1–19, 21–45; 48), and in the Bodleian (i, 1–48; ii).

of the first edition of *The Gazette* were distributed at the meeting 'and judging from its reception the future success of *The Gazette* appears to be a certainty.' At the conclusion of his address Mr. Portal said:

> Let us henceforth all work together for the development of the commerce of Zanzibar: let us make Zanzibar a great depot and a great market knowing that as we do we are helping materially in the great work of the civilization of the continent of Africa; and may God grant success to our labours.

From the first the official medium for official notices from H.M.'s Agency and Consulate General and H.M.'s Consular Court, *The Gazette* carried a good deal of general news. It was primarily a local newssheet, with local social news, trade, shipping and weather reports, a means of inter-communication for the European community and traders. Later it added a column of overseas news received by telegraph from the Reuters news agency. Except for brief periods there was little or no interest in the affairs of the Arabs or the native Swahilis. It was chiefly in English, with some parts in Gujerati.

On 24 October 1894 it became the property of the Zanzibar Government, and had numerous British officials as editors; none of whom of course were trained journalists. One left his post as editor to become the jailer at Mombasa.[13] The editors remarked: 'The establishment of a newspaper under the direct proprietorship of the Sultan's Government is a proof that His Highness [Sultan Ḥamad b. Thuwaynī] has still higher aims in view. We understand that H.H., having the interests of his own race at heart, proposes to have the chief items of news from week to week translated into Arabic and published as a supplement to *The Gazette*.'[14] It was a year or two before this wish was put into regular practice;[15] from June 1897 to 1899 a few news items (*akhbār*) and advertisements in Arabic started to appear occasionally, ranging in length from three or four items of international news in Arabic from Reuters/*Riyūtā* to a column or more of Reuters telegrams (*min ṭaraf riyūtir*).[16] The first notice in Swahili

---

13 James Francis Scotton, *Growth of the Vernacular Press in Colonial East Africa: Patterns of Government Control*, PhD (The University of Wisconsin 1971), 42.

14 *The Gazette*, 143, 24 October 1894, 2. It is available in the British Library 1^{49} –; the Bodleian 1–58, 1892–8, and in the Zanzibar Archives (A) 1892–, 1–, and can be purchased on microfilm. It cost two annas.

15 *The Gazette*, 248, October 28, 1896 and 252, November 25, 1896.

16 *The Gazette*, 253, December 2, 1896 and 283, June 30, 1897.

in *Gazette Amri ya gouverneuri* was a Government notice about Harbour duties.[17] Amongst the Arabic news covered was an item on the death of Commendatore Antonio Cecchi, Italian Consul-General, who had been killed up country in a Somali ambush.[18] To commemorate the 60th year anniversary of the accession of Queen Victoria a rare announcement (*i'lān*) in Arabic appeared.[19] Sometimes the paper carried no Arabic news for ages and all that appeared were various notices in Arabic.[20]

A new Swahili monthly newspaper, *Habari za Mwezi* (Monthly News), appeared in October 1895, edited, printed and published at the Universities' Mission to Central Africa at Magila in northeast Tanganyika; it lasted till 1910. It was especially intended for circulation in the Bonde and Zigua districts. *The Gazette* commented:

> We hold out the hand of greeting this week to a new venture in journalism in East Africa, which may be the beginning of a great change in the life and views of the educated native races around us. It is nothing less than a newspaper published entirely in Suahili, to be issued at present monthly, but which it is hoped before long will become a weekly publication. Here is the opportunity for the spreading of good and helpful advice to be pondered over and not forgotten as soon as heard. And here are the means for the extension of commerce by making the wants of one tribe known to another, and for uniting all interests in the huge civilised Africa, which is slowly but surely being built up. The evolution of society is working out before our eyes, there can be no retrogression, we have moved on from the past and there can be no return thereto, and the Press is one of the greatest factors at work even in Africa.[21]

In 1899 the weekly *East Africa and Uganda Mail* started at Mombasa on the Kenya coast, and the German language *Deutsche Ostafrikanische Zeitung* was published in Dar es Salaam in mainland German East Africa (Deutsch Ostafrika). The policy of the German administration was to promote the spread of literacy; they wanted an efficient and profitable colony staffed at the lower and intermediate levels by literate Africans. Swahili, widely known on the coast and along trade routes was selected as the language of the administration. A number of Swahili periodicals that proved very popular were published in German East Africa; there were no equivalent publications in Zanzibar. In 1905–16 with German government encouragement, a group of teachers and government clerks from the German Regierungs-Schule

17 *The Gazette,* 70, May 31 1893.
18 *The Gazette,* 254, December 9, 1896 and 256, December 23, 1896.
19 *The Gazette,* 281, June 16, 1897, 5.
20 *The Gazette,* 355, November 16, 1898.
21 *The Gazette,* 192, October 2, 1895, 6.

produced *Kiongozi* (The Leader) at Tanga. The Catholic Benedictine Fathers at Peramiho in southern Tanganyika began a religious monthly, *Rafiki Yangu* (My Friend) in 1908–14, and the Lutherans started *Pwani na Bara* (The Coast and the Hinterland) at Dar es Salaam in 1910–14.[22]

In April 1897 the Arabic news in *The Gazette* was 'to announce a most important project just set on foot in the interests of the shambas of Zanzibar and Pemba. It is intended to publish monthly at the Government *Gazette* Press a journal devoted to agricultural interests ..., and sold at a cost calculated to just cover its production. The journal ... will be essentially practical in nature, dealing with products and labour. Mr. Theodore Burtt of the *Friends' Industrial Mission* at Pemba has undertaken to deal with subjects especially affecting that Island.'[23] The Collector of Customs (*al-ḥukūma al-zanjabarīya Kustum Haws [al-Furḍa]*) and Messrs. Arnold Cheney & Co. would chronicle the monthly wholesale market quotations, Mr. L. Besson the prices of cloves and chillies, and Messrs. Hansing and Co. the price of India rubber and Orchella weed. The *Jazīt al-Shānba/The Shamba* appeared in June 1897/12 Muḥarram 1315, subtitled in English the 'Journal of Agriculture for Zanzibar', and in Arabic *al-Jarīda al-Ḥukmīya al-Zirā'īya Ikhtibār 'an al-falāḥa wa-'an al-akhbār al-mufīda* (A Government Newspaper Seeking Information on agriculture and on useful news), appearing in English and Arabic. It was edited by R.N. Lyne, the Director of Agriculture of the Zanzibar Government; the paper largely owed its existence to the enterprise of the Editor of *The Gazette.* In its first editorial it announced:

> A newspaper is an indispensable condition of progress. It stimulates activity, collects and distributes knowledge: voices the opinions of those among whom it circulates, and acts as a bond of union between them. But a newspaper is something more than a condition of progress. It is an indication that a certain amount has already been made, and it is also an earnest of future exertions. A community does not as a rule indulge in the luxury of a paper unless it has accomplished something worth writing about, and is voyaging towards prosperity. We, to a certain extent, may be said to have taken time by the forelock, through the latent forces of these islands, together with the great possibilities that lie before them, justify us in taking a step which might otherwise be considered

22 Scotton, *Growth,* 32–3. The German government had declared a protectorate over the area in 1885.
23 *The Gazette,* 273, April 21, 1897, 5. The Arabic word *Shānba=shamba,* Swahili, means plantation. Copies can be found in the Royal Botanic Gardens, Kew 1897–1903, the British Library nos. 23–4, April 1901–June 1903, Zanzibar Archives (A) BA 3/1, 24, June 1903, and US National Agricultural Library, 17–20, 23–4.

premature. We have yet another justification to plead. Many of the Arab Planters in Zanzibar and Pemba do not understand the European languages in which most current agricultural literature is written. One of the principal objects of the *Shamba* will be to act as a medium through which subjects of agricultural interest may reach them. Matters of local importance will naturally occupy considerable attention, though on the other hand we cannot afford to turn a deaf ear to what is being done in other countries.

'We ... trust that a real response will be given to a very earnest effort which is being made to give a helping hand to those who have for long past dwelt in and managed the plantations in these islands, who have now to accommodate themselves to a changed order of things calculated at the outset to somewhat embarrass them.'[24]

The London based *The Chemist and Druggist* noted: 'Zanzibar has become enriched by a commercial journal, *The Shamba (Plantation);* it promises from the first number to be 'very lively little paper.' Appealing to Arab and European planters, it proposes to educate the planters and keep a lookout on London and American brokers. 'The broker', it says, 'is a creature to be watched, and in watching him we shall fight him with his own weapons, because he watches us, and very closely too ... We have to watch the prices, not of cloves only, but of every product that we raise.' It is 'devoted entirely to the planting interests of the Island, which dealt in a practical manner with these things, and being printed in Arabic would give the Arabs all the information they needed and gave them further an opportunity of asking questions and of contributing remarks and recording experience.'[25]

The Shamba was for sale at *The Gazette* Office in Mnazi Moja; it later could be obtained, particularly by its Arab readers, at Mwera, Dunga, and at Tundawa in Zanzibar and Weti in Pemba. In the first issue there were six pages in English and seven in a parallel Arabic version, in the main a translation from the English. There was a regular section on catch crops and cloves (*al-qurunful*). A section in Arabic was not related to agriculture, but brought Arab readers the latest international news, 'telegraphic news from Reuters' (*akhbār al-sīm min ṭaraf Ryutir*), or Reuter's telegraphs (*tilighrāf Riyūtir/Rūtā*), for example items on Lord Salisbury, Gladstone, news from Bombay, and of Turkish ministers (*wuzarā' al-Rūm*). One issue carried a valuable tabular list of experiments carried out in Pemba by Theodore Burtt on clove

24 *The Gazette,* 281, June 16, 1897.
25 *The Gazette,* 297, October 6, 1897, 5 and 301, November 3, 1897, 6.

drying and the betterment of samples; experiments had brought the working of the Pemba shamba into line with European planters' estates.[26]

Lyne at the first meeting of its kind with Arabs (planters) at Mwera told them that any contribution to the paper would be gladly received; 'at the close of the meeting copies of *The Shamba* were distributed to those present and the pages were eagerly scanned by the Arabs.' [27] Lyne, in post for nine months, established government nurseries for tropical products, which he supplied to the Arabs, and introduced for the first time agricultural implements. He experimented with the drying of cloves, chillies and other staple products. He placed Zanzibar products side by side with those of their competitors in Singapore, Java, Sumatra and West Indies, so that the Arabs could have a complete object lesson of the quality of Zanzibar export.[28] An article on 'The agricultural movement in Pemba' detailed a meeting (*shauri)* of Arabs at Weti on 24 October, summoned by the Li Wali Hamis bin Salim to meet Lyne and Lister, the Government agent for Pemba. Lyne interested Arab plantation owners considerably in the present state and the future outlook of plantation culture there. The Arabs were encouraged to improve their neglected shambas; Mohammed bin Jumah of Kish Kash responded positively: 'The Arabs were too fond of sleeping and eating and never bestirred themselves to any work (*tadhakkar an ahl al-'arab yuḥibbūn al-istirāḥa wa'l-akl faqaṭ wa-abadan lā yasta'idūn anfusahum ilā shughl*), but the time had now come to make an end of all this.' Lister said 'they should all buy a copy of *The Shamba Gazette* which was written especially for Arabs. They could buy it every month from the Hindi Hashim in Weti for one anna [4 *bīs*]. The Arabs should write letters to the *Shamba* if they did not understand anything, and their letters would be printed and answered.' [29] *The Gazette* remarked: 'We are glad to hear that that enterprising little paper has already attracted considerable attention even amongst the Rip van Winkels of Pemba. To many it is a first revelation of Caxton's boon to mankind.'[30]

The Shamba carried its first photographs of horse and cattle pulling ploughs in March 1898. There were 'Notes on the Weather' in the issue of November-December.

---

26 *The Gazette,* 294, September 15, 1897, 4 and 6.
27 *The Gazette,* 303, November 17, 1897, 5.
28 *The Gazette,* 317, February 26, 1898, 4.
29 *The Shamba,* 6, November 1897 quoted in *The Gazette,* November 17, 1897, 6.
30 *The Gazette,* 301, November 3, 1897, 6.

Regular 'meteorological reports for East Africa', statistics on mean temperatures and rainfall (*tibyān fī akhbār al-maṭar* 'explanation of the news of rain') with comments appeared. Some adverts were published, even one for G. Bercovich's *The Splendid Bar,* opposite the German Consulate, also in Arabic *dī Sblindid Bār.*[31] Articles were carried, not in the English version, on 'The Djinn in Dunga' (*al-Jinn fī Dūnghā*), on the indigenous rulers the Mwinyi Mkuu (Muynī Makūh), on the sacred horn of the Swahili, the Sīwa;[32] even the odd line of Arabic poetry was printed. Occasional problems occurred in producing the Arabic version; the March 1898 issue no. 10 of the paper appeared in April: 'It was found impossible to publish a March number owing principally to the Ramazan, during which the fasting operators and translators could only work half time. Every thing of course was put out of joint and thrown into arrears, so we judged it wise to let the month go and allow our straggling remnant to close up for a fresh start in April.'[33] In May 1898 the Arabic section bore a new heading *al-Jāzīt al-mu'lin bi'l-bashā'ir wa'l-asrār*[34] *fī umūr al-shawānib wa-mā ya'tarīhā al-jazīra al-maḥrūsa Zanjabār. al-Jarīda al-nāṭiqa bi'l-ḥikma al-mū'īya li'l-'uqūl wa'l-adhkār li'l-zirā'a wa-mā ya'taliq bi-hādhā'l-shān* (The Gazette announcing good news and secrets concerning shambas and what happens to the protected island of Zanzibar. The newspaper speaking with wisdom enlightening minds and memories on agriculture and what is connected to this matter).

In January/February 1900 the paper announced: 'In consequence of the absence of the Editor the *Shamba* will not again be issued till the latter end of the year.'[35] After a gap of more than a year it re-emerged in no. 23, April 1901 completely in English; there was no longer any material in Arabic, only the Sultan's seal at the top was in Arabic. After that three pages appeared in November 1901 and then there was another unexplained gap till the last issue no. 24 in June 1903, when it ended abruptly with no explanation.

Dr Spurrier announced in December 1898 His Highness the Sultan Sayyid Ḥamūd's gratification of the work done by the Arabic press, especially with the

31 *The Shamba,* 3, August 1897.
32 *The Shamba,* 8, January 1898/Sha'bān 1315.
33 *The Shamba,* 10, March and April 1898, 1.
34 *The Shamba,* no 11, May 1898/al-Ḥajj, 1315. Fīlīb dī Ṭarrāzī, *Ta'rīkh al-Ṣiḥāfa al-'Arabīya,* (Beirut 1913–33), iv, 352–3 wrongly thinks that this was the title of an official magazine established 24 December 1899.
35 *The Shamba,* 22, January/February 1900, 5.

account of his son, Seyyid Ali's tour to the Cape Colony, with which H.H. expressed himself much pleased, saying 'it was some of the best Arabic work he had seen.' H.H. hoped soon an account of his own tour to the East African coast in 1898 would be put in hand; this eyewitness account, the only work published at the government press by a contemporary Zanzibari, was written by the judge and outstanding poet, Abū Muslim, Nāṣir b. Sālim b. ʿUdayyim al-Ruwāḥī (1856/7–1920), *al-Sīra al-Saniyya, al-Musammāt bi'l-Lawāmi' al-Barqīya fī Riḥlat Mawlānā al-Sulṭān al-Mu'aẓẓam Ḥamūd b. Muḥammad b. Sa'd b. Sulṭān fī'l-Aqṭār al-Ifrīqīya al-Sharqīya Sanat 1316 Hijrīya,* published in 1899.[36]

The thriving Indian commercial community established its own papers in Zanzibar. A Gujerati paper, the *Zanzibar Vepar Samachar* ('Zanzibar Business News'), was published on 9 July 1899; Gujarati was the language of the majority of the Indians in East Africa, who came from the Kutch. It was to be published every Sunday; *The Gazette* commented: 'judging from the first number, we think it is likely to be a success.'[37] The weekly *Zanzibar Akbar* ('The Zanzibar News') was established in 1900 in a house in Shangani by an employee of Smith Mackenzie & Co., later revealed to be Byramji Hormasji Mory. It later became a daily, and then a weekly again in Gujerati and English, published by the Mori Press. It was still appearing in 1917.[38] A contemporary historian on Zanzibar the Syrian Ḥikmat Sharīf in 1901 gives details of a paper he asserts was appearing: 'There are in Zanzibar today about 100 merchants from the Ottomans of huge wealth, some of them have two commercial ships that traverse the sea between Zanzibar and Bombay India. They have set up a mosque, a school, a public library, as they have set up a newspaper, called *'Irāq,* published once a month.'[39]

36 *The Gazette,* 361, December 28, 1898, 5. No copy has been found of the travel account of the visit to South Africa.

37 *The Gazette,* 389, Wednesday July 12, 1899, p. 7. The *Vepar Samachar* still existed in October 1899 (*The Gazette,* 404, October 25, 1899, 6).

38 *The Gazette,* 414, 3 January, 1900, 5. It had no connection with the *Samachar.* It is also referred to as the *Zanzibar Akhbar* or the *Akhbar.* Sources are all mistaken about this: Sturmer, 198 is incorrect, calling the paper *Zanzibar Akhbar* probably established in 1902; *Mwongozi* (Anon, 'Review of the History of Newspapers,' *Mwongozi,* Friday 20 February 1948, vol. 7, 2, 4.) says it was founded in 1907; Scotton, *Growth,* 470 describes it as a Gujerati and Arabic newspaper existing between 1905 and 1910. Sturmer and Scotton believe it later became the *Samachar.* At Criminal Appeal 2 in 1914 in H.B.M. Court for Zanzibar (Zanzibar Archives (A) HC 6/95), it is described as 'the Arab newspaper;' it may have carried material in Arabic.

39 Ḥikmat Sharīf, *Ta'rīkh al-Mamlaka al-Zanjabārīya* (Tripoli, 1318/1901), 15. This reference is mysterious. It seems likely that he is referring to Indian residents of Zanzibar, perhaps the Ismaili

The *Islam Samachar* established in Zanzibar on 28 July 1901 by Fazal Janmohamed Master (1873–1920), continued till 30 July 1903 as a purely Gujerati weekly appearing on Sunday; English columns were added later. It changed its name to the *Zanzibar Samachar* in August 1903; on 30 July 1906 it became a daily.[40] It stopped appearing in October 1911, when Master went to India.[41] On his return, the *Zanzibar Samachar* resumed under the title, *El Islam and Samachar,* first as a daily then a weekly, until the time came when Master could not get sufficient printing job work to carry on his press. At that time there were five presses in Zanzibar: the Union; the Meher; the *Najah;* the De Lord Press and Master's press (the Huseni/Hooseni Printing Press); in addition the Government Press accepted private work. Master 'saw that there was not work enough', so he closed the paper and took his press to Mombasa at the end of 1913, and started a paper there called the daily *East African Samachar* on 29 January 1914. His press and paper flourished;[42] it was the most important Indian newspaper in East Africa at the time and Indians wrote to it frequently to present their grievances. There was a tone of moderation in most of the complaints the paper carried; it made clear pleas for justice under British rule and offered no challenge to that rule.[43]

In the reign of Sultan Sayyid ʿAlī (1902–11) a new court system was established, and a government (*niẓāmīya*) school set up in 1908. The sultan's court and Zanzibari intellectuals kept up their links with Arab intellectuals, including newspaper publicists, elsewhere in the Arab world. Very early in his career the litterateur, jurist consult (*faqīh*) and *kathi* Shaykh Aḥmad b. Abī Bakr b. Sumayṭ (1859–1925) established and maintained ties with a few pan-Islamicists and reform thinkers.[44] Sayyid Mansab b. Ali Abu Bakr b. Salim, a descendent of the Mwinyi Mkuu, took an interest in the Egyptian reform newspapers such as *al-Manār, al-Hilāl, al-Muqtaṭaf, al-*

Khoja community. The reference to 'Ottomans' makes no sense, there being no Ottomans on the island. No date is given for this publication.

40 *The Gazette,* 803, June 19, 1907, 4.

41 'The Chequered Career of the "Samachar" and a Short Account of the Equally Chequered Career of its Founder the late Mr. Fazal Janmohamed Master', *The Samachar,* Silver Jubilee Number (1929), 10.

42 'The Chequered', 10. The Union Press working for the Indian community in 1914 was at no. 345 Sokokuu, a property owned by Mohsin bin Seif Khanjiri. The Meher Printing Press in 1914 was at no. 821 Kiponda, a property owned by Esmailji Jivanji & Co.

43 Scotton, *Growth,* 68.

44 Pouwels, *Horn,* 206 from Abdallah Saleh Farsy, *Baadhi ya Wanavyuoni wa Kishafi wa Mashariki ya Afrika* (Mombasa, 1972), 57, translated as *Shafi'i Ulema of East Africa, c. 1830–1970: A Hagiographic Account,* Translated, Edited and Annotated by Randall L. Pouwels. Madison 1989.

Liwā', and *al-Mu'ayyad;* in addition he read the famous *tafsīr* written by the Egyptian Islamic reformer Muḥammad ʿAbduh. Two Egyptians, living in Zanzibar, appear to have been very influential, particularly on the youth of Zanzibar: Muḥammad Jamal, called Turkiyya, a tarbush merchant was active in reading and promoting reformist papers and pamphlets, such as *al-Manār,* to the baraza, and Umar Lutfi was especially effective as a reformist propagandizer; acting on his convictions he gave lessons in the Jumaʿ mosque where he influenced various youths especially open to the new religious ideas he purveyed.[45]

Many daily single-page advertising sheets with some items of local news were published for short periods by Asian printers in East Africa. East Africa's first daily newspaper, *The Hindi,* appeared in Zanzibar *c.* November 1906 in Gujerati; it still existed in 1914. It was to be a rival Indian newspaper to the *Zanzibar Samachar.* The editor Cheturbhooj Jugjivan was deported for two years from the Sultanate soon after its appearance for publishing abusive articles.[46] 'A distinctly diverting circular' announced the publication with the New Year in 1907 of a weekly illustrated paper, *Praja Punch,* to be published at the Samachar Office in English and Gujerati, that 'promises amusement and edification by 'moralizing facts'.[47]

The *Zanzibar Gazette* (this is how *The Gazette for Zanzibar and East Africa* is described in its own columns) celebrated its fifteenth anniversary in 1907. Had F.W. Campin, one of the first editors survived to witness the 15th anniversary of 'the old lady of Zanzibar,' he might have considered his offspring had to some extent fulfilled his hopes.[48] Most of the articles were in English. Apart from regular translations of decrees into Gujerati and Arabic, Arabic material was rare. One article in both languages was about the sad drowning on January 27 1909 of the Weli of Mkokotoni, Seyyid Suleman bin Hamed, with his son Hamdan, Said bin Seif and his son Amur, two slaves Abedi and Mchenzi, and five sailors (*baharias*), who left Mkokotoni in a small boat (*falak saghīr*) bound for Zanzibar. In a heavy sea the boat capsized; all were drowned, except the baharias.[49] In 1911 small entries appeared in Arabic on the Zanzibar court (*Maḥkamat Zanjabār wa'l-Jazīra al-Khaḍrā' li'l-Sulṭān*). A full page

45 Pouwels, *Horn*, 206–7 from Farsy, *Baadhi*, 7–8 and interview with Farsy in 1975. The baraza is the stone bench outside Zanzibari houses, where people meet to relax and chat.

46 *The Gazette*, 803, June 19, 1907, 4.

47 *The Gazette*, 778, December 26, 1906, 2.

48 *The Gazette*, 785, February 13, 1907, 2.

49 *The Gazette*, 885 [sic], Wednesday February 3, 1909, 3.

notice in English/Arabic announced the commencement of a steam launch service (*I'lān Istīm Lansh*) to the south of Zanzibar departing every Monday and Thursday.[50] In January 1911 a two and half page list of the names of the shaykhs of Zanzibar (*Qā'imat al-Mashāyikh Zanjabār)* was published in Arabic.[51]

Many members of the cultured elite from Oman, the coast, the Comoros, and elsewhere emigrated to Zanzibar, looking for a better climate to express their aspirations at the reign of apathy and the precarious economic and political situation in their homelands. 'The first Arabic newspaper to be published in Zanzibar', *al-Najāḥ* ('Success') in September 1911 was not a paper of the diaspora (*mahjar*), but a nationalist paper;[52] circumstances did not permit the appearance of a paper in Oman. The *Gazette* called it *El-Hezbu el-Islah*; it was the organ of the Arab Association/*al-Jam'īya al-'Arabīya* or the Ḥizb al-Iṣlāḥ (The Party of Reform), its promoters; 'we give a cordial welcome to the publication as a means of bringing the Arab more closely in touch with official matters and with events taking place in other parts of the world.'[53] The editor said 'I have urged the Arab people to found an association to encourage agriculture, an independent agricultural bank, a trading association, and Arab religious schools.'[54] Sultan Sayyid ʿAli stood behind the establishment of the first society to take care of the affairs of the Arab community. It was directed specifically to Arabs in Zanzibar, but was read widely on the coast. On page one after the title the following description of its contents was printed: *Jarīda, waṭanīya, 'ilmīya, ikhbārīya, ta'rīkhīya,* and *tijārīya* (nationalist, scientific, news, historical and

50 *The Gazette,* 989, Tuesday January 10, 1911.

51 *The Gazette,* 990, Tuesday January 17, 1911.

52 Muḥammad al-Ḥārithī, 'Awrāq Majhūla min al-Ṣiḥāfa al-ʿUmānīya fi Sharq Ifrīqīya: al-Judhūr, al-Ruwwād, al-Nahḍa al-Ṣaḥāfīya fī Zanjabār,' *al-Quds,* 27 March 2000, 10; al-Ḥārithī saw a copy of the paper.

53 *The Gazette for Zanzibar,* vol. xx, 1030, Monday October 23, 1911, 9, Mwongozi, 4 and R. Axenfeld, 'Geistige Kämpfe in der Eingeborenenbevölkerung an der Küste Ostafrikas,' *Koloniale Rundschau, heft* 11 (1913), 654. The title of the Arab community society seems to be here confused with the title of the journal. Sturmer, *Sprachpolitik,* 195 says it appeared as a weekly from 1912–14. There are references to issues of *al-Najāḥ* appearing on 3 April 1912, October 1912, 2 January 1913, no. 56, 20.2.1913, no. 64, 17.4.1913, and no. 67, 8.5.1913.

54 John Iliffe, *Tanganyika under German Rule 1905–1912* (Cambridge 1969), 208 from *al-Najāḥ,* December 1912 quoted in Axenfeld, 659–60. August H. Nimtz, Jr., 'Islam in Tanzania: an annotated bibliography', *Tanzania Notes and Records,* 72 (1973), 57 commented at that time that it was not known where there might be old copies. Quotations from it may be found in the German file G9/48.

commercial newspaper).[55] Its slogan came partly from the Quranic verse Hūd, 88 and partly from a proverb: '*in urīd illā al-iṣlāḥ mā istaṭa't -kull man thābir 'alā'l-'amal adraka al-najāḥ*' ('I only desire [your] betterment to the best of my power-everyone who persists in a task, attains success'). It appeared thrice monthly at three annas per copy. In the first number an article by Shaykh Naser, in which he endeavoured to rouse the Arabs to a sense of their responsibilities, impressed upon them that indifference and lack of initiative were responsible for the decline in their prosperity. It became a voice urging that effective improvement was impossible under European control and to break European control required unity. Shaykh Naser called for a united Islamic nation (*umma islāmīya muwaḥḥida*): 'What is important for the East? People tell us: knowledge and work. But more important is effective unity.' The same writer contributed an article on Zanzibar and Pemba, dealing chiefly with the role of labour to the success of the clove crop. The Morocco question was dealt with at some length and much general information about the country was included in a discussion of the political situation. *The Gazette* remarked: 'We hope the management will see their way to extend the circulation of the paper by the publication of articles in simpler Arabic than that of the first number. In its present form the circle of its readers must be very limited,' adding a call for the paper to extend its readership. 'At the same time we feel confident that its usefulness would be increased and its circulation further extended if the more numerous section of the subjects of H.H. the Sultan were catered for and one page printed in Swahili.'[56]

The editor was Abū Muslim, Nāṣir al-Ruwāḥī ('Sheikh Naser') and the manager Jabir bin Saleh; some of Abū Muslim's poetry was published in it.[57] Sheikh Nāṣir b. Sulaymān al-Lamkī became the editor in October 1912; Naser was the son of an old loyalist, Suleiman bin Naser, the Governor (*Liwali*) of Dar es Salaam, who had risen to prestige and power serving the Germans.[58] Nāṣir al-Lamkī edited a volume of poetry in praise of the Imām of Oman, al-Shaykh Salīm b. Rashīd b. Sulaymān al-

55 Muḥammad b. Nāṣir b. Rāshid al-Maḥrūqī, *al-Shi'r al-'Umānī al-Ḥadīth: Abū Muslim al-Bahalānī Rā'idān 1860–1920* (Casablanca 1999–2000), 119 from his MA thesis 1995 in Kullīyat al-Ādāb, Sultan Qabus University.

56 *The Gazette for Zanzibar,* vol. xx, 1030, Monday October 23, 1911, 8–9.

57 al-Maḥrūqī, *al-Shi'r,* 47, n. 2. As a poet he did not win the fame of his contemporaries such as the Syrian Khalīl Muṭrān, and the Egyptians Ḥāfiẓ Ibrāhīm, and Aḥmad Shawqī. Shawqī said, referring to al-Ruwāḥī, when he was appointed by his peers prince of poets: 'How can I pay homage (*ubāyi'*), when the poet of Oman is absent from this gathering?

58 Axenfeld, 657.

Khurūsī, *Tahānī al-Imām,* at the paper's press Maṭbaʿat al-Najāḥ in 1914. It contained poems by al-Murr b. Sālim al-Ḥaḍramī, Shaykh ʿAbd Allāh b. ʿĀmir b. Muhīl al-ʿAzrī, Shaykh ʿĀmir b. Sulaymān al-Mālikī, and ʿĀmir b. Sulaymān b. ʿĀmir al-Ibāḍī. The press also published in 1915 a description of travels in Egypt, Syria, the Ḥijāz and Aden in 1914, *Riḥlat Abī'l-Ḥārith* by Abū'l-Ḥārith, al-Shaykh Muḥammad bin ʿAlī bin Khamīs al-Barwānī (1878/9–1953), a scholar (*'ālim*), poet and *adīb* (litterateur) like his father. It included poems at the end by Aḥmad b. Sumayṭ, Abū Muslim, Burhān Mukallā and by *al-shaykh al-'ālim,* author of *Silk al-Balāgha.*

Local journalists were active in local community life. A mass meeting in November 1911 of 6–7,000 Muslims of nearly 14 sects was held at the Ismaili[a] Baug to show sympathy towards the empire of Turkey, and declare contempt against the cowardly step of the kingdom of Italy in occupying Libya. The leading members of almost all sects were there; only the Ismaili Khoja community leaders were conspicuous by their absence. Janab Ali Sayyed Abbas, the head 'priest' of the Ithnasheri Khojas, chaired the meeting; Naser bin Suleman bin Naser Lemki was present. A sub-committee, including Shaykh Isa bin Ali, Vice President, and Fazal Janmahamed Master, was formed to raise funds for those rendered helpless by the war, the aged, widows, and orphans.[59]

A special issue in English, Arabic, and Swahili, *The Special Gazette for Zanzibar,* vol. xx, no. 1036a, Saturday December 9, 1911, published a proclamation from His Majesty's Diplomatic Agent and Consul-General that His Highness Seyyid Ali bin Hamed, the Sultan of Zanzibar, had informed His Majesty the King 'that the state of his health is unhappily such as to prevent his any longer fulfilling the duties incumbent on him as ruler of the Sultanate.' The Sultan asked to be relieved of the burden. The British Monarch offered Seyyid Khaled bin Mahomed bin Said, His Majesty's uncle the high position, but he asked to be excused on grounds of ill-health. His Majesty then offered Seyyid Khalifa bin Harub bin Thweini bin Said the throne. *The Gazette* continued to publish a few items in Arabic. An Arabic report [not available in English] contained a note (*tadhkira*) read by the *Wakīl al-malik* and the Consul-General at an assembly of the Arabs (*Majma' al-'Arab*), held by Sultan al-Sayyid Khalīfa b. Ḥārib on 10 October 1912 to discuss mosques in Zanzibar. There

59 Report of an Inspector in the Zanzibar Police dated 25/11/1911 in Zanzibar Archives, AC 1/151. Document 90 in AL 2/38.

were forty mosques: twenty-six under religious endowment (*awqāf*), fourteen (B) under the Government, which paid the salaries of the Imams and 16 private; the mosques in group B were funded from the private pocket of the sultan (*sa'ādatihi*).[60] An Arabic description of the Sultan's visit (*riḥla*) to Pemba (*al-Jazīra al-Khaḍrā'*) in 1912, covered nearly two full pages; His Highness visited a branch of *al-Jam'īya al-'Arabīya* in Weti. A full page announcement was printed in Arabic in 1914 on the admission of students to al-Azhar in Cairo (*mashaykhat al-Jāmi' al-Azhar al-sharīf i'lān 'an shurūṭ qubūl intiṣāb ṭalabat al-'ilm al-ghurabā' bi'l-Jāmi' al-Azhar* (the Professoriate of al-Azhar mosque on the conditions for foreign students to be accepted at al-Azhar mosque), intended to encourage Zanzibaris to study there.[61] The paper divided into two with a separate parallel edition to *The Official Gazette of the Zanzibar Government* with local non-official news called *Supplement to the Official Gazette* appearing in 1914.

In the First World War in 1914 Master 'started publishing a daily Gujarati translation of Reuter's cables' in Mombasa, perhaps a small afternoon mimeographed newsletter called *Ruta* ('*Information*') that appeared for the duration of the war. It attracted Indian readers eager to know of the developments in the war. It cost ten cents a copy.[62] Then when Martial Law was introduced, Master saw that the wisest thing was to stop the paper altogether 'as the whole atmosphere was too risky for a paper being kept going'. He survived earning a living as a tailor.[63]

Another self-interest group, the Indian National Association was founded in 1914, representing all sections of the Indian community, except the Parsees; there was a considerable amount of internal dissension in the body. A small monthly magazine, *The Journal of the Indian National Association* lasted between January 1916 and 1922, circulating in 325 copies.[64] It had four pages in English and seventeen pages in Gujarati. The Gujarati part included sections on the activities of the Association, commercial subjects, market rates, commercial intelligence, and an enquiry column. It

60 *The Gazette,* 1082, Monday October 21, 1912.

61 *The Gazette,* 1084, Monday November 14, 1912 and *The Official Gazette,* 1191, November 23, 1914.

62 A daily *Commercial Report* appeared during the war in Gujerati and English. The editor was J.P. Patel. It circulated amongst the Indian community; 100 copies were sold daily at ten cents each. It ceased in the late 1960s. See Hamdani, *Zanzibar,* 11. There is no other evidence for its appearance.

63 'Chequered ...', 10 and Sturmer, 198. Hamdani, *Zanzibar,* 11 believes it appeared in Zanzibar and that it also was in English

64 Zanzibar Protectorate, *Blue Book for the Year 1916* (Zanzibar 1917), Q5.

also carried important Government notifications. *The Journal* declared: 'The publication of the monthly journal of the Indian National Association Zanzibar is the new enterprise undertaken by the Association and the publishers crave for the indulgence of the generous readers for any imperfections that may have crept into it. The outgrowing demand from the members of the Association and the Indians here to remain in close touch with the activity of the Association was deemed to be quite just and fair as well as beneficial to all concerned. Unfortunately there is no regular paper in Zanzibar clearly representing the Indian Voice and treating so important subjects of Education, Trade, Commerce, Literature, Agriculture, etc; and it is to meet this long felt necessity to a certain extent that this publication is undertaken.'[65]

Various efforts were made by the British authorities to keep the Arab and Swahili speaking population informed of the progress of the war and to keep them on the British side. A three-page government leaflet in Arabic on the war, *Bi-Amr al-Ḥukūma* (On Government Order), entitled *Nubdhat al-Natā'ij al-Ḥarbīya ba'd Ḥarb Ithnā 'Ashar Shahran, ṭubi'a wa Nushira min Maṭba'at al-Ḥukūma, Zanjabār, fī athnā Shahr Aughst 1915* (Fragment on the Military Consequences after 12 Months of War, Printed and Published from the Government Press, during August 1915) trumpeted '1. England is still the Queen of the Seas' and has no rival; all enemy ships have been sunk that we have come across. Germany and Austria are besieged; most German people eat 'potato bread.' German trade from all parts of the world has been destroyed; British trade has not been affected. English notes and financial notes (*awrāq*) are negotiable anywhere; German notes and silver have less than half the value. The English Government has captured all the German colonies, except that in East Africa (*al-Ifriqīya al-Sharqīya*). It has the German colony in South West Africa, which now flies the British flag. It has conquered 'Kiya Gaw' (Kiautschou in China?), New Guinea, the Marshall Islands, the Bismarck Islands, Samoa, Cameroon, Togoland, Mafia Island (*Gawlah*), it rules over Egypt, Iraq and the Euphrates Delta, Cyprus, and Samoa. German submarines have sunk a large number of ships, but up to 2,000 ships leave and enter English ports every week. Though some old warships (*bawārij*) have been sunk by submarines, the English fleet is still the greatest power. The German fleet has taken refuge in the German ports, since the beginning of the

65 *The Journal of the Indian National Association,* 1. Some say wrongly that it appeared in 1915.

war it is afraid to confront the English fleet.'[66] It continued: one must not consider the temporary withdrawal of the Russians as an indication of their defeat, as Russia has a vast and large population. The Germans for a year have been unable to pierce the English and French lines; they have suffered great losses up to four million (i.e. 40 lac). The Italian army has entered Austria. Turkish attacks on Egypt and Aden have been dispersed.[67]

Major Pearce informed those present at the British Resident's monthly *baraza* held at the Residency on Wednesday [1915], including all leading Arabs, of his intention to have a newspaper in Arabic and Swahili published weekly, 'so that the subjects of His Highness the Sultan may be given greater facilities to learn the trend of the more important events of the war.'

> The need for a more satisfactory channel of communication with the Arabs and natives of Zanzibar than is provided by the *Official Gazette* has long been felt, for since the publication of *Nagar* (sic) was discontinued there has been no Arabic newspaper of any description published in the Protectorate.
>
> From time to time pamphlets in Arabic and Swahili in Arabic characters have been published by the Government Press, giving the outline of the more important events which have happened during the war. The eagerness with which these publications have been received by the Arabs and Swahilis and the frequent enquiries for further, more frequent and more detailed information, have led the Government to consider the possibility of publishing a weekly Arabic-Swahili newspaper.
>
> The first number of *Min Usbour illa Usbour* [From Week to Week] will be published on Wednesday next and while its immediate *raison d'être* is to meet an ever increasing demand for news of the war, there is every reason to hope that the new journal will prove of great value in furnishing information on all subjects of economic importance. It will also provide a medium for the conveyance of all official information to the farthest village of the Protectorate.
>
> It is hoped that Europeans by becoming subscribers, will contribute to the increase of the circulation of the paper amongst their native employees.

At the same time Pearce expressed the hope that the support given to the paper would be such to encourage the Government to increase the size of the paper and extend the sphere of its influence. 'The Arabs in expressing their pleasure at the

66 Ibid., 1–2.
67 Zanzibar Archives CA 1/10, 3.

fulfilment of a long felt want' assured the Resident that they would do all in their power to increase the circulation of the paper. After refreshments had been served a copy of the first issue was presented to everyone present.' The paper, called *El-Usbueyah/al-Usbū'īya* (The Weekly), appeared on 27 Dhū'l-Qa'da, 1333/7th October 1915, every Thursday at 3 cents/two pice per copy;[68] Printed at the Government Press (*Maṭba'at al-Ḥukūma*) in two columns, one in Arabic and one in Swahili in vowelled Arabic script, it had an edition of 600 copies.[69] Subscribers were told to contact the administration of *The Gazette* or Shaykh Ṣāliḥ b 'Alī; the latter may well have been the editor of the paper. The first editorial (*al-dībāja*) commented:

> We have found that the opportunities for the subjects of H.H. the Sultan of Arabs and Swahilis from the inhabitants of Zanzibar and Pemba to get to know the passage of important events, especially since the events of the present European war are confined to a limited circle. We thought to help them find a means to quench the severe thirst that befalls them, by which we mean the thirst of coming upon the spring of the correct news, which is clear and plain between the Arabs and Swahilis.
>
> As for the Indian communities, their Indian papers published for them are sufficient for their needs.
>
> Many Arabs and all those speaking Swahili depend upon getting the news on what friends are so kind to translate a small amount from some of the European and Indian papers.
>
> To block this deficiency that has happened, we have taken the initiative to offer the first number of *al-Usbū'īya.* We are confident that most Arab and Swahili readers will welcome it and turn to it with approval and support, back and help it, encouraging the government to continue to publish this fixed weekly. The purpose which led to issuing this weekly is to find a means to bring news of the Great War to all readers.
>
> We hope if we find acceptance from the readers by guaranteeing to issue it weekly, they will find it a means to bring useful information on health and agriculture, etc. and material containing benefit.

The first issue in five pages carried news of a great French and English victory in Flanders, news from the Russian front, news from the African mainland (*al-barr*),

68 *Supplement to the Official Gazette,* vol. xxiv, 1236, October 4, 1915, 402 and vol. xxiv, 1237, October 11, 1915, 411. Sturmer, *Sprachpolilitik,* 195 believes it appeared from 1914 to 1918. Scotton, *Growth,* 37 and 470 gives the name as 'El Usueyeh ... reportedly published in Swahili' 'between 1905 and 1910'.

69 Zanzibar Protectorate, *Blue Book for the Year 1915* (Zanzibar 1916), Q5; *Blue Book, 1916,* Q5; *Blue Book for the Year 1917* (Zanzibar 1918), Q5 and *Blue Book ... 1918* (Zanzibar 1919), A15.

describing German cruelty, harshness (*faẓāẓa*), and looting.[70] By 1918 the circulation had fallen to 200 copies. In December 1919 it was announced that 'owing to the apparent lack of demand for the Arabic weekly newspaper *El Usbueyeh,* issued by the Government Press, its publication will be discontinued.'[71]

Master returned to Zanzibar in 1916 and restarted the newspaper, *The Samachar,* as a Gujerati weekly on Sunday 1 May 1917, costing Rs. 10 a year and sold about 300 copies. It gave special attention to Islamic matters and the affairs of his community, the Ithnasheri. In July 1920 he left first for his native place of Cutch, intending then to go on pilgrimage to Karbala. He died en route to Cutch of a heart attack on 28 August 1920. He left the paper in charge of his son Hasanali F.J. Master (1920–38), under whom it 'became second to none amongst all newspapers in East Africa barring *East African Standard* and *Tanganyika Standard.*'[72]

Opportunities for publishing works in Arabic in Zanzibar remained limited, so that a number of Zanzibaris arranged to have their works published in Cairo. The chief Ibāḍī judge of Zanzibar, Shaykh ʿAlī b. Muḥammad b. ʿAlī al-Mundhirī (–1925) published *Nūr al-Tawḥīd,* a short text on the articles of faith (*'aqā'id*), in Cairo in 1901–2 and a work on jurisprudence (*fiqh*) for the young, *Kitāb Ikhtiṣār al-Adyān li Ta'līm al-Ṣibyān,* in Cairo in 1913–14. The leading Zanzibari Ibāḍī scholar of his time, Sayf b. Nāṣir b. Sulaymān al-Kharūsī (fl. late nineteenth century) published his *Jāmi' Arkān al-Islām fī Madhhab al-Ibāḍīya,* on the pillars of Islam according to the sect in Cairo in 1912–13.

Abū Muḥammad, Burhān b. Muḥammad Mkelle/Mukallā (1883–4/1949) taught the Arabic language for more than thirty years in the government school (1908–39); generations of young Muslims in Zanzibar and East Africa studied under him. He had extensive knowledge of the Arabic language and its literature, and became known as the Sibawayh of Zanzibar. He published various works for his students on grammar, *al-Alfīya al-Wāḍiḥa al-Mulaqqaba bi'l-Jawāhir al-Munaẓẓama,* in Zanzibar in 1916–17, *al-Tamrīn/El-Tamrin/Primary Lessons on Grammar,* written with Saleh bin Ali, and edited by Aḥmad b. Sumayṭ at the Zanzibar Government Printing Press in 1918,

---

70 *al-Usbū'īya,* vol. 1, 1, 1–2 in the Public Records Office, CO 618/12.

71 *Blue Book, 1918,* Q4 and *Supplement to the Official Gazette,* 1455, December 15, 1919, 396.

72 'Chequered ...', 12 and *Blue Book ... 1918,* Q4. Scotton, *Growth,* 36 says the *Samachar* first appeared in 1901; Hamdani, *Zanzibar,* 8 and Sturmer, 183 give 1902, confusing it with the *Islam Samachar.* The Zanzibar Archives have a copy of the issue vol. 15, no. 260, Saturday 30 March 1918 all in Gujerati. It ceased to appear in 1968. Few copies are available from these early years.

'teaching Arabic to Arab children in Z'bar who speak Swahili from their infancy as they do not understand the Arabic grammar easily,' and on rhetoric, *Murshid al-Bustān ilā 'Ulūm al-Bayān,* in 1923.

A new section in Arabic, *al-Qism al-'Arabī* or *al-Qism al-'Arabī min al-Gāzīt al-rasmī* (The Arabic Section of the Official Gazette) or *akhbār al-usbu' -rasmīya* (the week's official news) appeared in the *Supplement to the Official Gazette* for the first time in no. 1465, February 23, 1920, filling between one and a half columns to a full page of two columns, including official, local and foreign news (*akhbār rasmīya, maḥalīya,* and *khārijīya*).[73] It always began with news of the Sultan (*'iẓmat mawlānā al-sayyid*) and his movements/activities, the meetings of the British Resident (*rizidint*), and then foreign news. The local news covered were barazas, official engagements, weddings, 'īd celebrations (*al-iḥtifāl bi'l-'īd*), the sale of cloves (*qurunfūl*), and deaths of prominent figures. There was very little hard news. Most items were short, just a line or two; it can hardly be considered a substantial newspaper. In 1928 the Mudīr al-Qism al-'Arabī was Ṣāliḥ b. 'Alī b. Ṣāliḥ al-Shaybānī/Saleh bin Ali bin Saleh el-Sheibani, the Arabic interpreter at H.B.M.'s Agency and Consulate General, who had worked dedicatedly for 40 years for the British Government. In 1929 al-Qism al-'Arabī was still regular in the *Supplement*; by 1930 with the appearance in April 1929 in Zanzibar of a regular weekly Arabic newspaper, *al-Falaq,* it had stopped.

This section soon began publishing its own feuilleton. In an article in Arabic in *The Gazette* it was announced that the Resident (Major Francis B. Pearce, CMG) will publish in London a book, *Zanzibar: the Island Metropolis of Eastern Africa* (*Ta'rīkh Zanjabār wa'l-Ifrīqīya al-Sharqīya*) containing 'strange and scarce news', ornamented with beautiful drawings, with a picture of al-Sayyid and other Arab nobles (*a'yān al-'arab*) in Zanzibar.[74] *al-Qism al-'Arabī* announced: 'We hope to present our readers shortly with a translation of extracts from the book, *'Āṣimat al-Sāḥil al-Ifrīqī al-Sharqī* (Capital of the East African Coast) or *Kitāb Jazīrat Zanjabār 'Āṣimat al-Ifrīqīya al-Sharqīya* (The Island of Zanzibar, Capital of East Africa). It contains useful news. Only a limited number of copies have been printed of this valuable book. We inform

73 *Supplement to the Official Gazette,* 1467, March 8, 1920. *Mwongozi,* 4 states incorrectly that *el-Qism el-Araby* appeared during the Great War, mistakenly perceiving it as a separate publication, rather than part of *The Official Gazette.*

74 *Supplement to the Official Gazette,* 1465, February 23, 1920, 62 and 1467, March 8, 1920, 77.

everyone, who wants to peruse the past history of Zanzibar and what events pervade it, not to miss the opportunity of the existence of this book and rush to obtain a copy of it. Because it is one of the books, which each family of Arab origin should get a copy of.' At the end of the month of fasting the translation would begin; 'thus all our readers can study this valuable book.'[75] The translation began of a selection each week from the first chapter, filling regularly from one column to two full pages.[76] In it could be found details of the official visit of al-Sayyid Mājid b. Saʿīd to Bombay in 1863, of the Arabs uniting in Islam, their invasion of Africa, and the conquest of Syria, Persia, Iraq and Europe. At the end His Excellency thanks all those, who gave him information: al-Sayyid [the Sultan], Dr. Aydarus, Ṣāliḥ b. ʿAlī Ṣāliḥ, and the photographer Gomes.[77]

By 1920 the printing press and newspapers had become an established part of the cultural and religious life of Zanzibar. The Arab, Swahili, British, and Indian communities had grown accustomed to books and newspapers in their languages, and in 1929 with *al-Falaq/The Dawn,* 'a literary, political, moral and agricultural newspaper', established by the Arab Association an Arabic newspaper was to become a permanent feature of the media. The government press had played a major role in encouraging religious scholarship amongst Zanzibaris/Omanis and making Ibadi religious texts available to a wider audience in Zanzibar and Oman and other centres where the Ibadi community lived. Arabic printing presses in Zanzibar and Cairo had allowed Zanzibari writers from the Ibāḍī community and the islands' larger Shāfiʿī community to publish Islamic and other textbooks for their young and to make a contribution to the island's literary renaissance with works in Arabic of poetry and travel description.

75 *Supplement to the Official Gazette,* 1472, April 12, 1920, 129 and 1479, May 31, 1920, 114.
76 *Supplement to the Official Gazette,* 1485, July 12, 1920.
77 *Supplement to the Official Gazette,* 1476, May 10, 1920, 1478, May 24, and 1485, July 12, 1920.

الاسبوعيه

EL USBUEYAH.

العدد ١ من المجلد الاول زنجبار الخميس ٢٧ ذى القعدة سنه ١٣٣٣ الثمن بيستين

الديباجه

قد وجدنا ان الفرص التى لدى رعايا جلالة السلطان من العرب والسواحليين من سكان زنجبار وسكان الجزيرة الخضراء فى الحصول والتعرف على سير الوقائع والحوادث المهمة وعلى الخصوص وقائع الحرب الاروپاوية الحاضرة محصوره فى دائرة محدوده وقد راينا ان نساعدهم فى ايجاد وسيلة تطفى الظمأ الشديد الذى حل بهم ونعنى به ظما الورود على منهل الاخبار الصحيحه الذى هو بينا وواضحا بين العرب والسواحليين

اما جماعات الهنود بجرائدهم الهنديه تنشرلهم ما يكفيهم لاجل احتياجاتهم

انما كثيرا من العرب وكافة المتكلمين باللغة السواحلية يعتمدون فى الحصول على الاخبار فيما يتفضل عليهم الاصدقاء الذين يقدرون يترجمون لهم نتفا من بعض الجرائد الاروپاويه والهنديه

فلاجل سد هذا النقص الحاصل بادرنا بتقديم العدد لاول من الاسبوعيه هذه واننا واثقين بان عموم قراء العربية والسواحلية سيستقبلوها ويلتفتوا لها بالاستحسان ويعضدوها ويشدوا ازرها ويؤيدوها تاييدا يشجع الحكومة على استمرار اصدار جريدة مقننه اسبوعيه ـ اما الغرض الذى دعى لاصدار الاسبوعيه هذه فهو ايجاد واسطة تنقل فيها اخبار الحرب العظمى الى كافة القراء

انما نؤمل باننا اذا وجدنا اقبال القراء عليها بكفل صدارها اسبوعيا فانهم سيجدونها وسيلة تنقل اليهم

تموتن نجيا ونازا اندام وعرب نوسواحل وانغوج نيمبا كپاتى خبار يمامب مكوا يناى پيت نخاص خبار يفيت فليوك الاى ننجيا نيمبامبا سان نتمئون افضل كوسيدى كوپتيا نجى اتكاى واندلى كيو وليج ناج چشوق يكسوم خبار زلز كويل ـ اما هاو جماع وكهندى هوان شد يكپات خبار سباب مغازيت م يكهندى ينوتشبزى حاج زاو ـ لكن وعرب نوسواحل ولى رعى وسيد ونتمنى كپات خبار زاو كوواسط ومرفيك زاو ووزاو كواحسان ياو كوترجمى فپاند فپاند فدوغ فيخبار كتك مغازيت يكنغريزا تمغازيت يكهندى

باس كواجل يكزيب پنغوا هى تمئندوك كوتنزا وات وسماو كعرب نكسواحل كوهى عدد يكوانزا تلى ايتا الاسبوعيه نسيس تنامين كن كاف يوات وناو سوم كعرب نكسواحل وتاشنغلى نوتاسيدى حتى سركال افانى موى مكوبوا ايتو كل اجما ـ نسبب الى پاس كتنغازا الاسبوعيه هل هيف ساس نكيفنيا سباب يكوجوليش جميع يوات وسماو كعرب نكسواحل خبار زفيت فكوا فليوك الاى لكن

Figure 1.

الشانبة

الجريدة الحكمية الزراعية

تشيع في كل شهر مرة اخبارا عن الفلاحة وعن الاخبار المفيدة

١٢ شهر محرم سنة ١٣١٥ الجزو الاول الثمن ٤ بيس

المبادي

الجريدة الة لارتقاء مدارج الانسانية * وهي منبع العلم ومخزن الهمم * وبها تنبعث الافكار الصائبة وتمحى الكسالة الباطلة * وبها بين الانام رباط المحبة وقلادة المودة ولكنها اشارة على العلم فقط فثبوتها من العمل عليها في الاني * ونحن عجلنا لانتشار هذه الجريده بوجوه فمنها قياسنا على محاسن ارض زنجبار وقابليتها بتيقن حصول المنافع الوافرة لذا لانطيق ان نصبر * ومنها ان اهل البلد من زنجبار وفيمبا الذين يخدمون الزرع لا يعرفون شيئا من لغات يوروب واخص علم الفلاحة ومعارفها في هذه اللغات مستور ومعلوم ان علم الفلاحة هو اخص مسائل الزرع فالغرض القوي من هذه الشانبة (اسم الجريده) التعليم في حجب المسائل اللطيفة * ونحن نعد فيها اولا مسائلها خاصة لفلاحين البلد * وثانيا نذكر فيها اخبار البلد * وثالثا لا نترك اخبار بلدان اخرى * نحن لو نشتغل في تذكرة علم الفلاحة فقط دون امور اخرى فيمكن لا نحصل فائده تامة خاصة لنا في زنجبار

فهذه الجزائر بوسايط الشمس والمطر خضراء وعلى اعتدال كلي من الهواء * فلذا جرت القاعدة اهل الزرع لايدخلون في امور عالية ولايتعبون انفسهم كثيرا الا يزرعون البزر وينتظرون الحصاد وهم في البيوت جالسين (اما في زماننا هذا الكسل والبطل وهذا الاستغناء والفشل لا ينفع بشيء * كل من حرك حصل * كل من جلس بطل * لان الرقابة في البيع واسعه * وحوايج السوق في الرخص شائعه هكذا قاعدة الدهر ان كل شيء ينقص تدريجا في ثمنه * فينبغي لاهل الفلاحة التدبر والتفكر للفلاحة * لو تفكروا اهل الزرع وعجلوا في امورهم فلهم فواكه الفوائد ناضجة ومساعيهم من البركات منتجه * والا حصول القوت لهم الامر الاصعب وكل من تأني في الميسر فهو الاعقب ولنا لايس اليأس لان عندنا الجزائر الخضراء بقوة الارض وكثرة الماء * قصيرة المسافه طويله الامال * رخيصة الثمن كثيرة المال * هواءها للصحة كالدواء ولقرة العيون فيها الخضراء * لو خدموها اهل الزرع بقوانين الفلاحة وتركوا الكسل فهذه الجزائر ليختطفن كرة السبق عن اراضي جميع البلدان كلها خاصة في النارجول والقرنفل لا تسبق عليها احدى ارض بحلها *

فنحن نتوقع في الاني ان نذكر طرق الفلاحة باسرها تدريجا ونعلم اهل الشوانب المصالح لها *

ومن المعلوم التعليم والسعي منا لا ينفعهم الا بوجدان شغفهم في هذه الامور والشوق وتدقيقهم فيها *

Figure 2.

From Journalism to Promotion of Goods: Why and How Did Press Publishers Establish Advertising Agencies in Egypt, 1890–1939?

Relli Shechter

Ben-Gurion University

Introduction

Although there has been growing interest in the history of the press in recent years, most such research falls short of bringing together the content of newspapers and magazines and the operations of the publishing business.[1] Historiography, so far, has generally focussed on the press as a cultural institution or as a source for political, social, and cultural commentary on contemporary transitions.[2] The business history of the press has not been entirely ignored, but it is only secondary to the main topic. In other words, we still lack research discussing the influence of organisation and finance on the substance of the press. Nowhere is this more obvious than in the study of the development of the popular press, especially illustrated magazines, whose rise epitomised the entry of publishers into advertising and the search for new venues to carry advertisements successfully.

This article aims at closing this gap by bringing content (of advertisements) and context (the economics of publishing) together and discussing the interplay between the two. The article studies two periods in which press advertising developed significantly. The first, during the 1890s, a period characterised by a surge in Egyptian journalism, which coincided with an impressive local economic boom at the peak of Egyptian integration into the world economy. The second and more

1 Short sections from this article appeared earlier in a different context in 'Press Advertising in Egypt: Business Realities and Local Meaning, 1882–1956', *Arab Studies Journal*, 10:2 / 11:1 (Fall 2002–Spring 2003): 44–66.

2 For a cultural institution approach, see Ami Ayalon, *The Press in the Arab Middle East: A History* (Oxford 1995); Beth Baron, *The Women's Awakening in Egypt: Culture, Society, and the Press* (New Haven 1994). The literature that uses the press as a source of commentary on contemporary life is by nature more eclectic. For journalism as an interface between politics and culture see James Jankowski and Israel Gershoni, *Rethinking Nationalism in the Arab Middle East* (New York 1997). The press (especially popular magazines) has recently become a growing source of interest in studies on mass culture; see Walter Armbrust, *Mass Culture and Modernism in Egypt* (Cambridge 1996).

significant period, and that on which the article focuses more closely, was the 1920s and 1930s, when there were major developments in the operations of the Egyptian press accompanied by a significant increase in the number and quality of advertisements.

Press Advertising before World War I (WWI)

Press advertising began soon after the publication of the first Egyptian journal;[3] the earliest advertisements appeared in the official journal of the Egyptian government (*al-Waqa'i' al-Miṣriyya*) a large number of which were government notices.[4] In 1867 *Wadi al-Nil* was among the first privately owned newspapers to publish advertisements.[5] Private persons also placed ads in both the government and the private press announcing in simple terms the sale of goods, properties, or services in the standard format of classified ads. Besides being inconspicuous, advertisements also occupied little space: seldom more than 5% of the total space of the newspaper.[6] Real growth in advertising happened only when press publication in Egypt received a significant boost during the 1890s after the colonial government eased regulations on journalism.[7] An economic boom that lasted until 1907 enlarged the financial means that facilitated the progress of the press. During this period the Egyptian press came to play a significant role in contemporary political and cultural life. At the same time, there were also important developments in publications aimed at women.[8]

The period before WWI experienced a corresponding development in the business of advertising, mainly in selling advertising space. Even more the press played an active role in promoting the business and attracting potential customers. *Al-Hilal* was especially busy in such promotion.[9] Jurji Zaidan, the editor of *al-Hilal*, published several articles explaining the principles and benefits of advertising to his

---

3 Khalil Ṣabat, *al-I'lan: Tarikhuhu, Ususuhu, wa-Qawa'iduhu, Fununuhu wa-Akhlaqiyyatuhu* (Cairo 1987), 51.

4 Mona Russell, *Creating the New Woman: Consumerism, Education, and National Identity in Egypt, 1863–1922*, unpublished dissertation (Georgetown University 1998), 131–2.

5 Ṣabat, *al-I'lan*, 51.

6 Ayalon, *The Press*, 203.

7 Ayalon, *The Press*, 52; Russell, *Creating*, 132–3.

8 Baron, *The Women's*, 67–71.

9 Ayalon, *The Press*, 205. Ayalon cites the following examples: *al-Hilal* (1 Sep. 1892), 48; (1 Jul. 1895), 840; (15 Aug. 1895), 926–31; (15 Aug. 1900), 128. See also Russell, *Creating*, 134, citing *al-Hilal* (4 Sep. 1896), 344; (5 May 1897), 413–14; (10 May 1901), 151.

readers and *al-Hilal* frequently published calls for advertisers. After WWI Zaidan's sons continued to be in the forefront of publishers of keen business acumen who promoted press advertising in Egypt.

It was the larger and more established newspapers and magazines that received most advertising because they offered advertisers better exposure to potential consumers. Close ties with the political and economic elite of the country further improved their lot. Thus, *al-Ahram* had official approval to publish announcements by all the national and mixed courts, and it also secured the authority to publish stock-market announcements.[10] While advertising certainly became a significant source of income, especially for the larger publications, it probably could not sustain most newspapers and magazines.[11] With the possible exception of the better-selling magazines and newspapers, the vast majority of the press must have received some sort of subsidies from the government, political parties, private investors, or publishers.

With the developments in the press, the quantity (space and size), quality (especially new illustrations), and number of commodities and services advertised significantly increased. Egyptian advertisements were similar to advertisements elsewhere because, with few exceptions, they promoted modern imported commodities and services. Egyptian advertising also followed the universal trend in which the most highly advertised items of the period were patent medicines and cosmetics.[12] Other commodities advertised included alcoholic beverages, ready-made clothing, furniture, and home and office appliances.[13] Among professional services offered were law offices, doctors' and dentists' clinics, insurance, financial services, and translation offices. Still, limited literacy and circulation of the press during this period meant that even when local advertising followed the contemporary stylistic and thematic standards of Europe and the United States, it aimed at much more affluent consumers than those who would buy the same commodities in their countries of

10 Yunan Labib Rizk, 'Al-Ahram: A Diwan of Contemporary Life (205)', *Al-Ahram Weekly* (23–9 October 1997), 10.

11 Baron, *The Women's* (69) suggests the same for women's magazines of the period.

12 Russell, *Creating*, 135.

13 Russell, *Creating* (135–66), provides the best analysis of the content of advertising for this period. See also: Ayalon, *The Press*, 202–6; Rizk, *al-Ahram*, 10; Yunan Labib Rizk, *al-Ahram, Diwan al-Ḥayat al-Mu'aṣir* (Cairo 1995), 77–84.

origin. From this perspective, it is also significant that most locally produced commodities and the more traditional services were not represented in the press.

The restricted nature of the readership also meant that even some modern items were excluded from advertising. This was best illustrated in women's magazines, which were even more class-restrictive than the general press. Russell rightly points out the absence of labour-saving devices from the list of commodities advertised in *Anis al-Jalis*, the first women's magazine published and the heaviest publisher of advertisements.[14] Unlike women in Western countries, women of leisure in Egypt did not need such devices, since labour was cheap and abundant. The world of goods and services represented in the press was, therefore heavily biased and exclusive; it exposed only small, albeit developing, new markets rather than a clear picture of the commodities and services available to the majority of the population.

The Press and Advertising during the 1920s and 1930s

After WWI, the circulation of Egyptian newspapers and magazines began to increase significantly. One of the reasons for this was a rapid rise in literacy, albeit mainly in urban areas, and demographic growth, which also enlarged the absolute number of readers. In addition, the prices of newspapers were lowered by subsidies of all kinds, technological improvement, and growing revenues from advertising. In fact, newspaper prices dropped significantly in real terms between the turn of the century and the outbreak of WWII.[15] This enabled persons of small financial means to buy and read them. The expansion in newspaper and magazine circulation was also connected to the relative freedom of the press after 1923, with the introduction of a new constitution and the first Parliament.[16]

As during the 1890s, the press rapidly spread as the main form of democratic political expression. This, in turn, brought about a major increase in the circulation of existing newspapers and magazines and the establishment of new politically-affiliated ones such as *al-Kashkul*, *Ruz al-Yusuf*, and the short-lived weeklies, *al-Siyasa al-Usbu'iyya* and *al-Balagh al-'Usbu'i*.[17] Egypt also experienced an intellectual revival,

14 Russell, *Creating*, 151.
15 Ayalon, *The Press*, 193.
16 'Abd al-Latif Ḥamza, *Qiṣṣat al-Siḥafa al-'Arabiyya fi Miṣr mundh Nasha'atiha ila Muntaṣaf al-Qurn al-'Ishrin* (Cairo 1985, 2nd edition), 166; Ṣabat, *al-I'lan*, 56.
17 Ḥamza, *Qiṣṣat*, 169.

which manifested itself in all spheres of cultural production and found its fullest expression in new magazines such as *al-Thaqafa*, *al-Risala*, *Apollo*, and *Majallati*, which reflected conflicting visions of Egyptian cultural life and identity. The period further witnessed the establishment of many special-interest magazines: professional, Islamic, sport, women's, children's, etc.[18]

An important, but less discussed addition to the press of the period was popular illustrated magazines,[19] especially those of *Dar al-Hilal*. This publishing house, now headed by Emil and Shukri Zaidan, the sons of Jurji, was the leading promoter of this new trend and it became the largest press business of the period.[20] During the 1920s and 1930s, *Dar al-Hilal* produced a long stream of popular magazines in Arabic and French,[21] which created a different approach in the Egyptian press. The magazines discussed contemporary local and world events in less serious tones than did the political press and took a less highbrow approach to culture. Instead, the illustrated magazines introduced the concept of reading for leisure and they promoted a new style of journalism that highlighted new topics such as fashion, sports, tourism, and local and international cinema. They featured attractive layouts and high-quality illustrations, cartoons, and photographs, which were refreshing additions to the press of the day. Accordingly, they could cater for a larger audience which, unlike in the past, included semi-literate and even illiterate persons who could enjoy the magazines simply by looking at the graphic images. The advent of the illustrated press opened new options to advertisers. It promised high quality printing and graphic design. It further offered a modern ambience, which suited the advertised goods. Most important, illustrated magazines were among the best-sold press.[22]

During the period under discussion, the press actively promoted the sale of advertising space and owners competed to increase their share in the advertising

---

18 Ḥamza, *Qiṣṣat*, 172.

19 See an article on contemporary development in the press with special attention to illustrated magazines, 'Jara'iduna wa-jara'iduhum', *Majallat Miṣr al-Ḥaditha al-Muṣawwara* (25 Dec.1927), 3–6.

20 Ayalon, *The Press*, 78.

21 *Dar al-Hilal* publications included *al-Dunya al-Muṣawwara*, *al-Fukaha*, *Image* (in French), *Kull Shay'*, and *al-Muṣawwar*. Advertisement in *Taqwim al-Hilal* (1932), 11. It also included *al-Laṭa'if al-Muṣawwara*, Ḥamza, *Qiṣṣat*, 167.

22 *Al-Ahram*, the biggest newspaper of the time, had an average circulation of 70–80,000, *al-Muqaṭṭam* 10–15,000, *al-Siyasa* 5,000, and *Wadi al-Nil* also 5,000. In comparison, *al-Dunya al-Muṣawwara* had an average circulation of 30,000; *al-Muṣawwar* 21,000; *Kull Shay'* 19,000; *al-Fukaha* 15,000; *al-Laṭa'if al-Muṣawwara* 12–14,000 (the last four were published by *Dar al-Hilal*). *Balfour Trade Mission Survey*, 10–14.

business. The internal struggle in the press over advertisers became a major factor in the promotion of advertising. Most newspapers and magazines published information for advertisers on how to place advertisements (directly or via advertising agencies) and at times indicated the price of space. They also engaged in active advertising campaigns aimed at persuading businessmen to advertise. *Dar al-Hilal*, for example, ran continual promotional campaigns for advertising in *al-Muṣawwar* throughout the 1920s and early 1930s. The magazine ran slogans such as '[N]othing is more useful for you than the advertisement, which is the secret of success in this age.'[23] And, '[T]he best advertising is the one that is always in the hands of the customers. Advertise your merchandise in order to sell it to the people.'[24] Press rivalry over advertisements further stimulated integration between the press and the advertising business as a whole.

Initially, most publishers handled press advertising as part of the editorial office.[25] In time, the larger publishers such as *al-Ahram* established large advertising departments to cope with the growing business.[26] In addition to selling space, these departments provided customers with copy-writing and graphic services.[27] Later, the big publishing houses established their own advertising agencies in order to save on commissions paid to other agencies. *Al-Ahram* established *al-Ahram li l-I'lan*, *Dar al-Hilal* established *Wikalat al-I'lanat al-Afriqiyya al-Asiyawiyya*, *Akhbar al-Yawm* established *Wikalat al-Qahira li l-I'lan*, and *Ruz al-Yusuf* established *Wikalat Ruz al-Yusuf li l-I'lan.*[28] The larger agencies also had representatives abroad.[29]

In establishing their own advertising agencies the publishers followed the model of *Société Orientale de Publicité* (SOP) established 1906. SOP was the oldest, largest, and probably the most technically-competent agency of its kind. A close look at the structure and activities of this company illustrates the high level of integration between publishing and advertising. *The Stock Exchange Year-Book* for 1939 described SOP as 'newspaper proprietors, printers, and advertising contractors,

23 *Al-Muṣawwar* (28 Dec. 1924), 3.
24 *Al-Muṣawwar* (6 Nov. 1931), 13.
25 See, for example, *al-Nahḍa al-Nisa'iyya* (Apr. 1922), back cover. *al-Nashra al-Iqtiṣadiyya al-Miṣriyya* (27 Jun. 1920), 44.
26 Ḥamza, *Qiṣṣat*, 173.
27 See an advertisement for such services in a self-advertisement, *Majallati* (1 Feb. 1935), n.p.
28 Ṭal'at al-Zuhayri, *al-I'lan bayn al-'Ilm wa al-Taṭbiq* (Cairo 1975), 155–6.
29 See, for example, an advertisement in *al-Ithnayn* (27 May 1935), 33, directing advertisers to the agents of *Dar al-Hilal* in Britain (London) and France (Paris).

including poster, illuminating signs, and all classes of outdoor advertising.'[30] The company owned the English-language dailies *The Egyptian Gazette* and *The Egyptian Mail* and the French-language dailies, *La Bourse Egyptienne* (Cairo and Alexandria editions). In SOP, business interests overcame political rivalry and the company represented both *al-Miṣr,* the 'opposition party organ,' and *al-Balagh,* the 'government party organ'.[31] The chairman and managing director of SOP at that time was a Jew Henri Haim, but in the largely cosmopolitan business environment of the period, this did not seem to bother the owners of the national press.

A few years later the newspaper *al-Miṣr* bought half the SOP business and the company changed its name to the *Société Egyptienne de Publicité* (SEP).[32] *Al-Miṣr* had developed from a party organ to one of Egypt's largest newspapers, and its owner probably felt that it needed to keep up with other large publishers who had their own advertising agencies. At that time press-advertising agencies operated as the sole representatives of their publications and competed with other agencies for advertising space in the newspapers and magazines that were affiliated with it. Thus SEP operated as the sole representative of *al-Miṣr* and the SOP press. The agencies of *al-Ahram* and *al-Hilal* did the same and did not accept advertisements from SEP. All this indicates the high level of convergence between press publishing and advertising, and the monopolistic tendency in selling advertising space. These characteristics were not unique to publishing and advertising but fairly common in most Egyptian businesses of the period.[33]

The Operations of the Business

After WWI two inter-related developments in advertising accelerated in Britain and the United States.[34] The first was professionalisation, in which those recruited into the

30 *The Stock Exchange Year-Book of Egypt* (Cairo 1939), 609.

31 Ibid., 609–10.

32 Tom J. MacFadden, *Daily Journalism in the Arab States* (Columbus, Ohio 1953), 80–1.

33 On monopolies in the Egyptian economy, see A.A.I. El-Gritly, *The Structure of Modern Industry in Egypt* (Cairo 1948), Chapter 8. Charles Issawi, *Egypt at Mid-Century: An Economic Survey* (London 1954), 160–1.

34 On the development of advertising in Britain and the US, see Roy Church, 'Advertising Consumer Goods in Nineteenth-Century Britain: Reinterpretations', *Economic History Review,* LIII 4 (2000), 621–45; Jackson Lears, *Fables of Abundance: A Cultural History of Advertising in America* (New York 1994); Lori Anne Loeb, *Consuming Angels: Advertising and Victorian Women* (Oxford 1994). Roland Marchand, *The American Dream: Making Way for Modernity, 1920–1940* (Berkeley 1985); N. McKendrick, 'George Packwood and the Commercialization of Shaving: The Art of

business were required to go through prior training, usually in business and commerce. Professionalisation also encouraged a second and more important development in the business: the use of statistical tools to measure human behaviour and preferences. Advertising agencies began to conduct market research and provide data on the tastes of consumers that helped advertisers target specific groups of buyers for their commodities and services. Agencies also began to utilise advances in psychological research when preparing advertising campaigns. Scientific advertising services initially supplemented and gradually replaced the impressionistic slogans and illustrations and the simple sale of newspaper advertising space that had characterised early agency activities.

To what extent did international developments in the business of advertising influence the local Egyptian scene? Local economists and the commercial press publicised some of the developments in international advertising and tried to promote scientific advertising in Egypt. In 1921 Ḥasan Ṣalih al-Jadawi published a series of articles in *al-Jarida al-Tijariyya al-Miṣriyya* in which he discussed different advertising tools.[35] In April 1927 the official organ of the Commerce and Industry Authority (*Ṣaḥifat Maṣlaḥat al-Tijara wa l-Ṣina'a*) reviewed a book on advertising by Yaḥya Fahmi Effendi. In July 1928 *Ṣaḥifat al-Iqtiṣad wa l-Tijara* published an article on the importance of advertising in contemporary life in which it reported on advances in advertising in Europe and the United States.[36] In 1933 Milayka 'Iryan, a professor at the High Commerce College (*Madrasat al-Tijara al-'Ulya*), published a book on advertising.[37]

The attention paid to advertising by journalists and scholars had little influence on the business; scientific advertising of goods and services never reached the level of advanced countries in the West. This was mainly due to the fact that publishing and

Eighteenth Century Advertisements', in N. McKendrick, J. Brewer, and J.H. Plumb (eds), *The Birth of a Consumer Society: The Commercialization of Eighteenth Century England* (Bloomington, Indiana 1982); T.R. Nevett, *Advertising in Britain: A History* (London 1982); James D. Norris, *Advertising and the Transformation of American Society, 1865–1920* (New York 1990); Thomas Richards, *The Commodity Culture of Victorian England: Advertising and Spectacle, 1851–1914* (Stanford 1991); John Sinclair, *Images Incorporated: Advertising as Industry and Ideology* (London 1987); Susan Strasser, *Satisfaction Guaranteed: The Making of the American Mass Market* (New York 1989); Vincent Vinikas, *Soft Soap, Hard Sell: American Hygiene in an Age of Advertisement* (Ames, Iowa 1992).

35 See, for example, his article on catalogue advertising (7 Nov. 1921), 1.

36 *Ṣaḥifat al-Iqtiṣad wa l-Tijara* (July 1928), 275–8.

37 See advertisement for the book in *al-Usbu'* (29 Nov. 1933), 30.

advertising were controlled by a few leading companies which had little incentive to introduce these novelties into the business. As a result, advertising in Egypt largely remained the business of selling space in newspapers and magazines. Even in the early 1950s, when academic research was first performed on the state of advertising, the agencies in Egypt adopted few of the professional practices of businesses elsewhere.[38]

The underdeveloped operations of the business also reflected the slight trust local manufacturers and merchants had in advertising (for several good reasons). Egyptian commodity markets remained small and the overall volume of trade was confined to the larger cities. Moreover, local industry developed monopolies or monopolistic conditions that did not encourage competition and the widespread use of advertising as a tool in this struggle. Under contemporary economic conditions, services such as banking, insurance, and internal tourism, which would be big advertisers elsewhere, were still limited. In the Egyptian business culture sellers and buyers appeared to prefer personal and communal connections to an advertisement in the newspaper. Moreover, for most consumers price rather than quality or fashion continued to be the most significant factor in determining the purchase of commodities and services. Therefore promoting the image of commodities was less significant. The end result was that under normal conditions established local businesses did not feel the need to advertise in order to increase sales, and they would usually do so only under pressure of competition.

Another major factor that influenced the volume of advertising was the structure of the Egyptian labour market. Egypt, like many other developing countries, enjoyed an abundance of cheap labour that provided relatively inexpensive household services such as cleaning, cooking, sewing, and repairs. In addition, women rarely worked outside the home, making family members, especially daughters, more readily available for household-related tasks. Local households benefited little from ready-made, easy-to-use, labour-saving items, which were among the staples of contemporary advertising in the West.

During the period under discussion, advertising was mainly by foreign companies that imported and distributed foreign goods and services. Foreign

38 Abdel Aziz el Sherbini and Ahmed Fouad Sherif, 'Marketing Problems in an Underdeveloped Country—Egypt', *Egypte Contemporaine* XLVII (285) (July 1956), 71.

companies advertised because they believed, on the basis of their experience at home, that advertising would improve sales. They were unfamiliar with Egypt and searched for inroads into markets. The fact that many of the imported items were new to Egyptian markets further encouraged advertising in order to promote new habits and preferences of consumption. However, the most important reason to advertise was probably the fact that Egypt was experiencing growing business competition among European and later Japanese and American producers for local markets.

The Content of Advertisements

The content of advertisements well demonstrated the fact that advertising catered mostly to manufacturers abroad and local retailers who promoted imported goods.[39] After WWI, pharmaceuticals and cosmetics continued to be among the best-advertised non-durables, products increasingly manufactured by large multinationals such as Bayer, Colgate, Gillette, and Lux, rather than by the obscure chemists and doctors who had earlier controlled patent medicines. Household non-durables such as detergents and pesticides (Flit), which were a rarity before WWI, began to occupy growing space. The same was true for foodstuffs and canned foods such as baby food, biscuits, cereals, chewing gum, coffee, spring water, and tea, whose presence in advertisements became more manifest (see Fig. 1). This reflected a second trend according to which advertisers were aiming at a wider audience whose more humble means would suffice for practical day-to-day goodsising for ready-made clothing and the large-scale introduction of fashion to promote its sale. It further witnessed an increase in the promotion of imported mechanical products.

The period after WWI saw the spread of advert durables such as pens, sewing machines, and watches, whose consumption had been restricted in the past. Electric appliances like radios, refrigerators, and fans were a novelty in advertising. Such items, together with advertisements for European-style furniture, suggested a shift in the content of the home, which followed new notions of domesticity and family space

39 The analysis is based on the following newspapers and magazines: *Akhar Sa'a* 1948, 1951, 1956–9; *al-Ithnayn*, 1937–9; *al-Kashkul* 1924–8; *Majallati* 1934–7; *al-Muṣawwar* 1924–37, 1947, 1949–50, 1959; *al-Nahḍa al-Nisa'iyya*, 1922–32; *Ruz al-Yusuf* 1931–5; *al-Siyasa al-Usbu'iyya* various issues 1926; *Taqwim al-Hilal*, 1932–7.

(see Fig. 2).[40] Cars were also newly- and widely-advertised, but buying a car remained out of reach for the majority of Egyptians.

Advertisements of foreign manufacturers focused on persuading readers to begin utilising their products, to use them on a regular basis, and to prefer their items to those of the competition. In contrast, importers and distributors, while sometimes also promoting sales based on the qualities of the commodity, concentrated on advertising the retail establishment itself and inducing consumers to buy by introducing new fashions, suggesting low prices, announcing sales, and offering credit. The most devoted to advertising in this category were the large department stores such as Çicuril, Ṣidnawi, and ʿUmar Effendi (see Fig. 3). This was at least partly because, unlike smaller retailers, they also had the financial means to carry out such promotion.

With the exception of banks and insurance companies, services were not well-represented in advertising. In fact, ads by service providers such as doctors, lawyers, and translators, which were quite abundant in early advertisements, almost disappeared. This was probably because the price of advertising space increased beyond the means of private advertisers. It may also be that individual service providers did not see much benefit in advertising for services offered locally in the national press.

While advertisements for locally produced goods and services constituted only a small proportion of the advertisements, they brought something unique to the advertising of the period, as they often used national Egyptian sentiments to promote their items (Fig. 4). Such advertisements portrayed local production and consumption of items 'made in Egypt' as patriotic. Egyptian advertisers also played on national pride by suggesting the higher quality of local products and the superiority of local commerce and services. They further used the notion of 'Egyptianness' to gain leverage over the competition, which was usually from abroad. By doing so, they probably contributed to the politicising of economic thinking during this period and supported the creation of a nationalist economic ideology.

40 Nancy Y. Reynolds, 'Sharikat al-Bayt al-Misri: Domesticating Commerce in Egypt, 1931–1956', *Arab Studies Journal* (Fall 1999/Spring 2000).

Conclusion

The development of advertising in Egypt was the result of an interaction between demand for advertising space and the motivation of local press to provide it. Competition over Egyptian markets played an important part in promoting local advertising. However, both before and after WWI there was an even closer correlation between rapid periods of development in the Egyptian press, especially the introduction of popular magazines, and growth in advertising. While promoting and eventually monopolising the business, the large publishing houses curtailed further professionalisation of advertising, and Egyptian agencies adopted very few of the scientific practices that gradually became the norm in advertising elsewhere. The professional industry would only develop much later, during the Sadat era and under the impact of the Egyptian 'Open Door' policy—the *Infitaḥ.* Nevertheless, contemporary advertising was significant in the commercialisation of this rapidly evolving public sphere (the press), and in fostering the entry of modern commodities and services into Egyptian markets. For these reasons, the advertising business and its products deserve our attention in studying the history of journalism and, more broadly, in explaining the synergy between cultural change and the development of local capitalism in Egypt and elsewhere in the Middle East.

Figure 1. Advertisement for Horlick's: 'The original malted milk.'
Al-Muṣawwar (14 Oct. 1927), 17.

Figure 2. 'A happy family thanks to Bort Bonir clock.'
Al-Ithnayn (15 Jul. 1935), n.p.

Figure 3. 'Great clearance sale', an advertisement for 'Umar Effendi department store.
Al-Ithnayn (1 Oct. 1934), n.p.

Figure 4. 'Your Egyptian cigarette: produced with Egyptian capital and by Egyptian workers.' *Al-Ahram* (3 Mar. 1939), 5.

Arabic Typography: Call for a Cultural Rebirth

Huda Smitshuijzen AbiFarès

Typography is one of the most widely spread forms of visual communication. It is so integrated into all aspects of our daily lives that we simply take it for granted.

Four years ago, I embarked on a journey to rediscover what I have taken for granted all my life, Arabic Letterforms. I was invited to act as an Arabic type consultant on behalf of a renowned Dutch design studio. However, my professional education and training in the US, as well as my years of experience in Europe and the Middle East, had ill prepared me for the problems I was about to encounter. The design commission consisted of bi-scriptural signage for the reconstructed area of Beirut's Central District. Surprisingly, finding and selecting an Arabic font that is visually and technically appropriate for the design, became a daunting task. Firstly, the few fonts available on the market were either badly crafted or simply not befitting the visual style required by the design. There was no font that could harmoniously match a sans serif Latin type, and that was simple enough for use on large-scale signage. Secondly, the use of the fonts was limited by the typesetting software. I discovered that not all Arabic fonts can be used on all Desktop Publishing programs. Third, there was little information available regarding the historical background of each design, which often justifies the use of a particular typeface for a specific design application. I was faced with a frustrating situation, the like of which I had not previously encountered. I decided to turn this experience into a positive one.

I set about compiling a helpful guide and concise sourcebook on Arabic typography. Three years of research of a number of global resources and contacts followed. The book was finally published at the beginning of this year (fig.1).[1] I trust that it will fulfil its ultimate goal, that is, to facilitate the work of designers practicing in the Arab world, and that it will serve as a source of inspiration for the new generation of type designers in the Middle East. The book has marked my call to

1 Huda Smitshuijzen AbiFarès, *Arabic Typography, a Comprehensive Sourcebook* (London 2001); Saqi Books have kindly given permission to reproduce material from this book.

educate design students, and encourage them to attempt new design approaches for Arabic type.

I shall later outline the educational model I follow in the Arabic type design course I teach, and will elaborate with examples of the resulting case studies.

Typography is the Embodiment of a Culture's Identity.

Typography has been regarded throughout history as an influential representation of the prosperity, the political and cultural authority of a state. Alphabets represent a strong form of cultural identity through their embodiment of a culture's language, history and recorded thought. Their degeneration represents the degeneration of the culture itself. Like the Romans before them, the Arabs have seen their culture diminish in power and leadership, and that is clearly manifested in the state of the visual representation of their script. However, unlike the Romans, the Arabs have not seen their script evolve visually along the developments in printing and typesetting. Arabic calligraphy did not move forward after it was standardized in the tenth century. During that period many innovative designs followed, with the aim of beautifying the script to befit the Holy message it was meant to carry. Generally speaking, Arabic type today does not seem to be designed to meet the needs of contemporary design trends. It often conservatively emulates the past and alienates the younger generation of Arab designers.

The Problem with Emulating the Past.

When we limit our discussion of Arabic typography to historical facts, and we dogmatically follow the well-tread paths of the old masters, we are simply declaring the culture extinct. This is a far cry from the realities of design in the Arab world of today. Both design and the culture are very much alive, though their creative efforts are in a budding state. Clearly there are lasting lessons to learn from the past; however constructive discussions need to be concerned with the present and the future.

Visual culture has been stagnating in the Arab world for several centuries, owing to lack of enforcement of copyright laws, and lack of appreciation and funding of the visual arts. In addition, the suppression of freedom of expression strongly manifests itself in all forms of visual expression. The legacy of this long state of stagnation is a loss of confidence in the culture and all its identifying characteristics. Young designers in the Arab world shy away from their own culture because it fails to represent their complex modern identity. It is seen as repressive. It limits rather then fulfils their aspirations. This situation needs to change. It will only do so, when we assume the responsibility of taking creative risks that challenge the rules of the old establishment; of recognizing present realities of contemporary design and visual branding; of being ready to constantly question what we take for granted; and of setting the stage for constructive discussions around the subject of Arabic Type.

The ultimate emblem of Arabic culture.

The Shift from Calligraphy to Typography

Gutenberg's invention of movable type in the fifteenth century, and the mass-produced books that resulted from this invention facilitated the dissemination of knowledge. It sparked a cultural revolution that transformed Europe; liberating creative energies and advancing every area of intellectual expression. This invention also marked the birth of typesetting and the shift from calligraphy to typography in the printing arts. Historically speaking, the concept of the modern implied an inevitable break with the past. For Latin type, this meant a clear dissociation from the calligraphic past had to take place, in order for typography to flourish in its own right. Latin type has since been visually evolving along with the technological advancements of each era.

This same shift from calligraphy to typography has yet to happen for Arabic type. The belated introduction of Arabic typographic printing into the Middle East has had no effect on the visual representation of the Arabic script. It is only natural that the first cut types would be modelled after fine examples of calligraphy — as can be seen in this comparison of Gutenberg's fifteenth century Fraktur font used for the 42-line Bible, with Granjon's sixteenth century Arabica Grande font cut in 1585 for the Stamperia Medicea in Rome (fig.2).[2]

Yet Arabic calligraphy did not eventually evolve into typography. In fact, the technical and aesthetic developments were minimal and slow. Led by Western manufacturers, Arabic type became an unimaginative copy of fine examples of

2 Details of illustrations from *Arabic Typography, a Comprehensive Sourcebook* (London 2001), 48, 128.

handwritten scripts. Little was done to rejuvenate the design field with innovative typefaces. Arabic typography became merely a mechanized version of calligraphy.

Arabic type is at a critical point in its historical development where severing the ties with its glorious past is unavoidable. Arabic type is still stubbornly maintaining the values of its master calligraphers. It is not the copying of letters and aesthetic rules that need to be retained from the past, but rather the spirit of creative experimentation, and the pragmatic design solutions that show affinity with materials and media. With the technological possibilities available today, it is highly tempting to carry on emulating the past and to ignore issues of modernizing Arabic type design. Unfortunately, this is detrimental to the creative nature of typography, for the creative act is, by nature, an act of rebellion and adventure.

Twentieth Century Attempts for Reforming the Arabic Alphabet.

In the 1930s, and following the cultural Arab renaissance, a conference was held at the Academy of the Arabic Language in Cairo, with the agenda of reforming the Arabic language and its visual representation. Several proposals were submitted concerning the adaptation of the Arabic script to the modern means of typesetting.

The proposals were many and ranged from the outrageous (fig.4),[3] to the more pragmatic solutions of reducing the character set to its absolute minimum (fig.5).[4]

In fact this latter principal, though not officially adopted by the Academy, was later implemented for the Arabic typewriter keyboard. A similar Arabic keyboard, with minor modifications, is now applied to most PCs. Though a computer's keyboard resembles that of the old typewriter, it has become capable of triggering complex commands that enable us to use a far larger set of characters than what can be visible on the keyboard itself (i.e. the Unicode character sets which can contain thousands of glyphs). Economy of space is no longer an issue for type design today; it is the aesthetic reform that demands attention.

---

3 The proposal of Yahya Boutemène uses the Latin characters to represent the Arabic letters. Nasri Khattar's proposal is to create an Arabic alphabet that uses one shape variation per letter. Both proposals advocated non-connected Arabic letterforms, with the aim of simplifying the script and making it easier to learn (much like the Latin alphabet). Ibid., 73, 75.

4 The proposal of Ahmad Lakhdar Ghazal was to reduce the amount of characters for typesetting without sacrificing much of the traditional letter shape variations. The system was named ASV-CODAR (Arabe Standard Voyellé—Codage Arabe) the standard vocalized Arabic encoding systems for typewriters and typesetting machines. Ibid., 77.

The Educational Model for Arabic Type Design.

As the Arab nations fully embrace the new advancements in communication technologies, the need for serious professional involvement in type design is manifesting itself forcefully. Young Arab graphic designers are entering the field, and the need to provide them with a solid design background with respect to Arabic type is a pressing issue. At the dawn of every technological development, a need for setting new standards arises. This is never the work of one sole individual, but of a group effort of professionals sharing a common goal. It is precisely this degree of involvement, of past Arab calligraphers, which brought calligraphy to the high level of sophistication practiced from the tenth century onward. The tools of pen and ink, and the traditional dedication of calligraphers to their old masters, are no longer useful for type design; in fact, they may prove to be more of an obstacle. Arabic calligraphy is no longer sufficient for contemporary communication needs, or indeed appropriate for modern tools and media. Arabic calligraphic styles would not have developed, had the calligraphers not been progressive and experimental in adapting their script to the technological developments of their times. Every age has its requirements and its trends, and every medium its inherent aesthetics. Arabic type should be perceived, like any written script, as a collection of shapes designed to serve specific design objectives and media (fig.6).[5] Arabic type should not be merely concerned with traditional book design; it should also find a way to retain its aesthetic livelihood on unforgiving computer screens. Arabic type needs to be adapted to the low-resolution limitations that require clarity and formal simplicity.

The reading process and intelligibility of letters are practically the same for all scripts, including Arabic. It is based on recognizing the skeletal shape of letterforms and interpreting them within a specific word context. This explains why people can read a text regardless of the type style, as long as the skeletal shapes of the letters are not dramatically altered (fig.3).[6] Letters can only exist in co-dependant relationships and not as individual characters. Their interaction creates a much-needed dynamic

5 This figure, illustrated by Ziad Kadri (A final degree student project. American University of Beirut. 1996), shows Ibn Muqlah's *Nizam Al-Tashabuh*, his third principle on the construction of letterforms. It explains the similarities between parts of letters that are interchangeable and useful in the construction of different letters. Ibid., 98.

6 This figure shows one sentence set in five different type styles and illustrates the readability of a text even if the letterforms become distinctly different in shape. This image is a reproduction from Agfa-Monotype's catalogue of Non-Latin fonts. Ibid., 216.

fluidity that facilitates the reading process. This characteristic is essential to Arabic letters, since their pairing with, and connection to their surrounding letters often defines their shapes. Their individual form cannot remain static due to the connectivity of the letters within words.

A new digital aesthetic for Arabic type needs to be created. Designing a typeface requires thorough understanding of abstract shapes, and the skill to interpret handwritten letters into drawn forms. It is not the copying of calligraphic strokes, but rather the drawing anew, that takes into consideration the limitations of where and how these letterforms will be used. There is a need for expressive experiments that challenge the established calligraphic rules and conventions. The academic environment is traditionally a fertile arena for such experimentation.

Considering the multilingual nature of visual communication in most Middle Eastern countries, bi-scriptural typography — the simultaneous use of Arabic and Latin scripts — has become mandatory for any qualitative education in this field. A course on Arabic type should be designed to create the right open-minded and experimental environment that encourages progressive thinking. The new educational model should not stress abiding by the absolute rules of the old masters, but should instead encourage learning through personal research, questioning and critical analysis. It should stress the importance of the physical experience of creation and self-expression.

On the practical level, it should provide students with a simple framework for the design process. First. A theoretical framework for discussion of the needs of contemporary Arabic typography, and the ways to investigate innovative design solutions, through:

1. a historical overview of the origins of the script, its aesthetic, social, and technological developments.
2. a discussion on the relation between aesthetic freedom and technical limitations.

It is equally important, to establish a set of practical guidelines and conventions for type design, such as:

1. a description of the anatomy of the letterforms (fig.7).[7]

7 This nomenclature of the parts of Arabic letters is not an accepted convention since the calligraphic terms may be slightly different and far more detailed. Ibid., 181.

2. a basic grid for overall proportional measurements of a typeface (fig.8).[8]

3. a set of rules on the formal modification of letterforms for legibility in low-resolution digital environments.

4. a standard set of letters, words, and sentences for testing the feasibility of the design.

5. a basic knowledge of the software needed to execute the design.

6. a new type style classification based on functional applications rather than historical calligraphic models.

The students are encouraged to develop their design concepts based on researching examples of type design (both Arabic and Latin), and on experimenting with various drawing tools and techniques, other than the conventional pen and ink. The aim is to initiate a transformation from the calligraphic to the typographic aesthetic.

Here are some case studies:

1. *Saleet*, meaning 'sharp' in Arabic, is a hybrid display font that combines curvilinear forms encased in sharp-angled geometric shapes (fig.9).[9]

2. *Conrinthos* was designed for typesetting spiritual manuscripts and special edition books. It was inspired by the spiritual philosophy of Tawhid, using the metaphysical symbol of the circle as a basic structural element for the construction of the letterforms. The light weight and airy look of this typeface portrays the spiritual concept behind the design (fig.10).[10]

3. *Cryptic*. The name conveys the perception of the Arabic letterforms by the non-Arabic speaking designer of this typeface. Legibility in low resolution digital environments was the main objective for this design. The letterforms were drawn with a minimal amount of detail and generously open counterforms. *Cryptic* harmoniously combines a contemporary aesthetic with a pragmatic design solution (fig.11).[11]

4. *Megamel*, named after its designer's alter-ego, is a free interpretation of the calligraphic Diwani style. It incorporates the multi-level baselines with an oriental

8 The Arabic type measurements from left to right and top to bottom: the bounding box, the baseline, the loop-height, the tooth-height, the ascender and descender heights. Ibid., 181.

9 Poster illustrating the design process of the *Saleet* font, designed by Zeina Khalifeh for the Arabic Type Design course (Spring Term 2001) at the American University in Dubai. Huda Smitshuijzen AbiFarès, *Experimental Arabic Type* (Dubai 2002), 19.

10 Sample text of the *Corinthos* font, designed by Fadi Gwanny. Ibid., 11.

11 Sample text of the *Cryptic* font, designed by Shubha Goenka. Ibid., 16.

brush stroke. The letterforms are constructed on a diamond-shaped grid, meant to enhance the look of a true Italic font (fig.12).[12]

5. *Farfasha*, meaning 'playfulness and vigour' in Arabic, is a playful display font designed for use in animations and comics. It has a predominantly geometric structure with angular asymmetrical counterforms (fig.13).[13]

6. *Nebrass*, meaning 'the guiding light' in Arabic, is a low-resolution digital font. It is designed strictly for on-screen use (thus the reference to light in its name). It combines the Square Kufi style of lettering with the digital aesthetic of pixel-based imagery. This typeface addresses an important cultural issue by combining traditional Islamic art with a contemporary design aesthetic (fig.14).[14]

These case studies (which were not developed into full character sets or workable digital fonts) present innovative typefaces, with unique personalities, and diverse sources of inspiration. They deviate from the traditional calligraphic model and present a free interpretation of Arabic letterforms. Their ultimate role is to instigate a discussion about the formal and conceptual developments of future Arabic type design. In conclusion, I say, it is high time for Arab typographers and designers alike to share their knowledge; that they collectively assume the responsibility for shaping and promoting their script in a way that is suitable for contemporary design.

Arabic type is the visual branding of the Arab/Islamic culture. It is a cultural disgrace to let the world's second most used script become so improperly represented in today's influential communication media. The recent international political conflicts have created an urgent need for rejuvenating Arabic culture's image. Contemporary Arabic type can shake off the uniform and conservative image, and can promote a multi-faceted and diversified identity that represents more realistically modern Arabic culture. It only takes a handful of passionate pioneers to set into motion a new wave of creative energy. Their creations do represent a specific form of cultural production. It is our duty to facilitate the release of that creative energy; to set into motion a cultural mobilization through a new Arabic typography that will ensure the rebirth of visual culture in the Middle East.

12 Poster promoting the *Megamel* font, designed by Melvin Mathew. Ibid., 21.
13 CD and its packaging/booklet cover promoting the *Farfasha* font, designed by Qurat Sharif. Ibid., 12.
14 Poster promoting the *Nebrass* font, designed by Sara Al Ghurair. Ibid., 9.

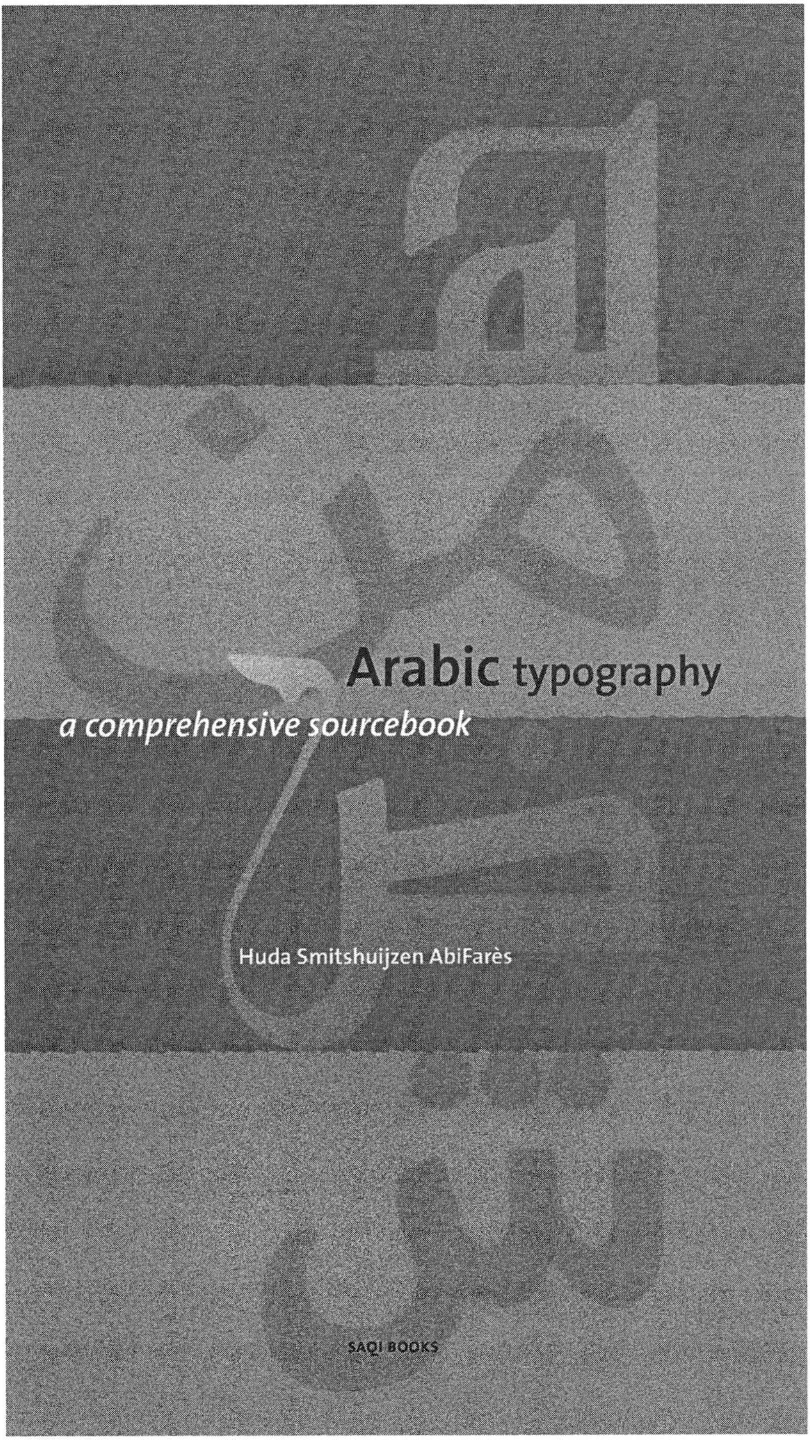
Arabic typography
a comprehensive sourcebook
Huda Smitshuijzen AbiFarès
SAQI BOOKS

Figure 1.

وَهَذَا ٱلنَّيْلُ لَهُ خَصْلَتَانِ ٱلْأُولَى بُعْدُ مَرْمَاهُ ఆperímentū querítís éius qui în me
ٱلْمَعْمُورَةِ نَهْرًا أَبْعَدَ مَسَافَةً مِنْهُ لِأَنَّ مَبَادِئَهُ loquit̃ xp̃c. Poſt đamaſcū arabiāq̃
جَبَلُ ٱلْقَمَرِ وَزَعَمُوا أَنَّ هَذَا ٱلْجَبَلَ وَرَاءَ خَطِّ luſtratā: aſcēdit iħeroſolimā ut uĩſit

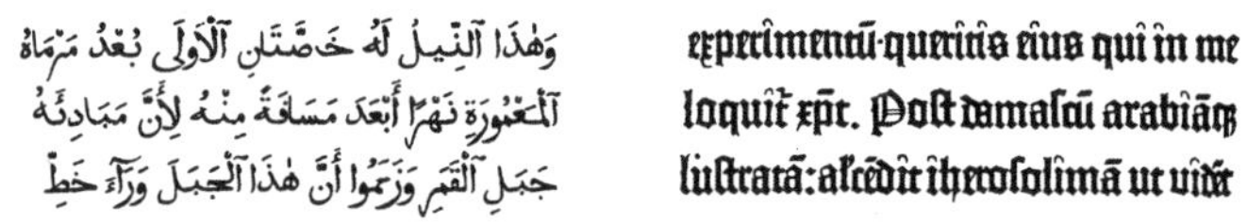

Granjon's Arabica Grande (1585) | Gutenberg's type for the 42-line Bible (1455).

Figure 2.

والخاء تحدث من ضغط الهواء

والخاء تحدث من ضغط الهواء

والخاء تحدث من ضغط الهواء

والخاء تحدث من ضغط الهواء

والخاء تحدث من ضغط الهواء

والخاء تحدث من ضغط الهواء

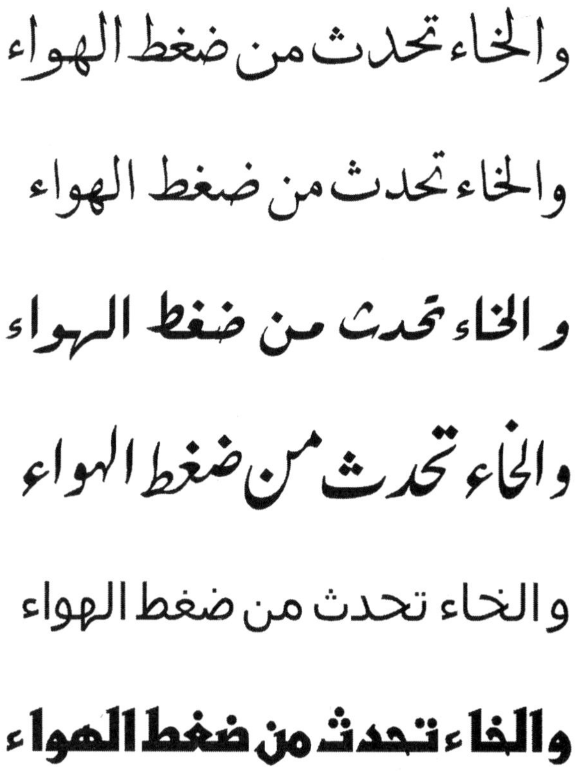

Figure 3. Various Arabic type styles.

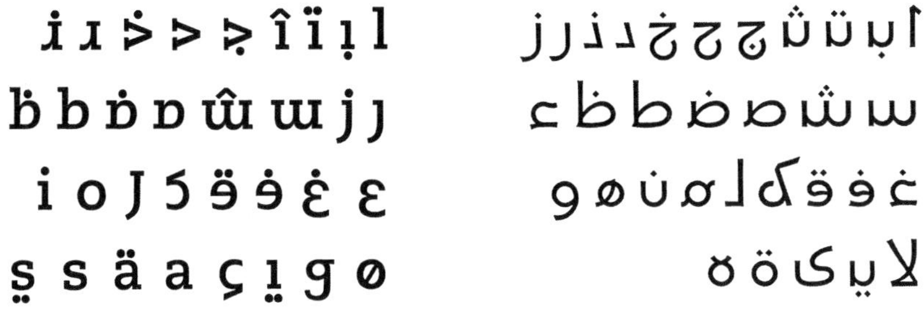

Yahya Boutemène's proposal for using the Latin alphabet to represent Arabic letterforms.

Nasri Khattar's proposal the *Unified Arabic* where each letter is represented by a single free-standing distinctive shape.

Figure 4.

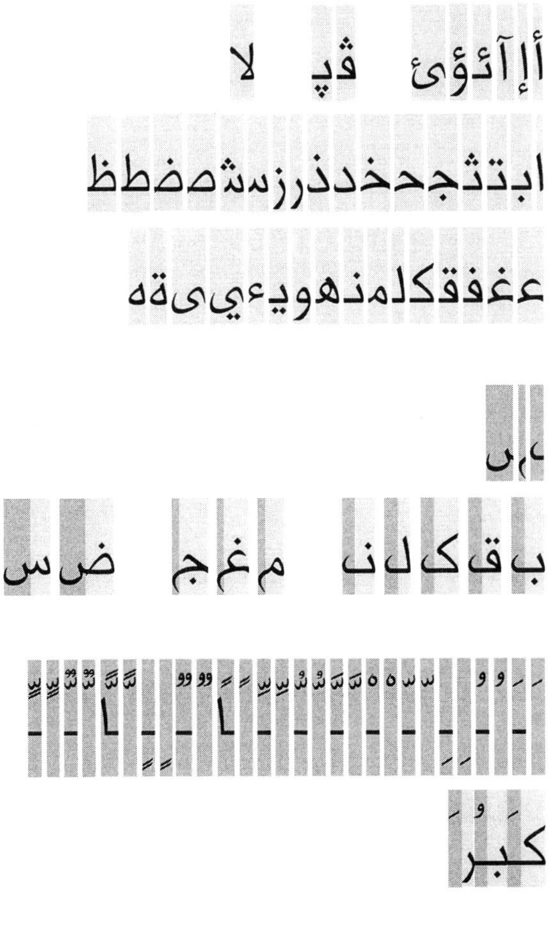

Figure 5. Ahmad Lakhdar Ghazal's proposal that reduced the Arabic character set to its absolute minimum combined with an ingenious system for ending tails and vocalisation marks as separate characters.

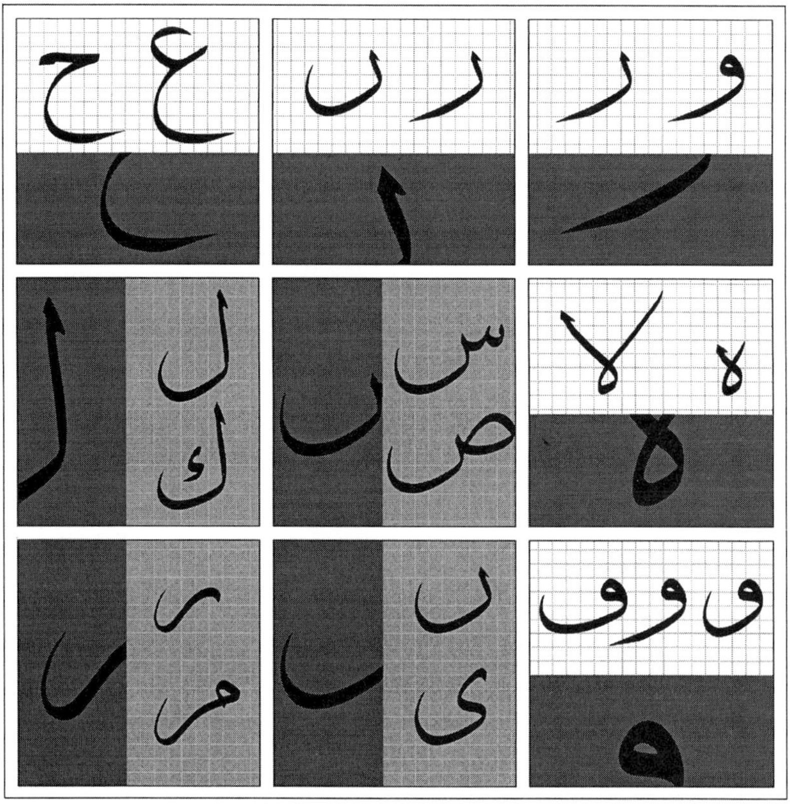

Figure 6. Ziad Kadri's study based on Ibn Muqlah's Nizam Al-Tashabuh. The system for bringing unity into a typeface by using similar parts of different letters.

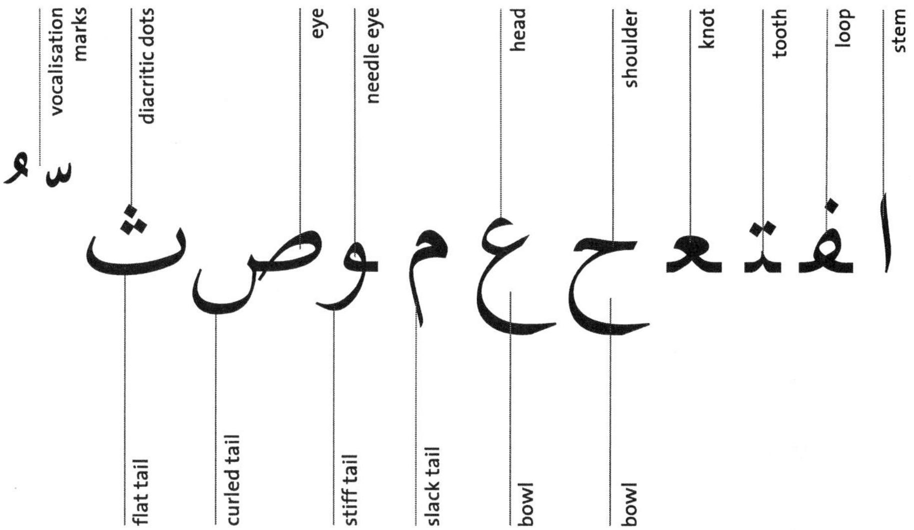

Figure 7. Unconventional nomenclature of the anatomy of Arabic letterforms.

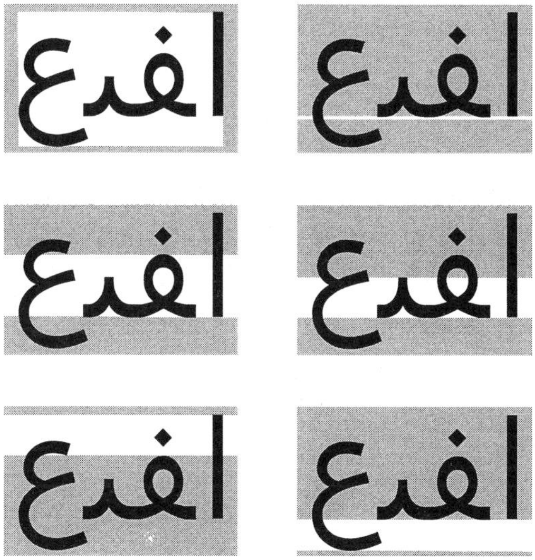

Figure 8. Arabic type measurements. From left to right, top to bottom: bounding box, baseline, loop height, tooth height, ascender height, descender height.

Figure 9.

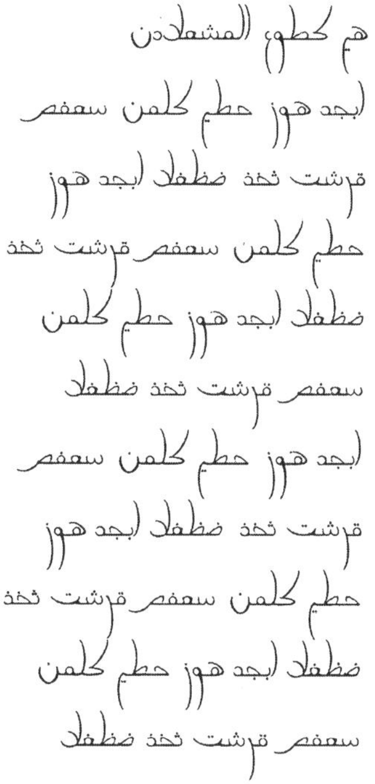

Figure 10.

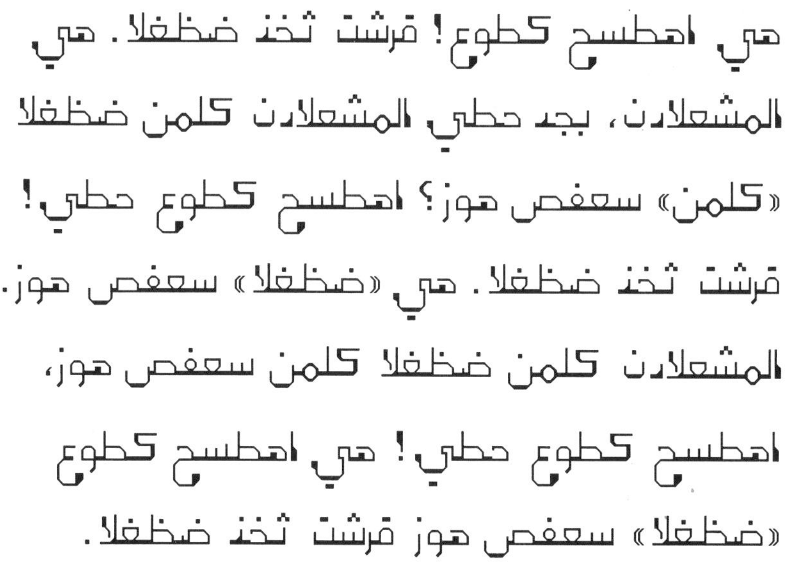

Figure 11.

ابجد
هوز حطي كلمن سعفص
قرشت ثخذ
ضظغلا
MegaMel first began with a simple idea,
to create an Arabic font that uses the lines of the Latin font Kendo,
with the irregularities of the Diwani Arabic font style.
Elements of the Diwani style like the multiple base lines and extended swashes are combined with Kendo's variations in thick and thin sharp curved lines.
MegaMel's construction is based on a diamond grid of intersecting 45 degree angle lines to create an italicized look.

Figure 12.

Figure 13.

Figure 14.